REST IN PEACE, LILLY

When Lilly got to the crypt, she went to the door and opened it. It swung easily, and she cursed.

"Sorry everyone, didn't mean to swear," she said, looking around. There were bits and pieces of crime scene tape still stuck to the door. She put her bag on the ground and fished through it until she found a trash bag. She started carefully pulling the tape off the door.

She had one foot on the lip of the mausoleum and was reaching up for the last bit of tape when she felt a hard shove. She toppled a bit and grabbed onto the door. She felt an arm go around her waist and clawed at the bright green jacket that was crushing her ribs. The arm shifted and she reached down and dug her nails into the hand that squeezed her waist. Her feet were lifted up off the ground and she was pushed inside the crypt.

She fell on her hands and knees, and looked back. She saw another flash of green, then darkness. The door was closed and she heard the lock turn . . .

Books by Julia Henry

PRUNING THE DEAD

TILLING THE TRUTH

DIGGING UP THE REMAINS

WREATHING HAVOC

THE PLOT THICKETS

Published by Kensington Publishing Corp.

A Garden Squad Mystery

The
PLOT
THICKETS

Julia Henry

Kensington Publishing Corp.
www.kensingtonbooks.com

KENSINGTON BOOKS are published by

Kensington Publishing Corp.
119 West 40th Street
New York, NY 10018

All Kensington titles, imprints, and distributed lines are available at special quantity discounts for bulk purchases for sales promotion, premiums, fund-raising, educational, or institutional use.

Special book excerpts or customized printings can also be created to fit specific needs. For details, write or phone the office of the Kensington Sales Manager: Attn.: Sales Department. Kensington Publishing Corp., 119 West 40th Street, New York, NY 10018. Phone: 1-800-221-2647.

The K and Teapot logo is a trademark of Kensington Publishing Corp.

First Printing: November 2022
ISBN: 978-1-4967-3310-8

ISBN: 978-1-4967-3312-2 (ebook)

10 9 8 7 6 5 4 3 2 1

Printed in the United States of America

To Tracy Stewart
"Life is partly what we make it, and partly what is made by the friends we choose."
—Tennessee Williams

Tracy, I'm so grateful for these many, many years of friendship. Here's to many more.

Chapter 1

If she was being honest with herself, which she usually was, Lilly Jayne had to admit that her days of slinking around outside peoples' houses should be well behind her. Standing beneath the window, she eyed the work she'd done and sighed. She rolled her hips, hoping that her back wasn't going to seize up on her way home. She resisted the urge to trim the bushes any more and sidled her way out of the leggy branches. She'd need to leave shaping them for another day. The important work was done. Helen Garrett could see out her front window again.

Lawns were overrated as far as Lilly was concerned, looking at the patchy green that marred the front yard. She'd used the push mower to do what she could, but that wasn't much. The grass was too tall, with dead patches that were beyond hope. After she'd run over a couple of sticks, she gave up. It didn't matter. Today, a perfect green lawn wasn't the point. Lilly's expertise was needed for the flower bed, currently a muddy patch, in Helen's front yard, by the sidewalk. Lilly used the side of the hoe to create rows of loose soil. Normally she'd kneel on the ground with a trowel precisely digging down, but a long-handled tool kept her upright. She looked over at the flat of wilting flowers, and tilled another row.

Using a combination of her experience, knowl-edge, and love of plants, Lilly laid out the pots, ar-ranging the flowers in what she hoped would be an interesting pattern. She took a deep breath and squatted down so that she could get the plants in the ground, whispering to them each.

"You're here to give Helen a view. Now, I know you've been neglected a bit, but those days are over. You'll get plenty of water and this is a lovely, sunny spot. I'd really appreciate it if you perked up a bit. There you go, my darlings."

She stood up slowly, putting her hands on her thighs and gently straightening herself to standing. Her back spasmed, but then it stopped. She moved her hips around and walked to the right-hand side of the house. Was the gardening hose still there? Yes, it was. Guilt tugged at Lilly. The hose had probably been out there all winter. The beautification commit-tee should have checked in last fall to make sure it had been drained, and the water had been shut off. The committee was an informal group who took on gardening projects around town. Helen had been a member, but now, close to her hundredth birthday, she was a candidate for their spring project list.

Nothing appeared to leak or burst when she turned on the hose, so Lilly gently watered the flower beds and bushes. She rotated the sprayer for a powerful stream, and rinsed off the front walk. The water re-moved some of the debris, but the encroaching moss could use a scrubbing. Still, it all looked better. She went back and turned the hose reel a few times, but it got stuck and she didn't have the patience to fix it. She coiled the rest of the hose on the ground and walked out toward the front, looking at the new flower beds.

"That looks wonderful!"

Lilly started and jumped back. She hadn't noticed anyone at the front door when she came around the side of the house, but then again, she hadn't been looking. She was in her gardening zone.

"I'm sorry," the younger woman said. "I didn't mean to startle you."

"That's all right, I'm fine," Lilly said. "I was fighting the hose winder."

"Don't worry about that. My son will be by to pick me up at four, and I'll have him take care of it. I'll also get him to clear those branches," the woman said.

What was her name? Jessica? Janice? Lilly couldn't remember, and stopped trying to. Names weren't her forte these days. "I'm sorry, I've forgotten your name."

"No worries, it's Kathy. I can't tell you how much I appreciate you doing this work. Helen is going to be delighted. She was getting frustrated by that bush out front blocking her view."

"I'll come over with some other tools to do a better job of shaping it," Lilly said. "I wanted to clear her view for now."

"And give her a better one to look at. You know, it was awfully nice of her cousin to buy those plants, and a real shame she didn't get them in the ground. I'm glad you noticed them on your way in today."

"I tend to notice plants in distress," Lilly said.

"When she wakes up, she's sure going to enjoy seeing that burst of color. Anything we need to do to make sure they don't die?"

"They'll need to be watered. I'll get some mulch over here, and that will help when it gets warm, but I think they'll be fine once they settle in. I hope that they give her some joy." Lilly's voice broke at the end of the sentence, and Kathy reached over and put her hand on Lilly's arm.

"Ms. Jayne—"

"Lilly."

"Lilly, Helen's lived a good life. Her cousin wants to keep her home and comfortable, so she's got a few of us taking shifts, tending to her."

"I'm glad that she's able to do that," Lilly said. "I hadn't realized Helen was failing so badly, but I haven't been able to get over here for a few weeks."

"She took a turn right after the first of the year. Her cousin thinks it was her choice. She's tired. A hundred years is a long time."

"It certainly is," Lilly said. "I've lived sixty-five years—make that sixty-six—and feel every one of them these days."

"I noticed you favoring your back a bit. You okay?"

"I took a fall on some black ice in January. Wrenched my back, sprained my arm. I'm just starting to feel like myself again. It's been a long three months."

"I can imagine."

"I'm glad that I came today. I hope she knew that I was here."

"Her pulse went up when you spoke with her," Kathy said. "I know she appreciated the visit."

"You're very kind." Lilly looked around at the yard, and back at Kathy. "I'll make sure people come by to help clean up from the winter. Helen was always fastidious about her yard."

"Honestly, I'm not sure there's a budget for that—"

"I work with a group of volunteer gardeners. Helen's given a lot to Goosebush; folks will be happy to do for her. Please let the other nurses know that I live close by, and if anything is needed, to let me know."

"I'll make sure your name and number are on the instruction list. Thanks again for the gardening. You've got the magic touch. Look how the flowers are starting to perk up already."

"Lilly! Where have you been? What happened to you? You're all dirty. Did you fall? Are you hurt—"

"Delia, stop," Lilly said. She'd let herself in the front door, hoping to be able to sneak upstairs for a shower, but alas. Ernie Johnson, in one of his many attempts of thanking Lilly for letting him stay with her, had installed a new security system: A doorbell with a camera that sent an alert whenever someone was approaching the front door. "I thought you had a date this afternoon with Stan."

"*Date* is such a weird word, Lilly," Delia Greenway said, reminding Lilly of their forty-year age gap by rolling her eyes and shrugging her shoulders. "We were going to get together, but he canceled."

"Again?" Lilly asked gently. Stan and Delia had been dating, seeing each other, involved, whatever the term was these days, for a year. Lately they'd been spending more time scheduling and cancelling dates than actually seeing one another. Not that it was any of Lilly's business, except that she cared about Delia, and knew that she wasn't happy.

"At least this time I hadn't gotten in my car yet," Delia said. She walked over to Lilly and took her coat from her, walking over to the closet to hang it up. "Enough about me. Where were you?"

"I went over to visit Helen Garrett. I told you that I was going to do that."

"But you've been gone for hours." Delia stood in the front hall with her arms folded and stared up at Lilly. Lilly was never sure how Delia didn't blink for so long, but it was disconcerting. And effective.

Lilly looked down at her watch, feeling like a teenager who'd broken curfew. She loved that her housemate took such good care of her. But she hated that Delia had developed the ability to intimidate her, despite being decades younger and six inches shorter.

"There was some gardening help required at Helen's house, so I did it. Thank you for your concern. Really, Delia, it means the world. But stop worrying about me. I'm fine."

"You shouldn't push yourself," Delia said.

Lilly took a deep breath and forced herself to smile. "Again, I'm fine."

"Why don't you come back to the kitchen. I'll make us some tea."

"Thank you, no. I'm going to head upstairs to take a shower. Perhaps a nap."

"You may have time for a quick one. Roddy will be over here in about an hour."

"Roddy? Why?" Not that Lilly didn't look forward

to seeing her favorite neighbor. But she really needed a nap.

"He wanted to come over early to talk, and then he's going to take you to the Star. Remember? The Garden Squad is having dinner out."

"Is that tonight?" Lilly sighed. "Why can't we have dinner here?"

"Because you're going to celebrate the work on Alden Park beginning," Delia said.

"What kind of celebration will it be without you? We should reschedule."

"Absolutely not. There will be other dinners. I wish I could be there, but I have to go to the university to do a run-through of my presentation with the tech team. The dean just wrote to me and told me that there will be a few high-profile alumni there tomorrow for the event, so I'm glad I'll be setting it all up tonight."

"They shouldn't have moved your lecture to Sunday afternoon and made it a high-profile event without your knowledge. What would have happened if you weren't available, or ready?"

"That's academia," Delia said. "I'm sort of flattered. There's a lot of interest in the talk." She'd been working on her lecture about the excavation of Alden Park for weeks, and had several items to display as well. Lilly had wanted to attend, but Delia had told her that she'd make her too nervous. Besides, Lilly had heard the script dozens of times.

"You'll be wonderful. Now, I'm going up to my room," Lilly said. "I can still fit in a nap and shower. For the sake of everyone, I think that's a good idea. A chance to get up on the other side of the bed, as it were. I'll text Roddy and let him know."

"Are you sure you're okay, Lilly?" Delia asked quietly.

"Seeing Helen was harder than I expected," Lilly said. "I could use an attitude refresher. Stop fussing. Go get ready for your rehearsal."

Lilly walked over to the side table to look at the mail. She shuffled envelopes until Delia went all the way to the end of the hall and took a left into the old breakfast room, her current office. As soon as Delia went in, Lilly dropped the mail and walked to the staircase. The walk home had helped, but her back still wasn't happy. She took one step at a time, resting on each riser. The only thing that kept her going was the promise of a restorative shower, nap, and heating pad.

Chapter 2

"Sorry if I'm late," Lilly said as she entered the back room a while later. She felt much better after her nap, and had taken some extra care in getting ready for the evening out. Her friends were worried about her, and a little mascara, some blush, and red lipstick helped her look healthier.

"No, no. You're fine," Roddy Lyden said, standing up from the couch as Lilly came in the room. Tall, handsome, with wavy silver hair, deep dimples, and an easy smile—Lilly sometimes forgot how good looking he was, especially if she hadn't seen him for a few days. Which she hadn't.

"Do we have time to sit, or do we need to leave for dinner?" Lilly asked. She sat down gently and smiled at Roddy, who sat beside her.

"We have a few minutes," Roddy said. "Are you well, Lilly?"

"I'm fine. I did a little yard work for a friend, and I'm feeling stiff. I'm out of gardening shape. I hate to admit it, but I should probably get a stool if I'm going to weed this weekend."

"Lilly, there's no shame in a gardening stool. I've been considering getting one myself. Staying ahead of the weeds is going to be a full-time job."

"Mulch helps—"

"I have a delivery slated for next week. I ordered the amount you suggested, though it seems like a lot."

"It won't be, trust me. Is your composting bin in place?" Lilly looked at Roddy and did her best to look severe. He'd been resistant to the idea, but she'd prevailed. Partly because it was a good way to reuse waste. But also because she knew he'd enjoy the process once it got going, and the compost would be good for his gardens.

"It is, but nothing seems to be happening."

"Roddy, it takes a while. A layer of newspaper can help, but be sure—"

"Patience has never been one of my virtues," Roddy said. "You can't blame a man for envying your compost, Lilly."

Lilly laughed and Roddy joined her. "I'm delighted I have something worth envying."

"You have much to envy. Good friends. A wonderful house. Stunning gardens—"

"A charming next-door neighbor," Lilly said.

"I wouldn't describe Mrs. Cotton as charming, but to each their own."

"You're terrible," Lilly said, laughing again.

"I am that," Roddy said, quietly. His phone buzzed and he shrugged apologetically at Lilly and took it out of his jacket pocket. He looked down at the screen, read something, and frowned.

"Everything all right?" she asked.

"My ex-wife wants to come and pay me a visit."

"Which one?" Lilly asked. She knew he'd had three wives, but didn't know much about any of them. He'd married the first young, had a daughter with the second. He never talked about the third, only that there'd been one. When she thought about it, she didn't know too much about Roddy's pre-Goosebush life. Of course, she hadn't asked. At this point in both of their lives, past history, and mistakes, seemed less important to dwell on, especially at the beginning of a friendship. Though they'd known each other for almost a year now.

"Fair question. The last one."

"From the look on your face, seeing her isn't something you're looking forward to."

"Adrienne is one of my great mistakes. We weren't married long. I should have known better. I haven't seen her in seven years. Seven wonderful years."

"She sounds delightful," Lilly said, smiling. Now she knew a bit more about wife number three.

"Ah, Lilly. Adrienne's a long story, and it will take much longer than we've got this evening to tell it."

"It's none of my business."

"I'd like it to be," he said quietly, locking eyes with her.

Lilly's breath caught, then she realized she wanted to know more, and wasn't sure what that meant. "You've got a rain check to tell me about your ex-wife, then."

Roddy nodded. "I won't say I'm looking forward to that, but the conversation is long past due." He looked at Lilly with such intensity she felt herself blush, and looked away.

"Tonight, I do have a favor to ask," he said, in a different tone.

"Ask away."

"Would you mind going to Alden Park and doing a walk-through with me before we have dinner? They've started to prep for the cement pour, and I'm having some concerns."

"Concerns? About your design? Or the work being done?"

"Both? Mostly my design. The cement is permanent, or close to. I want to make sure it's right, and that I've thought everything through. We have a few minutes before dinner. But I completely understand if—"

"I'd love to see it," Lilly said quickly. Roddy's design for Alden Park had won a contest last winter, and he'd spent the past few months with the project manager working out the details. "I may need some help getting in and out of the car, though. My back is a little stiff. Moving around helps."

"Would you prefer to walk? We can get a ride back with Warwick or Ernie."

"I wouldn't mind walking. But if you tell anyone I mentioned needing help, especially Delia, I'll kill you."

"Noted." Roddy stood up, put his hand under her elbow, helping her off the couch. He held on while she took a deep breath and steadied herself.

"Walking really does help my back," Lilly said. "I hope you don't mind."

"I don't mind at all," Roddy said. They were walking down Washington Street toward the Wheel, the main rotary in Goosebush. Like many New England towns, rotaries took the place of intersections and lights. They weren't for the faint of heart; rotaries required a mixture of patience and daring. It was only May, early in the season, so traffic was fairly light. Still, Roddy and Lilly had a job navigating the four crosswalks as they moved toward Alden Park. There would have been fewer crossroads if they'd taken a left instead of a right, but then they would have been walking along a stretch with some of the busiest businesses in town, including the Star, where they were having dinner. The chance that they'd see someone and be distracted from the task at hand was too great.

They stepped into a crosswalk, and Roddy pulled Lilly back a large sedan turned the corner quickly.

"Whoa, slow down!" Lilly called after the car, which had sped up.

"Are you all right?" Roddy asked.

"I'm fine. Did you see who that was?"

"No idea who the driver was," Roddy said. "But *Bradford Funeral Home* was painted on the side."

"Are you sure?"

"Their logo is hard to forget. A sailboat sliding toward the sunset with angel wings floating around the sun. The halo above the 'o' in *Bradford.*"

"Angel wings? I don't remember angel wings."

"Perhaps you're so used to seeing things around here you don't notice them. I found it, the logo, extraordinarily distasteful the first time I saw it. I can't help but notice it now, with a bit more humor."

"When you're the only funeral parlor in Goosebush, you don't worry as much about being tasteful," Lilly said. "Though I swear I don't remember seeing the halo or the wings, and I like to think of myself as fairly observant. They must be new additions to the sunset and sailboat. Likely Whitney's doing."

"Remind me which one Whitney is? The daughter?"

"No, no. That's Sasha. Whitney Dunne-Bradford is the second wife, and widow of Sam Bradford. The business was his parents'. And grandparents', I think. Theoretically it should be passed down to Sasha, Sam's daughter from his first wife. It will be interesting to see if that happens, now that Whitney's in the picture."

They slowed down and waited for a pause in traffic before they stepped into the crosswalk. "I think I met Sasha at a town meeting recently," Roddy said.

"I'd imagine you did. That meeting was the one I missed, about using more town property for a new cemetery. They were smart to have Sasha do the presentation. Whitney isn't terribly popular. I'm glad they put that idea on hold for a while. I have a few thoughts I look forward to sharing. Not about the cemetery per se, but about the use of town land."

"I look forward to hearing those thoughts, as do others, I'm sure."

"You're very kind, Roddy. I suspect more than a few people would rather I kept my thoughts to myself, but it's my duty to Goosebush to speak up about these things."

"I'm used to living in cities, and being a bit less directly involved with the complexity of local issues. Goosebush has helped me focus on civic responsibility. Ah, here we are," Roddy said.

One of the Alden Park improvements was designated entrances and exits, defined by gates in the new wrought iron fence. The fence was put in early, and the view was blocked from the outside by panels that included the history of the park. The idea was to have a grand reveal for the town when all of the work was completed.

"Who's going to use this entrance?" Lilly asked while Roddy unlocked the gate and slid it open. She walked in and he closed it behind them, making sure it was locked.

"This won't be a public entrance. When you slide both sides open, it's wide enough for trucks, and can be used for maintenance and deliveries. Generally, it won't be open during the day. The other three gates will be."

"I'm still not sure that the park needs to be locked at night," Lilly said.

"That's to be determined," Roddy said. The access to the park was a hot topic of discussion in Goosebush, one which Roddy was fairly agnostic about. "While construction is going on, the gates are locked, mostly for safety. And security of the materials. I wanted you to see the park from this perspective, since it's the best way to get an overall impression of what's going on."

"What's this? I thought that the paths were going to be cement?" Lilly pointed to an area of the path that was packed down and had an Astroturf-looking covering.

"That's the sample of the running track that will go around the park. There are loops built in at each end so that people can get more distance in. It was decided that this surface would be better for runners, and the look would differentiate their path. We've decided on a brick color, which I think will go nicely with the gray of the other paths."

"I like that idea," Lilly said. "What's it made of?"

"A rubberized track material. Better for people's knees and legs. The other paths and the maintenance track will be concrete. Pressed and stained, so that it looks more like stone. I know that people wanted cobblestone and gravel—"

"No, your plan is better," Lilly said.

"Certainly easier for people with baby carriages, wheelchairs—"

"And bad backs," Lilly said. "I've come to appreciate steady paths. Walk me through the plan."

For the next half hour Roddy walked Lilly around the park, showing her the edging that was in place and describing the altered plan, which included more infrastructure than Roddy's original design.

"What are all those pipes?" Lilly said, pointing to the piles of pipes in the construction area.

"The plan is to lay them down under the walkways, and run water pipes and electricity through them," Roddy said. "They will also have space for anything else in the future that needs to be run through the park, which will hopefully prevent major work being done as the use of the park changes. After the success of the garden sculpture event, the Board of Selectmen agreed that anticipating future events made sense. The engineer included some locations where lights and sound can be easily set up, in case we want to have another public festival, or a small concert here."

"That's smart," Lilly said, looking around and noticing one of places that equipment could be set up. "The tendency would have been to pretend there'd never be another event, and then people would be forced to deal with generators and cords and all sorts of nonsense."

"You're the one who suggested the changes," Roddy said.

"After participating in that ridiculous garden sculpture event in December, and seeing how successful it was, I knew that people would start coming up with ideas," Lilly said. Lilly had only participated in the event because her friends had cajoled her into it, though she had to admit that putting together their large ivy-covered heart had been fun. And all of the sculptures had made Alden Park magical through the holiday season, no small feat since it was a mud pit covered with hay at that point. "I merely pointed out how much easier it would be to build in the infrastructure. And that you'd done some of the work when you figured out the grid for the displays in December."

"Is there any particular reason you dislike taking credit for wonderful ideas?" Roddy said.

"I only say aloud what others are thinking," Lilly said, giving him a sidelong glance. "I do see that the gardening areas have changed. I'm confused. What's that ring between the running track and the garden paths? A bike lane?"

"No, no bikes in the park. It's been pointed out that people will use the park to walk their dogs, so not having grass didn't make sense. The ring around the edges will be a grassy area specifically for dogs. But generally, the entire center will be gardens, with benches and other seating areas."

"When is the planting starting?"

"Very soon. I'm concerned it's being rushed. Does the park look ready to you?"

"The topsoil looks a little—"

"Anemic?" Roddy said.

"It looks sandy," Lilly said, kicking at the soil with her foot. "Roddy, if I bend down to look at it, I won't get back up."

"Here, let me grab you a sample." He bent down and grabbed her a handful of soil.

"Show-off." Lilly reached over and took some, running it between her fingers and smelling it. "They've probably had to put a sand foundation down for the cement, and it got mixed in. Still, I would have thought that the layers of topsoil and compost we put down after the holidays would have done more work in general." The beautification committee had done some emergency repair work after the successful event in Alden Park in December. They'd mixed up some seaweed, fertilizer, lime, and compost with the hay that was there, put ground cloth on top, and left it there to ferment. Lilly hadn't had a chance to check on it, but she was surprised that the soil didn't look better. "Before you plant anything, I think you'll need to get some better soil in here."

"The expert the construction company hired indicated six inches of topsoil would be sufficient."

"The expert is wrong. The varied history of Alden Park, including the dumping that was done here over the years, means that the soil issues need to be addressed. I'd hoped our winter preparation would have yielded better results. If you don't deal with it now, you'll pay for it later with bad drainage and dead plants."

"I thought perhaps she was," Roddy said. "But she speaks with certitude that caused me to doubt myself. I may need some backup—"

"You've got it," Lilly said, interrupting him. She looped her arm in his and gently squeezed. "Don't look so worried, Roddy. We've got this. You should be proud; this all looks wonderful. I wish I could explain how thrilled I feel. Alden Park is finally coming back to life."

Chapter 3

The Star was busy, but it was, after all, Saturday night. The old Woolworth store had been re-imagined by Stan Freeland, a local entrepreneur. The first floor had been converted into a café, book-store, and restaurant. The second floor was a theater and the top floors were offices and storage. *Star* stood for Stan's Theater and Restaurant, but most people didn't know that. Lilly did, since she'd been looking at the business plans for the project since Stan first proposed them.

The crowd was four people deep in the café, so Roddy and Lilly couldn't walk side by side. He took her hand and made a path past the coffee drinkers and the bookstore. Once they got into the restau-rant, Lilly took Roddy's arm, and they looked around for their friends. The rest of the Garden Squad, save Delia, was waiting at the big circular booth that Lilly had come to think of as their table.

"Yay, you're here!" Ernie said, sliding out of his seat to give Lilly a peck on the cheek. He was her height, with a bald head and bright smile. "I was beginning to wonder if I was supposed to come to the house to get you."

"My fault," Roddy said. "I asked Lilly to walk around Alden Park with me. Here, Lilly, sit in this chair. I'll slide in next to Tamara. You don't mind, do you?"

"Mind sitting between two handsome men? Please," Tamara O'Connor said, moving closer to her husband Warwick to make room. Tamara's natural hair was cut short, with flecks of gray that were the only sign of her age. There was nary a wrinkle on her brown skin, except when she smiled and her laugh lines appeared. She wasn't smiling now, as she watched her best friend sit down carefully. "You okay, Lil?"

"I'm an idiot," Lilly said, sitting down in the chair that Roddy had moved over to the end of the table. He held it until she sat down, then slid in next to Tamara. "I went over to visit Helen Garrett this afternoon and did some gardening. I'm a little sore, is all. I'll be fine."

"How is Helen?" Tamara asked. Lilly shook her head, and both women looked down. Helen had been friends with both of their mothers, and was the last tie to that generation.

"What kind of gardening did you do?" Ernie asked.

"She's living in a front room on the first floor. I cut the bushes down so she could see out the window, and then I planted a couple of flats of flowers someone had bought, but hadn't planted."

"Jackie. That's her cousin. She's been in a few times, getting home repair items so she could take care of projects while she's visiting."

"Her cousin?" Lilly asked, trying to remember if she'd ever met her, and coming up short. She wished her mother was here to tell her about Helen's family tree. Her mother had always been a font of knowledge about connections.

A server came by with a bread basket, two bottles of wine, and glasses. She also put a plate of hot towels on the table. Roddy picked it up and held it out to Lilly, then took one for himself. Ernie looked at the wine, thanked the server, and waved her away. He loved the ritual of opening and serving wine. "I hope you don't mind, but we ordered some wine and appetizers to start. Service is slow at the Star these days."

"Her cousin doesn't live here?" Warwick asked, picking up the plate of towels and offering one to his wife.

"No, she lives down in New Jersey, but she's been coming up a lot," Ernie said.

"She's hired several nurses so that Helen has full-time supervision. Though at this point it's about keeping her comfortable," Lilly said, taking a glass from Ernie. "Sorry, gang, didn't mean to drag us all down. Helen's lived a long, full life."

"She has, but it's still hard," Tamara said. "It's nice of you to put the flowers in. I'm sure she'll enjoy them."

"Even if it did wreck your back again," Warwick said, looking over at Lilly. "I've got some more of that liniment in my car."

"Thank you, Warwick. I'll take you up on that. What's in that stuff, anyway?"

"My secret mixture," Warwick said.

"Catnip has to be one of the ingredients," Lilly

said. "The cats go a bit nuts when I put it on. They start meowing and dancing around. I have to lock them out of my room when I open the jar."

"Though you let them back in afterwards," Tamara said.

"Of course," Lilly said.

"The food isn't even that good," a voice said loudly.

Lilly tried to turn and look at the speaker. Her range of motion was limited, so she couldn't see behind her. Turning back to the table, she was about to ask what was happening, but Ernie anticipated the question.

"It was Whitney," he said, shrugging and wiping off his hands. "She's at the table next to the kitchen. The bar is crowded tonight. It's a lousy seat, but at least she's sitting down."

"I think she almost ran us down earlier," Lilly said. "We were in a crosswalk and a car from the funeral parlor went roaring by us."

"Someone else may have been driving," Roddy said. "I take it she's the older woman."

"Don't let her hear you say that," Ernie said, laughing.

"Who is the man with them?"

"The entire merry trio is here tonight," Ernie said, glancing to his right. "Dewey Marsh is the man. You'll never see him out and about without either Sasha or Whitney. He's been working for Bradford's for what, two, maybe three years? Handsome, but not the brightest bulb on the Christmas tree. Sasha looks more miserable than normal, which is really saying something."

"Poor Sasha, she's such a mess. Tell you what, let's

ignore them," Tamara said. "We're here to celebrate Roddy."

"Indeed we are. Cheers to you, Roddy. The game's afoot!" Ernie said. Everyone raised a glass and they clinked gently. "People, please, have some of these appetizers." Ernie put the chickpea and garlic spread on one of the homemade crackers, and closed his eyes while he tasted the combination. The Star had added a number of offerings over the winter, and started to work with a bread company in Marshton that provided fresh bread, rolls, and crackers to the menu.

Roddy looked around the table and smiled. He took another hot towel and wiped the rest of the Alden Park soil off his hands. "Thank you, Ernie, but I'm not sure there's that much to celebrate yet."

"Of course there is," Ernie said, chasing his cracker down with a sip of wine. "The fountain in Alden Park is plumbed, and it isn't even Memorial Day yet. The project is right on target. By the Fourth of July the park will be open."

"The warmer-than-normal spring moved it along," Warwick said. "I was worried that removing the old pipes would be more of an issue, but as it turns out, I hear it went better than expected." Warwick and Ernie traded ramekins, and Warwick took another cracker.

"It helps that the Board of Selectmen saw fit to do some public works projects over the past few months," Lilly said.

"What helped was that Delia spent a lot of time co-ordinating those projects so that a lot could be done without a ton of fuss. I wish she could be here today to celebrate. I give her all the credit in the world for helping keep Alden Park and other projects in the mix when they were doing repairs after that water main break in January." Tamara shook her head and took a cracker to nibble on. As a member of the Board of Selectmen, Tamara took the inner workings of Goosebush running well very seriously. When the Wheel had become a skating rink in January and all of the businesses had to shut down, she felt responsible though she hadn't even been born when the original pipes were laid.

"Delia has an amazing mind for details, and for putting pieces of projects together. But I credit you, Tamara, for taking advantage of the work to open possibilities for the park. Rerouting the water main solved a lot of issues," Roddy said. "I am sorry Delia isn't here, but she has to give a lecture as part of her tenure process. She's also mentioned that she has a lot of grading to do for the end of the semester."

"Having us all out of the house will help her concentrate," Lilly said. "She's more than ready to give the lecture, though." When Lilly's husband Alan got sick, Delia, his graduate assistant, moved in to help him finish his final book. When he died, she stayed to help Lilly work through her grief. Now the women were great friends, and Delia was settled into Windward, Lilly's beloved, eccentric family home.

Not that they saw much of each other, unless they wanted to. Lilly lived in one of the biggest houses in Goosebush, Massachusetts. The original house had been built on a triple lot over one hundred and fifty years ago by one of Lilly's relatives, a ship captain with a stubborn streak. He'd eschewed the norms of the day, and set the house back from the street with fences all around it. Over the years the house had been added onto, but Lilly was the owner who had raised it to its current glory. She'd added a large greenhouse on the side of the house, and her gardens were legendary. Not that most people saw them. Lilly loved her privacy and was grateful that the captain loved large fences.

When Ernie sold his house, he came to live with Lilly and Delia while he looked for another one. He was hopeful that the spring house-selling season would give him some leads, but Lilly half hoped it didn't. She liked having him around, and was glad that more of the house was being used.

Looking around the table, Lilly smiled. It was almost a year since she'd had her garden party and met Roddy, her next-door neighbor, for the first time. What a year it had been. Both she and her gardens had come back to life, something she didn't think was possible after Alan died. Her friends, her Garden Squad, had seen her through some dark days.

"Quick, everyone make yourself look like you're miserable. Whitney's looking over here," Ernie said. In a flash, everyone made somber faces and stared straight ahead. They held it for a few seconds, maybe a minute, before Lilly started to laugh, and everyone joined in.

Tamara looked over her shoulder and then back at the table. "Whitney looks like she ate a lemon while sitting on a tack. Heavens, is she miserable or what?"

"Maybe that's part of being a funeral director," Ernie said. "I've got to think that the work weighs on you."

"Sam Bradford, may he rest in peace, was far from

miserable," Tamara said. "In fact, he was a lovely man—"

"Come on, Tamara, Sam was a little odd—" Lilly said.

"Perhaps. But who amongst us is not? What I'm saying is he had the personality for a funeral director. Kind, competent, sympathetic. Like his father and his grandfather. His first wife had a similar personality. Whitney does not share those traits."

"Sasha is a lot like her father, but she's shy," Warwick said. Warwick had been a coach and PE teacher in the high school for almost twenty years, and remembered most of the students who had crossed his path. Sasha Bradford had been young when her mother died, and found solace in playing lacrosse and soccer. Her father married Whitney Dunne less than a year after the death of her mother, the year Sasha had gone all-star. Warwick believed in tending to the entire athlete, and made sure that Sasha got support in her training, and also in her grief. He'd been disappointed when, after a wonderful career as a student soccer player, Sasha didn't pursue the sport when she got an offer to do so. Instead, she came back to Goosebush and started to work with her father.

"Sam was a good guy," Tamara said. "I'll tell you what: We miss him on the business council. He was always the first to contribute to any cause, and he was great at getting other businesses to step up. Whitney couldn't care less. She doesn't even come to the meetings. I suggested she send Sasha, but she told me Sasha didn't have the authority to represent the company."

"So much for passing the family business down to the next generation," Lilly said.

"Whitney could always adopt Dewey. What kind of name is Dewey, anyway?" Ernie said.

"Probably a family name turned into a first name," Lilly said absently.

"Probably that," Ernie said, watching his friend spread some of the pub cheese on the last cracker. He watched with pleasure as she took a bite and smiled. "Isn't that delicious? Anyway, Dewey is a lot younger than Whitney, is all I'm saying."

"I don't see that that makes a huge difference in a working relationship," Lilly said, taking a sip of wine. She looked around the table. "What? Did I miss something?"

"Nothing confirmed," Tamara said. "But word on the street is that Dewey is more than an employee."

"So there's gossip," Lilly said. "Surely we're all better than spreading gossip, aren't we?"

Tamara shrugged her shoulders. "You're right, Lilly. We're all better than pointing out that Dewey's car is parked outside the funeral home day and night. I think he lives there."

"Can you imagine living in a funeral home?" Ernie asked.

"Quiet neighbors," Warwick said. The men laughed and Tamara shot them a look.

"I meant the house. They've got more of a compound, so there's plenty of room," she said.

"What do you mean by *compound*?" Roddy asked.

"They started with one house, and bought the house next door years ago. When the house on the other side came up for sale they bought that, leveled it, and put in a smaller house to live in, and a parking lot," Tamara said. "This was years and years ago, mind you. I don't think all of this would be able to happen now."

"I don't either," Lilly said. "But back then, the houses they bought weren't anything special, nor was the neighborhood. Now it's worth a bit more."

"I half expect Whitney to—"

"I told you to shut up," a loud voice rose above the din of the dinner conversation. No one at the table turned to look. They'd learned to recognize the voice. Buzz Freeland.

Buzz Freeland was Stan's father. Buzz and Stan had been estranged for years, but right after the new year Buzz had shown up in Goosebush, on Stan's doorstep. Since then he'd become a fixture at the Star. Lilly had asked Delia about Stan and his father recently, but Delia had shrugged her shoulders. "He doesn't talk about his dad," was all the younger woman would say. Lilly couldn't help but wonder if Buzz was part of the reason Delia and Stan weren't connecting lately. She'd noticed how having his father around had changed Stan, and not for the better. Lilly hadn't spent nearly as much time with the young man over these past few weeks as she had in the past, but she still recognized that he wasn't himself. She could only imagine the changes Delia had noticed.

Lilly had been recuperating from home until the final thaw, so she hadn't met Buzz until he'd settled in. From then on he always sought her out when she came into the Star, determined to settle into a long conversation. For a moment, a brief moment, she was afraid that Buzz was, as Warwick put it, making moves, but soon enough Lilly realized that Buzz talked to everyone, and showed them the same amount of attention. Buzz was a charmer, but it was a hollow sort of charm, full of empty promise with no follow-through. Something about him made her uneasy. He'd become a fixture at the Star, and Lilly couldn't help but wonder that she wasn't the only person who was starting to avoid the place.

"God, you're an awful woman," Buzz said again, loudly. This time Lilly turned to look over her shoulder, and noted that he was talking to Whitney Dunne-Bradford at the bar. The man had a point, Lilly thought uncharitably.

Whitney walked back toward her table, but Buzz grabbed her arm and started to stand up.

"Dad," Stan said loudly from the other end of the bar. Buzz let go of her arm and Whitney went back to her seat and tossed some money down on the table. The Bradford, Bradford, and Marsh trio stood up and walked out of the restaurant.

Stan watched them go, and then he grabbed a bottle and topped off his father's drink, leaning in to say something. Buzz settled back into his barstool and turned his back to the restaurant. Soon the din of the room came back to normal levels.

"I wonder what that was all about," Ernie whispered.

"Poor Stan, his father's more and more difficult to manage," Roddy said.

"What do you mean?" Lilly asked. She looked over at Roddy's handsome face and couldn't help but smile. Roddy was both complicated and open, with a clarity of vision about the residents of Goosebush that came from being a newcomer with an uncanny knack of reading people.

"When his father first got here, what was it, five months ago?"

"The end of January, so almost," Ernie said.

"Buzz was on his best behavior. Most people were pleased that Stan could reconnect with his father," Roddy said. "Though one thing I dislike about living in a small town is that everyone knows everyone's business, the return of the prodigal father was a nice story."

"Gave a lot of folks hope for mending fences with their own family," Warwick said.

"But lately, now established, Buzz has been showing his truer colors. That's been giving people more to talk about."

"He hasn't been making Stan's life easy, that's for sure," Ernie said. "He's been running up tabs all over town. Stan stopped by the Triple B earlier today to pay off what Buzz owed us." Ernie owned Bits, Bolts and Bulbs, the local hardware store and garden center.

"Buzz came by the office Wednesday and wanted to set up appointments to look at houses in town," Tamara said. "He indicated that he and Stan needed more space." She made air quotes around the word *space*.

"Did you show him places?" Roddy asked.

"No, I gave him to Pete Frank," Tamara said. "Something about Pete and Buzz smooth-talking each other made me giggle."

"You have an evil side," Lilly said. Tamara had a point, though. Lilly's first husband was a smooth talker if ever there was one. Buzz would be a challenge for him. "I haven't talked to Stan for weeks.

We've had a few coffees scheduled, but he's canceled them all."

"He's canceling on a lot of people these days," Ernie said.

"He's not his normal happy self," Tamara said. "It must be difficult. I'm grateful my parents were never a burden."

"Indeed they were not," Lilly said. She and Tamara had been friends since they were three years old, and Lilly had thought of them as her second family.

"Hello, folks. Nice to see you all. You ready to order?" The server came up and stood to Lilly's side. She looked up and smiled.

"Chase, when did you start working here?" Lilly asked. Chase Asher was the grandson of her friend Portia.

"Hey, Ms. Jayne. Nice to see you. I've started to cover shifts on the weekends," Chase said. "It's wicked busy tonight; I didn't even notice you were the party sitting here. Glad that they got you started. It's nice to see friendly faces."

"We'll be the easiest table you have all night," Ernie said. "We'll start with—"

"Let me tell you the specials," Chase said. "Stan likes me to go through the whole routine."

"Far be it for me to get between a man and his spiel," Ernie said. "Lead on, Macduff."

"Okay, cool. Tonight the appetizer is—hold on for a second, I'll be right back." Chase moved quickly toward the bar, where Buzz had tried to lean over to grab a bottle and had instead knocked over several glasses. Stan was trying to clean it up, and push his father back in the chair at the same time. Chase arrived at Buzz's side as the older man was about to miss his barstool as he sat back down. Stan leaned over and spoke to Buzz. Buzz nodded and stood up, with the help of Chase and someone else at the bar.

"See you at home, son," Buzz said loudly.

Lilly couldn't hear what Stan replied, but she saw him hand a bag of food to Chase as the younger man helped Buzz leave the restaurant.

"Poor Stan," Warwick said.

"Indeed," Roddy said.

Lilly looked at both men and wondered about the tone of sympathy in their voices, wondering if it came from empathy or shared experience.

"Let's figure out what we're ordering before Chase comes back," Ernie said. "I looked at the specials on the way in. They've got steak frites with a Gorgonzola sauce—"

"Call 911," Chase screamed as he came back into the restaurant. "Buzz is—call 911!" He ran back out, and Ernie slid out of the booth so that Warwick could follow the young man. Lilly looked over at Stan, who stood there slack-jawed. She fished her phone out of her bag and dialed.

Chapter 4

"Thanks for waking up early," Delia said a few mornings later. They were driving on the nearly empty roads of Goosebush, heading toward the town cemetery. "I wanted to check out the viability of this project before our next beautification committee meeting."

"I'm glad to be here," Lilly said. "Thanks for waiting until my back straightened out again."

"I'm glad you're feeling better," Delia said. "But between Buzz's death and the end of the semester, this is my first morning free."

"It's been a week," Lilly said, looking over at her friend. "How's Stan doing? I've reached out, but I haven't heard back."

Delia shrugged. "He's not saying much. When we speak, which isn't often. To tell you the truth, Lilly, it's been hard to be around him for a while, but I keep trying. Now it's even worse. I don't think he's processed what happened completely."

"Of course not," Lilly said. "Unexpected deaths are challenging."

"Especially when there are unresolved issues."

"Especially then. Is Stan going to have a ceremony of some sort for Buzz?"

"That's one of the things he won't talk about. He had Buzz cremated right away, but he bought a plot for him. I think he feels like he should have a ceremony of some sort, but he isn't talking about the plans."

"The ceremony would be more for Stan than for Buzz. He deserves to know how many people care about him. I'll reach out again," Lilly said gently. They drove past the parking area. She took the next right and parked along the cemetery fence. It wasn't an official parking space, but it was the one that the Jayne family always used.

"I haven't been here in years," Lilly said, getting out of the car with her new routine of gently unfolding herself, moving her hips and arching her back. She didn't mind getting older. Most of the time. But the slight aches and pains that came along with the extra years—those she could live without. "I used to love coming here when I was young."

She was waiting for Delia to close her door before she hit the lock door button on her fob. Her final stretch done, she hit the button, but the door still wouldn't lock. She looked over at Delia, who was staring at her, her door ajar.

"What's the matter, Delia?"

"What do you mean, you used to love coming here when you were young," Delia said. "Sometimes you freak me out, you know that? This is a cemetery, Lilly. Who hangs out at a cemetery?"

"When I was really, really young my father would bring me here to clean up the graves in the spring. He'd walk me through, point out headstones, and tell me stories about the person resting there. He told great stories. That's probably what got me comfortable being here. I loved my father's stories."

"Lilly, it's an odd way to spend time with your father. You've got to admit that."

"Maybe. But those were special days. We'd always end up at the family crypt, do some weeding. In the spring we'd plant flowers—"

"Crypt?" Delia asked, finally closing her door. Lilly clicked the fob, though why she bothered to lock the car eluded her. No one was around this side of the cemetery, nor would they be this early. Most people parked in the designated lot. But Lilly was not most people.

They walked over to the gate on the corner, but it was closed and locked. Lilly looked at her watch and shook her head. "The gates should have been open a half hour ago," she said. "I wonder what's holding up Mac Townsend?"

"Don't you remember? He doesn't open the cemetery up anymore," Delia said.

"Did I know that?"

"Maybe? He sort of retired last winter."

"Sort of?"

"He's still working at the crematorium, but he isn't officially in charge of the cemeteries anymore. Cutbacks. Maybe that happened after your fall."

"How do people get in to pay respects?"

"There's a visitors' entrance by the parking lot

for foot traffic. If anyone wants to drive in, they need to coordinate with Sasha Bradford and she'll let them in."

Lilly turned and looked at Delia. "What do you mean, Sasha will let them in?"

"The cemetery board outsourced taking care of the cemetery to the Bradford Funeral Home."

"When did that come up for a vote?" Lilly asked.

"It was announced at one of the town meetings this winter," Delia said. "I gave you the minutes, but you may not have read them all."

"Obviously I missed that part. You miss a couple of town meetings and it all goes sideways."

"There wasn't a vote. The cemetery board said since they were all appointed, and in agreement, they'd save some money and accept Whitney's proposal." The Board of Cemetery Trustees was, in fact, appointed by the town moderator, an elected position. The town moderator attended town meetings and made procedural rulings when needed. Goosebush was run by the Board of Selectmen, a strong group of individuals who didn't make the moderator's job particularly easy. A new person had been elected this past winter, but Lilly had also missed that meeting. She needed to remedy that. The position didn't have a ton of power, but it did appoint several committees, and Lilly was always happy to offer her opinion on those appointments.

"We'll see about that," Lilly said. She walked over to the square granite post and put her bag on top. She swung one leg over the split rail fence. Ungracefully, she got the other leg over. Another thing that was easier when she was young.

"Lilly, what are you doing? You're going to hurt your back again."

"No, it's fine. Honestly. I feel like a new woman between Warwick's liniment and the stretches I've been doing. This is the easiest way to get into the cemetery," Lilly said. "I'm not walking all the way around to the front gate, and I don't feel like moving the car. Come on, Delia, jump over. Surely this can't be the first time you've climbed a fence."

"As a matter of fact," Delia said, handing Lilly her saddlebag, "it is. I'm a rule follower, Lilly." Delia put her hand on the post, and swung both legs over in a graceful vault.

"Show-off," Lilly said, handing her back her bag. "Let me get acclimated here. That should be Mercy Peabody's grave right there." Lilly walked over and faced the gravestone. "Got it in one."

Delia walked over and looked that the gravestone. "How did you know that?" she asked, taking a notebook and pen out of her bag, then taking out a document and unfolding it.

"I told you, my father would walk me around here when I was little. I always liked that name. Mercy Peabody. Then when I got older, I'd ride my bike here and spend hours exploring, sketching, reading."

"Did Tamara ever come with you?"

"No, she didn't like graveyards," Lilly said. "I'd come by myself. Quiet time with my thoughts."

"I'm with Tamara," Delia said. "It always gives me the creeps to be around all these graves."

"That's because you don't know the stories," Lilly said. "Let me tell you about Mercy Peabody. She was born in 16—"

"Lilly, maybe we can save stories for another time? We need to look at this proposal for a beautification project first."

Lilly sighed and took out her own notebook. She hoped this proposal had legs, so that they'd spend more time exploring. By the time the project was done, Delia would be a convert to the wonders of the Goosebush Town Cemetery. The beautification committee was an official town committee, formed by Lilly and some like-minded citizens who were concerned with some overlooked projects in town, and were willing to use some elbow grease and limited funds to change them. Happily, some of the students on the high school sports teams were volunteers, thanks to Warwick. The Girl Scouts counted work with the committee toward several different badges, thanks to Portia Asher's ingenuity. There was also a cluster of town gossips who helped out, but they mostly behaved. The work was fun, which helped keep people volunteering. The projects they took on were usually bold, short-term, and seemingly impossible either because of scope or red tape. Lilly excelled at navigating both those obstacles.

The cemetery project was suggested when Portia Asher, town elder and master gardener, came to a committee meeting with pictures of the disgraceful neglect of some of the graves.

"The old graves, the ones the tourists come to see, those are in good shape," she'd said at a recent meeting. "And of course, the recent graves are fine. Folks are still visiting regularly. But there are swaths of graves that have lichen and moss covering them. There's a problem with some thickets along the edges that are out of control. The grass is mowed, but that's it. If someone was looking for their relative, they'd have a hard time finding them." After the meeting, Delia and Lilly had volunteered to do a reconnaissance and report back.

"Remind me where the graves Portia was talking about are," Lilly said.

"They're in the middle, against the back fence." Delia took out a map that Portia had drawn, and looked around. "I'm having trouble figuring out where we are," she said.

"Let me see," Lilly said. She looked at the map, and then around. "I have another map that has more markers. I brought you a copy." She reached into her bag and took out her notebook, handing Delia one of the folded pieces of paper inside.

"This is interesting," Delia said. "What's it from?"

"Cemetery tours," Lilly said. Turning around, she made her way toward one of the driving paths. Like many old cemeteries, and this was a very old cemetery, the driving paths used to be for horse-drawn carriages so they were narrow, and not up to cars. The outer perimeter of the cemetery was car friendly, but only for hearses and a couple of limos. Being buried here took advanced planning, and a lot of walking. But many people felt it was worth it. Spots were limited in the historic cemetery. This wasn't a Jayne family problem, but Lilly had heard grumblings over the years from people who weren't able to get a plot.

"All right, Delia, see how Portia marked Bertram's Folly?"

"You mean, Field's Monument?" Delia asked, looking up and toward where Lilly was pointing. "The short obelisk right there?"

"That's the one."

"Why did you call it Bertram's Folly?"

"Bertram Fields wanted a proper tribute to himself for after he died, so he designed a monument. He had the base built while he was still alive, and put quotes about himself on three sides and his name on the fourth. Problem was he didn't leave room for his wife, or children. Apparently Bertram was a bit of a—"

"Lilly, can you tell me the story later, when I can write it down?"

"Sorry, you're right. No stories. Bertram's Folly marks the corner that Portia wants us to look at."

"That's a ways away," Delia said.

"Closer than it looks," Lilly said. "You're thinking that the obelisk is proportional to the base. It isn't. That's Bertram's folly."

The women walked for a few minutes, and then Delia broke the silence. "You may as well tell me. Why's it Bertram's folly?"

"No, you're right, let's focus on the job at hand."

"Lilly—"

The older woman smiled and looked at Delia. "Bertram had the base designed while he was alive. He oversaw the quotes being engraved, and picked the font for his name. He never found the stone he wanted for the obelisk itself. He spent years looking, to no avail. He left a small fortune in his will for his wife and son to continue the search, but he didn't make it binding. He also didn't specify the size in the will. So they found a piece of granite, had it cut, and called it a day. Bertram had imagined a twenty-foot-tall monument of polished marble or some such material. Instead, he got five feet of common stone, and his family got a windfall. My father always said that Bertram's folly served as a reminder to act as someone worthy of having a monument rather than assuming you deserved it."

"You're right. That's a pretty good story." They moved closer and Delia looked at the base. "Where's his name?"

"That's the other thing his wife did. She put her own headstone up against the side with his name. That's my favorite part of the story."

"I'm going to look him up—"

"Look her up. She outlived him by thirty years, and had a good time spending his money."

"That patch over there must be what Portia was talking about," Delia said, pointing to an untended area.

"Looks like. I can see why Portia found this area upsetting."

Cemeteries sometimes had areas that were underused and served as memorial gardens or places for reflection. This area could be mistaken for that from a distance, but the ivy that drowned the stones and the unkempt thicket of shrubs along the back indicated that some graves had lost a fight with nature. Lilly walked over and pulled up some of the ivy, tearing it away from one of the headstones.

"Died 1952." She pulled more ivy. "In Korea. This is a veteran's grave."

Delia wandered a few feet away and rescued another memorial. "Nineteen-fifty-five." She stood up and looked around. "Look at the brambles over there. I bet there are graves underneath. Why is this so overgrown?"

Lilly stood up and sighed. "This cemetery is huge and had pockets of neglect over the years. Not sure what happened here. Portia's right, it would be a good project for us to take on."

"The headstones are in pretty good shape, they just need to be cleaned," Delia said. She took out her phone and snapped some pictures. "I'll do some research on the best way to clean them that's not toxic."

"Once we tear out the ivy and cut back the bushes, we'll need to get some grass in here. We could put some flowers on the graves." Lilly looked around. "If we get a good turnout, an afternoon of work, tops."

"Not that creative a project."

"But important."

"Absolutely," Delia said. She pulled on a bit more ivy, and looked up at Lilly. "Do you think they'll let us do it?"

"Who? The Bradfords? Oh yeah, they'll let us do it. This is neglect, pure and simple. If they're supposed to be maintaining the cemetery, they're not doing a very good job of it."

"I didn't think this would make you so upset," Delia said.

"We need to treat people with respect," Lilly said.

"Why don't you tell me some more stories." Delia said. "Let's take a walk and see what else needs our attention."

Chapter 5

"The Reed family looks like they're in good shape." Lilly pointed to a block of headstones, all with new flowers in front of them. There were four short granite posts marking the area. Lilly recalled a short fence, but that had been removed years ago to make maintenance easier.

"Did you know the Reed family?"

"No, but I remembered the headstones from my walks years ago. They were all from the early 1900s. I used to think about what their lives must have been like. Two couples, Sarah and Josiah, Myles and Priscilla. I think Myles and Josiah were brothers, but I may have made that up. They are the bigger headstones. Then there are markers on the plot, for their children who didn't survive. See the four short pieces of granite? That sort of marked their plot."

Delia walked around and looked at the Reed headstones, while Lilly moved forward, testing her memory by trying to remember the names on other gravestones. She was right about fifty percent of the time, which wasn't making her happy.

"Lilly, could you come over here? Does this look right to you?"

Delia was standing in front of the Reed plots, and Lilly joined her. She noted the two headstones, proud that she'd remembered the names. But looking up and around, she realized what Delia was pointing to. Lilly's memory was that the four granite posts indicated the entire Reed plot, but now the markers were lined up by the headstones and there were two other graves in the area.

"I might have I remembered it wrong," Lilly said, dubiously.

"Maybe," Delia said, making a note. "Those two other graves are more recent. That could be why the area looks well-tended."

"Would they have moved graves?" Lilly wondered out loud.

"They might. I was doing some research on cemeteries. You don't really own a plot; you lease the land. Maybe the Reeds' lease was up."

Lilly looked at Delia, slightly aghast.

"What do you mean, lease?"

"It depends on the charter for the cemetery. I'll look into this one before we start guessing." Delia stopped, made some notes on the map, and more in her notebook.

"I mean, I suppose that makes sense," Lilly said. "But still, it's a bit unsettling."

"You seem upset," Delia said.

"Frustrated. I used to be able to tick off names of

different headstones, but not anymore. My memory is frustrating me."

"Maybe it's not your memory," Delia said quietly. "Why don't we look around some more?"

"Let's walk over toward the Jayne mausoleum. I know all the graves around that."

"You mentioned a crypt before. Is it a group of family plots?"

"No, it's a real mausoleum, Delia. A building. Surely you had to know my family went over the top, as always."

"Where is it?"

"Do you see that granite building over there?"

"That whole thing? I always thought that was some sort of old chapel. It's huge."

"My family never did anything halfway."

As they walked, Lilly noted more of the names she remembered, in addition to newer headstones.

"Why do you write it down every time I get a name wrong? Are you keeping score?" Lilly asked.

"What? No, of course not. I want to do some research on the names. See if they're connected with the other graves."

"There do seem to be a lot of newer headstones and markers here," Lilly said.

"Stan got a plot for his father. In section A-3."

"A-3." Lilly pulled out the old family map her father had drawn years ago and looked around. "Bertram's Folly is A-2. The Jayne mausoleum is A-5. We'll be able to find it, I'd imagine. That was nice of Stan, to get Buzz a plot in here."

"Yeah, well, it turns out that Buzz bought a plot for himself through Bradford's. At least he'd put a deposit on it. Stan has to pay off the balance. Over four thousand dollars."

"Four thousand?"

"For Buzz's spot."

"That seems awfully high," Lilly said.

"I thought so too," Delia said. "But he got really upset when I mentioned it."

"I'm sure Stan will come around."

"I'm not," Delia said. "We're good together when things are good, but during these rough patches, he pushes me away. And you know me, I'm not that good at reading people, or figuring out how to help when people don't want my help. So, I've been stepping back."

"You're better at reading people than you think—"

"Then I don't like what I'm reading."

Lilly nodded sympathetically, but didn't say anything. Lilly valued privacy more than most, and gave it to others as a default. She didn't like to hear that Stan was closing Delia out, though. Not only because it wasn't fair to Delia. He needed to talk to someone. She made a mental note to give him a call later.

They walked toward the Jayne mausoleum, and Lilly started to name the neighbors. There were a couple of times where she missed, and Lilly took pictures of the headstones while Delia took notes. Most of the new headstones were of the right time frame, but she didn't remember them.

"There it is, the family tomb," Lilly said, as they walked over to the granite structure. She walked over and patted the side of the building. Though large and ostentatious, the warm granite always made Lilly proud to be part of the family that had built it.

"Look at the workmanship on this. It's really something," Delia said. She noted the Jayne name over the door, carved into the granite. "These details are really wonderful." She stepped closer, looking at the decorations along the front. Walking around the side, she started to read the names that had been carved into the side.

"Your parents are here," Delia said. "I thought you said they were buried at sea."

"And in my garden," Lilly said. Last fall, the fact that Lilly had a memorial garden in her backyard had become fodder for gossip, a fact that still made Lilly wince. "My parents wanted to be spread around, as it were. They've got urns inside here. And I had their names carved so they'd be remembered."

"That's so—"

"Eccentric," Lilly said. "Don't worry about the label. My family defines *eccentric* in Goosebush, and that's saying something."

"What about Alan?" Delia asked.

"His name is on the other side," Lilly said. "We're running out of space on the building, since it's a family tree as well. Running out of space outside, not in. There's plenty of room inside. Not that I've been in there."

"Could you go in if you wanted to?" Delia asked. She walked to the front and looked at the door. "That's an impressive lock."

"Isn't it? The key's back at the house, so I suppose I could, though I don't see the point. I do like the idea of being etched on the side. It's a nice memorial."

"What about your garden? Isn't that enough of a memorial?" Delia said.

"My gardens may change," Lilly said. "I don't want whoever takes care of them forty years from now to be restricted by memorials." She stepped back and looked at the outside of the resting place of many generations of Jaynes. "Delia, do you want to hear the story of the mausoleum?"

"There's a story?" Delia said.

"With the Jayne family, there's always a story," Lilly said. "The Jaynes have been in Goosebush for a long time. When this cemetery became established, a lot of families reburied their people here, so they could all be together. The Jaynes took over this entire corner, but then people started buying neighboring plots. One of the Jaynes, I don't remember which off the top of my head, decided to claim the family space. He put up this short fence and started to build a place where the family could get stacked up if space ran out."

"Stacked up," Delia said. "That's rough."

"Sorry, that was my father's phrasing. He actually applauded the move. He was never a big fan of land being used for the past. Anyway, as—what was his name? Eliot. I think it was Eliot. As Eliot started to build, he got to know some stonemasons. He decided to offer the project for apprentices, a sort of patronage. It helps explain the ornate, and varied, carvings. People were learning and Eliot gave them free rein. That's why there's no one style."

"That explains why there are hieroglyphs next to Shakespeare. And different arches."

"Isn't it wonderful?" Lilly said. "I used to spend hours doing rubbings, delighting on finding mistakes that were shown in the relief, but not visible to the naked eye. I loved spending time on the bench back here—"

"What bench?" Delia asked, looking around.

Lilly and Delia were standing along the side of the tomb, and Lilly stopped and looked around. "See where that granite pillar is? That's an old horse hitching post. The bench was right next to that. I wonder where it went." Lilly walked to the front of the building and looked around.

"Here it is," Delia called out. "It's along the back of the tomb."

Lilly walked to the back and stood next to Delia.

"Is this the bench?" Delia asked.

"The one and only. It's supposed to be over there," Lilly said, quietly. She took her phone out for a picture. Without saying anything, she turned and looked at Delia.

"Maybe it was moved for some reason?" Delia asked.

"Perhaps. I'll check my email. I may have missed a notification."

"Should we try to find Buzz's plot?" Delia asked.

"Of course," Lilly said. She patted her parents' names as she and Delia walked back to the front of the tomb, and made their way toward A-3, Buzz Freeland's final resting place.

"I don't see where it could be," Lilly said.

"Neither do I," Delia said. "I don't really understand how these things work, since the graves aren't all lined up."

"They are in the newer cemeteries," Lilly said.

"But this one's too old. Still, you'd think we'd see a marker—"

"Or an empty space," Delia said.

Lilly looked around. "I don't see either." She wandered around and took more pictures. She turned on the video and did a walking tour of the places she remembered, noting any differences between her memories and what she was seeing. Granted, her recollections were fifty years old. But still. She didn't think she'd be that off.

Lilly sidled up to Delia and stood close by until she was done writing some notes.

"I texted Stan. He thought it was A-3, and asked me to send him some pictures," Delia said. "He's pretty upset."

"Why don't you drop me at Helen Garrett's house and go visit him?" Lilly said.

"I should go with you to Helen's," Delia said.

"I'll pass on your good wishes. Go be with Stan. He may not realize it, or appreciate you enough, but he needs a good friend right now."

Chapter 6

"I'm home," Lilly called out as she let herself in the front door. She stopped and listened. Not a creature was stirring, at least as far as she could tell. But what was that wonderful smell? She took a deep breath and smiled. Ernie had been baking.

Lilly took off her muddy boots and left them by the front door, replacing them with the slippers she'd left there for the purpose. There was a moment of hesitation at the coat closet. Windward was a wonderful house, but it held the cold, even in May. The heat was off and would stay off. No matter what, the heat went off on April 15 every year, and didn't go back on until October 15. This May morning the house was chilly and keeping her coat on was tempting. She thought about what her mother would say about wearing a coat inside the house, and went to hang it up. Crossing her arms, she ran her hands up and down, trying to generate heat. She considered going up to her bedroom to get a sweater, but the kitchen would be warm enough, and the gas fireplace in the porch would take the chill off.

Windward was a rambling Victorian with rabbit warrens of rooms that had been added on as the family's fortunes ebbed and flowed. When Lilly's father inherited it, his brothers were grateful that they'd escaped what they considered the family curse. George Jayne, along with his wife Viola, had maintained the house, with some improvements on the first floor and outside. But they hadn't had the means to do a lot of work. Lilly's brother had no interest in the house, or the cost of maintaining it, so Lilly inherited it from her parents, and spent years and a small fortune on restorations, renovations, and repairs.

Walking in through the front door, which few people who knew Lilly ever did, showed a grand entry hall, off of which were several rooms, including a living room, parlor, dining room, breakfast room, and two libraries. The floors in the hallway were marble, not Lilly's favorite. She had several rugs strewn about to warm the space up, and to cut down on the echo. The deep green walls and polished woodwork showed the house off, and the artwork that adorned the walls displayed lifetimes of collecting, and the eclectic taste of both Lilly and her relatives. She was so familiar with the hallway that she used to go days without looking around, but since Delia and Ernie had decided to move the artwork around, with Lilly's approval, Lilly made a point to slow down. Where had they found that painting of the lizard? And what had happened to that awful bat statue? Ernie had pointed out that there was enough artwork for a museum, and she knew he enjoyed curating the collections. She was getting used to the daily discovery of the Jayne collection, a bit embarrassed that it took Ernie and Delia to help her appreciate it.

"Ernie, are you here?" she called as she got closer to the kitchen. She heard a scuttling sound and bang, and two fur balls propelled themselves out of Delia's office, the former breakfast room, hooked a right, and ran toward Lilly. She paused and leaned over to pat Max and Luna on their heads, rubbing their ears and scratching them between the shoulder blades.

"Hello, my darlings," Lilly said. "I'm glad you're happy to see me, but I wasn't gone that long. Honestly, you have to stop being so dramatic about being without humans for a while. Someone will always be here for you both." She gave them some more rubs and stood up. Lilly hadn't had a cat for years, but that changed last fall when Max and Luna both became part of the household, much to everyone's pleasure. Luna was still a kitten, discovering something new and wondrous every day. Max was a few years older, but he did his best to keep up with her. They loved running down the hallway in the house, slipping and sliding on area rugs, doing a loop in the living room by jumping from chair to couch to chair and then back down the hall. At least once a day something crashed to the floor, but so far nothing valuable had been lost to their exuberance. Ernie kept them well supplied with museum putty, which they used liberally on photos, vases, and artwork to keep it in place.

The cats followed her down the hall, to the closed kitchen door. They both looked up at Lilly and back at the door. "You're right, the door shouldn't be closed." She pushed it open gently, and the cats pushed their way in and rushed to their water dish, where they made a huge show of drinking.

"Hi Lilly," Ernie said, looking up from a bowl where he was mixing dough with his hands. "Don't they have a water dish in Delia's office?"

"They have a water fountain, but you know them. They hate being left out."

"They're spoiled rotten," Ernie said, smiling.

"What are you making?" she asked, looking around at the two bowls covered with cloth on the kitchen table, and the tray on top of the stove, also covered.

"I've been watching reruns of the Brits baking, and decided to make some bread."

"Now? Don't you have to go to work?"

"The brioches are a slow rise, so I'm starting them this morning. Sorry I kept the cats out. I'm trying to keep the heat in here to give the yeast a fighting chance."

"No worries, I'm grateful for the warmth. It's very chilly this morning. Good for a brisk stroll."

"You okay? You look distracted." Ernie looked up and gave her a smile.

"I'm just back from a visit to Helen Garrett. Delia dropped me off."

"How is Helen?"

"Same. They're expecting her to pass in the next couple of days."

"Oh, Lilly. I'm sorry."

"I'm glad I got a chance to say goodbye."

"I'd give you a hug, but I'm covered in flour."

"It's the thought that counts."

"Let me know, there are plenty of hugs available. Losing a friend is hard, even when she's lived a long, rich life."

"Thanks, Ernie. It's the passing of a generation. But she did live a long life, bless her." Lilly blinked a few times and walked over to the sink to busy herself by pouring a glass of water. "Do you need some help?"

"I've got my system down, but thanks."

"You've been busy. Do you have some sort of event that you're bringing bread to?" Lilly asked, looking around at the towels covering dough. Four batches of dough were a lot of bread.

"Sorry, no. I find baking stress-reducing. Don't worry, I'll bring some to work."

"Are you stressed?" Lilly said, walking over and taking the coffeepot out of the machine. She rinsed it in the sink and added water.

"Tamara called me this morning. I'd put an offer in on a house, and I was outbid."

"Which house?" Lilly asked, pouring the water into the reservoir. "Do you want coffee?"

"I'd love some," Ernie said. "The house over by Route Three."

"The new Cape? You didn't love that house. You said that it didn't need enough fixing," Lilly said.

"I prefer places that I can work on, but it was a house in my price range, and had some potential. I could have learned to love it."

"All relationships need a spark for passion to ignite. You have to love your home, Ernie."

"Finding a house to buy is tougher than I thought it would be."

"You'll find a place soon," Lilly said. "Don't settle

for less than what would make you happy. Plus, you know I love having you here."

"And I love Windward, but still. I've been here for six months."

"And you want your own space. I get it," Lilly said. "Any regrets at selling Minh your house?" Last fall Ernie sold his house, bought a new one, and then sold that one to Minh Vann, the town's new archivist. The second sale was partially because Minh had a connection to the house. But it was mostly because Ernie had almost died in the kitchen and couldn't face living there after the ordeal.

"No regrets. She comes into the store at least three times a week, gleefully telling me about the latest repair that needs to be made, asking for recommendations of all sorts of tradespeople. She's keeping half of the folks who do construction in business these days."

"The house had been patched together for a long time," Lilly said. "I'm glad Minh is able to do that many repairs."

"I think I dodged a disaster, to be honest. Now," he said, turning the dough onto a floured board, "for my favorite part, the kneading."

Lilly put the old grounds into the compost bin and replaced them with the blend she ground. Before Delia moved in, Lilly got cans of coffee. No more. Now she used different blends for different times of the day, measured carefully, and used the right temperature of water. The fact that Delia and Ernie got her a heavy-duty coffee maker and latte machine for Christmas added to her interest in brewing.

"Were you with Delia? You were both gone when I

got up." Ernie barely looked up as he kneaded the dough.

"We went to the cemetery—"

"Right. Reconnaissance. Was Portia right? Is there a beautification committee project there?"

"Yes, there's some military graves that are overrun with ivy," Lilly said.

"Be good to do that before Memorial Day," Ernie said, looking up.

"That's what I was thinking." Lilly took two mugs out of the cabinet and brought them over to the table.

"Is there more? You sound distracted."

"I am, a bit. I had trouble remembering some of the names on the headstones, but that's probably age. Delia and I are going to do some more research on the cemetery."

Ernie looked up. "That sounds ominous."

"There seem to be some odd things happening. The Jayne bench got moved."

"What Jayne bench?"

"And apparently Buzz Freeland bought a plot there, but we couldn't find it."

"Buzz has a plot there? How? I couldn't get a plot there. Course that was a few years ago." Ernie cleared his throat and went back to kneading. His husband had died five years ago, putting him in the same club with Lilly, a club that neither of them wanted to belong to.

"Delia mentioned Stan paying over four thousand dollars—"

"Whew. That's a lot—"

"I know. Something's off about the whole thing,"

Lilly said. She shook her head, and focused on measuring the coffee.

"You mentioned that Delia dropped you off. Where is she?" Ernie asked, slapping some dough on the flour-covered table.

"She went by to visit Stan."

"Stan. She's trying, I have to give her that."

"What do you mean?"

"She keeps reaching out, dropping by, but he's shutting her down. Not just since Buzz died. He's been pulling away for weeks. I tried to give her advice when she talked to me about it, but it's been years and years since I had a date."

"Am I wrong to be disappointed in Stan?" Lilly asked as she sat down at the table and watched Ernie.

"Not wrong, no. He's changed ever since Buzz came to town. I think he's processing a lot, but still. He should treat our girl better than that." Ernie punched the dough down and shook his head. Neither he nor Lilly had children of their own, and they were both protective of Delia.

"I mentioned to Delia that I'd like to know when Stan's planning on having a ceremony for Buzz, so I could be there. I want to show my support."

"Stan got him cremated so fast I wondered if he was planning on doing anything with old Buzz."

"Ernie, that sounds like gossip," Lilly said.

"There's been some," he admitted. "People are wondering how Buzz died."

"They are, are they?" Lilly asked.

"Any unexpected death looks like a murder around here, especially after the last year."

"Oh for heaven's sake."

"Some are calling it the Goosebush curse. Don't

look at me like that, I didn't make it up. Do you want to hear more?"

"I suppose so," Lilly said, leaning back in her chair and watching her friend. She didn't like gossip, but it was helpful to know what people were saying.

"Mary Mancini said she heard people wondering if Stan killed his father because that was the only way he could get rid of him."

"That's terrible."

"Absolutely," Ernie said, pulling the dough into a ball and putting it into a bowl. "I told her that and reminded her that Stan's a good guy. Though he has been a jerk lately, so I may not have supported him as vigorously as I once would have."

"I really need to reach out to Stan," Lilly said. "I've been sort of a mentor to him with his business."

"Sort of? You've helped him tremendously. Helped me too, for that matter."

"I enjoy helping people with their business plans," Lilly said. "Makes me feel useful."

"He may listen to you. He could use a talking-to, otherwise he's going to lose Delia. And I think she's one of the best things to happen to him in a long time, even if he doesn't know it."

"I'm not going to get in the middle of their relationship, but I will remind him of how wonderful Delia is during the course of our conversation. Unobtrusively, of course."

"Of course," Ernie said, walking over to the stove. He took the dishcloth off the top of the pan, and sprinkled some sugar on the balls of dough that had been hiding underneath. "I really hope that if they break up, it's mutual and that he doesn't break her heart. I'd hate to pick sides."

"As would I. Though there isn't a question in my mind of which side I'd be on," Lilly said.

"None. I pity the fool that messes with our girl. There. The rolls are ready to go into the oven. I'll have time to try them before I go to work."

"I'll catch you up on my trip to the cemetery while we wait," Lilly said. "But let me get some paper first. I need to make some notes."

Chapter 7

Yankee frugality was a trait shared by many in Goosebush. Resoling Bass Weejuns rather than buying new, patching Brooks Brothers blazers, upcycling furniture, celebrating a car's 100,000 miles—these were part of the Goosebush way. The same spirit went for old buildings. Rather than tearing them down, in Goosebush buildings found a new purpose that suited them just as well. Such was the case of the old elementary school, which had become the new town library. The deal was a win-win. The costs saved on building a new library were rerouted to the new elementary school building. And the library moved into the airy, spacious school that perfectly suited its needs.

At least it used to. Like any successful project, demand soon outpaced supply. There was a proposal before the board to build an extension off the back of the building that would add accessibility, study carrels, and storage. Lilly had every confidence that the plan would pass. It helped that she was the chairman of the board, newly appointed earlier in the new year.

She parked in the back of the library, which meant that she could get to the historical society with limited human contact. The historical society had been promised new digs by way of a house bequest over a year ago, but probate was holding that up. Not confident the probate would clear soon, the architect had significant new space for the historical society added to the proposed addition, complete with its own entrance, so that the riches held within weren't constricted to the bowels of the building.

Riches they were. The town hall held most of the official documents of Goosebush. The historical society held the stories. Letters, pictures, diaries, newspapers, journals, audio recordings, and video. For years the maintenance was left to volunteers, all of whom had different and varying abilities. Until now. Last fall Minh Vann had been hired to oversee the archives and collections. She was part-time at first, but was going full-time on June first. The difference Minh had made was palpable. Sorting, scanning, and storing. Minh called those her three S's for success, and Lilly was a believer.

Lilly texted when she was close to the door at the end of the long basement hallway. The society wasn't officially open, but Minh made an exception for Lilly.

"Hello, Lilly, how are you," Minh said, opening the door and stepping into the hallway to welcome her friend.

Lilly waited until she was closer, and kept her voice low. "I'm well, and appreciative of your being willing to help. How are you?"

"I'm happy to be here, and to see you," Minh said. "I had to leave my house anyway. Lots of work being done today, and I was in the way. Fingers crossed; I may have a kitchen by the end of the week."

Lilly made a crossed fingers gesture and followed Minh into the society reading room. She hoped that the kitchen was going to work out this time, but she was wary. The old Preston house had more issues than a magazine stand, and new ones cropped up every day. But they were all met with amazing energy and enthusiasm by Minh and her children.

"You mentioned that you were looking for some records?" Minh asked.

"I'm not sure you have the information I need, but I thought I'd ask. Do you have any cemetery maps? I have this one that my father had. It's dated from 1900. He used it as a basis for some maps he, or more likely my mother, drew later. But I'm wondering if you have anything more recent, and more official?"

"That's odd," Minh said.

"I know. My grandfather was on the cemetery commission, and that's where this came from. I could go there and ask, but I'm trying to do some clandestine work."

"The request isn't odd. Who's buried where is a question we get once in a while. For some families we have funeral programs and prayer cards that add to the story. The new scanner is making it easy to connect that information to different records. Once we're done—"

"Minh," Lilly said gently. She'd learned over time that Minh would keep filling in the silence with words and ramble down new paths unless she was stopped.

"Sorry. What's odd about your request is that it's the second time I've gotten the question in the past month. I pulled some interesting information for her. Some of the old filing systems make it tough to find those kinds of records. I'm determined to figure it out, so I've been exploring. It's almost like I'm getting to know some of the old volunteers by their filing style. Did you know Marle—"

"Who asked you for the records last month? Can you tell me? Or is it wrong to ask?"

"The requests aren't officially public records—"

"That's fine, I thought I'd ask."

"But I do log all requests in this book," Minh said, turning the ledger around to face Lilly. "And I need to go back and print out some things to help you. I'll be right back."

Minh walked through the gap in the countertop that gave her access to the office part of the space. There were no walls, but she made a show of turning her back to Lilly while she accessed some records and started to print them out. "I have some other items I was going to scan. I'll go get them."

Lilly smiled and opened the ledger, flipping to the more recent pages. She was surprised by the number of people who had come in to request information. She ran her finger over the *request* column until she ran into cemetery records. The requester was J. Ross.

J. Ross. Lilly furrowed her brow and pursed her lips. No, she didn't know who J. Ross was. But she'd figure it out, and find out why they wanted information about the Goosebush cemetery.

Chapter 8

"Can you pass the salad?" Delia asked.

"This? This, my friend, is not a salad," Warwick said, passing the bowl to his right. "This is salad dressing being held together by cheese and toppings with a few pieces of kale for color. Delicious, but more of a decadent side dish."

"The kale makes me feel virtuous," Tamara said. "Warwick, baby, love of my life, do not rain on this salad parade."

"That's kale?" Lilly said, moving her fork around her dish to look more closely at the leaves on her plate. Warwick was being facetious. She saw a good amount of green, albeit pooled with vinaigrette.

"If you take kale, mix it with dressing, and rub the leaves a bit to soften them up, it loses some of the kale chewiness," Ernie said. He was always delighted to see his friends enjoy a meal he created. The two soups, two salads, and fresh bread were a huge hit. Leftovers might not be an option for tomorrow's lunch, not after tonight. Everyone was on seconds.

Roddy ladled more of the squash soup into his bowl. "Thank you for this wonderful meal, Ernie," Roddy said. "I had hoped to contribute a stew this evening, but I underestimated the cooking time. Perhaps we can try it tomorrow night?"

"You're on," Ernie said. "Stew is always better the next day. I'll make more bread. I've been stress baking a bit today." When Roddy raised his eyebrows, Ernie explained. "House issues."

"Ernie, we'll find you your house," Tamara said. "Have faith."

"I have faith in you," Ernie said. "But I had a moment. The bread baking helped. Fair warning though, friends. I tend to go on bread baking benders. You'll be getting a lot of different loaves over the next few days."

"My kind of bender," Lilly said, putting more butter on her bread slice. "This is delicious."

"Over-proved, but thank you," Ernie said. "Tomorrow morning's brioche should be better."

"What time should we be here?" Tamara asked, laughing and bumping shoulders with Ernie.

"Eight-fifteen," Ernie said, bumping her back.

"Ernie, I'm glad you live here," Delia said. "Honestly, I really am. Before you moved in, it was so—"

"Quiet?" Ernie said, laughing.

"Yes, but not that. Things weren't as—"

"Sunny," Lilly said. "I think that's the word you're looking for, Delia. Ernie brought a lot of light with him."

"That's a good word," Delia said, taking another slice of bread.

"You ladies are the best," Ernie said. He cleared his throat and took a sip of water. "I'm enjoying being here, that's for sure. But I think that the addition of fur has also added some light to the house."

Everyone looked over at the chair where Max and Luna were nestled. They were sitting out in the porch, which had been well insulated over the winter and was now more like a family room. While Lilly had been laid up, Ernie had made some adjustments to the plans that included raising the floor to house level and adding a ramp rather than a staircase out to the greenhouse. He'd also extended the porch the full length of the house, and put a French door on Lilly's library. What had started as a winterizing project had become a small addition, but Lilly was delighted by the results. She'd always call it a porch, but now it was the center of the house. The wonderful views of the garden through the large windows ensured that.

Lilly had ordered a new round table for the porch, making sure it was large enough to fit all members of the Garden Squad. The sides could be lowered and the leaf taken out, if a smaller table was needed. So far, it had stayed open and well used. Lilly dreaded the day it wasn't. She sighed and looked around.

"I hate to bring up business," Lilly said.

"Did someone die?" Warwick asked.

Tamara hit him on his arm, and looked over at her friend. "What is it, Lil?"

"Delia and I went to the Goosebush cemetery today," Lilly said. "I hadn't been there to wander for years. I've been to funerals, of course, but hadn't spent time."

"Visiting your old friends?" Tamara said.

"Old friends?" Roddy asked. He'd finished his soup and leaned back in his chair.

"There were a couple of years where Lilly spent hours and hours in the cemetery," Tamara said. "It all started when her father did a walking tour to raise some money, and he brought her to practice."

"I don't understand," Roddy said.

Lilly sighed. "I was about twelve. Daddy used to take people on informal tours, but then some group asked him to do it as a fundraiser. He took it very seriously and spent a lot of time doing research, finding stories, connecting them to living people. He took me for rehearsal walks. Anyway, over time, it became something my father did a few times a year."

"The tours were interesting and entertaining. Your dad should have been an actor," Tamara said. "He had a presence."

"He always said that storytelling was an inherited trait. Apparently, his grandmother would tell him stories every time they went to lay flowers and clean off the family plots on her side of the family. There was one name, Rachel Hutchinson, who haunted me. She was the only Hutchinson in the cemetery, and died when she was fourteen. I wondered about her and her family. I asked my father about her, and he told me I should find out for myself. He showed me how to look up records at the town hall, sent me to the historical society, had me look in church records."

"What was her story?" Ernie asked.

"She died in the flu pandemic in 1919. Her father had been injured in World War One, so the family moved to New Hampshire to live with her mother's family. The father died in 1922 and the mother remarried. It took me months to figure it out. I always made sure her grave was cleared off. Anyway, whenever I'd visit the family crypt, I started to pay attention to the neighbors. That's what my father called the other headstones. I memorized names and tried to find out who they were."

"Family crypt?" Roddy asked.

"The Jayne mausoleum," Delia said. "I'd noticed it before, but didn't realize what it was until today. It's really beautiful."

"I always thought it was spooky," Tamara said. "Back in the day, Lilly loved hanging out there, bringing a picnic, sitting on that bench and reading for hours."

"The bench was moved," Lilly said.

"What do you mean?" Tamara said.

"It's moved. It's right up against the back of the mausoleum."

"What? Who would do that? How could they do that? Did they damage it?"

"It seemed to be in decent shape, but I didn't look too closely," Lilly said.

"Lilly noticed some names on the headstones weren't the same as she remembered, either," Delia said.

"That's probably a faulty memory. I kept thinking some of the neighbors have moved. But how would that be possible?" Lilly said.

"What do you mean?" Ernie asked.

"Like I said, I memorized the headstones, especially the ones near the family. They were all there, but there were some new people as well. I went to the historical society and Minh helped me find some cemetery records so that I could compare my memory to what's there. The only detailed record I could find backed up my memory. It was from 1987."

"Maybe they've moved graves to make room?" Roddy said.

"Maybe, but that doesn't explain how the bench got moved," Lilly said.

"Lilly, tell Roddy the story of the bench," Warwick said.

"The bench and base were all carved out of a single piece of granite. It hasn't been moved in over a hundred years," Lilly said.

"That must be quite something," Roddy said.

"It's not very large, but it is—"

"That's not the story Warwick was talking about," Tamara said. "The bench is called the bastard bench, Roddy. I remember Lilly's dad telling me once that the bench was outside the official family mausoleum boundaries by design, but it was still part of the family plot."

"Created to remember the Jaynes who were Jaynes by blood, but not by name," Lilly said. She didn't particularly love the nickname of the bench, though she had to admit it was accurate.

"Were there a lot illegitimate family members?" Ernie asked.

"No one's added to the bench lately," Lilly said. "But back in the day, three people who were officially recognized to be part of the family were buried in their own plots. The bench is their memorial so that future generations remember them. Other names were added over the years as family connections were confirmed, even if the owners of the names weren't buried in the cemetery. We did that to help clarify parts of the Jayne family tree."

"The bench is part of the Jayne plot," Tamara said.

"It never should have been moved without Jayne permission."

"That's what I think," Lilly said. "I'll admit I'm a bit befuddled lately. But the bench being moved? I certainly didn't approve that."

"We'll figure it out, Lilly," Delia said quietly.

"I know we will," Lilly said. "I'm being overdramatic. It's frustrating when you can't trust your own memory."

"What do you mean, Lilly?" Roddy asked gently.

"I kept misremembering names. Names I knew like the back of my hand. Listen to me. Delia's right. We'll figure it out, one way or the other."

After a pause, Roddy asked about Portia's idea for a beautification committee project.

"There are some graves in the cemetery that are suffering from neglect," Lilly said. "I think some cleanup would be a great project."

"Whitney doesn't love the idea," Ernie said. "She said that the care and maintenance of the cemetery wasn't a public effort, and needed oversight by people who knew what they were doing."

"When did you talk to her?" Tamara asked.

"She came by the Triple B this afternoon," Ernie said. "She was buying some weed killer."

"Someone must have seen us walking around," Delia said. "I guess that as long as it gets done—"

"Whitney spraying weed killer in the cemetery doesn't warm my heart," Lilly said.

"Lilly, why don't we drive by the cemetery tonight," Tamara said.

"Tamara, it's getting dark. What are you going to see?" Warwick asked his wife. "I've got some grading to do."

"I want to see the bench," Tamara said. "Lilly can drop me home afterwards. You go ahead and start your grading."

"What's the big deal about this bench?" Ernie said.

"The Jayne family gave a lot of money to the Goosebush cemetery to take care of their family plots in perpetuity. If the bench was moved, there's shenanigans afoot. I want to see," Tamara said.

"I'll go with you," Ernie said.

"I'm going to stay here and clean up," Delia said. "I have a few more projects to grade."

"I'll help Delia clean up, and start grading," Warwick said. "Roddy, buddy, you go with the three of them and keep them out of trouble. I'll see you all back here."

Tamara's car was large and comfortable, since she used it to take clients to see houses. Ernie sat up front, and Lilly and Roddy got in the back seat. They drove over toward the cemetery, and Tamara pulled in alongside the fence. The sun hadn't set yet, but it was getting dark.

"There's the Jayne crypt," Tamara said, slowing down and pointing.

Roddy leaned over Lilly to look out the window. "The big gray granite house? That's for your family?"

"I believe I used the term mausoleum," Lilly said.

"You did, but I pictured a much smaller building," Roddy said. "That's very impressive."

"Even more so up close," Lilly said. "The facade is highly decorated."

"I'll admit, I thought it was an old caretaker's cottage. Nice location, back there in the corner," Ernie said. "Since Lilly usually undersells, not oversells, I can't wait to see it up close. We could try and go now, but it's quite a ways back."

"The location speaks to the relative who picked it," Lilly said. "He wanted it to be difficult to get to, and fairly secluded."

"Was it the same relative who built your house?" Ernie asked.

"His son," Lilly said. "He made the same larger-than-life choices, though. Normally you could have seen the bench from here. Now it's along the back side of the building."

"How large is the cemetery?" Roddy said. "I'll admit, I haven't driven past here much."

"This is the oldest cemetery in Goosebush," Tamara said. "There are two more, which you've probably driven past. They were more planned. This neighborhood is pretty residential, expect for the cemetery campus."

"Campus?" Roddy asked.

"There's a crematorium, small chapel, a few parking lots," Lilly said.

"The crematorium also has a chapel, but it's more modern since it's a more recent addition," Ernie said.

"A crematorium? Who runs it?" Roddy asked.

"Officially, the town," Lilly said. "For Goosebush residents, it's a local service at a very reasonable rate. For nonresidents, the cost is higher. It's one of the few crematoriums in this area."

"I'll drive you back and show you," Tamara said. "We might get a better look from there. I'd love to see the bench, but I don't feel like jumping the fence in the dark."

"Scaredy-cat," Lilly said.

"You bet," Tamara said, putting the car in gear.

She did a U-turn and went back out, taking a left, and then another left. "This road was built specifically to make sure funeral processions had a place to go. As you can see, it goes into a rotary. Off to the left, you can get out to the back road. The rest of the roundabout leads to the chapel there, and some parking. Let's go back—see that building, that's the crematorium. Hmm, I wonder what's going on?"

"What?" Lilly asked. It was her turn to lean over Roddy to look out the window.

"The crematorium looks lit up, but it should be closed this time of day. What's that?" Tamara drove around so that her headlights flashed on the cars outside the building.

"Looks like a Bradford Funeral Home hearse," Lilly said.

"And that gray Mercedes? Unless I'm mistaken, that's Whitney Dunne-Bradford's car."

Chapter 9

Lilly and Tamara met at her office the next morning. Lilly was wearing her workout clothes, leggings and sneakers under a tunic-style shirt and a jacket. Once Lilly had started to feel better, she realized that walking helped, so she made a pact with Tamara to join her for walks. They'd been meeting three times a week since the beginning of April.

"Let's go by Alden Park first," Lilly said.

"Fine. But let's walk to the shipyard afterwards. The long way," she said, giving her friend a side-eye.

Lilly nodded. She was not going to fight Tamara on this. She knew, or suspected, that Delia and Tamara had cooked up these walks to help Lilly get more fit, and she didn't mind the caring or the intention. She knew too many sixty-six-year-olds who could barely walk anymore, so she practiced gratitude and rolled her hips to get them warmed up.

They couldn't get into Alden Park, but Tamara knew where they could stand outside and peek in through a gap in the boards. Lilly was impressed. A lot of work had been done. The edging stones were set and the rubber rims were in place on the paths. They watched as concrete was poured in small batches, then flattened, colored, and stamped.

"I'll admit, when Roddy was insistent on concrete, I thought it was going to look terrible. But this looks decent," Tamara said.

"Decent?" Lilly said. "That powder they're throwing on the concrete gives it a lot of depth. It looks like fieldstones. Without the uneven surfaces. Fascinating."

Lilly had smiled at the thoughtfulness of Roddy and his plan for Alden Park. Grateful, as always, that he'd bought the house next door a year ago, she was getting to the point where she couldn't remember what life was like before Roddy, and didn't want to imagine life without him. She shook her head. Her mind was wandering to places she wasn't emotionally prepared to go.

"The progress is looking good," Lilly said to Tamara.

"Looking great," her friend corrected. "I can't tell you how excited people are about the park. Really excited. Did Roddy show you the running paths?"

"He did, including the different surface on most of them."

"Roddy's so smart. There are running groups who are dying to use the park."

"Goosebush does lack walking, and running, paths," Lilly said.

"Unless you know where to go, like we do. Ready?" Tamara held up her water bottle and smiled at Lilly.

"Ready," she said, lifting hers up and clinking Tamara's.

Goosebush was not a big town. It was founded in
the 1600s, and was known for shipbuilding for a short
period of time. Soon other towns took over the in-
dustry, and Goosebush was forgotten and slightly neglected. Then the town became a fashionable place
to summer in the late 1800s, which brought it back fi-
nancially. That didn't last either, but by the 1970s the
town had become a hidden gem with good schools,
great views, and beach access. The town beach was a
spit of land that faced the Atlantic Ocean on one
side, and a bay on the other. There were oyster beds,
clam beds, nesting areas, and other interesting at-
tractions on the beach, but for Lilly, the main attrac-
tion was the unspoiled beauty.

Tamara and Lilly walked into the main rotary in
town, the Wheel, so named because it was supposed
to look like a captain's wheel. Some people called it
the Hub, which made a bit more sense since this rotary was the center of most activity in Goosebush.
There was a flagpole in the center and six roads fed
off of it. The road to Lilly's house was directly across
the street, but instead of going there, Tamara took
the second right, and they walked down Standish
Street. Both women knew exactly where to turn to
get to the shoreline of Goosebush.

There wasn't much they didn't know about the
town. They'd both been born and raised there.
Tamara's family had been in Goosebush almost as
long as Lilly's, but neither of them knew that when
they met at three years old. All they knew then was
that they made each other laugh, and liked the same
things. Over the years since, their friendship had
deepened and changed. They'd seen each other

through heartbreaks and joy. Because of their friendship, Lilly had learned a lot about racism in her beloved town, and she'd committed herself to creating change where she could. They'd both seen each other through the loss of a spouse and their parents. Lilly had also learned the joy of loving children and grandchildren unconditionally, thanks to being part of Tamara's life and being "Auntie Lil" to two generations.

Over the years, Lilly had helped Tamara embrace her talents for leadership and business. And Tamara had helped Lilly embrace being a Jayne, eccentricities and all. When Lilly had given up cashmere sweater sets and wool pants for patterned dresses, Tamara had seen her friend flourish and move into this new phase of her life, the phase of being Lilly Jayne. This was after Alan had died, so Lilly no longer had any part to play except the role of being herself. She was no longer the professor's wife, or George and Viola's daughter. The Lilly walking with her friend had always been there, but she'd been hidden by social norms.

"Do you remember when we used to ride our bikes down here?" Tamara said as they made their way down the barely paved street toward the water. Some side streets, like this one, were left in bad shape intentionally to discourage cars from taking shortcuts and speeding. With every winter the residents got their wish, and the potholes grew.

"We were both, what, nine? My parents weren't going to get me a bike, but when you drove up in yours, they gave in."

"What freedom. We rode all over town."

"Remember the double baskets your father bought us? That really opened things up. We could pack enough stuff to be gone for the entire day," Lilly said.

"Of course, looking back, I do wonder what they were thinking, letting two nine-year-olds ride around for hours."

"We were good kids and always got home for dinner," Lilly said. "They really didn't have to worry about us then, or all through high school."

"We were nerds, Lil," Tamara said, laughing. "We studied hard, barely dated, and focused on getting out of town."

"And we did, for a while. Then we came back."

Tamara nodded. "Tyrone asked me if I regretted moving back to Goosebush, and staying. I really don't. When I was young, I lived in my parents' shadows. But now, I've created my own. And so all my kids have moved out of town. Though, I'm happy to say, Rose and Gordon may be moving back."

"How wonderful," Lilly said. Tyrone was Tamara's youngest child, her only son. He was in graduate school, and home for spurts of time between internships. Rose, Tamara's youngest daughter, lived close to Boston with their toddler, Alan. "Why the move?"

"The schools are good here, and Gordon's got a new job that lets him work from home more, so the commute isn't as much of a factor. Goosebush is only one place on their list, but there are benefits to being here. Including built-in babysitters. I include you in that, Lilly."

"I adore baby Alan," Lilly said. "I'd love to have him visit more. I was planning on putting the fence back up, the one along the driveway, to keep Luna in the backyard if she gets out. Alan's another reason to get that done."

"Alan is a dear baby, but he's a terror," Tamara said. "Warwick and I were talking about the baby-proofing we need to do at the house, and there's a lot to be done. But he's worth it."

"You must be thrilled that Rose wants to move back," Lilly said.

"Honestly, I think it's Gordon's idea. She still takes Goosebush for granted, having grown up here. He loves the town."

"She'll appreciate it more now," Lilly said. "You know, when I married Alan I was more than happy not to live in Goosebush. We lived in Cambridge and came down on weekends. But after my father died, and left me the house, he wanted to live here. Partially to be there for my mother. But also because he loved it here. He gave me a new appreciation of the town."

They had made their way down to the shoreline. To walk over to the shipyard there would be a complicated zigzagging of walking on the beach, up on the street, across parking lots, and through a couple of lawns.

"You sure your back is up to this?" Tamara asked.

"I'm sure. I may need you to give me a hand once in a while, but I'm feeling better than I have in months."

"I'm glad to hear it. Listen, I called a couple of people on the Board of Selectmen to talk about the cemetery," Tamara said.

"Learn anything?"

"Nothing that made me feel better. In fact, quite

the opposite. You know how the cemetery board is appointed by the town moderator? Well, the checks and balances seem to have gone off the rails. The Bradford Funeral Home somehow got contracted to oversee the grounds, and they're also selling plots for the town and getting a small commission."

"Surely there are only so many plots, especially in the original cemetery," Lilly said.

"That's a gray area," Tamara said. "When you buy a plot, you lease the land."

"Delia mentioned that."

"They could be finding new space by looking at unused plots, gaps, that sort of thing."

"Sounds like they may be within their rights—"

"Something tells me that Whitney's pushing it. Who's paying attention to what's going on, that's what I have to wonder. She's got herself, or Dewey or Sasha, on every decision-making board that affects her business. That feels like a bad idea for anyone to have that kind of influence, never mind Whitney."

"What are you going to do?"

"Start looking into it, what else?"

"Are the rest of the board agreed?" Lilly asked. She'd served on the Board of Selectmen and knew how challenging that could be. The town hired a manager to run things, but the board made all the decisions. Needless to say, there were a lot of politics involved.

"Ray Mancini said that by asking questions we may be opening a can of worms. I told him to take out the can opener."

"Thanks, Tamara. There's something odd going on."

"The Jayne bench being moved is what got Ray willing to take a look. Ray is reaching out to Mac

today to ask if he oversaw that before he retired."
Cormac Townsend had overseen the Goosebush
cemetery for over thirty years before he retired in
December, and knew more about what happened on
those grounds than anyone else alive. Lilly had never
warmed to Mac, but she didn't hold that against him.
A lot of folks didn't warm to her either.

"I can't imagine Mac moving the bench and not
giving me a call," Lilly said.

"Neither could anyone else. The Jayne bastard
bench is a piece of Goosebush history."

"I hate that nickname."

"Come on, that's pretty funny. How many families
create a memorial to all of the illegitimate relatives
in generations?"

"The bench was my father's great-aunt Agnes's
idea. Family history painted her as an uptight spin-
ster, but with a modern lens I think she was a woman
who lived outside her time. She never married,
though she did have a friend named Ellen who she
lived with, probably a Boston marriage. She inherited some money and taught school. She also had the
means to support some members of the family, and
was not a fan of her brothers, both of whom had several affairs. My father called it the spite bench."

"Bless Aunt Agnes. Her spite bench has given us a
new mystery to solve. Good thing. I was getting
bored."

"Are you sure you don't want to walk right back to
your office?" Lilly teased as they made their way up
the front path of Lilly's house.

"Oh, I'll walk back, but first let me collect myself. Take a load off for a minute."

"Why don't you have some lunch," Lilly said. "There's more soup and we can make some sandwiches with Ernie's bread." She put the code into the front door and it unlocked. Though she'd resisted the new locking system when Ernie had suggested it, she had to admit that she no longer worried about forgetting her keys. And being able to see who was at the front door without having to walk the length of the house delighted her, though she didn't usually have her computer on when the doorbell rang.

Both women went upstairs to refresh themselves. Lilly took a quick shower and put on her normal uniform—a cotton dress with a nipped waist and full skirt. Today's dress was covered with red cabbage roses. She slipped on some flats, grabbed a cardigan, and went downstairs to the kitchen.

She walked over to the cabinet and took two glasses out, then over to the refrigerator, where she filled them both with water. She took a long sip and took a deep breath. She enjoyed the long walks she and Tamara took, even though she complained about the pace her friend set. Sure, she was a bit achy and would need a nap, but still. The exercise, and spending time with her best friend, were the best thing for her.

"I'm glad that I left some clothes here," Tamara said. She walked into the kitchen, looking pulled together with black wool pants and an oatmeal-colored sweater. She was tying a scarf around her neck—Lilly recognized it as one of hers. She smiled. The colors looked much better next to Tamara's brown skin, complemented by her gold earrings. Or were they Lilly's?

"They're your earrings," Tamara said, taking the glass of water from Lilly while she read her mind. "So's the scarf. Hope you don't mind. I saw the scarf lying on the bed, and was inspired."

"The scarves on the bed are all part of my purge," Lilly said, opening the refrigerator and pulling out containers of soup and sandwich makings.

"Let me go through them before you give them away," Tamara said. "What made you decide to purge?"

"I don't wear scarves often and if I do, they're the same ones. That was one of my mother's. It looks much better on you."

"Yeah, that's because I'm a fall. You're a winter, Lilly."

She laughed, remembering the conversations about color seasons from several years back. Lilly had never paid much attention to fashion, preferring instead to dress as she pleased, especially now. When Alan was alive she'd played the part of faculty wife and businesswoman, complete with wool suits, cashmere sweaters, silk blouses, and fashion-first footwear. Now that he was gone and she was retired, she dressed for herself, and comfort.

"What I am is hungry," Lilly said. "What sounds good? I'm thinking squash soup and maybe a turkey sandwich?"

"Perfect. I'll make the sandwiches," Tamara said. "I'm sorry that Ernie's stressed about the houses, but I'm thrilled that he's working through the stress by making bread."

"I'm going to gain ten pounds—"

The kitchen door swung open and Delia walked in. "Delia, you gave me a start," Lilly said.

"Seriously," Tamara said, putting her hand on her chest. "I didn't even hear the car."

"Delia's got a new hybrid," Lilly said. "It barely makes a noise."

"Sorry, I didn't mean to scare you," Delia said. "I'm supposed to be at the library, but I needed to come home . . . I just saw Stan." She reached up and rubbed her eyes, further smearing her mascara.

Lilly stopped stirring the pot and walked over to Delia, opening her arms a bit. Delia stepped in for a hug, but didn't stay long.

"I went by his house this morning. He said he was glad to see me, but he was distracted. He was going to the cemetery to look at his father's plot, and I offered to go with him."

"Did you find it?" Lilly said. She took Delia by the elbow and had her sit at the kitchen table.

"Yes, he'd given me the wrong coordinates before. The new grave is over by the Jayne family area. I took a picture to show you. There didn't seem to be enough room, but Stan said it was only a marker. I tried to ask him questions, but he shut down."

"I'm sure he's upset," Tamara said. She put a sandwich in front of Delia and smiled. "Eat. I'm making tea."

"But why won't he talk to me?" Delia said. "He acts like he's mad at me, but I don't know what he's mad about. It's like I can't do anything right."

"Oh, honey," Tamara said.

"What? Why are you looking at me like that?"

"Delia, I have three daughters, and they've all been through this."

"Through what?"

"I don't know how to say this, but how are things with you both?"

"Okay, I guess. We haven't been seeing each other much these past few weeks. Months. Since Buzz came, and the semester got busy. Why do you ask?"

Tamara looked over a Lilly, who shrugged. "It's just that, well—"

"Delia, sweetie, it's been a long time since I was your age," Lilly said. "But sometimes when a man acts like a jerk—"

"Stan's not a jerk," Delia said.

"I know he's not," Lilly said, looking at Tamara.

"But when he acts like one, he may be trying to get you to break up with him," Tamara said.

Delia looked over at Lilly, who nodded.

"That sucks," Delia said. "Do you think that's true?" She looked over at Lilly.

"I don't know what he's thinking," Lilly said.

"That's probably *not* what's happening here. He's a good guy, with a lot going on. Hang in there, Delia," Tamara said, putting the tea on the table.

"I don't think our relationship is the only reason he's distracted," Delia said. "Stan said that they'd taken some samples from Buzz, and they were running tests. He's freaking out a little."

"Samples? What samples. Who's *they*?" Lilly asked gently.

"You know, blood and tissue samples. Whatever they use to try and figure out how Buzz died. Bash told Stan it was routine. Stan cursed him up one side and down the other, and got really upset when I said Bash was only doing his job." Sebastian "Bash" Haywood was the Goosebush chief of police, a job that had gotten very complicated in the past year.

"Running tests seems pretty normal," Tamara said, giving Lilly a look as she set the teapot down on the table.

"I'd imagine so," Lilly said.

"They haven't found anything," Delia said. "I texted Bash to ask about it, and that's what he told me. Just routine."

Lilly nodded and turned to start ladling the soup. She knew that unless they knew what to look for when they were running tests, finding out what might have caused Buzz's heart attack would be very difficult, if not impossible. Still, she had to wonder, was there something odd about Buzz's death? Was that what worried Stan?

Chapter 10

Delia went to her office after lunch, and hadn't emerged since. Lilly had knocked on her door, but Delia told her she was fine, and would keep working on her dissertation.

That worried Lilly. At this point she was double-checking sources, formatting footnotes, and going over her advisor's notes for the umpteenth time. She'd been given an extension on her deadline after Alan died, but the clock was ticking and she needed to hit *submit* so that she could defend it. Delia was ready, but self-doubt kicked in. Lilly couldn't help her get past that; she'd tried, but the end result was usually Delia locking herself in her office for twenty-four hours and ignoring the rest of the world while she went through it all again.

Lilly walked into her back porch. Part of the work that had been done over the winter included re-thinking the flow of the room, and its purpose. The width had been extended, and a new wall of French doors looked out into the gardens, so that the sight lines were clear from the front of the house through to the back wall. A small gas fireplace had been relocated to the right as you entered the porch, with a small sitting area nearby. The door to Lilly's library was to the side of the couch.

To the left, along the side wall, another doorway had been added, one that led down a ramp into a mudroom where boots, gloves, and other gardening paraphernalia could be stored, but kept for easy access. At the other end of the mudroom was the entrance to the greenhouse. Lilly made her way down the ramp and opened the door, making sure that neither cat followed her in.

The greenhouse was temperate, as always. Lilly misted the seedlings, separated a few plants that Ernie had brought home, and repotted some others. Bits, Bolts and Bulbs, Ernie's store, had a flourishing garden center, partially thanks to Lilly. She spent a couple of hours a week in the store watering and weeding, taking plants home that needed some extra TLC, required a new pot, or were now off-season. Ernie had texted that he was bringing home some plants that she'd find of interest. She cleared off a workbench and checked her watch. He'd be home soon.

Lilly went out to the mudroom again, and out another exit to the gardens. She still wasn't used to the new cobblestone area, complete with a tiled potting table, sink, and faucet. The surface doubled as a food prep station for the grill. They hadn't christened the area yet—it was still a bit too chilly for outdoor dining, but it would happen soon. Warwick and Ernie were excited about the cooking, since they'd both designed the adjacent grilling area. Lilly was excited about the eating, and the dinners they'd be hosting.

Though April showers were supposed to bring May flowers, April had a couple of snowstorms that threw the cycle off. May had been rainy early on, but now it had been dry for a few days. Ernie had suggested that Lilly add rain barrels next to the greenhouse, where gutter runoff could be reused to water her gardens. She'd been hesitant, but was glad she'd listened. She checked that the soaker attachment was on one of the rain barrels and turned the lever, setting the timer on her watch for ten minutes.

She heard a short horn and looked over toward the driveway. "Hey, Lilly, I'm glad you're there. I have some flower flats," Ernie called from his car. He was parked three quarters of the way down the driveway, where the retaining wall was five feet instead of its twelve feet closer to the garage. "Can you come in the garage to help?"

Lilly walked over to the garage and opened the side door. The garage was a feat of design. The driveway dipped down below grade, but the garage had been designed to ensure the cars' safety from floods by having an interior incline so that the cars were a story higher. From the outside the building looked like a garage with an in-law apartment. Inside, the cars ended up on the same level as the gardens.

"Let me get the wagon," Lilly said to Ernie, who had parked and lifted up the hatch on the back of his SUV.

"Excellent," he said. "That will make it easier."

The flatbed wagon was soon full and Lilly pulled it toward the greenhouse, thinking about the dozens of tepid tulips that were moving in. She unloaded the flowers and pulled the wagon back out to the garage. Ernie had finished unloading and was waiting for her. This trip was full of more tulips, potting soil, and several pots. Ernie carried a couple of bags and followed her into the greenhouse.

"What are these for?" Lilly asked him. They'd put everything on the stainless-steel potting table she'd cleared.

"They were a special order for Helen Garrett," Ernie said.

"Helen ordered them?" Lilly said.

"No, her cousin did. But she over-ordered and panicked. I told her not to worry, we'd use them."

"You know, I didn't realize that Helen had a cousin," Lilly said. "I didn't think she had family left. But then again, we hadn't talked about family much." Lilly was well aware of the fact that she didn't talk about her own family that often. Reticence about discussing personal matters was the New England way.

"Jackie's a lot younger than Helen, but they seem pretty close. She's taking care of all of Helen's needs right now, but it isn't easy. She's been driving back and forth to New Jersey. I hadn't realized that we shared that back wall with the Garrett house until I went by to talk with Jackie about the tulips. It looks different from her yard."

Lilly looked toward the back of the garden at the tall stone fence that separated the two houses.

"A double fence. The stone one that my relatives built, and the brick one that her relatives built. Now, explain the tulips?" Lilly said, looking around at the dozens of plants.

"Helen loved pink tulips," Ernie said.

"I don't think I knew that, but most of the plants I put in last week? Two weeks ago? Most of them were pink and white. But there weren't any tulips," Lilly said.

"There are now," Ernie said. "Jackie raved about the garden fairies, that's what she called you, who helped Helen have a view that gave her such joy. She ordered tulips to add to the mix, but hit an extra zero when she ordered online."

"That's a shame—"

"She was in a dither about it. I dropped some by the house and brought the rest back here. I thought we could repot them and sell them for Mother's Day. I can order more when Jackie needs them. This is going to sound macabre, but she wants some on hand for Helen's grave, when it's time."

"Helen's hanging in there," Lilly said. "It's smart of Jackie to plan ahead, though. It will make everything easier when it comes time."

"Planning is what Jackie does best. According to her, she's glad she started now. She's dealing with quite a mess."

"What sort of mess?"

"Problems with the Garrett family plot. I got the story from Jackie this afternoon, over multiple cups of tea. Delicious tea, by the way. She called it a chai latte, but it wasn't like anything I've had before. More tea, less sweet. Anyway, sorry, did I say there was a lot of tea? Too much caffeine. Helen has a spot in the Garrett family plot."

"Of course she does," Lilly said. She thought she knew where the plot was, but would need to double-check. She lined the tulips up on the table, and waited for Ernie to tell her his plans. "She was the last one in the line."

"Jackie's been trying to prepare the arrangements, and went by the cemetery. But according to the records Sasha showed her, the Garrett plot only had four graves, and they've been used. Sure enough, Jackie took a walk, and there is another headstone in the area that Helen always told her they owned."

"Does she have a record?"

"Jackie's been searching for one," Ernie said. "No luck so far. She thinks that Helen assumed it was all taken care of, especially since her name's there."

"What do you mean?"

"When Helen's father died, her mother had her name and Helen's put on the tombstone as well." Ernie shuddered.

"I've seen a few folks do that," Lilly said. "It saves money."

"Still, who'd want to visit their family and see their name on a headstone? Not this guy, that's for sure. Anyway, Jackie's beside herself. She's turning the house upside down, looking for old records."

"What's her last name?"

"Jackie's? Ross."

"Jacqueline Ross. She went to the historical society a few weeks ago to look at cemetery records."

"She's determined to figure it out. In the meantime, I've got some pink tulips to sell."

"What do you have in mind?" Lilly said, looking at the sea of pink.

"These look great," Ernie said, turning the pot around and examining his handiwork. The tulip was centered in the decorated pot, with a bit of Spanish moss on top to help it look more posh.

"They do," Lilly said. "Who painted the pots? They're really cute."

"There was another ordering issue, and we ended up with six dozen white ceramic pots. Someone suggested decorating, so the staff has been having a ball with paint markers."

"All happy accidents. They look great," Lilly said. "A perfect Mother's Day gift."

"Do you think the tulips will be healthier looking for the weekend?" He turned the pot around, and looked over at Lilly. "No one wants to give their mother a saggy tulip."

"Let's water them and then we'll put them under the lamps tonight. That will perk them up. And the fresh soil always makes plants feel better. You can take some pictures and post them on social media. I bet they'll fly off the shelves."

"I can't believe it's mid-May already," Ernie said. He put some moss around the top of another pot. "Do you think a bow would be too much?"

"I'd let the decorations on the pot stand on their own," Lilly said, partly because she believed it, partly because the idea of tying dozens of bows didn't thrill her.

"Yeah, you're right," Ernie said, filling another pot with soil.

"How's the house hunting going?" Lilly asked. Ernie had been to several open houses in the last few days, but they hadn't had a chance to talk about them.

"Not well, but I'll keep looking."

"A lot of people put their houses on the market

this time of year." Lilly wasn't sure if that was true or not, but she wanted him to feel some hope.

"Whitney Dunne-Bradford came by today to get some paint samples. Apparently, Sasha is thinking about moving into an apartment, so Whitney's thinking about downsizing."

"As in selling her house?"

"She hinted at that."

"Are you interested?"

"Only in seeing the house," Ernie said. "I've driven past it a few times. It's a nice place from the outside. But like you and Tamara said, it's pretty tied to the business."

"It used to be worse. The family lived upstairs and the funeral parlor was downstairs. But then they bought the second house, and built one for the family. I can't imagine selling them separately," Lilly said. "If I recall correctly, there's an embalming room in the basement of the house, or something like that."

"Then that's definitely out," Ernie said. "Can't imagine how I'd reuse that space."

Lilly laughed. "Where is Sasha moving?"

"I have no idea," Ernie said. "Whitney said something about them both needing a bit more privacy these days."

"I wonder where Dewey Marsh lives," Lilly said, gently shaking a plant to make sure the soil was settled into the pot.

"There's an apartment over the garage," Ernie said. "I wonder if he'll be moving and where, though."

The two friends stopped potting plants for a moment, and looked at each other. Lilly shook her head, determined to change the subject away from Whitney Dunne-Bradford's love life.

"What was the paint for, did she say?" Lilly asked a couple of minutes later.

"She said that Dewey was going to help her paint the bathroom in the master bedroom. The paint color she chose was black. Apparently, the tiles and fixtures are white, and she's looking for drama."

"That would do it," Lilly said.

"She also asked about the best way to adhere mirrored tiles to the walls."

"Perhaps she's going for an art deco look."

"I don't think Whitney has a particular design esthetic. She'll probably put them all over the house so that Dewey can look at himself all the time."

"Ernie, stop—"

"Lilly, have you ever watched the man? Granted, he's good-looking. But he knows it. There isn't a mirror, pane of glass, or any other reflective surface that he walks by where he doesn't stop, flex his muscles a bit, and smile at himself."

"You're terrible," Lilly said, laughing. "He is an odd one, though. I saw him last week at the grocery store. I said hello, but he just nodded. Does he ever speak?"

"Whitney runs a tight ship. He only says what she wants him to say, and does what she wants him to do."

"Do you think he and Whitney have been dating?" Lilly asked.

"Dating. Such a quaint term," Ernie said, laughing.

"Delia said the same thing to me. What's the matter with the word *dating*?"

"In this case, I don't think it fully describes what's

going on at the Bradford compound. Who knows who'll be living where, or with whom."

"I wonder what the house is worth?" Lilly said.

"I offered to go over and give her some decorating ideas," Ernie said. "I want to get a look inside. It must be a good-sized house, what with Sasha and Whitney both living there since Sam died. They never struck me as terribly close."

Lilly laughed. "That's an understatement. I couldn't blame Sasha for not liking Whitney. She married her father so soon after her mother died. Still, I do think Whitney tried her best."

"Her best?"

"Her best may be terrible. Likely was. I'm trying to be kind," Lilly said, taking a scoop of soil to top off the tulip she'd just transplanted.

"Did I ever ask you why you didn't use the Bradford Funeral Home when Alan passed? Most people in Goosebush do."

"It wasn't because of Whitney. My father and Sam Bradford had a falling-out years ago. My family has gone to Marshton ever since."

"What was the falling-out about?" Ernie asked.

"My father felt that Sam was always selling and pushing too hard. He had a friend who went into serious debt paying for his wife's funeral, and that didn't sit well with Dad."

"What did he do about it?"

"What could he do? It was Sam's business. But he did tell anyone who'd listen that it was a shame that a funeral could bankrupt a person. Business fell off for the Bradfords for a while afterwards. But then my father died, and Sam married Whitney. She brought a little more polish to the business. It's still the default for most people."

"She may have brought polish, but not a lot of warmth," Ernie said. "I didn't use Bradford's either, back when Steven died. I didn't get a good feeling from them."

"So much depends on reputation," Lilly said. "With Sasha moving, I wonder if they've decided to cash in and sell the business."

"My sense is that the business is growing, not shrinking. But I'll see what I can find out. She liked the idea of my help."

"Maybe while you're helping Whitney you can find out a bit on the Garrett situation," Lilly said. "Turn on the charm."

"For charm we should probably send Roddy over, but I wouldn't do that to the poor man. I'll see what I can find out."

Chapter 11

"Where are you off to this early?" Ernie asked Lilly the next morning. He waved her toward the fresh brioche rolls on the kitchen table. "Coffee?"

"Yes, please. Has Delia come down?"

"She's in her office," Ernie said.

"Still upset?"

"She's very quiet," Ernie said. "What happened? I've never seen her like this."

"She and Stan are still having issues," Lilly said quietly.

"I hoped things were getting better."

"Maybe if you try to talk to her? Tamara and I did, but I think we made a pig's eye of the conversation. I've never been good with advice on love lives."

"What makes you think I'll be any help?"

"You are a sympathetic shoulder," Lilly said. "And you're making bread."

"Brioche."

"I stand corrected. Brioche can help start any conversation."

"I'll make her some tea and bring in rolls when they're ready."

"Wonderful. Do you need some help getting the tulips back in your car?"

"Delia can help me," Ernie said. "I peeked at them this morning. They look great."

"I'm glad. Perhaps you can leave one in the greenhouse for Tamara? I'll let Ty know, in case he doesn't have a Mother's Day gift."

"Done," Ernie said. "And now back to my original question. Where are you off to this early?"

"I emailed Mac Townsend last night, and told him I had some concerns about the Goosebush cemetery. He called this morning, wondering if I'd like to take a walk with him, and show him what I'm worried about."

"Do you want me to go with you?" Ernie asked.

"No, I'll be fine. But first, a roll and some coffee. Brioche. Bless you, Ernie. This is my favorite breakfast. Did I ever tell you about the cruise Alan I and took the summer of 2007?"

"Thanks for meeting me, Mac," Lilly said. She'd parked in visitor parking and met him by the front gate.

"I take a daily constitutional around the place. Old habit. Hard to break, even now."

Lilly looked over at the former caretaker of the Goosebush cemeteries. He had his uniform on—well-worn khakis, boat shoes, a navy polo shirt that had begun to fade in places, a yellow jacket that a lot of sailors wore for foul weather. His had *Bradford Funeral Home* embroidered on the right-hand side. When he turned to the side, she noticed it was printed on the back as well. Goosebush frugality at work. His close-cropped gray hair was the same cut he'd had for as long as she'd known him. There were a few more wrinkles, mostly from spending so much time outside, she'd guess. His eyes were hidden behind dark glasses. He had a *Bradford Funeral Home* ball cap in his hand and he put it on.

"Then I appreciate you letting me tag along on your walk."

"Sounds pitiful, doesn't it, Lilly? Me taking a walk through the cemetery, after they let me go."

"It must be very difficult," Lilly said.

"Taking care of this place wasn't just a job. It was my life. Still got the job at the crematorium, so that's something. Keeps me occupied. But I miss this place."

Lilly nodded and watched as Cormac Townsend took out a large key and opened the gate to the cemetery. He put his finger up to his lips and gave her a wink. "Don't tell. Couldn't bear to give this back. They use the newer key these days. Whitney didn't think the old key worked, was going to toss it out. That's how she deals with anything that's old: Toss it."

Lilly took a minute to look at the gate. Sure enough, above the old key was a more modern keyhole. "How can both keys work?" she asked.

"The newer mechanism tumbles the older lock. When I talked to the locksmith, we decided to go with that as a solution. Cheaper than replacing the entire gate."

"I'd imagine so," Lilly said, pursing her lips together. "Why do they lock it up, anyway? All you have to do is come in from the side and jump the fence." And, she thought, dozens of people probably had keys to the old gate.

"It keeps people from driving in, which helps. You'd be surprised at the mischief people get into at night. Especially teenagers. Goosebush can be a boring place to be a kid; cemetery dares can add some excitement. I pointed out the security breaches all the time," Mac said. "But the fence—"

"Would cost a lot to replace," Lilly said. "Is the budget that tight?"

"It's limited, but enough, depending on how you spend the money, and who gets to decide," Mac said. He closed the gate behind them and she heard a *click.* "Now, tell me what's got you worried."

"Let me show you," Lilly said. She'd brought some of the old maps with her, but decided not to show him right away. She wanted to see how he reacted to the bench. She wasn't sure what was holding her back, but she'd long since learned to trust her gut.

"You know, when I was a young girl, I used to wander through here a lot. Doing rubbings, sitting—"

"You ever see the play *Our Town?*"

"Of course, several times." *Our Town*, New England's own Thornton Wilder's 1938 play, was one of Lilly's favorites.

"Goosebush Players wanted to do a version where the third act took place here, in the cemetery. This was back in the eighties, when Mel John was alive. Always regretted that we said no to that. Yeah, we missed a moment there."

"That would have been something," Lilly said.

"Thornton Wilder saw places like this the same way I do. I don't see headstones. I see people who once lived, and then died. They depend on family, or visitors, to tell their stories. I used to collect them, their stories, when I worked here."

"That's lovely. I love the stories as well. Learned a lot of them from my father. He used to give tours of the cemetery."

"I remember. I offered to do them again, but Whitney wasn't interested. A real shame. I remember going on a couple of your dad's tours, and how his stories helped me know the folks who decided to rest here."

As they walked slowly to the Jayne mausoleum, Mac mentioned the stories he'd learned about the names on the headstones. She knew some of them already, but listened anyway, anxious to hear a new tidbit or two.

"Does it seem more crowded to you?" Lilly asked gently.

"More crowded?"

"It must be me. I used to pride myself on knowing all of the Jayne family neighbors, but I could swear there were some new ones."

"Can't imagine," Mac said. "This is the older part of the cemetery. Historical. Folks come to visit. I can't see how's they'd make any changes."

Lilly nodded. She was glad she hadn't shown him the older maps. Mac was wrong. But surely he knew that, or maybe he'd forgotten? How old was he, anyway? He seemed old when she was young, and she was old now. Lilly wondered why they'd let him go. And who had made the decision. She shook her head. Time enough to learn that. They walked over to the Jayne corner of the cemetery.

"You know, I grew up with the Jayne largesse, and was used to the hubris of my ancestors. But seeing the family crypt through other eyes—it really is an abomination, isn't it?"

"Far from it," Mac said. "There's a level of efficiency to the place. Buy up several plots, build a place where the family can be together, but vertically. Takes up less space. Pardon the imagery, but it's true. All relatives are welcome and remembered. Even the ones born on the wrong side of the blanket, as it were."

"The Jayne family is very eccentric," Lilly said. "I include myself in that assessment. Here we are. Follow me, I want to show you the bench. It's around back."

"Course it is," Mac said. "Has been for over a hundred years."

They walked around the building and Lilly pointed to the bench, still located up against the back wall. Small wonder. It must have weighed close to a ton and would have to be lifted with expertise in order to keep the stone in one piece. She walked closer, but didn't see any cracks in the bench.

"That shouldn't be there," Mac said. He sounded angry.

"It shouldn't be," Lilly said. "Look over here, where it was. Doesn't it look like that area's been dug up?" They walked over and Lilly looked around. It was obvious where the base of the bench had been. But the area around it also showed signs of disturbance. The grass had been dug up and laid back down. Someone hadn't spent time on the seams, and there was browning on the edges.

"Looks like," Mac said. He took a small notebook out of his vest pocket and fished in his jacket for a pencil. "I'm going to make some notes and put a report in about this. Anything else look odd to you? Have you checked inside?"

"No," Lilly said, shivering slightly. "No need. We haven't opened it for years. I think I have the only key, don't I?"

"You sure enough do," Mac said. "Your mother saw to that years ago. Didn't like the idea of your uncles moving in without permission."

"She was so protective, though my father wouldn't have cared. I think she worried more about the Jayne legacy than he did."

"Good thing she did. Her will saw to it this place was well tended for years to come. A good woman, was your mother. I always figured if Viola didn't like someone, they weren't worth liking."

"Family is complicated," Lilly said. "Anyway, the outside looks fine, though it could use some weeding. I'm happy to do that. I am concerned about the land grab in the back, though."

"I'll look into that. You can trust me on that. You good seeing yourself out? I'm going to look around a bit."

Lilly went home and sat on her back porch, glancing up at her garden while she looked things up on her computer. The Goosebush Cemeteries Committee had a website, complete with the charter for the spaces. She downloaded it for later, but read it through quickly. The rules and regulations were laid out, but she could see where there might be wiggle room on the interpretation.

One thing was clear to Lilly. The Bradfords technically could serve in several different capacities. It wasn't a good look for them, or for Goosebush, as far as Lilly was concerned. She'd bring that up with the Board of Selectman. But was it illegal? Was anything untoward happening? She didn't know enough about the Bradford business, but she did know how she could learn.

Taking out her phone, Lilly sent a text to one of the most frequently used numbers on her phone.

Doing some research. Want to take a ride?

She went back to her web surfing, resisting the urge to check her phone. Roddy's reply came a few minutes later. **Give me fifteen minutes. I'll drive.**

Lilly sent another text to make an appointment in Marshton. She got a thumbs-up emoji in reply.

Chapter 12

Lilly let Delia know she was leaving, but neither she nor the cats moved from the couch. She printed the materials she'd been reading, and went into her office to grab a file folder and a fresh pad of paper. Spending time with Roddy always inspired new ways of thinking.

So far, the bench was an issue. And Helen Garrett's plot, but that required more investigations into town records. She wanted to wait to talk to Helen's cousin before she took that on. Better not to step on toes, especially during these challenging times for the family.

She freshened up her makeup and put on a nicer sweater before heading next door. Walking through the back gate, she was tempted to grab a couple of weeds, but she resisted the urge.

Roddy's back door had been replaced by two French doors that both let out onto a low deck. None of it was historically accurate, but it was a lovely place to sit outside and look at his gardens, which were still a work in progress. Coming together, but not quite there yet. Lilly had faith in the gardening muses, where Roddy had none. By the end of the summer, he'd be delighted. She'd see to that.

She looked in the kitchen. He wasn't there, but there were two cups on the table and a folded newspaper. The living room was empty as well, at least as far as she could see. Leaning forward, she thought she saw him at the front door.

She walked over to the patio and sat down on one of the Adirondack chairs he had set up around the firepit. She slid to the back of the seat and sighed. The chair needed a small back pillow, but otherwise it was perfect. The ottoman nearby was tempting, but she resisted. Best not to get too comfortable. She texted him that she was there.

"I need to get a doorbell on the back of the house," Roddy said, opening the French door and stepping onto the deck. "You could have come in—"

"I'm fine out here," Lilly said. "The ground cover looks wonderful."

"Patience has never been one of my virtues, Lilly. I want it to fill in more quickly."

"Trust me, it's going to be great. You don't want to overplant that."

"I do trust you," he said, sitting down in the chair across from her. "Otherwise I wouldn't agree to go on research adventures with no information. Where are we going, by the way?"

"You don't have to come, but if you're free, I want to visit a friend of mine over in Marshton. She owns a funeral parlor."

"Any particular reason?"

"To understand the mechanics," Lilly said. "I need

to know what I'm talking about. I realized this morning I don't understand how the business works. Or is
supposed to work."

"I always love research. As I said, I'm happy to
drive."

"That would be delightful," Lilly said.

"I'll go grab my notebook and—"

"Roddy? Darling? Are you back here?"

Lilly was facing Roddy, so she saw his reaction first.
His jaw clenched and he looked at Lilly quickly, then
over her head at the person who was making her way
to the backyard.

Roddy had installed freestanding gates on either
side of the garage to block the view from the street
into the backyard. Lilly heard one open, and she
tried to sit forward so that she could turn around
and see who was coming through.

The woman was beautiful, with deep auburn hair,
a trim figure shown to its advantage in her designer
suit, and deep mauve lipstick wonderfully offset by
her porcelain skin.

"Darling, I forgot to give you—oh. I'm so sorry. I
didn't realize you had company." She looked over at
Roddy, and then took a step toward Lilly with her
hand outstretched. "Hello, I'm Adrienne Lyden."

Lilly turned back in her seat, and used the arms of
the chair to lift herself out of her seat. She desperately wished that movement had been smoother, but
alas. The seat was deep, and Lilly was stiff. She got up
without making a grunting noise, which took effort.
Roddy took her by the elbow and held her next to
him.

"Lilly Jayne, this is Adrienne. Lilly is my neighbor."

"Over in that big old house?" Adrienne said, shaking Lilly's hand. "That's a beauty. As is this house. When I'd heard that Roddy moved to the suburbs, I expected a small cottage where he could live out his fantasy of being a country squire. I had no idea he'd make this sort of investment."

"Adrienne is my former wife," Roddy said quietly.

"It's very nice to meet you," Lilly said.

"Isn't this the part where you say you've heard so much about me?" Adrienne said. She looked Lilly up and down, and her smile grew.

"It would be if I had, but Roddy hasn't mentioned you," Lilly said, plastering a smile on her face that she imagined looked as fake as Adrienne's. This was not who Lilly had imagined for Roddy's ex-wife. And she had spent some time, more than she wanted to admit, wondering about the ex-Mrs. Lydens.

"Nor has he mentioned you."

"Considering we haven't seen one another for several years, that's hardly surprising, Adrienne. Did you forget something?"

"I wanted to give you this," the younger woman said, taking a flash drive out of her purse and handing it to Roddy. "Some more information pertaining to our earlier conversation. I could stay and go over it with you—"

"No need," Roddy said. "I'm more than capable of understanding spreadsheets. As I said earlier, I sincerely doubt that your proposal holds any interest for me."

"But you *will* think about it."

"I will be in contact with you in a few days," Roddy said.

Adrienne took a step closer to Roddy and ran her

fingernail down his lapel. "We were good together once. We could be again," she said. She stood on her tiptoes and went to kiss him. He moved his face, but she caught him on the jaw.

"Nice meeting you, Lilly. I'm sure I'll see you around," she said, letting herself back out of the gate.

"No, she won't," Roddy said. "Bloody woman. Sorry about that, Lilly."

Lilly reached into her purse and took out a tissue. She turned Roddy's face toward her, and wiped the lipstick off his jaw.

"You have nothing to apologize for," Lilly said. "When I heard her last name, I wasn't sure if she was a former wife, or a long-lost daughter."

Roddy's face went blank and then he laughed. "Well done, Lilly. Yes, she is quite a bit younger than I am. I thought we were well suited, though. She was as driven as I was. More driven, as it turns out."

"She's very beautiful," Lilly said.

"She's very pretty," Roddy said. "Beauty comes from within. There's nothing there but ambition. Let me lock the back door, and we'll be off."

"What's in that folder?" Roddy asked Lilly. They were in his Jaguar, making their way to the next town over. She'd been explaining what she'd read in the cemetery charters.

"Those are some maps of the Goosebush cemetery," Lilly said. "Nothing official, mind you. Mostly maps from past tours—"

"Is touring cemeteries a favorite pastime here in Goosebush?" Roddy asked. Lilly rifled through the small stack of papers Minh had copied for her, and showed Roddy a couple of the maps when he stopped for lights.

"They're fairly popular, or were. You know, on founders' days, for ghost tours, things like that," Lilly said. "There are lots of stories in a cemetery that can be turned into an interesting afternoon for small groups."

"You sound like you know a lot about this," Roddy said.

"My father loved doing cemetery tours," Lilly said. "I have a couple of his tour maps in the mix."

"Right. Tamara mentioned that he was quite the raconteur."

"He loved it. He'd spend hours tailoring his talks to different audiences. I'd go with him when he practiced."

"Have you done tours on your own?"

"No. Believe it or not, I don't relish the idea. I'd be happy to help someone else research the stories and practice, but the idea of leading a tour makes me nauseous."

"I can see that," Roddy said. "Since I've known you, I've noticed that you recede to the background when the spotlight shines."

"My parents were both big personalities," Lilly said. "My brother's the same."

"You don't talk about him much."

"No, I don't suppose I do. He was more than happy to pass on the family inheritance for a cash payout. Especially since Windward was a money pit for most of his life. Richard—his name is Richard—made his way in the world and had his own success. He brought his family to see my parents once a year, called on birthdays and holidays, but that was it."

"So you aren't close?"

"He's twelve years older than I. He left home before I was seven and never came back. I never really knew him. When his children were born I thought we could have a new relationship, but that didn't happen. I'm much closer to Tamara's children, and they to me."

"Is he still—"

"Living? Yes. We exchange cards, but that's it. My family relations are one of my failings in life."

"Or theirs," Roddy said. "You said that your parents had big personalities."

"They were always the life of the party. Bon vivants, offering to host parties, do fundraisers, you name it. They lived way beyond their means for years and years. As soon as I started making a living, I cleaned up their messes. Happily, mind you. But my life in finance was mostly motivated by figuring out money, making it, and keeping it."

They rode in silence for a while. Lilly didn't ever paint her life as perfect, but the imperfections weighed on her. She thought about the pro forma cards, with checks, she'd sent to her niece and nephew over the years. Paper in lieu of a relationship. The checks were always cashed and thank-you notes sent, but that's as far as it ever went. What had she missed over the years?

"Where are we going?" Roddy asked finally.

"Sorry, yes, that's where this started. Here, I'll plug the address in your GPS. We're going to the Marshton Funeral Home."

"The Marshton Funeral Home? Where is it? Let me guess. It's in Kingsfield." Roddy chuckled at his own lame joke.

"There were two funeral homes in Marshton up until twenty or so years ago, then they merged. They couldn't agree on a name and chose Marshton as the placeholder. The name stuck. The business was sold a few years ago and the owner kept it. Her name is Evelyn Crocker, by the way. The owner. That's who we're going to see."

"How do you know her?"

"I met her at a women in business luncheon a few years ago. When my father died, he left his body to science. I think I mentioned his falling-out with Sam Bradford. My mother wanted to let bygones be bygones, but I didn't want to do that to my father. I asked Evelyn to work out the details with the medical school, which she did. By the time my mother died, Sam Bradford had died and Whitney had taken over. I decided to have Evelyn take care of her. A couple of years later, she took care of Alan."

"Don't most people in Goosebush use Bradford's?" Roddy asked.

"Most, not all," Lilly said. "Sam's first wife, Carol, was the public face for years. She was lovely. When she got sick, Sam took over. And he and my father fell out. There's the thing about funeral homes in small towns. It's all about relationships."

"So we're going to visit Evelyn and . . ."

"Ask some questions about the funeral business."

Evelyn Crocker was busy when they got to her office. Rather than wait inside, Lilly suggested they sit in the car to wait. She hated funeral homes. Not for the work that they did. That was a necessary part of life. But the grief of the people there, making arrangements? That raw emotion always got to Lilly. She couldn't bear sitting in the waiting room.

A group of four adults came out of the front door, hanging on to each other, walking to a minivan and taking their time getting in. After they drove out of the parking lot, Lilly and Roddy got out of the car and went in.

"I thought I saw you out there," Evelyn said after she and Roddy shook hands.

"I didn't want to intrude," Lilly said.

"Yeah, I've got to figure out a better waiting room," Evelyn said. "Some people make appointments. But these days, a lot of people stop in to ask questions. I've realized that drop-bys can be good for business."

"Drop-bys?"

"People who want to ask questions, or make pre-arrangements to help their family. You remember that book about death cleaning? Cleaning out your stuff now so your kids don't have to? It's started a trend. Lots of people are coming in to make their own arrangements, or start the process."

"That seems a bit macabre," Roddy said.

"No, it's actually a gift to their loved ones. No one likes to make those decisions for someone else."

"My mother made her own arrangements, with Evelyn," Lilly said. "And it was a lovely funeral."

"Your mother was a trip," Evelyn said. "I'm glad I got to know her a little bit. Anyway, it's good to see you, Lilly. Been way too long."

"It has," Lilly said. "Thanks for making time."

"No problem. I don't want to rush you, but I have an appointment in an hour."

"Of course. You mentioned that on the phone. I'll

cut to the chase, shall I? Can you tell me how your business works?"

"What do you mean?"

"What your relationship is to the town, how and when you work with other funeral homes, that sort of thing."

"Sure, I can give you an overview, if you promise you'll tell me why you're asking."

"Deal."

For the next twenty minutes Evelyn gave them a brief overview on the business. She talked to them about packages, working with people on planning, and cash flow considerations.

"That's an overview, but I don't think you want to go into the business," Evelyn said.

"It's really helpful," Lilly said. "I have a couple of other questions. What can you tell me about cemetery plots?"

"Cemetery plots? I thought you had the Jayne crypt. Or have you run out of room?"

"Funny you ask," Lilly said. She told Evelyn about the moving of the bench. Then she mentioned the added headstones and markers nearby. "Of course, it may be my faulty memory."

"Or not," Evelyn said. "Places like Goosebush cemetery are hundreds of years old. They may be burying people in found spaces, between graves. Could be dozens of reasons." She paused and took her business cards out of the holder and tapped them on the desk.

"What aren't you telling us?" Lilly asked. "I promise whatever you say will stay in the room."

"You know Bradford's is now selling the plots in Goosebush?" Evelyn said.

"I heard something about that."

"It's only been a few months. But funny thing. Suddenly there's a lot more space available in the old cemetery."

"What does *a lot* mean?" Lilly asked.

"No one's been turned away, or sold a plot in one of the other cemeteries in Goosebush. There hasn't even been a waiting list. Course the price has gone up."

"Do you think something's going on?"

"I was looking through some old files the other day. Seems to me that there used to be a lot more paperwork involved when I was securing a plot in Goosebush," Evelyn said.

"Maybe they've found more space?" Roddy said.

"Could be," Evelyn said. "I don't do many funerals there."

"But something seems off to you," Lilly said.

"For what it's worth, I'd keep looking into it," Evelyn said.

"Could you let me know more about the paperwork issue?"

"I'll have my admin look through our old files to see if I'm remembering correctly. I'll let you know what I find."

"Thanks. Like I said, it's probably my imagination."

"Trust yourself, Lilly. That's not the only odd thing I've heard about Bradford's lately."

"What do you mean?"

"Listen, I didn't love Sam, but he ran a good business. I could work with him."

"Do you still work with Bradford's?" Lilly asked.

"No. And I'm not the only one."

"What's going on?"

"This is hearsay, mind you. I'm hearing that they're cutting corners, getting sloppy. I've picked up a few customers, and I know a couple of other homes have as well. So Lilly, to answer your question, there could be a good answer for the extra graves. But my gut says you're not wrong to ask questions."

Chapter 13

Roddy glanced to his right, where Lilly sat in the passenger seat. "You don't look satisfied," he said to his friend. She'd been looking through her notes, and was now staring straight ahead.

"I should probably mind my own business," Lilly said. "The memory of an old woman can be faulty—"

"Who is this old woman of whom you speak?" Roddy asked.

"You're driving with her. Honestly, lately I feel every one of my years."

"You've had a challenging few months."

"But usually this time of year, I come to life. Spring is my favorite season. This year I'm exhausted."

"I think too much of you to try talk you into feeling better," Roddy said. "But if platitudes about your zest for life, overall loveliness, and breathtaking smile are called for, I'm here."

Lilly smiled, but didn't reply.

"You're not the only person feeling their age. You

know, Buzz dropping dead like that—it threw me," Roddy said.

"That was awful," Lilly agreed.

"He's younger, was younger, than I am by almost ten years."

"No, not really? Wow. He looked much older. I think Buzz lived a hard life."

"Still. It's sobering. I've been much more reflective lately."

They drove for a while longer before Lilly spoke again.

"Roddy, about earlier."

Roddy glanced over at Lilly and then back at the road. "Earlier?"

"I'm sorry I made that crack about your ex-wife being your long-lost daughter," Lilly said. "It's a terrible habit of mine, one that I thought I was past. When I'm nervous, or feel off my game, I tend to be, well, sarcastic. I do apologize. It was very unkind of me."

"It struck me as funny," Roddy said. "The only moment in the entire morning that was at all amusing."

"She seemed happy to reconnect," Lilly said. She wasn't sure how much to ask, or how far to push the conversation. Or how much she really wanted to know. Roddy had mentioned his ex-wives, but only in passing. On the one hand, she didn't want to pry. On the other hand? That other hand was confusing.

"Only for business," Roddy said. "Upon reflection—as I mentioned, I've been in that space a great deal lately—upon reflection, the only thing we had in common was the business."

"Is that how you met? You worked together?

"I used to be a partner in a management firm."
Roddy mentioned a name, which Lilly recognized.
"She was a junior partner when we started dating.
Moved up to senior partner after we were married.
On merit, mind you. She was very bright. About busi-
ness."

"Lacking in other areas?" Lilly said.

"At first it was refreshing to be married to someone as obsessed with work as I was. No berating me
for checking email over dinner, or working seven
days a week."

"It's nice to share the same interests," Lilly said.

"I realized fairly soon that we had no other shared
interests. For that matter, we weren't interested in
learning from one another. She had no interest in
theater. We had different tastes in music, and they
weren't compatible. She hated to travel. All we had
in common was business. I should have ended it
then. But she made me feel young. And, in retrospect, that made me foolish."

"Interesting that she took your name, and kept it."

"Interesting, or strategic. It was good to keep a
Lyden at the firm, especially after everything that
happened."

When Roddy didn't say more, Lilly decided to
change the subject a bit. "How long were you married?"

"Less than a year. We'd only dated for a few
months beforehand."

"That's not a lot of time."

"It was enough time to implode my entire life. We
may have been married longer, but she chose the
wrong side in a business deal."

"The wrong side?"

"She'd disagree with that assessment, and stand by her decision. Even now. For me, that's the worst part. The part that makes me feel foolish, even now."

"You must have felt strongly about this deal you're referencing—"

"There were different business interests that the partners oversaw individually, but on large deals we all had to agree on moving forward or not. There was a deal that I objected to. Vehemently. I didn't like the people we'd be working with, and felt that it would damage our reputation. It went to a vote of all the partners, and I was the sole vote against it. They took on the client."

"That's frustrating, but surely it had happened before?" Lilly asked, thinking about her own similar situations.

"The discussions, arguments, we'd had brought up several issues about the mission of the business. I came to realize my partners and I had diverged into different paths, and had different values. The breach was irreparable, so we decided to part ways. That was the end of my business partnerships, and my marriage."

"Adrienne voted against you?"

"Indeed she did. She thought we could stay married, but didn't make too much of a fuss when I suggested that wouldn't work. Needless to say, we'd been arguing a great deal. I think she was relieved that it was over. I know I was."

"What happened?" Lilly asked quietly.

"I took a buyout. Got far less than I deserved, but I wanted cash, and to walk away. Which I did. No alimony, thankfully. The divorce was part of the deal."

"That's when you retired?"

"Not retired, no. I consulted for a bit, and still do that. It was a terrible time in my life. I lost a great deal of confidence in myself, and second-guessed a number of things that shook me to the core. But in the end, the entire situation gave me the gift of clarity. I reached out to my daughter and began to rebuild our relationship. After some soul-searching, I thought about what I wanted from the rest of my life. That's how I ended up here."

"But now she wants you back?" Lilly did her best to make her voice sound light.

"In the business, my dear Lilly. They've made some bad decisions, and having me come back could help mend some fences."

"That's flattering," Lilly said. "It is nice to be needed. My old firm rolls me out every once in a while to connect with older clients."

"I'm less than flattered, but agreed to consider the request, mostly so that she'd leave," Roddy said. He looked over at Lilly and smiled. "I'm grateful you brought up Adrienne, Lilly. Honestly, I am. I didn't want you to wonder about her. She's a mistake from my past."

"Roddy, you don't have to—"

"Let's change the subject, shall we? Was the conversation with Evelyn helpful, do you think?"

"Sort of," Lilly said, taking a breath. If she were honest, and she always was, she was just as glad to change the subject. "I'm still not sure there's anything afoot, but it was interesting. Between our conversation, the information on the Goosebush site, my conversation with Mac? The things I noticed in the cemetery could be on the level."

"Except for the bench."

"The bench is odd. Though that could be an honest mistake someone made when they were redoing the paths or some such in the cemetery."

"Could be."

"But still, I can't shake the feeling that something's wrong."

Roddy nodded. "We need more information about the Bradford practices. Tell you what, why don't I look into buying a plot in the Goosebush cemetery? We can see how the process works firsthand."

"That might be an interesting idea."

"Excellent. How about if we discuss it over lunch?"

Rather than go to the Star, they decided to have Roddy's stew. They parked and Roddy went in and got the container to bring to Lilly's house, the site of homemade bread. Delia made an appearance while it was being heated up, and even joined them while they ate. Roddy was good at small talk, and Delia seemed cheered by both the meal and the company. After lunch she went out for a walk, another good sign.

"Poor Delia. She's having men trouble," Lilly said.

Roddy nodded. "She and I spoke last night while we were setting the table. She asked me for the male perspective, and I did my best."

"That's very nice of you," Lilly said.

Roddy sighed. "As I mentioned, I've been introspective lately. I blame it on the time I've been spending with my ex-wife, Emma's mother. She was the closest I had to a chance at a decent marriage. She's happily married now, and loves pointing out my flaws."

"That must be delightful," Lilly said.

"They are, unfortunately, all true. And she would know. Anyway, if having a male perspective helps Delia sort through things, I'm happy to help. What are you smiling about?"

"It's very generous of you to offer her insights into Stan, but I think that you're very different men."

"Not so different. The first thing to understand about men is that fear is a powerful motivator. Secondly, she mentioned Tamara's observation about men forcing a breakup, and I confirmed that. Not true of every man, obviously. But true enough that I can offer it as an observation, and I've never met a woman who doesn't nod. Including you."

Lilly forced herself to stop nodding. "Thank you for being there for her. We all enjoy having a knight in shining armor around for emergencies."

"I wasn't there for my own daughter, so I'm glad to be there for Delia. Besides, I love our conversations. She has a marvelous brain, don't you think? She's more curious about the world than I am, and that's saying something. Have you talked to her about the cemetery issues?"

"She was with me the first day, when we were looking for Buzz's grave. She got distracted."

"We should catch her up later. Her perspective will be useful," Roddy said. "Let's get this call made, shall we? I'll put the phone on speaker, so behave yourself."

Lilly nodded, and got up from the kitchen table to get her notebook out of her bag, which was on another chair. She sat back down, pen poised, while Roddy made the call.

"Bradford Funeral Home. This is Sasha Bradford. How may I be of help?" A sultry voice answered the phone.

"Sasha, I'm not sure you'd remember me, but my name is Roddy Lyden—"

"Of course, Mr. Lyden. We met at the town meeting in February."

"We did indeed," Roddy said, raising his eyebrows. One of Roddy's favorite parts about living in Goosebush was the democracy of the monthly town meeting. The Board of Selectmen made decisions, but anyone could bring something to the town meeting for a vote as long as they followed procedure. In February Sasha Bradford introduced a proposal to use some town land as a new cemetery, to be opened in 2027. The proposal had passed to the next stage, and afterwards she'd worked the crowd, passing out business cards, one of which Roddy was using now. "You have a good memory."

"There aren't that many handsome men in Goosebush," Sasha said. "You stand out." Now it was Lilly's turn to raise her eyebrows.

"You're very kind," Roddy said. "Let me tell you why I'm calling. My daughter's father-in-law died a few weeks ago, and hadn't made any plans. I promised myself that I wouldn't leave her in those straits, so I thought I should start at the beginning. I checked the Goosebush website, and it sent me here to buy a cemetery plot."

"First of all, Roddy—do you mind if I call you Roddy?"

"Not at all."

"Roddy, your inclination is spot-on. Making your

desires clear is a gift to your family. It also ensures that your last intentions will be carried out."

"Exactly. I'm not sure I'm ready to plan the entire event, but I understand it will take a while to get a plot secured."

"It used to," Sasha said. "But we've been able to re-organize things to help folks out. Do you have a location preference? Maybe in the new cemetery?"

"I've become very fond of the history of the Goosebush cemetery. I'd love to be there. Are there any spots available?"

"You are in luck, Roddy. A few have come up, since we did a new inventory. Space is precious, though. There are many more spots in the Standish cemetery."

"I have my heart set on the old one. Do you think that would be possible?"

"Let me see. Yes, I may be able to help you, but you'll need to act quickly."

"I am prepared to do exactly that. Tell me: You don't happen to have a map of the free spots, do you? I'd love to be able to see them."

"I'd be happy to give you a tour—"

"No, really. I know it's odd, but I'd rather go on my own."

"Roddy, I understand. Tell you what. I have a couple of maps that I can scan and send over. Can you give me your email? Once you've taken a look, make sure to give me a call if you're interested in more. Things are busy these days."

After Sasha hung up, Roddy turned to Lilly and smiled.

"Well done," Lilly said. "I'm very sorry to hear about Emma's father-in-law."

"Oh, I made that up. I thought it would give the story more impact."

"You are a very facile liar, Mr. Lyden."

"A trait that has come in very handy over the course of my life. How about a cup of tea while we wait for Sasha to send that email?"

Chapter 14

"This is a much better place to have tea," Lilly said, settling into a table at the Star café. Roddy put the tray down on the table, and she took the tea things off and put the tray on the floor.

"Particularly while we were waiting for Sasha," Roddy said. "How long does it take to scan a map?"

"A while, apparently. I suppose that being thorough takes time, and that may be a good sign. Besides, the walk felt good, didn't it? I'm glad you suggested it," Lilly said to Roddy.

"Thank you for being a good sport and indulging me," Roddy said. "I thought we could use the waiting time to pick up the books I ordered, and it is a beautiful day."

"Stan has really expanded the bookstore offerings," Lilly said. "I've become addicted to having him order me books, and then buying more when I come and pick them up."

"The marvelous audacity of Stan in creating this wonderful business always gobsmacks me. Books, food, and theater all in one space. I can't imagine having that sort of vision for a building."

"Don't forget the gallery," Lilly said, looking around at the artwork Stan had hanging on all available wall spaces. Underneath each piece he had a blurb about the artist and a price tag. "Stan is an entrepreneur, and Goosebush is the better for it."

"It is a marvelous use of an old space," Roddy said, looking around.

"I'm glad he didn't completely gut it and start over. The old Woolworth's was one of my favorite places growing up. Did you ever go to one of those stores? Did they even have them in England?"

"No, I don't think so," Roddy said.

"They were wonderful. You could get anything there—craft items, goldfish, cosmetics, ice cream, grilled cheese sandwiches, books, magazines, medicine, fabric. I never thought it would go out of business, but alas."

"Why wasn't the building torn down?" Roddy asked. "Those were the days of demolition, weren't they?"

"And then replacing the old with terrible modern new that completely lacked character. There are a couple of blocks that surrendered to the wrecking ball, and the results were mixed at best. Several people felt that the old Woolworth building was too important to the character of the town."

"Were you one of those people?"

"I was, as was my mother. It took Stan's vision to see what it could be, while keeping the spirit of what it was."

"It really is a marvel. Does he still have the artist studios on the fourth floor?"

"He calls them offices now," Lilly said. "Cal Pace still has a writing studio, but Stan's using the others for offices to support the Star. I understand that Virginia Blossom is moving in up there." Much as she didn't enjoy spending time with Virginia Blossom, Stan hiring her to help with booking the theater had been a good idea. In a few short weeks the audiences had increased. The Stanley Theater was closed for renovations, but Virginia was positioning herself to program that space as well. She was making a good case for being able to do both.

"What is Virginia—"

Roddy stopped talking when Stan walked up to the table.

"Lilly, Roddy, I didn't see you come in. I just checked the bookstore and they told me you picked up your books. I'm glad you're still here."

"I will never forego an opportunity to have a kitchen sink cookie and pot of tea," Lilly said, smiling. "Join us, if you have a minute."

"I'd love to, thanks," the young man said. He pulled a third seat over and Roddy moved closer to Lilly to make room. She felt the heat of his arm next to hers, but she didn't move.

Stan had dark shadows under his eyes. He looked thinner and his complexion looked waxy.

"How are you, Stan?" she asked him gently. She didn't like the idea of having to choose sides between Stan and Delia, and would avoid it if at all possible. She and Stan had spent a great deal of time together earlier in the year, working on his business plan for the Star. Buzz moving to town had disrupted the meetings, but she hoped that the planning was moving forward. Lilly wanted the Star to succeed almost as much as he did, and the business was at a tipping point.

"I owe you a call, Lilly," Stan said. "I wanted to thank you for the nice basket of food, and the messages. They both helped me through."

"You don't owe me anything," Lilly said. "I hope you know that I'm here if you need me. The basket was a joint effort from all of us, but Ernie took the lead. We wanted to make sure you had some comfort food laid in—food you couldn't get here."

"Cheese boards, gourmet chocolate, artisan meats. It was perfect. Thanks. Dad's death has been harder than I expected."

"I can only imagine," Lilly said. "The finality of death is always difficult."

Stan sat forward in his chair. "He wasn't a good father by any stretch of the imagination. He made my mother's life a misery. We both flourished when he left. But when he came back and apologized this past winter? I felt like I needed to give him a chance, you know?"

"Of course you did," Lilly said.

"He did try to help out around here. Actually, he was pretty good at the bookstore."

"He was very helpful whenever I came in," Roddy said. "We'd have a conversation, and the next time I saw him he'd have a suggestion of books that may be of interest, or he'd show me new books he'd ordered inspired by our conversation."

"He was always good at selling people what they didn't necessarily need, or want," Stan said. "He'd done that his whole life."

"Maybe he'd changed?" Lilly asked gently.

Stan looked at her and his eyes filled with tears.

"Nah. He was good at talking me into the idea that he had, and I bought in for a while."

"Stan, you don't have to—"

"I've been meaning to call you, Lilly. The business is in trouble."

"What sort of trouble?" Lilly said. She lowered her voice and looked around, but she needn't have worried. No one was sitting nearby.

"I could leave you two—" Roddy said.

"No need," Stan said. "My dad being a disaster isn't going to be a secret I can keep much longer."

"What happened?" Lilly said.

"I hired a bookkeeper, like you and I talked about. She started to notice some discrepancies, and tracked them all back to Buzz. She created some ways to test her hypothesis, and he failed every single one of them. Turns out he was pocketing money wherever he worked—the bookstore, the bar, the theater. Not a lot, but every little bit matters in a business like this."

"Did you talk to him about it?" Roddy asked.

"Yeah. He said he needed spending money. I started paying him more, but the bookstore was still coming up short. Then there was the rest of it."

"The rest of it?" Lilly asked.

"He'd moved in with me when he first got here, promised he'd find his own space. Then I found out he'd been looking for bigger houses for us."

"Perhaps he was trying to make a family—" Roddy said.

"Maybe. I think he was having fun figuring out how to spend my money," Stan said. "I shut that down pretty quick. He'd offered to leave town, but told me he needed some seed money to start again. I'll admit,

I was getting frustrated, but we talked it through, and decided to try and start again."

"I'm sorry," Lilly said. "It's always difficult to lose someone when there are issues that need to be resolved."

"You said it," Stan said.

"Delia mentioned that you'd bought Buzz a plot in the Goosebush cemetery. That was very generous of you."

"Yeah, she told me that you both looked for it, but Whitney gave me the wrong location. That's another Buzz-related cash flow issue. She did give me a deal since I paid cash—" Stan turned his head when he heard his name being called by the coffee bar.

"Sorry, I've got a meeting." Stan stood up to go.

"Stan, let's talk, soon. I'm happy to look over anything you'd like, and we can figure out a plan to get you back on track."

Stan reached over and put his hand on hers. She turned hers over, and gave his a squeeze. "Thanks, Lilly. I'll definitely let you know."

"You take care," Lilly said. Stan stood up and turned away. He turned back and gave Lilly a kiss on the cheek.

They watched him walk up to the coffee counter and pick up a mug that was waiting for him.

"He seems tightly wound," Lilly said.

"He seems like he's struggling," Roddy said. "Losing Buzz unexpectedly must have been a blow. But, I wonder if on some level it wasn't a relief."

Lilly nodded. "Stan needs to know that the dichotomy of those two feelings is perfectly normal."

"It's good he came over to talk. I was hoping we'd see him today," Roddy said. "He's a complicated young man, with a complicated life." Roddy looked at Lilly and tilted his head toward the front door. Virginia Blossom arrived, a sea of black and gray fabric offset by her pale skin and auburn hair. Virginia never walked, she appeared. She moved toward Stan and gave him a kiss on his cheek. He moved closer to her to talk, and then looked around.

Roddy and Lilly made a point of looking at each other in time to avoid Stan's gaze.

"Complicated indeed," Lilly said.

"Stan asked me to bring you some more tea."

Roddy and Lilly both glanced up from the book they were looking at together.

"That's very kind," Roddy said, closing the book and putting it on his lap to make room.

"It's a new blend. He wanted your opinion," Virginia said, putting the pot and two mugs on the table. "I'm rather fond of it myself, but it's an acquired taste."

"Won't you sit down?" Lilly asked, hoping she'd say no.

"Thanks, just for a minute," she said. She sat and poured a bit of tea into the two mugs. "Bottoms up."

Lilly smelled the brew and winced a bit. "This smells sour."

"It is, but you may enjoy it," Virginia said. "I remember how you liked that blueberry shrub at the last business council meeting."

Lilly had enjoyed the shrub—a mixture of simple syrup, cider vinegar, and blueberries that were mashed together and allowed to ferment. She'd had it with soda water and enjoyed the tang. She'd had them in the past, but Virginia had added rosemary, which added another level of flavor.

She took a sip of the tea, which was indeed sour. But also delicious. She smiled and nodded. Virginia lifted the pot and Lilly held up her mug. Roddy followed suit.

"Is this a new offering?" Lilly said. She prided herself on being knowledgeable about the entire tea line offered by the Star. Not that there were many. Stan always believed in fewer choices and higher quality.

"I went to a tea festival a few weeks ago, and bought several blends from a small company in Philadelphia. Stan is testing them out. They're an acquired taste for sure. But delicious."

"Agreed," Lilly said. "I'd love to learn more about the company."

"I'll send you the information," Virginia said, beaming.

Roddy and Lilly both took a sip of tea, but Virginia didn't say anything more.

"How go the renovations at the Stanley?" Roddy asked. "Ernie tells me that you've been keeping tabs on the process."

"I just got back, as a matter of fact. Renovations are going well. Some setbacks with old infrastructure that needs to be replaced," Virginia said. She pulled the cuff of her silk shirt down past her jacket sleeves, and adjusted her collar.

Lilly nodded. The Stanley Theater closed in December after its owner, Leon Tompkins, had died. In his will he left a sizable amount to the theater, so the renovations had been reconsidered, with several elements added. Ernie was a board member of the theater, and he was working closely with Virginia on the renovations. She wasn't guaranteed a future role in the management of the theater, but she was making a good case for her ability, at least according to Ernie.

"I'm glad to hear that," Lilly said. "Ernie's been keeping me apprised, but I'll confess that I don't get as excited about sound systems and lighting grids as he might wish."

"He's been really smart about getting a lot of input into the design. The theater is going to be well equipped, but he's also paying attention to the audience experience, and the operating expenses that will be required to run the place."

"I know you've been helping him a great deal," Lilly said.

"I'm not going to pretend that I don't want to run the theater once it's open again. But this place is keeping me pretty busy, and I'm still settling into Goosebush. Trying to fit in."

Lilly and Virginia locked eyes, and both women smiled. In February, Virginia had come to Lilly and asked her point-blank why no one liked her. Lilly explained that she needed to try and be part of the community, not just take what she wanted from it. It had been a blunt, difficult conversation, but Virginia took it all in. Since then she'd volunteered for several committees and helped run a fundraiser for the new youth arts center that had taken over the old church buildings.

"I got a postcard for the concert schedule," Roddy said. "I'm a chamber music fan, and looking forward to them."

"I'm glad you're excited. The acoustics are surprisingly good in the space."

"I'm very excited to see the concert on Sunday. Scheduling those artists was quite a coup."

"I'll admit that when I booked them I wasn't sure that the tickets would sell, but I should have trusted Goosebush more. We're completely sold out. I'm looking forward to the concert as well. I'm not as much a chamber music fan, but I appreciate their musicianship. I've heard wonderful things. Are you coming, Lilly?"

Lilly looked over at Roddy and smiled. "I am, and I'm looking forward to it. I haven't been to a concert in a while." Lilly looked around and saw Stan busing tables. "Stan seems awfully busy."

Virginia looked over her shoulder and smiled. "He's down some staff. Stella Haywood got an internship. He's hoping he can hire some college students this summer. And, well, I hate to speak ill of the dead, but Buzz chased a few people away."

"Chased them away?" Roddy said.

"He was difficult to work with," Virginia said. "Made terrible jokes, and always talking. Was either manic and doing everything or quiet and did nothing."

"Still, it's hard for Stan—"

"Of course it is," Virginia said. "Not that everyone believes that. I've been hearing rumors, scuttlebutt really. About Stan."

Lilly nodded slowly. "People in small towns talk."

"People are saying that he had something to do with his father's death," Virginia said. "Ridiculous, of course. But the rumors about running tests to determine the cause of death haven't helped."

"Tests are not necessarily out of the ordinary," Roddy said. "I'm sure that the medical examiner wanted to make sure there's nothing untoward."

"Especially in Goosebush," Virginia said. "Stan had nothing to do with anything. I'm sick and tired of people acting like he did."

"You're very protective of him," Lilly said.

"I enjoy working with him. He's got an amazing imagination, coupled with a great business sense," Virginia said, meeting Lilly's gaze. "I'm seeing what he's going through up close, is all. We work together every day. This is really taking its toll on him."

"I'm sure it's very challenging," Lilly said. "I hope that Stan remembers that he has a lot of people who care about him."

"I'm trying to get Stan to schedule a ceremony for Buzz by the end of the week, so we can get the rumors buried at the same time," Virginia said.

"I'd like to be there," Lilly said. "Please keep me posted."

Virginia said goodbye and walked out of the café area toward the restaurant area. Lilly watched as Stan followed her a few minutes later.

"She's very concerned about Stan," Roddy said.

"Isn't she?" Lilly said. "Maybe a bit too concerned."

Chapter 15

After they'd finished their tea, they walked over to the bookstore section to check on another gardening book Lilly suggested might be helpful to Roddy. He'd brought a small backpack with him, but was running out of space. He'd decided to get the book anyway and carry it home. "I'll risk the upper back strain if it will help the hedges," he said as they were waiting in line to pay.

The busyness of the bookstore always did Lilly's heart good. Of course, the puzzles, stationery, and magazines helped as well. Lilly picked up a knitting magazine and added it to her pile of gardening quarterlies. Usually she gave up knitting in the spring, but this year she'd committed to creating several squares for a fundraiser for the beautification committee. She didn't quite understand what the project was all about: All she knew were the colors, the size required, and the number of blocks Portia Asher needed by August 1 so that the assembly committee would have time to do the work. Having committed to making a dozen, she was looking for inspiration.

"Is the restaurant open yet?" She turned and saw Whitney Dunn-Bradford and Dewey Marsh glide past the café without waiting for an answer. Dewey caught her eyes when he was walking by and tilted his head, giving her a smile.

"I wonder where they're going?" Roddy asked. "It's barely four o'clock. Of course, given the size of that young man, he probably has to eat three or four times a day to keep up his strength."

Lilly laughed. "I suspect he has lots of reasons to want to keep up his strength. Whitney likely keeps him very busy."

Roddy laughed and Lilly joined him. She loved his laugh, which came often and easily. "Perhaps we should come back for dinner?"

"I have a chicken in the crockpot," Roddy said. "Delia mentioned that chicken and dumplings were a favorite. I could bring it over, or you could all come to my house—"

"Get the hell out of here." Stan's voice rose above the murmur of the room, and everything else stopped.

Lilly and Roddy looked over, and saw Whitney and Dewey retracing their steps back through the store. When they were almost at the door, Whitney turned around and stared at Stan, who stopped in his tracks. "Listen, you," Whitney said. "I thought I'd give you a chance to do right by your father, but you blew it."

"You leave my father out of this," Stan said, lowering his voice and staring at Whitney.

"Your father's the reason for all of it," Whitney said. She looked around, but didn't even blink in the face of the rapt audience. "Maybe everyone's right about what they're saying. You're just as glad he's dead. Some son." She turned on her heels and left.

To his credit, or not, Dewey stayed behind and took a step toward Stan. "Listen, man, tempers are frayed."

"Get out of my restaurant," Stan said. "Both of you. I never want to see either of you again."

"Stan, man, take a beat and think about it." Dewey flashed his million-dollar smile, the one that got most people to do what he wanted. A reaction that Lilly could understand, even though more than twenty yards separated them. Tamara had recently surmised that Dewey's smile kept Bradford's in business. Seeing it in action, Lilly didn't doubt it.

Except. Except that Stan wasn't having it. Any of it.

Stan walked up to the taller man and poked him in his chest. "You tell your girlfriend to stay out of my way, otherwise I'll kill her. Can you remember that message, or should I spell it out?" Stan turned ran up the stairs to the second floor and disappeared.

The walk home was pleasant, mostly because they didn't talk about what had happened at the Star. After a bit of back-and-forth they'd decided to eat at Lilly's house.

"Again," as Roddy put it. "Not that I mind. I love eating at your house, especially in that wonderful back room. But I wouldn't mind getting some use out of my new dining set."

Lilly laughed. It was a lovely mid-century dining set, though not very comfortable. Of course, she'd never tell Roddy that. He took great delight in his interior design, as well he should. His old Victorian had a mid-century decor that somehow worked. She suspected he may have had some help in putting it all together, but she didn't press. Roddy had been intent on making a home for himself in Goosebush. So far, he was succeeding. But still, Lilly's house was too perfect for entertaining, especially when the exact number for dinner was always in flux.

That had not always been the case. For the first two years after Alan died, Lilly ate meals with Delia, and only if the younger woman was cooking. They went to Tamara and Warwick's on occasion, but other than that, Lilly's world was small, dull, and flat.

And then last spring, had it only been last spring? Last spring Tamara and Delia talked Lilly into having a garden party on the scale she hadn't had in years. They'd brought the idea up in February, to give Lilly plenty of time to get used to it, and to plan her gardens. She hadn't been enthusiastic, but they'd talked her into it. The event had been a success, helping both Lilly and her gardens come back to life. And, happily for them all, Roddy had crashed the party. He'd become a fixture in her life, in their lives, ever since.

Now that Ernie had moved in, the gravitational force was definitely at Windward. In her renovations Lilly had prized comfort above all else, so there was ample room to eat, lounge, and relax. She didn't think that Roddy really minded. He'd taken to bringing meals over to share a couple of times a week. In order to earn his keep, he insisted.

"I'll be over in a few minutes," Roddy said, veering off to his front door while she continued toward hers. She keyed in the code and closed the door behind her. She listened, but didn't hear the cats tumbling toward her. Delia must be home. She hung up her coat and walked to the back of the house. Looking to the right, there was no Delia in the kitchen. To the left, she wasn't in her office. She walked straight out to the back of the house and the back room. Over to the right she saw Delia sitting in the large rocking chair, staring at the fireplace.

"I got a knitting magazine," Lilly said. "There was a leaf pattern I thought might be fun—" She walked around to face Delia, and stopped when she realized the young woman was crying. The cats were both on her lap, leaning into her, trying to stop the sobs. Lilly took the footstool and pulled it close, putting her hands on Delia's arm.

"Oh, my sweet friend, what's happened?"

Delia trying to talk, but all that came out were rattled breaths. She handed Lilly her phone and pointed to a text. Lilly got up and grabbed a pair of glasses. She kept several around the house for moments like this. She opened the text, which was from an unfamiliar number. It said: **I thought you should know**. Lilly scrolled up to see the picture, and realized it was of Stan and Virginia Blossom kissing. She opened the picture and realized that they were in the Star restaurant. Looking closer, she recognized the jacket Virginia was wearing.

"Who sent this?"

"Don't know," Delia said.

Lilly clicked on the number and dialed. The call went to voice mail. "This is Whitney. Leave me a message, I'll call you right back."

She looked at the time stamp. The text had been sent ten minutes ago.

Chapter 16

"How's Delia this morning?" Roddy asked. He waited until Lilly settled into the seat and buckled her seat belt before putting the car in gear.

"Ernie's with her," Lilly said. "Bless him, he's commiserating with her over her broken heart. He's also making her laugh with some of his dating stories. I should let you know, he offered to have you go over and punch Stan out if she'd like. He assured her you'd do it."

"I've punched men for less," Roddy said. "And I'm very fond of Delia."

"Oh dear."

"My past, Lilly," he said. They drove the rest of the way in silence. Delia had been inconsolable last night, and gone up to her room to be alone. Roddy's chicken and dumplings did entice her to eat when Lilly brought her a tray.

"You mentioned a way to get into the cemetery without having to go in the front gate," Roddy said.

"Yes, park right over there."

"Here? This is a fence—"

"Indeed it is. Do you have the map Sasha sent you?"

"I have better than that." Roddy reached to the back seat of his Jaguar and brought up a leather folder. He opened it and handed a manilla folder to Lilly.

"The bottom is the map Sasha sent. Then I made copies of some of the maps you gave me, and put them on vellum so we could do overlays."

She flipped through the papers and looked at Roddy, smiling. "This is wonderful. How did you figure out the scale?"

"The Jayne tomb and Bertram's Folly are on most maps. I used them as anchors. I thought it might be helpful."

"Very helpful," Lilly said. "What do you have in there?" She pointed to the bag Roddy pulled out of the back seat.

"Paper for doing rubbings," Roddy said. "I've heard such wonderful things about your crypt, I thought I'd take a rubbing for study later, if we have time."

"I haven't jumped a fence in a few years," Roddy said.

"That little side hop of yours was impressive," Lilly laughed. "I want to go over here first."

Roddy followed Lilly, who was walking without looking at her map. She stopped after a few minutes, and walked into the middle of a section of graves, looking at the names on different headstones.

"No wonder her cousin is a wreck," Lilly said.

"What?"

"Sorry. I wanted to remind myself about the Garrett family plot. I'm not trusting my memory anymore."

Roddy walked around and stood next to Lilly.

"The family plot. What does that mean?"

"Early on, older families bought several plots so that the family could be together. See here? That headstone are the Garrett parents. Then this one is Helen's brother Raphael, and his wife. Two double plots."

"Helen's name appears to be on the headstone with her parents," Roddy said. "But there's a marker in the middle." He walked around to read it.

"Not a Garrett," Lilly said.

"No. Ted Jones. He died ten years ago."

"I wonder if that space was supposed to be Helen's resting place. She's outlived everyone by years and years. Her understanding was that there was space for her."

"You think they thought it was an abandoned grave, so they used it," Roddy said.

"That's what it sure looks like. Why would her parents and her brother and his wife all be there with enough room in the middle, and the space be used for a stranger? Unless her plot was somewhere else around here?" She went over to look at the headstones across from Helen's parents. Both were dated from the early 2000s.

"I can't imagine where there's space nearby," Roddy said.

"Helen thought there was. I hope Helen's cousin can find the paperwork to prove it." Lilly shook her head and looked up at Roddy. Wouldn't Helen have noticed Ted's headstone at some point in the last few years? Or maybe she hadn't visited; she'd been fairly housebound for the past few years, and you had to walk through the cemetery to get to their graves. A mystery for another day. "Let's go look at the spots Sasha wants to sell you."

They spent the next hour walking around, looking at the map that Sasha sent, and comparing it to the records they'd been able to find. They both took notes and pictures with their phones.

"Here's the last one," Roddy said. "It's close to the Jayne family."

"Very close," Lilly said, furrowing her brow. "Let's go check it out, shall we?"

They started to wander over toward the Jayne crypt. They found the spot for sale. Lilly looked around, again wondering where they'd fit another casket.

"These all look like legitimate spaces," Roddy said.

"They do," Lilly said. "But it's room that's been sliced out of other plots."

"When we get back we'll try and figure out how the space was made," Roddy said. "Your instincts, as always, are spot-on. Something's amiss. But first, let's go over and look at your family crypt. Delia raved about the carvings."

"Of course," Lilly said. "It's funny; I take it for granted, but it really is amazing. The historical society will have more information about the carvers. Of course, there are also some records at my house, in the family archives."

"Where are those archives?"

"There's a library downstairs where all the family records are kept. The doorway is built into a panel.

Alan used it for his office. He loved the gloom and doom."

"Gloom and doom?"

"The only light comes from transom lights on the second floor. It runs two stories. It's an odd space. I'll show you later. Ernie and I have been discussing where we might be able to install an elevator, and using part of the library is an option. I'd like your thoughts on that as well."

"I'd love to see it," Roddy said. They'd arrived at the mausoleum, and Roddy put down the bag he'd been carrying.

"This is wonderful," he said. "Look at the work-manship. Sort of a Greco-Roman influence."

"On this side," Lilly said. "And on that corner. But look down there. That area's Gothic. There are Egyptian influences on the back. And then there are the figures. They do all seem to be telling a story, but none of us know what it is."

"When your relatives left it to people to learn their craft—"

"They gave them free rein," Lilly said. "My father said that the work continued for years and years. Some people even came back later in life to clean up their earlier work."

"It's marvelous," Roddy said. "Would you mind helping me tape the paper up? I'll get one side today, and then come back."

Lilly held up one end while Roddy meticulously taped the paper down flat. She was impressed—he'd bought the flat-sided crayons that made the rubbings easier, and the paper he'd bought was good quality. He'd get good details.

"You came prepared," Lilly said.

"I've always loved doing rubbings, and Delia suggested it may be interesting to study the work. I won't be but a few minutes."

"Take your time," Lilly said.

She walked to the back of the building while he got to work. The bench was still in the wrong spot. She took pictures and wandered around, seeing if anything was amiss. She walked to the other side of the crypt. She made notes of the plants that would look nice, and the tools she'd need. The space was maintained, but neglected. The Jaynes deserved better.

She turned to pull the weeds along the side of the granite building. Yes, all of this needed to have new plants. She vaguely remembered seeing flowers along the edges, but couldn't remember the last time they'd been tended to. Her mother probably did it, right after her father died. That was almost twenty years ago.

She finished pulling one side and turned the corner toward the front. Here it was a little bit better, but not much. The ironwork around the door was tarnished. Lilly leaned in and took a closer look. There was a little rust, but it was mostly in good shape. Still, it needed tending. She looked at the door handle to check for rust, and then she looked closer.

The door. Something was off. There seemed to be an odd shadow by the door.

It took her a moment to register, but when she pulled down on the handle, the door gave with a groan and creaked open. She pushed the door and stepped back. There were dozens of urns inside, piled along the floor. There were also a number of wooden boxes stacked on top of one another. Lilly let out a cry and took a step backwards.

"Lilly, what's the matter—what's this?" he asked, standing beside her.

"The door was open," she whispered.

"But I thought you had the only key," he said, putting his hand under her elbow to steady her.

"I do," Lilly said. She wiped her eyes and looked at Roddy. "Sorry. It's just that—I have no idea who all these people are."

"What do you mean?" Roddy asked.

"All of these urns. Do you see that vault, over there by the wall, the second one from the floor? That was going to be for my father, but then he decided to be cremated. We scattered his ashes at sea and some in my garden, but I put an urn with his name in it in the vault, for future generations. Then I did the same for my mother, and dear Alan."

"The door to the vault is closed," Roddy said. The inside was very dark, since the only light came from the open door itself. Roddy took his cell phone out and turned on the flashlight.

"Do you see that urn, the one that looks like a Greek water pitcher? That's Alan. He shouldn't be on the floor like that. He should be in the vault."

"Perhaps it's an urn that looks like Alan's?" Roddy said.

"I had it specially made," Lilly said. "That's his."

She tried to take a deep breath, but couldn't. What was Alan doing on the floor? Where were her parents? She was going to go inside, but Roddy put his hand on her arm.

"I'll go in," Roddy said. "You wait here. I want to

see something. So, all of these vault doors on either wall? Most of them seem to have a seal on them."

"They're all places for coffins. The seals were put in place to ensure no one disturbed the contents," Lilly said. "There aren't many spots left, which is why my parents decided to share rather than build a new row of vaults. Do you see that newer plate? That's their spot."

Roddy moved carefully and made his way over to the vault. He took a deep breath and steadied himself. He gently pulled the door and quickly opened it. He walked out and stood next to Lilly.

"I know why Alan's on the floor," Roddy said. "There's a metal casket in that vault."

"Who is it?"

"No idea," Roddy said. "Come here, let's step out. Let me see this door. Yes, I see. Older lock. Though it doesn't appear to be forced."

"Someone may come back," Lilly said.

"We'll be back very soon," Roddy said, squeezing her hand. "Here, let's close the door. Now rip me off a piece of the tape I used for the etching. Thank you. Let's put it on the bottom of the door. Sort of like a seal."

"If it's broken, we'll know someone came back. Should I go and get Alan?" Lilly said.

"I think we should talk to Bash first," Roddy said.

"And tell him what?" Lilly said. She wiped her eyes and looked up at Roddy.

He put his arm around her shoulder and gave it a squeeze. "We've got a breaking and entering to report. Let's start there."

* * *

The police station was all too familiar to Lilly. Not that she was on the wrong side of the law. Not that at all. But she'd made it a habit to stop by regularly and visit with Bash Haywood, the chief of police.

Bash fell into the job of being the chief mostly because of the opportunity arising for him, rather than him pursuing that career path. He'd given up his dreams of being an artist when his parents died in an automobile accident, and he'd had to take care of his younger siblings. Stella, who was very young at the time, still lived with Bash in Goosebush, though these days she took as good care of him as he did of her.

Over the past couple of years, Bash had grown into the job of chief. He'd been learning more investigative techniques, developing confidence, and exploring more ways to help Goosebush move forward. Lilly had always been Bash's secret weapon, with a clarity of vision that he needed, and a mind that was always open to more possibilities than the obvious.

Lilly visited Bash on occasion, but more often Bash visited Lilly, helping her with chores, sharing a meal, and talking through what was on his mind. Though it had been quiet in Goosebush since last fall, when all hell broke loose after Leon Tompkins's death, he still sought her out. Bash was exploring new ways to do community policing, and to have the police play a positive role in the town. Bash, Warwick, and Lilly had been talking about new initiatives with the high school that were coming up for approval later in the summer for the coming school year.

Bash smiled when he saw Lilly and Roddy come into his office, but his smile soon waned when he saw her face. She'd been crying and held heavily onto Roddy's arm. He walked around his desk and sat at the edge, taking her hand into his.

"Lilly, what's the matter?" Bash asked. Roddy closed the door and sat down in the chair next to her.

"It's all . . . I'm not sure . . ." Lilly took a deep breath and looked over at Roddy.

"We came from the cemetery," Roddy said. "What we were doing there is a little complicated, and I'll get to that. But we wanted to come and talk to you about the Jayne mausoleum. It's been broken into. We found the door open."

"What was taken?" Bash said. He went back around his desk and opened up a notebook, pen at the ready.

"Nothing was taken," Lilly said. "It's what was added that's the problem."

"Added?"

"We didn't look too closely, but there were several urns on the floor," Roddy said.

"Dozens—" Lilly said.

"Including one that Lilly recognized. That which belonged to her late husband, Alan."

"What was that doing on the floor?" Bash asked. "Was it knocked over?"

"No, everything seemed to be upright. You may or may not know this, but Lilly had used her father's vault as a resting place for her parents, and for Alan. I checked the vault, and there was a body in there."

"A body?" Bash sat forward and stared at Roddy.

"Sorry, a casket. Which presumably had a body. I didn't check."

"And you don't know where that came from?" Bash asked Lilly. "Did you give anyone else permission to use the vault?"

"I have the only key," Lilly said. "Maybe it belongs to a relative who decided to squat, but I have no idea who the rest of those urns belong to."

Bash took some notes. "That does sound odd," he said.

"It's not the only odd thing that has been happening in the cemetery."

Lilly and Roddy went on to tell Bash about their inquiry into cemetery plots. Bash listened and took notes. Lilly knew if anyone else had come to him with these concerns, he may have listened with a critical ear. But it was Lilly and he trusted her. He'd relied on her judgment and good sense more than once. If she thought something was going on, something was going on.

"And then there's the Garrett plot," Lilly said.

"Helen Garrett? What about her plot?"

"Her cousin came up to take care of her, and she went to the cemetery to pay her respects to the rest of the family. She noticed that the plot seemed smaller, and has been doing her own research. It looked like someone else had joined the family. A Ted Jones."

"What do you think happened?" Bash asked.

"I'm all jumbled." Lilly shrugged. "It's not like that is the only resting place for my parents and dear Alan. You know that we also had burials at sea—"

"Yes, I was there," Bash said.

"And of course there's also the memorial garden. But still. All of those other people. It all felt . . . impersonal."

"Bash, couldn't Lilly file a breaking and entering complaint? Would that start you asking some questions?"

"Absolutely," Bash said. "Lilly, you up for a trip back out there now?"

"I suppose so," Lilly said.

"Great. I'll bring Steph with us, to take some pictures. Roddy, would you mind going over to talk to Ernie? We should get that lock repaired. Don't worry, Lilly. We'll get to the bottom of this. I promise."

Chapter 17

Ten days later, the new green of spring had finally popped in Lilly's garden. She'd been getting rid of winter debris; weeding, planting, pruning, mulching, and watering all spring, and now it finally felt as though the effort would pay off. She finished moving some grasses and stood back to look at her handiwork. Perfect. Well, not perfect; perfection was unattainable. But still, she persisted.

"I like those grasses," Roddy said, coming through the gate. "I assume they'll get taller over the summer?"

"No, not much taller," Lilly said. "It's Hakone grass. I'm going to try and keep it contained a bit, but I do like the spots of color that grasses offer."

"What are those pots for?"

"I've split some and thought I'd bring some over to Helen Garrett's house, and offer to put them in for her cousin."

"That's very nice of you," Roddy said. "I am sorry

about your friend, Lilly. I know it was expected, but it's still sad."

"It's the passing of a generation," Lilly said. "The grasses are an excuse to go by the house and pay my respects. And finally meet her cousin."

"It looks like there might be more to split," Roddy said, looking around Lilly's garden. Though it was her domain, he'd begun to understand her thought process around gardening. If she was going to thin grasses in one place, she'd do it throughout the garden.

"There are. I can put some in pots and send them to the store with Ernie."

"Or you can send some my way," Roddy said. "I hadn't realized how big my backyard is, and how many spots need to be filled."

"Patience, Roddy, patience. The garden muses will visit you all summer, giving you ideas. What doesn't work will become clear, but let your garden tell you what it needs."

"What happens if I don't speak garden? Will you come over and translate?"

"Gladly," Lilly said, laughing. "I happen to be fluent."

"You are indeed that, Lilly. What a sanctuary this place is. Everything is wonderfully green."

"A week of rain should have some benefits," Lilly said. "Since you're here, I have a favor to ask. Would you help me move some of the bigger plants out of the greenhouse? I moved several indoors for the winter, but they're ready to come out. I could probably lift them myself, but I promised Ernie I wouldn't. I want to get the cement planters filled—"

"You aren't going to believe this," Ernie said, running down the back stairs. "Oh, hey, Roddy. Glad you're here too. Look."

He held out his phone, but Lilly shook her head. "I don't have my reading glasses. Tell me."

"It's a breaking news item from the *Boston World*. Here's the headline. *Goosebush funeral home closed. Owners charged with illegal disposal of human remains.*"

"What? Bradford's?" Lilly said.

"The same," Ernie said. "See, I told you that Bash was working on something."

"I should have had more faith," Lilly said. "But it has been almost two weeks."

"Ten days," Roddy said. He'd taken Ernie's phone and was reading the article. "These are some significant charges. Here it says that this was a result of a longtime investigation."

"Bash is mentioned, and they said they were reaching out to him for a quote," Ernie said.

"Lilly, Bash is here to see you," Delia said. She was standing in the doorway of the back porch, holding both cats. "He's parking his car."

"Well, what's say we all go in and have a cup of coffee with Bash? The plants will have to wait."

"This room really did turn out great," Bash said, stretching his long legs out in front of him, mug of coffee in his hand. Both cats had run over as soon as he sat down. Luna sat on his lap, and Max found a place next to him on the chair. He used his free hand to pet the cats, one at a time. "It's a shame that these two obviously lack for attention."

"Don't even start," Ernie said. "There aren't two more spoiled cats in the entire world. Now, enough with the pleasantries. Spill. What happened?"

"I tried to get over here before the news broke, but I promised I'd keep it close to my vest until they were ready to file the charges. Something must have happened, because the timeline got moved up."

"Timeline?" Roddy asked.

"That's jumping ahead in the story. I'll get there," Bash said, shifting in his seat to give Max more room. "After I got your complaint about the Jayne crypt, Lilly, I opened an investigation. I also decided to make some calls to figure out other possible crimes I might be dealing with, aside from breaking and entering. Since you were worried about other things you'd noticed, I thought I should do some research. Because of the nature of the issues, I didn't want to call the Bradfords directly and ask them any questions."

"What do you mean, other issues you might be dealing with?" Lilly asked.

"I'm comfortable working with breaking and entering, but I wondered if there were other rules having to do with cemeteries. Was it illegal to put the urns in your family's mausoleum? Or could that be legal, but a bad practice? Or was it common practice, but people don't know because they don't go visit family mausoleums? Maybe someone was using it as temporary storage. Then there was the casket in the vault, the one that Roddy found. Was there a body inside? How could it be identified? Was there a standard way to track things like that? Like I said, I wanted to know what was what before I talked to

Whitney and Sasha. Good thing I did." Bash took a long sip of coffee, enjoying holding everyone's attention. Usually Lilly was explaining things to him.

"Why's that, Sebastian?" Lilly asked, looking at him pointedly over her glasses. She rarely used his given name, and knew it had an effect.

Bash smiled and looked at Lilly. "Seems there are a few active investigations on the state level into Bradford family business practices."

"Like what?" Ernie asked.

"Helen Garrett's niece, Jaqueline Ross—"

"I know her," Ernie said.

"She's been raising hell about Helen's plot. You were right, Lilly. She did have the space next to her parents, but someone else was buried there," Bash said.

"Did Jackie finally find the paperwork?" Ernie asked. "She'd been looking high and low for it."

"Jackie seemed to remember Helen mentioning that there was room for her too, so she got someone to come in with ground-penetrating sonar. Helen's space was actually across from her parents, and there was room for a fourth person, or two markers. Basically, Ted, the marker between Helen's parents and her brother, was put into a space that wasn't supposed to exist. I'm trying to track down information about who he was to see if I can talk to the people who made the arrangements. Two other bodies were put in the family plot. It's a good thing Jackie was dogged in pursuing this. And that she wasn't afraid to make waves."

"She takes good care of her family," Ernie said. "She's been in the store a few times while she was visiting Helen. I know that there are several home improvement projects that she's taken care of, mostly to keep busy. I've seen her twice in the past week, but she didn't tell me any of this."

"No, she wouldn't," Bash said. "The cone of silence was tight, so that as few people as possible knew about the investigations. Anyway, Lilly, that's why I didn't have Ernie rekey the door. There was surveillance set up to see what happened, if anything."

"I should have taken the urns," Lilly said.

"I got Alan and your folks out of there," Bash said. "They've been safe in my office."

"Were they investigating anything else?" Delia asked.

"Can't say," Bash said.

"I'll take that as a yes," the younger woman said, giving Bash one of her rare smiles.

He blushed slightly and then looked around the room. "Anyway, I'll know more soon. I promise to let you know what I can, when I can."

"One question," Ernie said. "Is it only Whitney being charged?"

"Whitney, Sasha, and Dewey. It's a big deal, my friends. Do me a favor, though. Don't try to get involved. There are a lot of factors at play, and it's pretty complicated."

Later that afternoon, Lilly was walking down the stairs when the doorbell rang. Her philosophy was that anyone worth opening the door to would either let her know in advance, or have the code and let themselves in the gate, so she usually ignored the bell until it rang three or four times. But, since she was close by, she decided she may as well open the door.

To her frustration, there was no one there. She went to close the front door again and glanced over at the wreath hook. She screamed, jumping back. There was a dead rat hanging on the hook by its tail. Her heart was racing and she swallowed hard. She slammed the door shut, and ran her sweaty hands down the front of her dress. She called out for Ernie and Delia, but remembered that they'd both left for the afternoon. She was alone. And there was a rat on her front door.

She fished her cell phone from her pocket, looked at her recently dialed numbers, and pushed down on Roddy's face. As soon as she heard the call go through, she spoke.

"There's a rat on my front door," she said quickly.

"I'll be right there," Roddy said.

True to his word, he came over within two minutes, through the back of the house. She heard him greet the cats on his way to the front hall. Ever since they'd been able to open the gate between the houses, Roddy had used the back entrance regularly. No need to give Goosebush information about their comings and goings.

He found her sitting on the stairs to the landing. She shrugged and shook her head. She pointed to the front door and shivered.

He opened it slowly and took a step back. Then he took a step forward and picked the rat up by the tail. "It's rubber," he said. "Very realistic, though. This is some sort of fake blood. Nice touch, though a bit much. What a mess." He took his handkerchief out and wrapped the rubber rat up. "Wait, what's that?" He opened the mouth and fished out a piece of paper.

"*Rats die*," he read, looking up at Lilly.

"That's succinct," she said.

"That's a warning," he said. "I wonder who left it there? How long was it between the doorbell ringing and you answering it?"

"Less than a minute. I was on my way downstairs when I heard it. When I opened the door no one was out front," Lilly said. "No human was there. Please, can you put that away? I hate rats."

"Yes, of course, sorry," Roddy said. He looked around the foyer, and put the bundled-up rat in a large urn that was sitting on one of the hall tables. He took a picture of the note with his phone, and then dropped the note into the vessel. "I'll move it later. In the meantime, let's see if we can figure out who left you this gift on the front door. The doorbell camera probably caught the person doing the deed."

"I don't know how to log in," Lilly said.

"You've logged in before, when we first set it up. Let's fire up your computer," Roddy said. "Your password may be recorded. I'll need to wash my hands first." He walked over to the washroom and quickly washed his hands.

"My computer's in the back porch," she said, after he'd dried them. "I'm doing some garden planning," she said. "I was coming down from the upstairs library—that's where I keep the gardening books—when I heard the door ring, otherwise I would have ignored it."

"Or checked the app on your phone to see who was there?"

"I removed the app from my phone. It kept pinging at me anytime anything moved. Since Ernie put a camera by the gate, every car created an alert."

"We can probably set it up so that it doesn't ping you," Roddy said gently. He loved tech and gadgets, but was aware of Lilly's reticence and knew that she needed to come to new ideas on her own.

"Then why don't we put it back," Lilly said.

"We'll do that in a bit," Roddy said. They were walking toward the back of the house slowly.

"Mind you, I would have called you anyway. Because, rat." Lilly shuddered and made a face.

"I'm not terribly fond of rats either," Roddy said, putting his arm around her shoulders and squeezing gently before letting go. "Let's see who the rat hanger was."

Roddy sat down at the table and Lilly slid her computer to him. It took him a few minutes to log into the doorbell camera site, since she didn't have the password and he needed to reset it.

"I'm going to go and get my own computer," Roddy said. "Resetting your password seems to be a bit of a process. Keep an eye out for the verification email. If you don't mind, I'll work on my projects over here this afternoon."

"I don't mind at all. My computer is very slow, but I'll keep working on the password situation," Lilly said. While he was gone, Lilly made some tea and put together a plate of cookies. There was plenty of space at Windward, and Roddy and Lilly could work on their own projects, but together. Not a bad way to spend an afternoon.

But first, they needed to figure out who was hanging rats on front doors.

After he came back, he set up his computer. By the time he'd logged in, Lilly had reset the password, and he wrote it down.

"I'm going to get a glass of water," she said. "Would you like one?"

"Sure," he said. "Could you leave your phone? We're going to get a text to verify that you're you."

"This site is more secure than Fort Knox," she said, turning her phone on and leaving it next to Roddy.

"You'd hate for someone else to be able to log in," he said. He logged into the site, and by the time Lilly was back with two glasses of water, he was in. Roddy clicked a few buttons, then he pushed the computer in front of Lilly, leaning in to watch. They waited for a few minutes, and then they saw a car pull up in the space in front of the driveway gate. After a few moments the passenger got out, and ran up the front walkway. She took the rat out of her pocket and shoved a piece of paper down its throat. When she stepped onto the porch, her face came into focus as she hung the rat and squirted the fake blood on it.

"Sasha, oh, Sasha. What would your mother say, young lady?" Lilly said.

"Perhaps you should talk to Bash," Roddy said.

Lilly's phone rang. "Speak of the devil. Hello, Bash, I was just about to . . . what? Of course. I'll meet you at the mausoleum. An hour, sure. Yes, I'll bring Roddy with me."

Lilly parked by the cemetery, this time in a legitimate spot, where she'd agreed to meet Bash. Well, Bash and his guests.

"This looks like it's more than a walk-through of the cemetery," Roddy said. "I see two people with cameras."

"He mentioned wanting to get my thoughts on the record. I guess he meant it," Lilly said.

"No worries, Lilly. Trust yourself, and your memory. I'll be right there with you." She reached over and gave his hand a squeeze.

Bash introduced Roddy and Lilly to the investigative team from the state. The person in charge, Darlene Daniel, shook their hands. Her navy-blue suit and white shirt were large on her. She wore short boots that were covered in dried mud, and she took a scrunchie off her wrist and pulled her hair back. Her assistant handed her a clipboard and she turned toward Roddy and Lilly.

"Ms. Jayne, Mr. Lyden, I appreciate your being willing to come here at the last minute."

"Bash mentioned that you needed my help with something," Lilly said.

"The Bradford story has been picked up by the news. I'm not surprised, it's a story that captures the imagination. So far no one has tracked the investigation back to the cemetery, so the reporters aren't here. But that's only a matter of time. We thought it would be good to get you on the record, Ms. Jayne, before you talk to the press—"

"I have no intention of talking to the press, Ms. Daniel."

"Good. Glad to hear that. Still, I should have talked to you earlier. We're exploring several other avenues of inquiry, and you may be able to help us. Chief Haywood mentioned that you noticed a few issues in the cemetery."

Lilly looked over at Roddy and he handed her a

folder. "Ms. Daniel, this is for you. With Roddy's help, we put some cemetery maps together. See these numbers? They correspond to the notes at the back."

"This is very helpful. Did you know I'd need them?" she asked, flipping through the pages.

"This was more of an exercise for myself," Lilly said. "I'd begun to think I was losing my mind. Roddy and Delia—"

"Delia?"

"Delia Greenway, a friend. They both suggested I write down my memories of who was where. I did that and I also took some pictures. Together we put together this document. It includes official records and some unofficial. It helped pass the time over these past ten days."

The younger woman flipped through the document and nodded. She lifted up the pages on her clipboard and put the booklet behind them. "We have a lot of this information, but not with this detail. Is it possible to send it to me over email?" Darlene handed Lilly her card.

"Of course."

"Let's do the walk-through, anyway. I'm a visual learner. It's helpful for me to see exactly what you're talking about," she said. "The chief mentioned that you used to give tours of the cemetery?"

"I've given some, but my father's tours are the ones people remember," Lilly said.

"But you know the cemetery well enough to be aware of things that had changed?" The six of them walked through the gate and Darlene paused. She nudged her assistant's arm and he nodded to the cameraman.

"I spent a fair amount of time here when I was younger. Visiting different family members."

"Do you have a lot of family in this cemetery? Aside from those who are interred in the family mausoleum?"

"I have my mother's family and other distant relatives sprinkled around."

"I've seen photos of the mausoleum, but haven't been here in person until today. We didn't want to tip anyone off that there was an investigation. It's an impressive building."

"My family never did anything halfway," Lilly said.

"The building was also a public works project of the time," Roddy said. "I've been doing a bit of research at the historical society. Goosebush had shipbuilding here for a number of years, but then it moved further down the Cape. The town elders created a few projects to give folks jobs, and to retrain people in other crafts. The Jaynes also privately hired people."

"They still do," Bash said.

"The carvings on the crypt are very interesting," Roddy said. "There are some amazing artisans who participated in the project."

"I look forward to seeing the work. But in the meantime, we're ready to start when you are," Darlene said.

"You just want me to talk?"

"Give us a tour."

"Let's start at the Garrett family plot, then. I suspect you'd heard about the issues there."

"We have, but that sounds like a good place to start."

Each stop took a while, because Darlene asked questions, and videos and pictures were taken. They walked over to the overgrown part of the cemetery, but Lilly noticed some changes.

"Is something wrong?" Bash asked her.

"Some of the weeds are gone," Lilly said. "And I thought I saw more headstones along that back path, but I may be wrong. Delia may remember." Lilly sighed. She'd like to visit one day and not notice any changes.

Darlene stopped and took more notes. "Ms. Jayne, don't doubt your memory," she said. "Could be that they were clearing more space."

"Is that what's been happening?" When no one answered her, Lilly continued. "All right, now this is getting to be what my father used to call the Jayne neighborhood." She pointed out the headstones she remembered, and the ones she didn't.

"Here's the family vault," she said, stopping.

"Very impressive. You're right, Mr. Lyden. The carvings are magnificent. Now, I understand that there was also an issue about a bench?"

"The bench was the thing that made me understand it wasn't my imagination," Lilly said.

"Tell her the nickname," Bash said.

"It's called the bastard bench," Lilly said, flushing slightly and shrugging her shoulders. "It was a way for a distant relative to create a place for the Jaynes who were Jaynes, but not in name. Over time, it became the family tree for the illegitimate family members, though I do hate that word. I'm glad that the shame of those days is behind us, aren't you? Anyway, there are a lot of names on the bench. Its normal spot is back there, behind the crypt. Do you see that

large granite hitching post? It used to be the right of
that."

"Is that all the Jayne plot?"

"A lot of it, yes," Lilly said. "Do you see the four
granite posts?" Lilly pointed out the three that were
visible from the front of the building. "Those were
the unofficial markers of the Jayne plot."

"It goes quite a ways back."

"Originally it went to the back fence. The path
along the back was added later, for trucks and cars,
but the family members were moved to make way for
that. My grandmother oversaw that."

"When did that happen?" Darlene asked.

"The early fifties? The exact dates are in those papers I gave you. There have been a few infrastructure
improvements that have required some moving over
the years. That was one of them."

"We should check that out," Darlene said to her
assistant. They kept walking on the path, and took a
right to go to the back of the building. "And here's
the bench in question—oh my. Is that?" She stopped
in her tracks and took a step back. Roddy rushed forward to grab her elbow.

"Lilly, don't—" he said, thrusting his arm out to
try and block her. He couldn't do more. Darlene was
starting to wobble, and he was holding her up.

Lilly didn't listen. She stepped around Darlene
and looked to her left. Whitney Dunne-Bradford was
lying in front of the bench. A broken headstone was
lying beside her, with pieces strewn about. Lilly saw
the name *Roy* on one of the pieces.

Bash went over and got down on one knee, checking her pulse. He looked up and held up his hand to stop Lilly from moving forward. He shook his head and pulled out his cell phone. While he was making the call, he squatted again, and Lilly leaned forward to see what he was looking at. There was a gun in Whitney's hand.

Chapter 18

Finding a body with the chief of police made the follow-up interrogation much easier.

"Can you account for your whereabouts this afternoon?" he'd asked Roddy and Lilly while they waited for the other officers to arrive. Darlene was sitting in the front seat of her car, and her assistant was squatting beside her, trying to calm her down.

"We've been together ever since Sasha left the rat at my door."

Bash looked up and squinted. "Explain," was all he said.

Roddy did exactly that, also letting Bash know about the video.

"When was that?"

Lilly looked down at her watch. "About two hours ago."

"Can you send the video to me?"

"Of course," Roddy said.

"I don't suppose you can tell when this happened?" Lilly asked.

"The coroner can help with the time of death. Body's still warm, so not long ago. There are some surveillance cameras, but they're focused on the front of the tomb. If someone came in from the back, they wouldn't be seen. Listen, why don't you both get out of here? I've got to get statements from Darlene and her crew."

"Surely she's not a suspect," Lilly said. "She practically fainted at the sight of the body."

"But she was here twenty minutes before I was. She may have seen something. Roddy, send me that video as soon as you can."

"Will do," Roddy said. They both got into Lilly's car and she quickly pulled out of the cemetery parking lot. They passed a news van while on their way back to Lilly's house.

"At least we're spared the press attention," Roddy said.

"For now, anyway," Lilly said.

"Are you all right, Lilly?"

"It's such a shock. I never would have imagined that Whitney would kill herself."

"Is that what you think happened?" Roddy asked.

"She had a gun in her hand. Why, don't you think that's what happened?"

"I couldn't get a close look," Roddy said. "Ms. Daniel was in quite a state and I was trying not to let her crumple to the ground."

"Do you think she was sincere?"

"I do," Roddy said. "Though I'd imagine seeing your prime suspect dead would be shocking as well."

"True. What should we do now?"

"Head back to your house. Everyone should be there shortly—"

"What do you mean, everyone?"

"Ernie was planning a dinner tonight to discuss the case, remember?"

"Darn it. Yes, of course. This morning feels like a million years ago."

"Should we cancel?" Roddy asked.

"Why? The only people making a special trip are Tamara and Warwick, and I wouldn't want them to feel left out."

Lilly was waiting at the head of her driveway for the gate to close, a precaution she always took to make sure that no one followed her in. Someone else pulled in and beeped.

"Tamara's early," Roddy said. He looked at his watch and shook his head. "Actually, she's right on time. How did it get to be so late?"

"It has been a very full day. Should we tell them all about Whitney?" Lilly said. She pulled down the driveway and opened the gate again.

"We may as well. It will be on the news, or in the Goosebush gossip circles, shortly," Roddy said.

"I feel odd having a dinner that feels in any way celebratory," Lilly said, driving slowly and closing the gate with her remote. She looked in her rearview mirror and smiled. Tamara was waiting to make sure no one snuck in. Then she thought of Whitney, and shook her head to get the picture erased. It didn't work.

"We're not doing that at all," Roddy said. "Ernie suggested it after the news about the investigation broke, but so much has happened since. No one knows about the rat situation, and telling everyone at once is much easier."

"I suppose that's true," Lilly said. "You'll need to download those videos for Bash."

"I'm going to do that first thing. I'll also edit the parts he needs, so he doesn't have to wade through hours of video."

"We haven't had a Garden Squad dinner in a week. I'm not sure what we'll eat—"

"Warwick is picking up a pan of chicken and broccoli, and Ernie's getting salad makings. I'm in a group text with them both about the details."

"You are very efficient," Lilly said, pulling the car up and into the garage. She wanted to make room for the other cars that would be arriving.

"What's going on in that mind of yours?" Roddy asked, opening his car door.

"Not much, I'm afraid. I'm exhausted all of a sudden," Lilly said, opening hers. "Would Whitney kill herself?"

Roddy looked at Lilly and shrugged. "I didn't know her at all. Perhaps she felt hemmed in and didn't want to tell her tale?"

"I have to wonder what her tale was?" Lilly said. "I couldn't help but overhear Darlene when she was talking to Bash. Whitney had called her office to make a deal of some sort. That's why Ms. Daniel wanted the tour today, so that she could get a handle on anything that may add to the potential scope of the investigation." She opened the side door of the garage and stepped out into the backyard.

"We'll meet you in the kitchen," she called out to Tamara. Roddy closed the garage door and followed Lilly up the back stairs into the house. "I'd have thought that before they went public with a news report they would have had their ducks lined up."

"Maybe the story leaked," Roddy said. "Or perhaps Ms. Daniel was the source of the leak in order to put pressure on someone. The story parameters were fairly broad, after all. Perhaps there are other funeral homes involved."

"I could give Evelyn a call," Lilly said.

"Let's see what Ernie and Tamara have found out first," Roddy said.

"Did I hear my name?" Tamara said from the kitchen.

"You did," Lilly said. "Roddy, could you—"

"Check on those files?"

"Please," Lilly said. "I'll get you a drink. Wine?"

"Water for now," Roddy said. Lilly smiled. Roddy was finicky about his wine and food pairings, so he'd likely wait to see what Warwick brought home for dinner. No one could go into the Italian market and walk out with what they came for, and nothing else. Ernie, Warwick, and Roddy on a group chat about dinner promised surprises.

"Where's Delia?" Lilly asked when she walked into the kitchen.

"I'd imagine she's in her office," Tamara said. She was taking cheeses and spreads out of the refrigerator and putting them on the counter. "I let myself in with my key. What's up? Where's Roddy?"

"He's downloading the video of Sasha hanging a rat on the door," Lilly said.

"Of Sasha doing what?" Delia said, coming into the kitchen, followed by her two furry friends. They both sat and stared at Lilly, then pointedly looked at the cabinet where their food was kept.

"You two will be fed in a minute," Lilly said. "After

you and Ernie left the front doorbell rang. I was coming down the stairs, so I opened it. There was a rat hanging on the wreath hook."

Tamara stopped and stared at Lilly. "A what?"

"Rubber, but very lifelike. I called Roddy to rescue me. Which he did."

"Did you cry? I would have cried," Tamara said. "Thank God for Roddy."

"Thank God for me for what?" Roddy said. He brought Lilly's computer with him and set it on the kitchen table.

"Rescuing me from the rat," Lilly said. She took a glass out of the cabinet and poured Roddy a glass of water, no ice.

"The bloody rat with a note," Roddy said. "Inside its mouth."

"Speaking of which, I need to go and clean up the front door." Lilly started to stand up, but Roddy put his hand on her arm.

"Later," he said quietly. "Have some water and gather yourself a bit first."

"What did the note say?" Delia asked. She went to the cabinet to get the cats' kibble and put some in their bowls.

"*Rats die.* Not very imaginative. But from the look of the video, she wrote the note in the car," Roddy said, clicking on a video feed.

"How could you tell?" Lilly asked. She went over to her wine cooler and took out a red blend. She held it up to Tamara, who nodded.

"The camera by the gate picked up the car. Sasha wasn't driving. When she went to get out, the light went on, and I could see what was happening. Whitney was driving. She handed Sasha a pen and piece of paper and made her write a note. They were arguing."

"Whitney was in the car?" Lilly stopped opening the wine and turned to Roddy. "Did you tell Bash?"

"I texted him that I'd be emailing the videos in a bit, but I let him know that. I'd imagine it will be helpful for timelines. I offered to edit them, but he told me to send the entire feed, and let him know what the time stamps were. There we go. That's done, I sent him the link."

"Well done," Lilly said. "But you may also want to do the edits. He may not be able to get to his desk for a while."

"Already working on that," Roddy said. "The videos are processing now. Bash did ask if we still had the rat and the note, and I told him we did. He asked that we not touch it any more than necessary."

"Why is Bash involved with a prank?" Delia asked. She looked back and forth at Roddy and Lilly. "What's happened?"

Roddy patted the chair next to him and smiled at Delia. "Delia, come sit for a moment." When she did, he turned to face her, and closed the lid of the computer a bit. Not enough to shut it down, but enough to let her know that she was his focus.

"Lilly and I went to the cemetery. Bash asked us to come down and meet with the person in charge of the investigation. She wanted to hear about Lilly's observations."

"It's about time," Delia said. "Lilly's the one who noticed that things were amiss."

"She did that. We brought a copy of the narrative you'd suggested she write after we found the urns in the crypt. They'll find it very helpful once they can focus on it. Anyway, we started at the main gate and walked through. Lilly pointed things out and they asked questions. The last stop was the Jayne crypt."

"The bench being moved was the first proof that something was amiss," Delia said.

"They wanted to see the bench. When we went to show it to them, we found Whitney."

"What do you mean, you found Whitney?" Delia looked at them both.

Tamara stopped what she was doing and sat down next to Lilly.

"She was out near the bench, on the ground," Roddy said.

"Was she—"

Lilly shook her head. "She may have died by suicide," Lilly said.

"Suicide? What makes you think that?" Tamara asked.

"There was a gun in her hand," Lilly said. "She was lying down and there was a broken headstone nearby. I saw a piece with the name Roy."

"I noticed pieces of the headstone on the bench as well. It must have been an older piece to break like that. I didn't see much else. Bash rightfully got us out of there quickly," Roddy said.

"Do you have any idea why?" Delia asked.

"Why what?" Ernie asked, walking into the kitchen from the hallway. He was carrying a tray and balancing two grocery bags under his arm. Roddy got up to help him. "Don't anyone think less of me, but I got a ready-made salad," he said, putting the tray on the kitchen table and lifting up a corner of the white cardboard cover.

"Why Whitney killed herself," Delia said.

"Why she what?" Ernie turned and stared.

Roddy and Lilly both told him the story of their visit to the cemetery. He looked at them both. "A suicide?" Ernie said. "I saw her this morning, holding her head up high and daring anyone to cross her. She sure didn't seem like she was in that frame of mind, but I suppose you can never tell."

"If her life was falling apart," Lilly said. "Perhaps she found herself in a pit of despair?"

"The woman I saw on that video was not in any sort of despair," Roddy said. "She seemed angry, if anything." He'd been squatting next to the wine refrigerator and stood up and opened the door, taking out two bottles. He showed them to Ernie, who nodded.

"That's what I thought," Ernie said. "She was royally pissed off at the world. Now she's dead?" He leaned up against the counter and looked down at the floor.

"I wonder if they made any other rat deliveries?" Tamara said. "What are you two looking at? Sure, they could blame Lilly, but seems to me that there were other people who could have brought things to the authorities' attention. That Jackie Ross woman—"

"Helen's cousin? I have no doubt that she was rattling cages," Ernie said. "What's this about a rat?"

Ernie shook his head after Lilly finished the story. "Whitney is, was, a piece of work. By the by, there's scuttlebutt that Dewey moved into a hotel last night."

"That's interesting," Lilly said.

"Whitney's life may have been falling apart in ways we don't understand," Roddy said.

"Stan had his issues with her," Delia said, quietly.

"A lot of people did," Lilly said. She took the glass of wine Roddy handed her and passed it to Delia. "He did have that terrible argument with her. I wonder if he was questioned during the investigation? He had been doing business with her."

"I don't know. We haven't spoken since . . . since I broke up with him. Have any of you spoken to him today?"

"I haven't been to the Star since you broke up," Ernie said, putting the salad on the counter and taking the top off.

"Neither have I," Tamara said, getting a salad bowl out of the cabinet.

"Nor I," Roddy said.

Delia looked around the room and smiled. "If the Garden Squad stops going to the Star, he may go out of business. I really appreciate the gesture, but you don't have to boycott it for me."

"It seemed like the least we could do," Tamara said. "Though it would be helpful to have seen Stan lately. He may have blamed Whitney for your breakup."

"She did send the picture," Ernie said. "But I can't imagine Stan would hurt Whitney, no matter how angry he was."

"I hated Whitney for sending that text, but I never wanted this," Delia said.

"Of course you didn't," Roddy said quietly. "You're not the sort of person to wish another person ill."

"I, on the other hand," Lilly said. Delia smiled at Lilly and reached across the table. Lilly took her hand and gave it a squeeze.

"I'll be all right," Delia said. "I'm going to go and get some fresh air. I'll be right back." She got up and went out of the kitchen toward the back room.

"I may go by the Star tomorrow to say hello to Stan," Lilly said.

"I don't think he'd do anything, but you've got to admit, he had a few reasons," Ernie said.

"Maybe it was suicide," Tamara said.

Lilly looked over at Roddy. He raised his eyebrows, shrugged, and shook his head.

Chapter 19

Lilly woke up the next morning and stretched. Suicide? She still couldn't believe it. Though she didn't know Whitney well, suicide didn't seem like a choice she would have made, no matter how dire the circumstances. Perhaps she wanted to go out on her own terms. Lilly thought back to the scene, but no clues jumped out. She did wonder about the broken headstone. What was the name? Roy?

As she was getting dressed, Lilly thought about Sasha. The proper thing to do would be to call on her. But then Lilly remembered the rat. The younger woman was likely coerced by Whitney, but still. Sasha was over thirty by now. She could have said no at any point.

When she went downstairs, the house was quiet. She found her phone where she'd left it on the kitchen table, charging. Picking it up and turning it on was rote, and gave her a sense of completeness. Addiction to the steady stream of information and connection was an issue she'd hear people complain about for the younger generation, but she recognized the signs in herself. If she hadn't been exhausted when she'd realized she left it downstairs last night, she would have come down to get it. Knowing that Ernie or Delia would come and get her if she needed to be woken up was what stopped her.

Three texts. One from Delia: **Gone to the historical society. Checking on new cemetery history Minh found.** Lilly wasn't sure what the history was, or how it would be helpful, but Delia would fill her in.

Ernie's text told her he was going in to open the store, and that she should text him with any updates.

The third text was from Roddy. **Let me know when you're up and about. I thought breakfast at the Star may be in order**. She checked the time stamp and then her watch. He'd only sent the text ten minutes ago. She hesitated over the keyboard, and then decided to go old-school and call. Aside from the efficiency, she enjoyed hearing Roddy's voice.

"Good morning, Lilly. Sleep well?"

"Embarrassingly so," Lilly said. "Didn't think about Whitney or what we'd seen until I woke up. Which wasn't that long ago, if I'm honest."

"Then you haven't seen the news?"

"What news?"

"The police issued a statement that her death was being investigated as a possible homicide."

"Oh no," Lilly said. "But wouldn't that be natural? I mean, it looked like she shot herself, but perhaps they need to keep the options open?"

"From what I can ascertain, and I don't speak social media fluently, mind you, someone in the investigation is leaking information, and the police are playing catch-up. Perhaps Delia could translate for me?"

"She's at the library," Lilly said. "I haven't had coffee yet. You'd mentioned something about breakfast at the Star, which sounds wonderful. I'm ready to go now if you are. Maybe afterwards we should bring a cup of coffee and some pastry over to Bash."

"I'll meet you on the front walk in five minutes. Unless you'd rather drive?"

Part of her would rather drive, but she shook off the feeling. Between Roddy and Tamara, the step obsession had been contagious. "No, let's walk."

After she'd checked on the cats, she put her notebook in her crossbody bag, along with other tools she might require: her phone, an extra pen, lipstick, hand sanitizer, a tube of sunblock, and a large scarf. She checked herself in the front mirror and then smirked. At this point in her life, her face was what it was. Her blue eyes were still bright, her white curls did what they wanted to do, and her wrinkles were present no matter what her expression. Smiling softened them, so she put that into good use and plastered one on now.

She made sure she had her keys and closed the front door, ensuring it was locked. She armed the security systems and walked down the front path, putting her medium brimmed straw hat on top of her head. Roddy was there, waiting. The smile got wider.

"Good morning, neighbor," Lilly said.

Roddy smiled and offered Lilly his arm, which she took. "I had an ulterior motive for walking," Roddy said. "I wanted to ask you about the plant choices three houses up. The house with the violet shutters and yellow front door."

"The Spences," Lilly said. "I love the color of that front door. All right, we're almost there. What's the question?" She skimmed the yard, taking in the choices that they'd made this spring. Roddy's house and Lilly's house were both built on larger lots. Both houses were set back a bit, with Lilly's much further back than any other. The rest of the houses were much closer to the street, with smaller lots that backed up on a dead-ended side street. Though the frontage was small, every house took pride in their yards. Partly that was because of the location, since Washington Street was a main thoroughfare in Goosebush. Also, there were ordinances that had to be followed in the historic district, and town shaming had an effect on behavior.

"Do you see that purple plant?"

"Phlox. Aren't they a lovely color?"

"They are," Roddy said. "I like the smaller flowers. I haven't noticed that in your garden."

"I move things around," Lilly said. "There were a couple of years when I neglected the gardens for various reasons, and I lost some plants, including the phlox. I haven't replaced them, but should. They remind me of my mother; they were one of her favorites. I'm sure if Ernie doesn't have it in stock, he'll order you some."

"I'm gathering the puzzle pieces," Roddy said.

"Puzzle pieces?"

"I'm realizing how many personal choices can go into a garden. Colors, plant heights, greenery versus flowers, shrubs or bushes. Never mind mulch colors, stones, and the like. Your gardens remind me of you.

I'm wondering what pieces will come together to make my gardens remind people of me." He took another look around and started walking again.

"Are you thinking phlox may be part of the puzzle?" Lilly asked.

"I was. Do you have other suggestions?"

"Boxwood," Lilly said. "A thicket of boxwood."

"That feels awfully dull," Roddy said.

"Au contraire. Boxwood is a great hedge for sculpting. For whatever reason, I can see you creating garden sculptures as part of your puzzle. Or maybe a maze. Our garden sculpture entry last December showed that you have great talent. Don't laugh. Our entry was simple, but complicated up close. Effective at a distance. You might have fun adding some sculptural elements to your gardens."

Roddy stopped and looked at Lilly, then he started walking again. "Boxwoods. That could be brilliant."

"There are also other hedges that could work," Lilly said. "It may be fun to think about ways to use your gardens that suit your creativity. Paint a tableau with your garden. Channel your inner Englishman. You have a wonderful yard for it."

Roddy and Lilly spent the rest of the walk discussing gardens. Before they knew it, they were at the Star, and Roddy held the door open. They ordered their breakfast sandwiches and brought coffee back to their table to wait. Lilly walked over to the bookstore and bought Roddy copies of the gardening magazines she'd bought herself. She arrived back at the table at the same time as the sandwiches.

They both ate in silence for a couple of minutes. Homemade brioche, thick cut bacon, sharp cheddar cheese, and a perfectly poached egg with a splash of hollandaise. Perfection.

"I was going to give you my copies once I was done, but this is a great issue," Lilly said, sliding the magazine over to Roddy. "If nothing else, maybe you can cut out some pictures and start a vision board for your garden."

"Thank you, Lilly. I'm going to do some sketches today, and add some shrubbery. I love the idea of using greenery as well as hardscapes to outline the Winslow design," Roddy said. Florence Winslow had been a garden designer in the Gilded age, but she'd never gotten the proper credit. When Roddy realized she'd designed his gardens, he decided to honor her ideas while adding his own. Her architectural aesthetic matched his. He looked around the Star, which was quiet. "I haven't seen Stan, have you?"

"I haven't," Lilly said. "Hopefully he'll hear that we were here. It's awkward, his breakup with Delia."

"It is, though she seems better," Roddy said.

"You're very good with her, you know," Lilly said. "She doesn't open up to people easily."

"I wasn't there for my own daughter when she went through struggles in her love life. I'm happy to be there for Delia. Even if it is only to lend a shoulder to lean on."

"You've got a good set of shoulders," Lilly said. She'd meant it figuratively, but then she looked at her friend. He had wonderful, strong shoulders that strained slightly against the jacket he was wearing. His button-down shirt was open at the collar, and his neck and face were both tanned from spending time outdoors. She forced herself to look back at her sandwich and take another bite. She took a sip of coffee to wash it down and looked over at Roddy, who was finished with his sandwich and was flipping through the magazine. "I want to make sure it's clear to everyone that if I need to choose sides, I choose Delia."

Roddy smiled. "No one would expect anything different. I hope that they—"

"Did you hear?"

Roddy stopped talking and they both looked up at Virginia Blossom. Her auburn hair was pulled back and she didn't have makeup on. She was still lovely, Lilly thought, but she looked exhausted.

"Hear what?" Lilly asked, putting her coffee mug down.

"Stan's been arrested," she said flatly.

"Why don't you sit down," Roddy said.

Virginia pulled over a chair and sat—well, actually she flopped—down.

"What's he been arrested for?" Lilly said, making sure her voice was lower.

"Technically he hasn't been arrested. Bash came by and asked him to come in for questioning. Immediately. Bash said he had some questions about Whitney's death."

"I had heard that they didn't think it was suicide after all," Roddy said.

"I have no idea what they're thinking. What I do know is that Stan left with Bash, and according to Stella Haywood, half the town saw him leaving. She called me and I came right down. You have to do something, Lilly."

"What do you mean, 'do something?' "

"Help him," Virginia said.

"I'm sure he'll be fine," Lilly said. "Stan isn't capable of murder."

"He's got motivation and that matters," Virginia said. "Listen, Stan hated Whitney. Everyone knows that."

"*Hate* is such a strong word," Lilly said.

"He hated that she took money from his father and didn't deliver on a place to bury him. He hated that she sent Delia that picture of the two of us. Don't look shocked. He's noticed that you haven't been in since. He hated her. But he wouldn't hurt a fly, you know that."

"Of course I do," Lilly said.

"Now I could definitely have killed her, but I was in Boston all day and didn't get back until midnight. Course, no one can verify when I got back. But I was with people until five o'clock, in case you want to check."

"Virginia, I don't think you could kill anyone," Lilly said. "You may inspire people to kill you, but that's another story."

"Don't try and make me laugh, Lilly. I'm too upset. I mean, look at me! I never go out in public looking like this."

"My sarcasm gets me in trouble, as Roddy well knows," Lilly said. "I agree, Stan is a gentle man. What should I do?"

"Go talk to Bash and see what's up? Help Stan however you can? Let me know what I should do? I'm losing my mind."

"It seems to me that you could help Stan by running this place today," Roddy said.

Virginia nodded and smiled at Roddy. She looked down at her sweatshirt and tugged on it. "Good thing I have clothes here. And makeup. You're right, of course. That's what I can do. We all need to do what we do best, right, Lilly?"

"I'll go over and see if I can speak with Stan," Lilly said. She looked over at Roddy and smiled. "Let's place an order to go."

Chapter 20

Since the Star was on a rotary, walking to the police station, which could have been a fairly straight route, required a more curved and longer walk. No worries. It gave them time to devise a game plan, or try. The best that they came up with was try to talk to Stan, and check in with Bash.

They took an earlier right and cut through a municipal parking lot to get to the police station, just like every other pedestrian in Goosebush had since time immemorial. They were chatting and almost missed seeing Dewey Marsh scurrying to his car. If he hadn't been obvious in his intent to avoid being seen by them, he might have been successful. But stopping a few feet away, making a noise, and quickly walking in the other direction didn't help his case, never mind the bright green jacket he wore, with *Bradford Funeral Home* embossed on the back. Then he walked in front of a car that was trying to park and got beeped at by the driver. These sorts of things got people noticed.

"Dewey," Lilly called out.

He had to stop and turn. "Ms. Jayne, Mr. Lyden. How are you this morning?"

"More importantly, how are you?" Lilly said. "I am very, very sorry about Whitney. Truly."

"As am I," Roddy said, shaking Dewey's hand.

The sincerity in both of their voices appeared to catch Dewey off guard. He paused for a moment, and then said "thank you" and nodded. The three of them stood around awkwardly, but Dewey rose to the occasion.

"I'm wicked sorry about the trouble with your family plot, Ms. Jayne," Dewey said. "There was some work that was set to be done on the watering systems this spring, and the bench got moved to keep it safe. We should have told you."

Lilly nodded. She wanted to ask a question about the urns in the family crypt, but she wasn't sure if that was public knowledge or not. "I wish you had," Lilly said. "It gave me a bit of a start, let me tell you. It's hard when you come to expect something one way, and it's changed."

"Absolutely. The letters about the work we were planning were supposed to go out this week. When Whitney had some heavy lifting being done in another part of the cemetery, she decided to move the bench to save on having to call the crew back in."

"That makes sense, I suppose," Roddy said quietly.

"It did to Whitney. Not to speak ill of the dead, mind you. But she was always looking for ways to cut corners, and moving ten steps ahead of everyone else. She made it hard to keep up. Or to know what was going on, to be honest."

Lilly stared at Dewey, being certain to smile, grateful that she was wearing sunglasses so he couldn't see the cool assessment of her eyes. Whitney was, proverbially, being thrown under the bus by Dewey. If he was coordinating with Sasha—

"Bradford's was always a lean machine, with a lot of work," Lilly said. "I'd heard that Sasha was moving soon. Hopefully not too far away, since she'll be running the business solo. I'd assume Whitney left it to her."

"Actually, I bought into the business, so Sasha and I will be working it together. Which is all good. We get along well. Very well."

The smile on his face made Lilly's blood run cold. Instead of continuing the conversation, she simply said, "Please give her my best."

"Will do," Dewey said, turning and walking away.

"Is that his car?" Roddy asked. "See the crystals hanging from the mirror? That's the same car Whitney was driving yesterday." They both turned and kept walking toward the police station, slowing down as Dewey passed by them. Lilly repeated the license plate aloud until he had turned onto the rotary. Then she took her notebook out and wrote it down.

The door buzzed gently as they walked in. The front desk had a line of Goosebush residents there to deal with the business of paying fines, securing beach permits, ordering construction parking signs, and the other business the police department oversaw. The officer looked up, gave Lilly a nod and buzzed the door so she could go behind the counter to the offices. She chose to see it as a good thing that everyone knew her well enough to wave her back.

"Come in," Bash called out when she knocked on his door. He looked up and made a face, not a smiling face, and pointed to the phone. He made some more "sure," "of course," and "you got it" comments before he finally ended the call he was on. "Lilly, I can't talk about anything."

"We brought you coffee and a breakfast sandwich," Lilly said, putting the cardboard carrier on the desk. "I got you a second cup, just in case. I know you have coffee here, but if memory serves, the Star's is much better."

Bash looked at the carton and back at Lilly. "Sit down. I can always use more coffee." He took the lid off one of the cups, and inhaled the coffee deeply before taking a sip.

"We also came by to take Stan home, if he's finished," Lilly said.

Bash sighed and unwrapped the sandwich.

"He hasn't even started," Bash said. "He asked for a lawyer as soon as he sat down. We're waiting."

"I see," Lilly said. It might not be a good sign that Stan felt that he needed a lawyer right away, but Lilly tried not to judge. "Could you let him know I came by asking for him?"

"Sure thing," Bash said. He took a bite of the sandwich and smiled at Lilly. "I promise."

"We saw Dewey in the parking lot," Roddy said. "I think that the car he was driving was the same car Whitney was driving yesterday. That may mean nothing, but I thought you should know. Lilly wrote down the plate number."

Lilly tore a page out of her notebook and rewrote the number on it. She and Roddy would be checking themselves, of course.

"We had a short conversation with him. The longest I've ever had with him, if I'm to be honest.

He blamed Whitney for my family's bench being moved. Said that she was cutting corners and taking advantage when another job was being done," Lilly said.

"There's a lot of work being done in the cemeteries," Bash said. "At least on paper. Not a lot to be seen for it. I'll check on the timing of the bench move, and the reason."

"Now that she's gone, I suspect she'll be getting a lot of blame for a lot of things," Lilly said.

Bash was struggling, Lilly could see that. He finished his sandwich and threw the paper away. He started flipping a pencil up and down and staring at his blotter, while he sorted through his thoughts.

"Dewey had decided to give evidence against Whitney in exchange for immunity," he said. "I did not tell you that, by the way."

"I thought I heard that Whitney was going to testify?" Roddy said. "I'm not sure where. I got lost in a haze of information online."

"I've heard that rumor, but I don't think it was true. Darlene says that she was adamant about fighting all charges. Whitney also mentioned making a trade, but Darlene has no idea what she was talking about. One thing that Darlene said was that Whitney was juggling a lot of balls when she died."

"I wonder what's going to happen when they start falling," Roddy said.

"It's hard to imagine," Bash said. "But I'm thinking you're right; Whitney's going to get a lot of the blame for what was going on."

"Is suicide off the table?" Roddy said.

Bash looked at him and nodded his head.

"You can't possibly think that Stan would ever do anything to hurt her," Lilly said.

"He's been under a lot of pressure these past few weeks," Bash said. "More than any of us knew. Now, I know Stan, and like him. But you know as well as anyone, Lilly, I need to follow the facts and see where they lead."

"Of course you do," Roddy said, putting his hand on Lilly's arm and giving it a gentle squeeze. "But you also know that other perspectives can be helpful in gathering those facts. I assume that Dewey and Sasha are on your list."

Bash nodded. "The window between the rat delivery and her death is short. Thanks for the video, by the way. That was very helpful. Anyway, Dewey said that he was with Sasha during that window of time."

"Any idea why she was there, in the cemetery?" Lilly asked.

"None. No one seems to know."

"And the cameras you had positioned?" Lilly said.

Bash sighed and looked at Lilly. "They didn't catch anything." Bash's phone buzzed and he picked it up. "Stan's lawyer's here. I'll tell him you both stopped in to check on him. And listen, I'm officially telling you both this: Don't go looking into this, understand?"

"Bash, we have no intention of getting involved in your investigation," Lilly said.

The young man nodded, and then stood up. He walked around his desk to offer Lilly a hand getting up. When she got close to his height, he leaned in and whispered in her ear.

"Tell me everything you find out," he said. He gave Roddy a wink and picked up his coffee, and the other one from the tray. He waited by the door until they both got up and followed them out.

Chapter 21

"Where were you?" Delia was waiting for Lilly as she opened the front door.

"Delia, don't do that," Lilly said. "Lurking by the front door isn't why we installed that security system."

"After what you told me happened yesterday with the rat, I put my alerts back on to see who was outside—"

"You'll have to show me how to do that," Lilly said. "It would be helpful. We took the long way home. Roddy and I ordered lunch on the way back. We got plenty; I hope you'll join us. He'll be over in a few minutes."

"Where were you?" Delia asked again.

Lilly took a deep breath. "At the police station. Now, don't fuss. Wait here for the food. Roddy's coming in the back door. He's bringing his computer over so that we can do some work. Stop making that sputtering noise, Delia. I've been walking all over

Goosebush, and I need to go upstairs and freshen up. I'll be down in a few minutes."

What Lilly really wanted to do was lie down for a quick nap, but she resisted. After Bash had dismissed them, they'd stayed at the police station for a few more minutes, in case the questions were answered quickly and Stan was released. Twenty minutes later, they realized that Stan wasn't going to come out any time soon and came up with plan B, which was going to see Tamara. Unfortunately, she was out with clients. Plan C was stopping by to talk to Ernie. The store was packed and he couldn't get away from the register.

At that point they were both tired, frustrated, and hot. Nothing some Thai food couldn't cure, Roddy suggested. On their walk back to the house he called and ordered takeout, factoring in plenty of leftovers.

Lilly changed her shoes and put on a fresh dress that had a little more room around the waist. If she was going to sit at the computer for the afternoon, breathing was a must. She threw some cold water on her face and ran her fingers through her curls.

She smelled lunch as she was coming down the stairs. Yum. Perfect timing. She walked down the hall, following the voices of Delia and Roddy from the back room.

"Then we came back here," Roddy said.

"Sorry, that took longer than I expected if you're already at the 'we came back home' part of the story," Lilly said, sitting down. Two containers of pad Thai were open, and there was a bowl of soup in front of each of them, with another quart on the table. Roddy put spoons in the noodles and gestured to Lilly to serve herself, which she did.

"There wasn't much to tell," Roddy said.

"You mentioned the Dewey part of the story?"

"Yes, though probably not in as much detail as you would like," Roddy said. "That was an odd conversation, wasn't it?"

"Especially since he spent time trying to avoid us at first," Lilly said. "He was surprisingly forthcoming."

"Could we get back to Stan," Delia said. "He's being questioned? Do you think it's serious?"

"Stan must think it's serious," Lilly said. "He asked for a lawyer."

"Who did he get, do you know?"

"I have no idea," Lilly said.

"I hope it's a good one. Someone who knew what they're doing. Who's taking care of the business?"

"Virginia was there when we left," Roddy said. "I think that was her plan."

Delia nodded and looked down at her plate. She moved her silverware around, but didn't serve herself any food. Lilly put some noodles on Delia's plate and smiled over at her friend.

"You have to eat," Lilly said.

"We have to help him," she said.

"I'm sure he'll be all right," Lilly said.

"You don't understand. Something's wrong, really wrong. He called me last night, late. He wanted me to tell anyone who asked that we were together all afternoon."

"Were you?" Roddy said.

"I saw him for a minute, at the library," Delia said. "We didn't really talk. He stopped by the historical society for a packet of information Minh pulled for him. She wasn't there and I told him that. I went back to work and eventually he left."

"What time was that?" Lilly asked.

"I don't know. Early afternoon? He said he was going to run some errands, and he'd come back. I left early to come home and didn't see him again."

"If he was running errands—"

"He didn't have an alibi," Delia said.

"I wonder if he went by the cemetery?" Roddy asked.

"He may have," Delia said. "When he was trying to get me to talk to him he mentioned that he was still waiting to get Buzz taken care of. I don't know what that meant, and I didn't ask. Anyway, Lilly, we have to help him."

"We will," Lilly said, taking a bite of her pad Thai. "Can I eat first?"

"Please check with Bash to see if there are any updates," Delia said.

Lilly sighed and took another bite. She fished out her phone and glasses from her pocket, and after some fiddling sent Bash a text. She broke her own rule and put her phone on the table to wait for the return text. She was on her second helping when it came in.

"Oh my," she said.

"What?"

"Stan's being held. They may arrest him," Lilly said. She asked to be excused and took her phone outside, and sat on one of the new chairs in the dining area. They needed cushions, but that would need to wait. She was back in a few minutes. "I called my lawyer. She's going to make sure bail is posted if necessary," Lilly said, sitting back down at her place. She pushed her plate away, her appetite gone.

"We have to help him," Delia said again.

"You're right," Lilly said. "But aside from posting bail, I'm not sure what more we can do until we hear back from Bash."

"I need to meet Mary Mancini at Alden Park later this afternoon," Roddy said. "I could stop by the police station again, though it might be easier to get him to talk if you're with me."

"I'm happy to go to Alden Park," Lilly said. "Delia, you find out what you can. See if Minh will tell you what information Stan asked her to find. We'll be home for dinner."

Chapter 22

"Alden Park isn't a ruse for our investigation," Roddy said to Lilly. They'd driven into town this time, in Roddy's Jaguar. Getting in and out of the car was always a bit of a challenge for Lilly, but he always came around and gave her a hand.

"We're not here to find out more gossip about what happened to Whitney?" Lilly said.

"Whitney's untimely demise will likely come up in conversation. But this meeting is about plants. Mary and I had planned to meet to discuss some soil samples."

"That will be interesting."

"And we planned on starting to order plants, a task that neither of us feel equipped to do on our own. I told her I'd bring you along. Honestly, I'd forgotten about the meeting until she texted me at noon."

"How does this help Stan?" Lilly asked.

"I'm not sure it does," Roddy said. "Though I'm not sure it doesn't either. We're out and about, running errands. Bound to run into other people. Though we'll be talking about plants, they may want to talk about Stan, or Whitney. It's polite to respond to conversations, don't you think? Oh, there's Mary now. Her mother's along; good. The more the merrier. Hello, ladies. Wonderful to see you both on this lovely spring day."

"Thanks for meeting me, Roddy," Mary said. "I was talking to my mother this morning, and she was asking about soil, and plants and all sorts of things I thought we should check in on. Since I have no idea about most of what she was talking about, I brought her along."

"You don't need me, with Lilly here. Though I am surprised to see you, my friend. I thought you'd be out helping get Stan out of jail," Meg said. She looked more like Mary's sister than her mother, and she and Lilly exchanged brief hugs. "I was sort of counting on that."

"I'm not a lawyer," Lilly said. "I'm sure he'll be out on bail soon."

"That's not what I meant—"

"Mom, Lilly, could I ask you both to focus on the park for a minute? Thanks. Let's go over here, so we don't get run over by a backhoe. Here's what started the conversation. I've been doing soil tests and I don't understand the numbers. Here, take a look."

Lilly and Meg stood side by side, and looked at the documents Mary had shared.

"Well, of course, the land was ill-used for a number of years," Meg said.

"And remember, last summer folks were trying to poison the plants to stop the project from going forward. Still, I thought that the treatments we gave the soil last fall would have helped more," Lilly said.

"Could all the digging have had an effect?" Roddy said.

"It shouldn't," Mary said. "I've been really clear on where to dig, and being careful of the soil displacement."

"I thought there was going to be a second delivery of new topsoil," Roddy said, looking at his notes. "Lilly had suggested that. Would that help with the numbers?"

"Yes, especially if they delivered the mix I suggested," Lilly said. Lilly took out her notebook and found the page where she'd made the note, showing it to Meg and Mary.

"If that was laid down, the soil shouldn't look like this," Meg said.

Mary made some notes and walked over to the foreman to check in with him.

"This is a great opportunity for Mary," Meg said. "Thanks for recommending her, Roddy."

"She's doing a wonderful job," Roddy said. "At first there was some resistance to hiring Goosebush oversight, but she's more than paid for herself by keeping track of all of the subcontractors."

"She's also establishing relationships with them," Meg said. "I asked if she planned on going out on her own as a project manager, but she wants to keep working with Ernie at the Triple B, offering this sort of service to customers."

"She did a wonderful job on my back room," Lilly said. "She and Ernie, I should say. They're a great team."

"The delivery was delayed, so that offset the levels," Mary said, walking back to them. "The company we hired is behind schedule. I'm not sure, but from what I can gather, I think it may have something to do with the cemetery scandal."

"In what way?" Roddy asked.

"We're using the same subcontractors as Bradford's," Mary said. "They're part of the investigation, so they haven't been able to do deliveries this week. It makes me wonder—"

"Wonder what?" Lilly asked.

"I'm not sure I should—"

"Oh, for heaven's sake, Mary, of course you should. By now you should have learned it's always better to share your burdens," her mother said. Meg looked at Lilly and shrugged slightly. Last fall Mary had run into trouble, and she was still wary of opening up too much.

"Wonder what?" Lilly asked again, quietly.

"I've been watching what's being ordered, and the order itself always has a bit of a surplus in case of problems. The numbers looked good to me. But at every stage of the job, we've come up short. Short on concrete. Short on edging materials. Short on gravel."

"Have you talked to Louise about it?" Roddy asked. Louise Schmell was the project manager for the construction company. Louise acted as though she knew everything and needed no counsel, which is one of the reasons the Board of Selectmen had hired Mary Mancini. The more safeguards to keep this project on track, the better.

"I mentioned my concerns about the concrete, but she dismissed me. I've been keeping track, though."

"Why would she dismiss you? You've got more experience than most people—" Meg said.

"Thanks, Mom. I do, but I'm not licensed here. As I said, I've been keeping track. That's part of what I wanted to talk to Roddy about."

"These community efforts can be tricky," Lilly said. "Roddy, you should make sure people know that Mary is in charge, don't you think?"

"Absolutely. In fact, if you'll excuse me, I'm going to make a call."

"Roddy, don't—" Mary said.

"Don't worry, Mary. He could charm the stripes off a tiger," Lilly said. "He's also very good at getting information. You know, we did a lot of work on the soil last fall. It should be less sandy, Meg, don't you think?"

"I wondered about that," Meg said. "Mary mentioned that they'd removed the topsoil before they started work."

"Then where is it? I wonder if our soil was used on another site?"

"Like the Goosebush cemetery?" Mary said. "After I heard about the investigation, I started to wonder if that's where some of our materials have ended up."

Roddy came back to the group and turned toward Mary. "Could you call Louise later and talk to her about the shorts you've noticed? We had a conversation and I suspect she'll be more receptive to your insights."

"We were wondering if some of the materials are being used in the cemeteries? Do you remember that clearing we saw yesterday, with the new footpath being edged?" Lilly said.

"I do indeed," Roddy said. "I wonder if I should mention that to Louise?"

"How about if you let me take a look first?" Mary said. "If the materials are the same—"

"It could add to the evidence against the Bradfords, but I don't think it will help Stan," Meg said.

"I've got to say, Stan hasn't been himself these past few weeks," Mary said. "Not that I think he killed Whitney, because I don't. But something's been bothering him."

"Yeah, I don't remember the last time I saw him smile. And I hear that he and Delia broke up?" Meg asked.

"They're taking a break," Lilly said.

"Thanks to Whitney," Mary said. "She was proud of herself. Told everyone about finding Stan and Virginia together, and that she made sure Delia knew what was going on. She tried to make it sound like she'd done Delia a favor, since if it were her, she'd want to know. Makes me wonder if anyone told her about Dewey and Sasha."

"Dewey and Sasha?" Lilly asked. She watched as Roddy wandered away, talking to some of the workmen who were laying the cobblestones in the center of the park. The cobblestones would be part of a fountain in the summer, and an ice-skating rink in the winter. It was an homage to what had been there over one hundred and fifty years ago, and had taken some engineering to pull off within budget.

"Whitney was too old for Dewey," Meg said.

"Less years between Whitney and Dewey than Dewey and Sasha," Lilly said.

"Maybe, but I always wondered what Dewey saw in Whitney," Meg said.

"Um, a robust business and a good paycheck?" Mary said, laughing.

"Mary, that's not very kind."

"Oh, please, Mom. Butter wouldn't melt in Dewey's mouth. He takes good care of himself. What I wonder is if he had anything to do with Whitney's death. Or were he and Sasha in it together?"

"I can't imagine Sasha doing anything of the kind," Meg said.

Lilly thought back to the rat episode and shook her head. "You never know who could be pushed to do what. I wonder how involved Sasha was with the business these days."

"Up to her neck, I suspect," Meg said. "It's a small business, but the three of them had fingers in a lot of pots. They run the funeral home, they took over the cemetery, and they're helping to run the crematorium. There's no way they could be as busy as they are without everyone being involved. Especially since they cut Mac Townsend off."

"What do you mean, cut him off?" Lilly asked. "What happened anyway? I thought that he retired."

"Was retired, from what I heard," Mary said. "I wouldn't be surprised if he's the one who dropped a dime on the whole thing."

"Dropped a dime? What's that, gangster talk?" Meg asked.

"Dad uses that phrase all the time. It means called in a tip. Comes from pay phones and when calls cost a dime—"

"I know what it means," Meg said, shaking her head and smiling. "The last time I saw Mac he was still working at the crematorium. He seemed fine."

"I went out for beers with Dad one night last win-

ter, right after Mac left the job. He and Buzz were
there, warming their barstools—"

"Warming a barstool?" Meg said.

"I enjoy Mary's colorful phrases," Lilly said. "Go on."

"It seemed that Mac was there a lot. The bartender
served him without being asked, that sort of thing.
Anyway, he was pretty bitter, complaining about Whitney and Dewey. Buzz said something about them getting theirs, but Mac hushed him and said 'not in front
of the police' and pointed toward Dad. They were
both pretty drunk."

"When was this?" Lilly asked.

"March? Buzz hadn't been here long. Long enough
to get to know everyone."

"I wonder what that meant, that they'd get theirs?"
Lilly said.

"I don't know, but he and Buzz spent a lot of time
together at the bar. Dad and I avoided them after
that night. Dad always said bitterness was contagious." Mary checked her watch and smiled at Lilly.
"Much as I'd love to stay and talk, can we get back to
the plants? If we want the park to open, we'll need to
get the gardens in place. You're two of the best gardeners I know. Help."

"You'll need to get the topsoil in," Meg said.

"First sweeten the base again, don't you think, Meg?"

"Absolutely. And let's double-check the drainage.
We want this place to thrive. Lilly and I will take a
walk around, and I'll write up the notes for you. How
does that sound, Mary?"

"Perfect. I'll go back to the Triple B and let Ernie
know you're on it."

* * *

Meg and Lilly took a walk around the park. They made a list of the basic steps to make the gardens flourish, and then another list of some of the plant suggestions based on Roddy's plans and the architect's drawing. Roddy joined them and added a few thoughts, but he mostly listened.

"I'll walk this over to the Triple B and tell Ernie and Mary that the exact plants are a work in progress, but we can start here," Meg said. "Roddy, I'd love to see what you've been thinking."

"Lilly's been a great help. We're working on updated plans now," Roddy said.

"Would you email me those drawings?" Meg said.

"As long as you promise to give me feedback," Roddy said, smiling.

"That's a promise. Though Lilly and I make a good team. We think a lot alike with these garden projects."

"Hearty, easy to maintain—" Lilly said.

"Plants that bloom in different seasons. And lots of green," Meg said.

"You'll get an email by the end of the day," Roddy said. "Thank you for coming today. I feel as though the project is back on track. Thanks to the two of you."

"This is so exciting; I'm thrilled to be part of it. Lilly, I hope you're able to help Stan. Call Ray if you need him." Ray Mancini was the former chief of police, and a good friend of Lilly's.

"Will do," Lilly said. "Roddy, are you ready to go?"

"Fifteen more minutes? I'm sorry, but we're getting some issues straightened out—"

"No worries. Tell you what, why don't you meet me over on the Wheel. I'll get dessert for tonight."

Chapter 23

The Cupcake Castle was one of Lilly's favorite shops, which still surprised her. The owner and master baker was Kitty Bouchard. Her previous life as a town gossip and home-wrecker had landed her on Lilly's wrong side, but of late she was redeeming herself by baking unbelievably delicious cupcakes, and going out of her way to support town events and fund drives. At first she'd done it to redeem her reputation after an unfortunate event last November, when one of her cupcakes was used as a murder weapon. She'd continued because it was wonderful for her business.

Lilly was a firm believer that baked goods could cure many ills, and she'd decided that Delia might benefit from her favorite cupcake, the triple vanilla. Since she didn't want Delia to eat alone, she was going to get enough for the entire Garden Squad.

When Lilly walked in, the smell of cake and sugar wafted over her. She stopped and took a deep breath.

If someone could bottle that scent, she'd wear it as perfume. The counter was being manned by someone new, and Lilly looked around for Kitty. She heard her back in the office, talking to someone. There were three people in line. Fingers crossed that there would be a triple vanilla left at the very least. Kitty only baked a certain number of cakes a day, and when they were gone, they were gone.

"What can I get you, Ms. Jayne?" the young woman asked when it was Lilly's turn at the counter. She sorted through her brain, but couldn't come up with a name. She smiled anyway. Lilly had worked on so many projects over the past year she couldn't keep everyone's name at the ready.

"Hello, thank you. What do you have left?"

"Let's see, two triple vanillas, one mocha, a red velvet, and a double chocolate surprise."

"I'll take them all," Lilly said.

"Oh, thank you! Ms. Bouchard stays open until the last cake is sold. You've just given me an early afternoon."

"Always happy to help."

"It will take me a minute to box them up. But first, I'm going to put the *closed* sign on the front door."

"Don't worry about anything," Kitty said as she opened her office door. "I'll take care of it."

"Thank you so much," Sasha Bradford said, walking out the door behind Kitty. "I'd forgotten that we were going to host the business council event. Even though I won't be there, I don't want to let folks down. At least not any more than we've already let them down."

"Sasha, it's going to be all right. Oh wait, you for-

got your paperwork. Let me go and get that for you."
As Kitty held the countertop up so that Sasha could
get through to the other side, she nodded at Lilly.

When Sasha turned and saw Lilly, she paled even
more than usual, which was significant. "High roads
are where the Jaynes walk," she heard her father say
to her, as if he was standing right there. Tempted
though she was to ignore the advice, particularly in
lieu of the rat, she decided to take heed.

"Sasha, let me first say how sorry I am for your
troubles," Lilly said.

"Thank you, Lilly. That's really nice of you, considering everything."

Lilly took a step forward and lowered her voice.
"You mean the rat?" she asked the younger woman.

"How did you know it was me?" Tears filled her
eyes, and she leaned back on the counter.

"Security cameras," Lilly said.

"Who else knows?"

"A few people, I'm afraid. Including Bash Haywood. I was there when they found Whitney, and
there were lots of questions. The rat came up. When
we checked the second camera, we saw that Whitney
was driving the car. It helped Bash narrow the time
frame around when Whitney was—when it happened."

"I'm so embarrassed," Sasha said. "It was all her
idea. She wanted to send people a signal."

"Did other people get the same token of her es-
teem?"

"A couple of others," Sasha whispered.

"What was the message about? A warning to not
talk? Or to be afraid?"

"Both. It was all her idea. She made me do it, in

case there were cameras. She didn't count on more than one, I guess."

"You know, I hate to speak ill of the dead, but Whitney was a fool. How did she not think that was going to blow up in her face?"

"She didn't think," Sasha said. "She just acted. That's how she lived her life, and how she ran the business. She kept doing these really nutty things, but somehow it always worked out for her."

"Not always, surely," Lilly said, tilting her head and watching the younger woman carefully.

Sasha flushed. "It's all pretty awful."

"It is. My friend, Stan Freeland, seems to be caught up in the mess. For the record, I don't think Stan is capable of hurting anyone."

"Whitney sure had a way of pushing people to the brink," Sasha said.

"Including you?"

"Yeah, me too," Sasha said. "But for me it was more of a numbing and not caring. When Dad married her he seemed happy, so I tried to be supportive. Then Dad got sick, and she stepped in and took care of everything. And I let her."

"That's understandable," Lilly said. She noticed that Kitty had come back out front, but was hanging back.

"I let her do things her way, and squashed myself in the process," Sasha said. "It's all so awful."

"Didn't I hear that you were moving? Were you leaving the business?"

"I tried, but I didn't leave in time."

"Did you know that there was an investigation going on?" Lilly asked quietly.

"Investigations. Plural. I'm finding out about more every day." Sasha took a deep breath.

"Sasha, did you—"

"I've got to go," Sasha said. "Please tell Stan I said I'm sorry, would you? Also, tell him I said 'thank you' for doing what I wasn't brave enough to."

Sasha turned and ran out of the shop. Lilly watched her go and turned toward Kitty.

"Lilly, are you helping Stan?" Kitty asked.

"I'm not sure what I can do," Lilly said.

"*Puh-leeze.* We both know that Merilee Frank's killer never would have been caught if it wasn't for you. And I probably would have lived under a cloud for the rest of my life. I really hope you're helping Stan, because he doesn't deserve to live under a cloud either."

"Are you friends with Sasha?" Lilly asked.

"Friendly."

"Did you think she could kill Whitney?"

"I don't. But—"

"But?"

"I think she could help someone kill her. Sorry, that sounds harsh, I know. But Sasha was, is, at the end of her rope. I don't know all the details, but it feels like Whitney's fast-and-loose business model was catching up to her. Sasha was caught in the undertow."

"I'd imagine Dewey was as well?"

"Dewey caused his own riptide," Kitty said. "Sorry, I don't speak ill of handsome men. Goosebush has a dearth of them, that's for sure. But he's trouble, and Sasha doesn't see it."

"So they're—"

"Not as far as I know. That's one of the reasons Sasha was thinking about leaving. She's confused by Dewey, and felt like she needed to get away. But could he talk her into covering for him if he hurt Whitney? That he could do. Hey, speaking of handsome men, isn't that your friend Roddy out there double-parked? He just moved his car. Don't forget your cupcakes, Lilly."

Lilly walked out of the door and looked to her right. She should have looked left. Perhaps then she would have avoided the human tank that plowed into her. She stumbled, but someone caught her by the arm and steadied her.

"Sorry, Lilly, didn't see you there. I hope I didn't squish your cupcakes." Mac Townsend didn't look that sorry. Lilly looked around and saw Roddy parked in a spot.

"No worries, Mac. Good seeing you," she said, turning toward the car.

"Nice to see you twice in as many weeks," he said, walking next to her. "Expect you're in the middle of this mess with the Bradfords."

Lilly turned and gave Mac an icy glare. He didn't blink. "I have no idea what you're talking about, Mac. From what I hear you've got your own Bradford business to sort out."

"Listen, Lilly, I need to talk to you," he said. "Thing is, Buzz and I were . . . well, Buzz was helping me with some payback with Whitney. Got messy towards the end. Honestly, I'd forgotten about it until all this with Stan started up. I don't want to cause Stan any more trouble than he's got, you know?"

Lilly stopped and turned toward Mac. "If you have something Bash should know—"

"Nothing that he needs to know, least not from me. Give Stan my best, will you? Tell him I'm keeping his business to myself. Got to get back to work. You take care, Lilly."

Mac turned around and walked in the opposite direction. Lilly walked to Roddy's car, and saw Mac drive by after she'd finished putting the cupcakes in his back seat.

"What was that all about?" Roddy asked as she settled in and buckled her seat belt.

"I think he was telling me that he had information that could make it worse for Stan. Mac's always been a little cryptic."

"He was waiting for you, you know. I saw him walk by the store, look in and see you, and then hang around. You were in there a while."

"Sasha Bradford was talking to me."

"Is that who left the store in such a hurry?"

"That was her. Did Mac see her?"

"He stepped into a doorway as she was leaving," Roddy said.

"I need to go home and write things down," Lilly said.

"We've got one more stop today," Roddy said. "Delia called. The Harmon estate lawyers need a report from you in order to release the funds for the nesting study."

"Dammit. I was supposed to do that last week."

"She suggested we go by, take a few pictures, and then head home. She's working on the report now. I told her I'd take a picture of you with the nests."

"Can't we do it tomorrow—"

"The report is due today," Roddy said.

Lilly looked at him in horror. "How did my life get so out of control? I've never missed a deadline like that in my life."

"Your record remains intact. We'll go by, take some pictures, and you'll get the report in."

Chapter 24

When Harmon Dane left money in his will for a bird sanctuary, but no other instructions, he couldn't have imagined how complicated that wish would be. By leaving Lilly in charge of said sanctuary, he must have assumed it would be done the right way. The first thing—well, maybe the tenth thing—that Lilly had done was to reach out to a local university, and to partner with Dawn Simmons, a scientist with a great reputation and bold ideas. Dawn had loved the idea of using the funding for a study, and she'd been part of a fall and winter project that was finally coming to fruition.

Shipyard Lane was unique in Goosebush. Originally, over a hundred years ago, the land on the side of a hill was flattened out, and the sides were built up with retaining walls, in order to help with yearly erosion that had been affecting the area. Since a few houses had been built up on the side of the hill, the concern wasn't minor. The project was significant and changed the coastline of the town. To offset the costs, three identical houses were built on the land by the town, with the purchase price going toward the project. The lane that ran behind them was for their use only, as was the staircase down to the small, rocky beach. Over time the houses had been sold, two of them in the past year. Yet the town still controlled the use of the land, which was leased to the owners with a lot of caveats as to building and maintenance.

The first house at the top of the stairs was, in Lilly's opinion, the crown jewel. The owners of that house, for many years the Dane family but now the O'Connors, had always helped set the boundaries for the use of the common space. Warwick had stepped into that role with gusto, making sure that the path that ran along the front of the houses discouraged strangers and encouraged birds. He'd also suggested that the egress road finally get the work it needed. The New England embrace of potholes in order to discourage fast driving was all well and good, except when the potholes could take out a transmission.

The other owners on Shipyard Lane were just as happy to have Warwick oversee the shared property maintenance. Clara Marsden owned the center house, as a result of her father's incarceration. She'd closed the house down for the winter and hadn't returned yet. She didn't love Goosebush, so there was some question of whether she'd come back at all. Rentals were forbidden by the street's charter; it would be interesting to see what she decided to do.

The third house had been in the Preston family forever. And it still was, thanks to the generosity of Ernie and the curiosity of Minh Vann in discovering her family history.

Roddy parked the car in Clara Marsden's spot, and then he and Lilly went back toward Minh's house, so they could walk on the pedestrian path where it started. There were two fences, one on the outside of the path, the other on the inside. The path itself was crushed gravel, which had been replaced recently. After much discussion the fences had been replaced with heavy-duty plastic fencing that looked like split rail from a distance. The safety of the old fence was questionable, mildly put, and Lilly felt good about the upgrade, especially with the nesting areas that were included in the design. Roddy and Lilly walked the length of the path. She'd taken to making voice recordings, and made a few as Roddy took pictures of the nesting areas in the rocks below.

"This is one of the best views in Goosebush," Lilly said, stopping in front of Clara's house. "You can see all the curves in the bay."

"It's a much rockier shore here. Were all these rocks originally here?"

"No, they weren't. They were moved here to help with the erosion issues. They also create a natural barrier so boats don't come too close to shore."

"I can imagine they'd be a deterrent."

"A few years ago they dredged the area to deal with the huge boulders that were under the water. They were submerged most of the time, and were a real hazard unless you knew the coastline. Now the channel is deeper, and this part of the shoreline is protected. There was a time, back in the fifties and early sixties, where there were at least three boats damaging their keels each summer because they didn't know about the boulders. Mostly out-of-towners, but still."

"Out-of-towners don't get the Goosebush hospitality rolled out for them, do they?"

"Used to, back when we were a resort town and needed the business. But now that Goosebush survives on her own, not so much," Lilly said. "See over there, on the right? All those moorings? Those are public docks. The next group of mooring, a bit farther down? Those are for the yacht club. Mooring at either place costs a pretty penny. The shipyard is further down."

Roddy used the camera on his phone to zoom in, and then looked over at the water.

"What's that?" he asked, pointing to a rowboat heading out from shore.

"Someone going to their mooring," Lilly said. "What's that, a Boston Whaler on the mooring? That's odd. A small boat for a deep mooring like that."

"The person rowing has on the same coat as Mac Townsend," he said.

"Let me see." Roddy handed her his phone, and showed her how to zoom in. "That sure looks like him."

"Did you know Mac Townsend owned a boat? Is he a fisherman?"

"Not that I know of," Lilly said. "That type of boat is more for getting around the shore, not for deep-sea fishing. As far as I know Mac's life was all about the Goosebush cemeteries. But I don't know him well."

Mac drifted for a minute, and then he picked something up from the rowboat and put it on the Whaler. He climbed aboard and cast off from the mooring, pointing out toward the center of the bay. Lilly and Roddy watched as he went out a bit, and dropped something over the side of the boat.

"This visit was unexpected, but wonderful," she said to Roddy. They were close to the staircase, and had stopped to look around.

"The sea air is always a tonic," Roddy said. "The fence and path look terrific, don't they? And I'm not afraid I'll slip and fall over the side."

"Yeah, it isn't a long drop, but those rocks. Falling would hurt. I know that Warwick was worried about the grandchildren taking a tumble."

"Hey, Aunt Lilly, that you?"

Lilly looked over and saw her godson Tyrone coming out of his back door. He opened his arms wide, as did Lilly.

"Ty, when did you get home?" Tyrone was in graduate school, but he'd decided to come home for the summer for the first time in years.

"I got home yesterday," he said, giving her a hug and lifting her up off the ground. "My internship starts tomorrow. Hey Roddy, good to see you." He reached over and shook the older man's hand.

"That's a quick turnaround," Lilly said. "I hope you won't be too busy to spend some time with your old godmother."

"I don't know who this old person you're talking about is, but I'll be spending time with you. Delia told me she's going to help me get my thesis ready to be approved next fall. You'll be seeing a lot of me. Where's your car?"

"We parked at the Marsden house," Lilly said. "I'm actually here doing some Dane bird work."

"Everything okay?"

"Looks great to me. What do you think?"

"Dad showed me where the nests are, and talked to me about how to track what's going on. We have this big spreadsheet that Dr.—"

"Simmons. Dawn Simmons."

"That's her. That Dr. Simmons set up for Dad. It's voluntary, but he's taking it seriously, and adding data every day. He expects me to help, especially while I'm taking care of the lawns."

"Taking care of the lawns?"

"Yeah, didn't he tell you about that? Seems there's been a lack of consistency the past few years. Clara's dad was big into green lawns, but he used pesticides, which is a no-go with the nesting areas. She's cool with the plan Dad laid out. So is Minh. This summer we're going to change things up, and treat all three yards as one for mowing and maintenance."

"Sounds ambitious," Roddy said.

"He'll be dragging Aunt Lilly into the planning pretty soon. He wants to get some bushes in, and flower beds."

"We've been talking," Lilly said. "It's a great summer project for Warwick."

"Otherwise he'd be sitting, staring out at the water even more than he does now—"

"Hey now, son," Warwick said, coming out of the back of the house. "Don't be talking trash about your father. Hey, Lilly, Roddy. You here working on the report?"

"We are," Lilly said. "I'm embarrassed to admit I forgot all about it."

"I emailed you some thoughts, and printed out these reports when I saw you out on the path. They may be helpful for you to take notes while you're walking. I emailed them."

Lilly flipped through them and smiled at Warwick. "They will definitely help." She handed them to Roddy, who began to pat his pockets for a pen. Lilly smiled and handed him one. "I needn't have worried. You're doing a wonderful job overseeing Harmon's wishes."

"My pleasure," Warwick said. "Buying this house, I feel like there's an unspoken compact that comes with it. Honor the land, and the history. Make it better."

"Warwick, I'd love to talk about putting you in charge of the sanctuary if you're up for it," Lilly said.

"Up for it? I'd love it. It will give me a good reason to study up. I've got to admit, when Dawn and the students come by, I ask a million questions. I'm probably driving them all crazy."

"Far from it," Lilly said. "Dawn feels like the success of the sanctuary is in no small part due to your care. I can't help but think how thrilled Harmon would be about all of this."

"It's a beautiful place to live," Warwick said. "I never thought I'd love sitting and watching life. I've always been go, go, go. This place relaxes me, even with all the work it's taking."

"Do you watch the comings and goings on the water?" Roddy said.

"There's a surprising rhythm to the activity."

"We saw Mac Townsend go out on a Whaler—"

"Burial at sea," Warwick said.

"Pardon me?" Lilly asked.

"There are urns that are made out of salt. Environmentally friendly. Mac does burials at sea. Takes them out, says a few words, and then drops them in. The salt dissolves and the environmental impact is lower. He makes a note of the longitude and latitude and gives the family a certificate. Sometimes he goes out on his own, and other times he takes folks with him."

"Is he always the one who does it?" Lilly asked.

"Sometimes it's him. I've seen Dewey do it too," Warwick said. "Why are you asking?"

"I thought that he was out of the business, that's all," Lilly said.

"People like Mac always keep a hand in," Warwick said. "Can't imagine that there's a huge rush of people who want to take over this particular task."

"I'd imagine not. But that's a big mooring for a small boat."

"I did notice that. I've been wondering if he's going to get a bigger boat this summer."

"Keep us posted," Roddy said. "Lilly is very concerned about this mooring situation."

"Moorings are at a premium," Lilly said. "I can't imagine there isn't some grumbling about this."

"I'm sure there is," Warwick said. "I don't spend much time at the docks, but I'll let you know if I hear anything."

"Warwick, are you and Tamara available for dinner tonight? You've heard about Stan?" Lilly said.

"Who in town hasn't? Tamara's been texting me updates."

"I think we need to help him, don't you? Ty, you're welcome to join us."

"I'd love to, but I'm heading into Cambridge for a lecture," Ty said. "Rain check? Stan's a good guy, I'd be happy to help out."

"I'll keep that in mind," Lilly said, giving Ty a hug. "Warwick, we'll see you later."

They went over to the staircase and Lilly made some more voice recordings. Roddy leaned down and took pictures to correspond with her notes, scribbling on Warwick's documents. It took them a while, but they finally got to the bottom of the stairs and walked over to the parking lot. The area was empty, which wasn't uncommon. This beach was rocky and small. Not good for sunbathing or swimming, which kept the crowds down. That was one reason the birds did so well there.

The original staircase along the cliffs had been there for a hundred years, an egress for the houses on Shipyard Lane to access the beach. Over time they'd also become cover for a few nesting spots. Rebuilding and reengineering the stairs had been the first part of the project.

"The new stairs are marvelous," Roddy said. "I know that was quite a process."

"Quite a process?" Lilly laughed. "We had to get the old steps out without disturbing what was there, and then fly in the new staircase so there was as little noise and commotion as possible. Add to that, the work needed to be done in the wintertime, when the birds weren't there. Dawn was a nervous wreck that the birds wouldn't come back. But they're here."

"I'm surprised that using the stairs isn't disruptive to the birds nesting."

"The stairs are built so that they jut out, see? There's actually more room underneath. Dawn has all sorts of measuring systems, and wants us to walk up and down the stairs and let her know when, so she can see if there's anything that happens as a result. I'd promised her that I'd walk up and down and let her know when, but I've been remiss."

"How complicated is this report you have to do?"

"It's more of a cover sheet for Dawn, showing that the project is meeting the desires of Harmon's estate. Blah-blah-blah. She's using the report and the work she's doing to apply for other grants, so it has to have some heft to it. Warwick's information makes my work even easier. I needn't have worried, but I am glad we came by. Come back over here, take a look."

Lilly gave Roddy the complete tour. She showed him the nesting grounds underneath the stairs, and what they'd put in place to discourage predators. They climbed back up the stairs slowly, stooping down to look underneath the rungs. When they got to the top of the stairs, they stood on the platform and looked out. After a while they got back on the path, and walked back toward the car.

"Mac's rowing back," Lilly said. "He's hard to miss in that yellow jacket. I forgot that it says *Bradford Funeral Home* on the back. Makes me wonder: Is the mooring a Bradford business expense? Or a town expense?"

"The boat he uses seems modest enough. Tell me about the crematorium," Roddy said. "You mentioned that he works there. Evelyn mentioned it as well. Is having a crematorium in town a big deal?"

"It took a lot for Goosebush to approve that," Lilly said. "Town funds supported the project and there were a lot of hoops to jump through with the state. Sam Bradford had a lot to do with it passing. Been around for over thirty years at this point. I'm not surprised that there's a limited number of people who can do the work. Or that Mac is one of them."

Chapter 25

"So, we're agreed?" Ernie said. "Plan Help Stan is underway." He handed the beet salad to Lilly, and leaned over. "Just try a bite. This is delicious. Roasted beets and fresh goat cheese. Don't make that face, you'll love it."

"I'll try it later, I promise. I'm very full now. But yes, I agree, Plan Help Stan begins."

"I wish we had more information," Delia said, moving the rest of her roasted tofu around on her plate. "We don't even know who knows what, or what the investigation into the Bradford business has found, what other peoples' motives might be—"

"Time for the whiteboard," Roddy said, getting up and rolling it in from Delia's office. The back porch renovation had taken the lip off the back doors to the porch, so the French doors to Delia's office, the former breakfast room, could be open. Lilly had re-designed the porch so that nothing was in front of Delia's doors, ensuring that she could get some sunlight and a bit of privacy. The eating area was set a bit to the left of the back door, and the living area to the right.

"I'm glad you thought to get it ready," Lilly said. "Who wants to take notes?"

"I'll do it," Delia said. "It will help me make sense of it. Where do we start?"

"Who killed Whitney?" Tamara said.

"What are the investigations about?" Ernie added.

"What have they found?" Warwick offered.

There was a pause. Lilly looked around the table and poured herself another glass of wine. "All right, friends, let's brainstorm. This room is safe, none of these conversations will leave. Here's a question: Why did Mac Townsend leave the cemetery?"

"I thought he retired?" Warwick said.

"That's the story. But I've also heard that he was retired. What's the real story?"

"What about Helen Garrett and the family plot? How upset was Jackie about all of that?" Ernie offered. "Not that I think she did anything, but who else had this happen to them?"

"How involved was Sasha in the business?" Delia wrote down. "Your conversation with her was interesting, Lilly. Question is, was it true?"

"Ray and Mary Mancini overheard Buzz Freeland say that he and Mac were going to make sure Whitney got hers," Roddy said. "It may have been two men with too much liquor bloviating. Or maybe Buzz was up to something?"

"Buzz hadn't been in town that long," Lilly said. "How did he and Whitney come into conflict so soon? Remember that night in the restaurant?"

"The night he died? That was tense," Warwick

said. He picked up a piece of steak and put it on his plate.

"I wonder if that was a coincidence," Lilly said.

"What, that he died that same night? Are you insinuating that Buzz was killed?" Tamara said. "I thought he died of natural causes."

"The coroner couldn't determine a cause of death, but they wrote it off as a heart attack. That's officially what killed him, but who knows what caused the heart attack?" Delia said.

"I have another thought. What's Dewey's deal?" Ernie said. "I could have sworn he and Whitney were an item, but now he's indicating that he's been with Sasha for months."

"Where did you hear that?" Delia asked.

"Mary mentioned it after a conversation she overheard at the store. She asked me if I thought it was true."

"Do you?" Lilly asked.

"If Sasha said it, I'd be more inclined. But I don't trust anything Dewey says, to be honest."

"He's too good-looking," Tamara said, picking up a breadstick. "He uses his smile, broad shoulders, and deep voice to get his way. I think we should definitely be looking into Dewey."

"He doesn't get his way with you, I hope," Warwick said, flashing a smile at his wife.

"He tries, but he doesn't get anywhere, don't you worry, babycakes. Tell you what, I'll ask around about Dewey."

"Delia, would you mind looking into the inner workings of the cemetery, and Mac's role?" Lilly asked. "I'm confused by who's doing what. There's supposed to be a board making decisions, but Whitney was on the board. Appointed. I'd like to know if they cut any corners when they put the Bradfords in charge of selling plots."

"That's fine," Delia said. "Can you and Roddy get me all of your cemetery research? Minh and I are meeting about it tomorrow. I've been curious about the same thing. I'll add Mac to the research list."

"Mac's an odd duck, but he cares about the Goosebush cemetery," Ernie said.

"He may care about it, but—"

"But what?"

"This has to stay in this room," Tamara said. "The Board of Selectmen were trying to get rid of him a few years back, before I was serving. I had lunch with Ray Mancini, and he told me that Whitney filed a couple of complaints with the cemetery committee a few years ago. Nothing happened and they seemed to have made peace."

"How long ago was this?" Lilly asked.

"Ten, fifteen years ago? You know who else was on the committee at the time, according to Ray? Portia Asher."

"Portia? Really? I promised to bring her some grasses," Lilly said. "I'll stop by her place tomorrow. I'd love to hear more about the committee."

"She'll let you know what's what for sure," Tamara said. "What else do we need to know?"

"Seems to me we need to talk to Stan," Warwick said. "See how much trouble he's in and how best to help." Everyone turned and looked at Lilly.

"Why me?"

"Because Stan likes you and respects you," Delia said. "If he's in trouble of his own making, you can help him figure out how to get out of it, without judging him."

"Lilly, Stan needs to know we're on his side," Tamara said. "Delia's right. You'll be able to get him to listen and to accept the help."

"I'll see him tomorrow," Lilly said, sighing. She took another scoop of guacamole and put it on a small flour tortilla. She added some steak and folded it up. She cut it in half and put the other half on Roddy's plate.

"I'd like to go over and talk to your friend Evelyn again," Roddy said, picking up the tortilla. "Maybe she'll give us some more information about the investigation. But you'd need to be there."

"I'll talk to Portia in the morning, then I'll reach out to Stan. Why don't you see if Evelyn is available in the afternoon?"

"Will do," Roddy said.

"I'll reach out to Jackie Ross," Ernie said.

"I'll talk to Sasha," Delia said.

"And we'll check back tomorrow," Lilly said. "Now, who wants a cupcake?"

Chapter 26

"Good morning, Roddy," Lilly said. She loved seeing his face in the morning. Even if it was only his picture as it flashed on her cell phone screen when he called.

"Good morning! Evelyn can see us today at three," Roddy said. "I have some errands to run this morning, but I should be back in time to drive with you. If I'm not, I'll let you know."

"That's fine," Lilly said. "I'm going to see Portia later this morning."

"Alas, I'll have to miss that conversation. Please give her my best. I've got to go over to Alden Park."

"Is everything all right?"

"Apparently, Mary mentioned the questions about the materials for the park coming up short to her father. He called Bash, and Bash connected with some people doing the other Bradford investigations. Misuse of funds was one of them."

"Another issue with Whitney?"

"Or Sasha. Or Dewey," Roddy said. "Louise asked

me to come in and meet with some people this morning."

"Surely they noticed the ordering issues," Lilly said.

"That's one of the issues, I'd imagine. Louise must have noticed, but she didn't bring it to anyone's attention."

"While they're asking questions, could you try and find out if any topsoil went to the cemetery lately? I've been looking at the results of those soil samples, and they don't make sense, unless the top layer we worked on last fall—"

"Was taken to the cemetery. I'll see what I can find out. Have you talked to Stan, yet?"

"I wanted to wait until Delia had left before I called him," Lilly said. "I feel as if I'm being unfaithful."

Roddy laughed. "Text me when you're going to meet him, and I'll try and join you. Wish me luck this morning, Lilly. I suspect we opened yet another can of worms."

"These are the ones that grow tall, right?" Chase Asher asked as he lifted the flat of grasses out of the back of Lilly's car.

"Right. They also get browner at the end of the season. Those other ones? They stay shorter and green. And these are midsized and purplish. Don't worry too much about it, Chase. They're great fillers, and create borders. Use them sparingly. They fill in quickly. Your grandmother said that you were both working on the yard and that they may come in handy."

"They will for sure," Chase said. "I keep reminding

myself of what you told us in that class. That gardens plans can take years to take shape, that you have to adjust as needed, and that well-placed annuals make all the difference."

Lilly laughed. When Ernie had asked her to teach a three-part course on garden planning last month, she'd done it as a favor. But she'd enjoyed it as much as the people in the class, and she'd enjoyed hearing about how the work was going for people. She'd thought Chase was there because the girl he was dating had dragged him in. But he'd asked a lot of questions, and it became obvious to her that Portia's grandson had inherited her gardening interest.

Lilly and Chase walked around their yard. The house backed up to public lands, which meant that they were somewhat limited as to what could be done in the backyard. For years Portia had focused instead on the front and the side yard, though they were much smaller. Chase was doing stonework in the back to create some raised beds, and had created a round patio area in the center of the yard. Lilly complimented him on the design and he beamed.

"We're getting some wooden raised beds over there," Chase said. "My friend works with the Urban Farming Institute, and they're selling them as a fundraiser. They'll help keep the vermin from eating the lettuce."

"I hope so," Portia said from the back deck. "I'm sick of planting food for the deer, let me tell you."

"We'll give it a shot, Gram. I'm going to try to put pepper flakes around the plants. I've heard that works really well."

"I'm glad you're here, Chase," Portia said.

"Not as glad as I am, Gram."

"Lilly, come up and have some tea with me. That will give Chase time to unload the plants and come up with any questions he might have. But come around front, these back stairs aren't very safe."

Lilly did as she was told. Portia's house was in disrepair, though Chase had been working on it over the winter. Lilly noticed that there were new windows, and she complimented Portia on the look. They were larger and Portia had left the bottom half clear.

"Not historically accurate," Portia said. "But a lot sunnier. Chase has been finding all sorts of programs that help the house be more efficient. He got new insulation blown into the outside walls last fall, and that made a huge difference this past winter. The new windows will make this place downright toasty, let me tell you."

"It looks wonderful," Lilly said. She carried the tea tray into the living room and put it on the table.

"You sure that's not too heavy for you, Lilly?" Portia said, hovering close to her elbow. "Your arm was in pretty tough shape."

"I'm feeling remarkably well these past few weeks. How have you been, Portia?"

"Better now that spring is here, thank you. The damp cold really does a number on my arthritis." She sat down and turned the cups onto their saucers. "We'll give that a few minutes to steep. Now, before we start visiting, do you know anything about services for Helen Garrett?"

"Nothing yet, I'll let you know."

"Heard there's nowhere to put her," Portia said. "That Whitney sold her space."

"It looks pretty crowed in the Garrett family plot,

but I'm not sure. Her cousin's looking into it from what I understand. I haven't met her yet. I've gone by a couple of times, but she hasn't been home."

"Terrible, just terrible. Of all the things to have happen to poor Helen. Glad she didn't know about it. That Whitney Dunne-Bradford was a piece of work, wasn't she? Now, tell me what's up with Stan. I heard he was arrested. That can't be true."

"He hasn't been arrested, yet. But he may be."

"Unless we all do something," Portia said. "The idea of Stan killing anyone is ridiculous. Though Whitney could certainly push people, that's for sure."

"I understand you used to be on the cemetery committee?" Lilly asked.

"I stepped on after my husband passed. He'd served for years."

"I should know this, but what exactly does the committee do?"

"Oversees the care and maintenance of the public cemeteries. The group meets to rethink the plots. They do the budget for the upcoming year. And, of course, they raise funds as needed."

"What does *rethink the plots* mean?"

"Some people buy plots they never use, so they get cycled back into what's available. The cemetery has unused land it opens up. Also, there are the un-marked graves. Sounds terrible, but after a certain amount of time, like a hundred years, they get put back into the availability."

"What happens to the remains?"

"Most of those folks weren't embalmed and they are put in pine boxes, so there aren't remains to speak of. They're very respectful and rebury them deeper down, and have the new graves on top. Me, I like the idea of being a tree more and more." Green funerals were becoming more popular and Lilly wasn't surprised that Portia liked the idea.

"Why were they unmarked? I don't remember seeing them."

"Sure you do," Portia said. She picked up the teapot. Her hands were shaking, but Lilly didn't jump in to help. Portia took the tea towel and steadied the pot so she could pour. "The monument to the folks who died in the 1918 flu epidemic? They couldn't keep up with the demand, so they took care of the burials and made a memorial. There are a lot of them, trust me. Working with the committee, I got to understand how a cemetery is a living thing that constantly changes. Course, people like Whitney force some changes, which isn't right."

"What do you mean?"

"Mac Townsend was always good about keeping us up on the plots, and how they'd been used. Whitney lit up when he talked about making room. This is back with Sam was alive, mind you. He was different than Whitney, knew just how much to push. I left the committee the year he died and Whitney took his place. They didn't replace me, so she had a lot of sway. Used it too. Not that it was all bad. The reserves have grown, and she took care of a lot of deferred maintenance."

"I don't remember the details, but I feel like the maintenance of the cemetery always had a fairly robust line item on the town budget."

"It does," Portia said. "But Mac was always asking for more money to do this or that. The place got a little run-down. Like that area I thought we should look at for the beautification committee. What did you think of that project?"

"I thought I'd talked to you about it. I think it's a good idea," Lilly said. "I got distracted by all of the new headstones and dropped the ball on that, sorry. We can do that project fairly quickly. Though I'm not sure who to talk to about it now."

"We'll get back to it once the clouds have blown over. What do they think happened to her?"

"I have no idea," Lilly said. "I'd imagine they're focused on Stan, because they'd had a couple of public spats."

"He wasn't the only one fighting with Whitney in public," Portia said. "I go by there a lot, to visit Hank's grave. I was there for his birthday, to leave some roses for my sweetie. I was getting in my car and noticed Whitney over by her car, screaming at someone. I couldn't hear what she was saying, but then she got in her car and drove away."

"Do you know who she was talking to?"

"Buzz Freeland stepped out and screamed 'This is the last time, you bitch' to her car."

"Yikes. When was this?"

"Like I said, it was Hank's birthday. April twenty-fourth."

"He died a few days later," Lilly said.

"Sure did," Portia said. "Course, that probably won't help Stan, will it?"

"If you remember anything else, let me know," Lilly said.

"So, you are looking into it?"

"I'm trying to help Stan," Lilly said. "He's a good guy."

"A good guy who cheated on Delia, is what I hear," Portia said. "Which puts him in the not-good guy column in my book."

"Delia wants to help him," Lilly replied, giving Portia a look.

"Well then, I guess that's all that matters. But she deserved better than to be two-timed like that. Not that this was all on him, mind you. Virginia's been working on him for months."

"How did you hear?"

"Chase. He's been working at the Star. Hard to miss the gossip from that close."

"Hello, Bash," Lilly said. When she saw his name pop up on her dashboard, she pulled over to answer the phone. She knew, or had been told, that she could answer her phone using buttons on her steering wheel, but she'd never been able to do it without help.

"Lilly, how are you?" he said. "I've half-expected you to be sitting on my doorstep today, wanting to talk."

"Whatever for, Bash?"

"I'd imagine you've been looking into Stan's case."

"Not at all. I did a run over to Portia's house. I'm giving her a few grasses to fill in the landscaping. We had a nice visit. She has new windows that look wonderful. But you didn't call to hear about her windows. What can I do you for, Bash?"

"Thought you might like to know. Sasha Bradford was just in here. She filed a missing person report.

Normally I'd want her to wait for the full forty-eight hours, but given what's been going on, I thought I'd make an exception."

"Who's missing?"

"Dewey Marsh."

"Dewey? Really? When did she see him last?"

"Yesterday afternoon. About an hour after we let Stan go."

"Oh dear," Lilly said.

"Yup. Stan's got lousy timing for alibis. Said he took a drive yesterday afternoon to get his head on straight. Same alibi as when Whitney was killed. He was at the restaurant last night, but not until seven or so."

"I was thinking about going by and saying hello to Stan," Lilly said.

"You may want to do that sooner than later. Right now the investigation into Dewey is informal. But I'm going to need to open it up soon. A man doesn't just disappear."

"Unless it's in his own best interest to do so," Lilly said. "He must be a suspect in Whitney's death."

"He was. And is. There's seems to be some clothes missing, and his phone and wallet are gone as well. I don't know what happened, and Sasha wasn't any help. I'm working on tracking his phone and his credit cards. Which presents its own challenges."

"How so?" Lilly asked. Someone slowed down and looked at her, but she smiled and waved, pointing to her phone. One of the nice things about a small town was that people stopped to help.

"He used a burner phone and seemed to only use the company credit cards. I can't find any in his name."

"That's odd, these days," Lilly said.

"According to Sasha, he'd had some financial difficulties and relied on his banking card. He'd put money on different gift cards to get coffee and things like that."

"Dewey seems to be a complicated man," Lilly said.

"Much more than I expected," Bash said. "Anyway, I wanted to give you a call. I'm going to need to bring Stan in for questioning about Dewey. And this time I don't think I can let him go."

"Thanks for the heads-up, Bash. I'll plan on seeing Stan soon."

"If you do, don't mention this call, all right? And don't tell me about your conversation, unless you have to. Whitney's dying turned up the heat on the Bradford investigation, and a lot of people are looking for a fall guy. Fall person. Sasha's not off the hook, by any means. But I have to act on any pieces of information, even the gossip. If you have something to tell me, make sure you've got facts backing it up."

"Understood," Lilly said. She ended the call and took a deep breath. If she'd been doubting the urgency of Plan Help Stan, she wasn't any more. Looking guilty might be enough to get him into more trouble than he could handle.

Chapter 27

"Delia, I'm home," Lilly called out as she walked in the back door. Luna and Max came out of Delia's office, stretching and blinking at her. She bent down to give them both pats. Their duty done, they walked over to the couch on the porch to take another nap.

She pulled her phone out and texted Roddy that she was home. She'd barely hit *send* when the front doorbell rang. Why was he coming in the front? The doorbell camera was operating, but she hadn't put the app back on her phone, and booting up her computer felt like a waste of time. She slowly walked the length of the house to answer the door. When there was an impatient second ring and knocking, she realized that it might not be Roddy. She finally got to the door and looked through the peephole.

That was convenient, she thought. Stan Freeland had come to her, so she wouldn't need to go looking for him.

"Stan, come in," Lilly said when he was in the middle of his third round of doorbell rings. "I heard the door the first time. It's a big house, and I don't run. Come in, come in."

"Sorry, Lilly. I was hoping to see Delia."

"She is not, to the best of my knowledge, here. Let me double-check." Lilly sent a text and smiled at Stan. "Come back to the kitchen. I was going to make myself something to eat."

"I'm not hungry—"

"And a cup of tea. Come have tea with me, Stan. Make sure to close the door behind you." Lilly started to walk, expecting that he would follow her, which he did.

"I don't suppose I could trouble you to make some sandwiches?" Lilly asked. "We have so many leftovers, but I am an uninspired sandwich maker, and would likely resort to a ham sandwich with a slash of mustard." Sandwiches were a specialty of Stan's and she suspected he'd enjoy the challenge. Ernie's bread was still plentiful, and Stan remarked on it when he did his taste test.

"Ernie bakes when stressed, much to the benefit of us all," Lilly said. "His brioche takes a couple of days to pull off, but it doesn't last long. He may need to double his efforts on that front."

Stan pulled out the condiments and Lilly handed him what he requested. Small bowls, spices, forks and knives. He concocted three separate sauces and slathered them on different pieces of bread. He moved very quickly, so Lilly stepped back to watch.

Lilly felt her phone buzz and pulled it out of her pocket. "Delia's at the library, doing some cemetery research." She texted Roddy and told him to stay put, that Stan was there.

"Cemetery research? Why?"

"To help you, of course," Lilly said. "We're trying to figure out who killed Whitney, and starting with the cemetery seemed like a good path. Besides, you know Delia. She's best when she has a research project."

"Who's *we?*" Stan asked quietly.

"There's a few of us," Lilly said. "Roddy, Tamara, Warwick. Ernie, of course."

"All of you are trying to help me? Why?" Stan stopped cutting sandwiches and looked at Lilly.

"First of all, because Delia asked us to," Lilly said. She let that hang for a bit. Though she was trying not to get involved, Delia was her friend. And Stan had hurt her. Deeply. She looked over at him as she poured the hot water over the tea. Satisfied that he looked sufficiently miserable, Lilly went on.

"Also, we all care about you. Even if you get off, or never get charged, none of us want to see the shadow of doubt in your life. You deserve better. You've actually saved me a trip. I was going to go and talk to you this afternoon."

"To see if I killed Whitney?" Stan turned and started cutting the sandwiches with much more force than necessary.

"Of course not," Lilly said. "To find out why they think you may have killed her."

"She was a blackmailing, conniving—"

"Blackmailing? Whom did she blackmail?" Lilly handed Stan a large plate, and he stacked the sandwiches. She brought two smaller plates over to the table to set it. Together they brought over the tea things, napkins, and some chips to round out the meal.

Lilly didn't bother to remind Stan that he wasn't

hungry. He ate two sandwiches and put a third on his plate. She went to take a nibble of one, but soon ate that as well: Delicious combinations of cheese, spreads, olives, meat, and other leftovers in small sandwiches. She poured them both tea and handed him the milk and sugar, neither of which he used. He took a sip and smiled.

"This is a Star brew," he said.

"It is," Lilly replied, smiling. "Roddy and I had some a while ago, and loved it. Delightful. I understand that Virginia has been buying tea for the Star lately."

Stan nodded and looked down at his plate. "You told me that I needed more help to move the business to the next level, and she's been doing that. She's got the theater running better than ever. And she's got great ideas about the café and bookstore. I don't know what I would have done without her for the past few weeks. But then . . ." He looked up at Lilly briefly, and then down again at his plate.

"What happened?"

"We were friends. Colleagues. You know. We worked together every day. But then my father died, and she was helping me clean up the mess he made. She understood. And didn't judge. I started to trust her, which is hard for me."

"You trust Delia, surely," Lilly said.

"I did. I do. But Buzz brought a lot of darkness into my life. I didn't tell Delia everything, and then it got so big I didn't know how to. But Virginia knew, and stuck with me. She was a good friend."

"Stan, I have many good friends. I don't kiss them like you kissed Virginia."

"Yeah, that. You're not going to believe me, but

that was the first time—I mean, we'd flirted, but nothing had happened. Whitney wound me up and Virginia came by to check on me. Next thing I knew—"

"And Whitney was there to take a picture."

Stan nodded and moved his glass around on the coaster. "I'll be honest with you, Lilly. It was the first, but then Delia broke up with me. Anyway, it wasn't our last kiss."

"I want to believe you, Stan. But you know how much Delia means to me—"

"I didn't mean to hurt Delia," Stan said quietly. He sounded miserable and couldn't look Lilly in the eyes. "Delia's one of the best things that ever happened to me. But Virginia? She's like a drug. I keep trying to break it off, but Virginia pulls me back in."

Lilly shook her head, her appetite gone. "Stan, as my late husband used to say, it takes two to tango. If you didn't want to dance, you'd say no."

"Fair enough," Stan said.

"Your business is your business. But you should have talked to Delia instead of pushing her away. You didn't believe she'd stand by you, and we both know she would have. She deserved much, much better than to find out from a text."

"I know. Delia and I had a good thing going, you know. But then we both got busy, and my dad moved in with me. I felt like my life was falling apart, but I thought I had to figure it out on my own."

"I'll leave it to the two of you. I have my thoughts and opinions, but they don't matter." She poured herself some more tea and turned toward Stan. "Do you mind if I change the subject?"

"Go ahead," Stan said, slowly breaking a chip down into many pieces.

"I heard that your father and Mac Townsend were talking about Whitney getting hers one night in the bar. Do you know what that was about?"

Stan sighed and pushed himself back from the table. "Man, you don't beat around the bush, do you?"

"Stan, it's best that you talk to me," Lilly said. "I'd imagine you think it all sounds like it will make you sound guilty. Here's the thing: I don't think you are. But I need to know what Bash is going to find out so that we can help you."

"My father was a first-rate bastard," Stan said, quietly. "He left my mother and me when I was seven. She struggled, but got it together. She talked about him, mostly about the good stuff. But after a couple of years of missed visits, birthday checks that bounced, and IOUs for Christmas presents, I stopped caring. When she got sick, I thought about reaching out to him, but I didn't try too hard."

"That must have been very difficult," Lilly said.

"When she died, I was really at a loss. I came to Goosebush to go to an art show and fell in love with the town. You know the rest. This place helped me move forward, and find some happiness. Then, out of the blue, Buzz found me last winter."

"Do you know how?" Lilly said.

"He read an article about the Star," Stan said. "He tried to act like a long-lost father coming home, but I called him out on that. Then he told me that he was sick, and wanted to make amends."

"Sick? I'm sorry," Lilly said.

"He wasn't sick," Stan said. "The autopsy actually confirmed that. He wanted into my life. And I let him in, idiot that I was."

"Not an idiot," Lilly said. "It's human nature to want to assume the best of people."

"Yeah, well. Old Buzz came to find me for a reason. He was running away from a heap of trouble and a mountain of debt."

"What kind of trouble?"

"Whitney found out before I did," Stan said. "She had a sixth sense about people, that's for sure. Turns out that dear old dad had some outstanding warrants. He'd been using another name, of course, but it was still him. Larceny, blackmailing, that sort of thing. He was a low-level con man. He'd spent a life running away."

"How did Whitney find out?"

"When he showed up, she did research on him."

"That's odd," Lilly said.

"Sasha told me that she always did research on people, to find out what they were worth, family ties, that sort of thing. She called it business preparation."

"What did Whitney do when she found out about Buzz's past?" Lilly asked, pouring herself some more tea. Her hands ached for her notebook, but she didn't want to break the flow of conversation. She'd need to do her best to remember.

"She started to blackmail him, so he had to find sources of money. He asked to borrow money, and I gave him some. Then I started noticing the till was short, even though he never had any cash. She was bleeding him dry. Course, I had no idea, not till much later. I wish he'd come clean."

"What would you have done?"

"Probably kicked him out, but I also would have gone after her. I have no time for people like Whitney."

"How did you find out?"

"He and Mac became great drinking buddies. Mac got him some side work, but it wasn't enough. Buzz eventually told me what was happening. I was furious. Furious at him for living up to my lowest expectations. Furious at her for blackmailing him. After we hashed it out, I told him we were going to go to see Bash. He didn't like that idea, but that was the plan. He promised not to confront Whitney in the meantime. That didn't stop him from making snide comments to her, though."

"When were you planning on going to see Bash?"

"Monday morning. But he died on Saturday."

"When had he confessed all to you?"

"That morning. That night, at the restaurant, I could barely focus. When Whitney came in, I didn't know what to do, but I played it cool. I didn't want to tip my hand."

Lilly nodded. "Did you tell Bash afterwards?"

"Whitney got to me first. She told me that she'd blow up my life. But then she told me that she'd bury it all with Buzz as long as I bought a plot from her."

"Which you did," Lilly said.

"I did. Ends up it wasn't even a real plot, but I didn't worry too much about that. I wanted it to be over."

"Was it?"

"Of course not. She came back for more, but I told her to drop dead. I said I'd go to Bash if I needed to."

"How did she take that?"

"She sent Delia that text. And called me, and said that was just the beginning of my miseries."

"Oh my. It's always depressing when people live up to our lowest expectations, isn't it? I wonder if blackmail was a normal way of doing business for Whitney?"

"She was really good at it," Stan said. "With Dewey as her muscle."

"What do you mean?"

"He came to pick up the money from me," Stan said. He stood up and started to pace. "Saying all of this out loud to you? I'm an idiot."

"Bash needs to know all of this."

"I know he does. Like you said, I didn't do it. Maybe it will help Bash figure out who did. I can't be the only sucker in town. I bet he could get Dewey to flip."

"Stan, Dewey's missing," Lilly said.

"Missing? What? Are you sure?"

"Bash called me a little while ago. He's only been gone a day, but Bash is concerned. It's not public yet, but you should know. Have you told your lawyer everything you told me?"

"Not everything," Stan said. "He was a public defender. Honestly, he was in a rush. Got me out of there and told me to keep my nose clean."

"Okay, Stan, sit down. You're making me nervous. Here's what we're going to do. I'm going to call my lawyer. Do you have your car?"

"No, I walked."

"Fine, I'll drop you by her office. I called her yesterday and told her that you may be a new client."

"Lilly, I can't afford—"

"Listen to me. Delia asked me to help you and I'm doing that. You are going to talk to my lawyer and tell her everything—and I mean everything—you told me. And you're going to tell her the parts you left out. Then you're both probably going to talk to Bash, but that's her call."

"Lilly, I can't—"

"Don't argue with me, Stan. Don't be stubborn about money right now. You can't afford your pride. I don't think you did this, but you've got to admit the frame is looking pretty solid."

"Dammit. I never should have—" Stan pushed the plate of sandwiches across the table.

Lilly stood up from the table and walked over to a drawer, opened it, and pulled out a roll of plastic wrap. "Would you mind wrapping those up? I'd appreciate that, as would Ernie and Delia. You have a real talent for making delicious food, Stan. I'm going upstairs to freshen up. Roddy and I have a meeting at three, but we've got plenty of time to drive to the office. Don't argue with me, Stan. There's no point. We'll leave in five minutes."

Chapter 28

A while later, Roddy and Lilly were in Evelyn's office, settling into the chairs in front of her desk.

"Hey Roddy, nice to see you again. Lilly, I've been meaning to call you. What did you do?" Evelyn Crocker had double-checked that they didn't need coffee, and then launched right in.

"What do you mean?" Lilly asked the younger woman.

"You're over here asking questions, next thing I know the ish hits the fan and Bradford's is shut down, and a few more funeral homes are put on notice."

"A few others?" Roddy asked.

"Yeah, I haven't been able to get a definitive list of who, but I've got some ideas. The gossip is flying, as you can imagine. There were a few folks Whitney was tight with, probably got themselves into trouble because of it."

"That's why we're here," Lilly said. "We're trying

to get a better sense of what the investigation entailed."

"Entailed? I'm not sure what you mean. How did they do it?"

"More like why. Bradford's was shut down because of some sort of code violations. What might that mean?" Roddy asked.

"A lot, from what I hear," Evelyn said, leaning back. "Financial records are where they started. That's where these things usually start. From what I hear, the audit is ongoing."

"I suspect the financial trail is going to be a mess," Lilly said.

"I hear that you found a bunch of urns in your family crypt, is that right, Lilly?" Evelyn asked.

"It is," she said. "Plus another body in my father's vault."

"Yikes. I hope for the sake of those families there's paperwork somewhere."

"So do I," Lilly said, shuddering.

"There is a lot of gossip," Evelyn said. "There have been mentions of bribes, but those are harder to prove. Now that she's dead they may not pursue that avenue. From what I hear, she covered her tracks well."

"I've also heard that Whitney wasn't above blackmail," Lilly said, watching Evelyn closely.

"Wouldn't surprise me in the least. She was a real piece of work. Sam Bradford wasn't my favorite person in the world, but he deserved better."

"Maybe Sasha will carry the torch forward."

"Oh Lilly, you're funny," Evelyn said. "Have you met Sasha? She's a follower, not a leader. The girl's never sent me a piece a paperwork that didn't have to be redone. Not once. Don't laugh, I'm serious. She's a disaster. Poor Sasha, I have no doubt Whitney ran all over her. I have no idea what Whitney was able to get her to do over the years. One thing I do know is that I doubt her father would approve."

"I wonder why Whitney kept her on," Roddy said.

"Sasha owned ninety percent of the business, that's why," Evelyn said.

"How do you know that?"

"Sam told me years ago. We were at some conference or another. He'd had a few, to be honest. Sasha is only a few years younger than I am, and he kept wondering where he'd gone wrong, since I was starting my own business. Later he offered to bring me in as a partner at Bradford. I said no, but I wish I had in retrospect. I would have bought Whitney out."

"Dewey mentioned that he'd bought into the business," Roddy said. "What do you think he meant?"

"Maybe Sasha sold him a share? Sasha is the primary owner of the business as far as I know. But the side hustles, they're all Whitney."

"Side hustles?"

"The deals with different cemeteries to sell plots, or oversee maintenance? She had a dozen side businesses going at once."

"I wonder how long she'd been overseeing maintenance of the cemetery," Lilly said, thinking about the waterlines that were being repaired.

"I'm not sure how long it's been official, but unofficially she's been in charge for a while," Evelyn said.

"She did it all on her own?" Roddy said.

"No, but the team was small. She put a lot of balls in the air, but Dewey helped her juggle them."

"How do you know about what she was up to?"

"She didn't hide things. She considered all of the side businesses a feature, not a bug. They were how she wanted to run things, though I don't know how she kept it all going. Listen, for all I know it was all on the up-and-up."

"You don't really think that, do you?" Lilly asked.

"In order to succeed in this business, you need two things. First, you have to care about people. Second, people need to be able to trust you. Whitney had the compassion of a hungry boa constrictor. And she'd burned a lot of people. The trust was eroding if not gone. So, no, I don't think she was altruistic."

"How about Sasha, or Dewey?"

"Sasha still has a reputation for being honest."

"Even with messed-up paperwork?" Roddy asked.

"For all I know, Whitney was making her redo it," Evelyn said. "Because of her folks, she still has a lot of goodwill."

"Do you have any idea who might have killed Whitney?" Lilly asked.

Evelyn paled a bit and shook her head. "None. I know a lot of people didn't like her, but to kill her? It's still hard to believe. Do you know anything about the services?"

"I don't," Lilly said. "I'd imagine it would be soon, but Sasha may want to wait until the investigation has—"

"Died down? It's okay, Lilly. Bad puns are part of the business. I hear they've arrested someone for her death."

"Not arrested, not yet. The man they're looking at is a friend of mine. Of ours," Lilly said, putting her hand on Roddy's arm.

"You're trying to help him out."

"I am."

"If I hear anything I'll let you know," Evelyn said.

"That would be wonderful," Lilly said. "You have ties to a community I don't know at all. Tell me, you mentioned Sasha running the business with help. Might Dewey be a good fit? What do you think of him?" Lilly asked.

"Aside from the fact that he was handsome as hell?" Evelyn laughed and shrugged. "He was a good wingman for Whitney."

"What about for Sasha? Do you think he'd be a good wingman for Sasha?"

Evelyn looked down and pursed her lips. She looked up and leaned forward. "I'm going to tell tales out of school, but Sasha called me yesterday. She wants to talk about me buying the business. She wanted to stay on, but said that Dewey would be leaving. Which, if you ask me, is a good thing. From what I hear, Dewey may be in some sort of trouble."

"Maybe he is trouble," Roddy said.

"You said it," Evelyn said. "He left a bunch of broken hearts; I know that for sure."

"I always thought he was dating Whitney," Lilly said.

"Oh, Lilly. They were an item, for sure. But it wasn't exclusive. At least not on Dewey's part. Don't ask me how I know that."

"I won't ask you," Lilly said. "Evelyn, if you find out anything else, would you let me know?"

"I will, Lilly. I hope you figure it out. In the meantime, I'll stay in touch with Sasha. I offered to help her with anything that comes up over the next few weeks."

"That's nice of you," Roddy said.

"We all work together," Evelyn said. "I use the Goosebush crematorium a lot, so I'm back and forth."

"Won't that shut down for a while?"

"No, Mac can keep taking care of that part of the business."

"Mac Townsend?"

"Yeah. He's been running things there for years. It's the one contract that Whitney didn't get total control over, which is why I still use it."

"Tamara wants us to come by her office," Lilly said, reading her phone. They were almost at Roddy's driveway, but he drove past. "She's got an appointment, so she has to stay put."

"We can do that," Roddy said. "Do you know what it's about?"

"She says she's been pulling information all day. Have you ever seen Tamara when she's gathering information? It gives Delia hives. She makes piles and piles all over the place that make no sense to anyone but herself."

"That's why she never gives us a piece of paper without explaining it first," Roddy said.

"That's why."

May was still before the official summer season, but downtown Goosebush was picking up. Roddy had to wait for three cars to pass before he could merge onto the rotary. Of course, Lilly wouldn't have waited, but she drove an older Jeep and had grown up learning how to drive around rotaries. Every few years there were discussions about changing them into intersections, but they never got past the discussion phase.

Roddy pulled his car into a space near the door to Tamara's office. He walked around to offer Lilly a hand, but she was able to get herself out of the car. She smiled at the offer.

"I'll probably need help next time," Lilly said. "I'm not built for a sports car. But I'm getting the hang of it."

"I'm not sure I am anymore," Roddy said. "Especially after driving an SUV all winter. But I do love this car." He gave it a pat and stepped back so that Lilly could take the lead.

The door buzzed when they walked in, and Tamara stuck her head out of her office.

"Hey you two, back here. Grab a cup of whatever on your way if you'd like."

Lilly resisted making herself a cup of the instant cocoa. Roddy smiled and tilted his head. "I'm going to make myself a tea," he said.

"Cocoa," she said. "Thanks."

"I've got a buyer coming in any minute to sign a purchase and sale," Tamara said as Lilly walked into her office. "And another buyer coming in to sign a counteroffer."

"You've got a lot going on this spring," Lilly said.

"It's always the busy time of year, but yes. The office is doing well. I'm doing well. I'm not going to complain. These two offers have been taking up a lot of my time this week, though. I hope they both go through."

"Tamara, I brought you a cup of cocoa," Roddy said, balancing three cups as he walked into the office. "I knew once you saw Lilly drinking hers you'd want one."

"You're a good man," Tamara said, standing up to take her cup. "All right, let me walk you through this so you can read it over if my clients come in. Lilly, here's a pen and highlighter for you. Roddy, here's one for you. Ready? I know you'll be itching to make notes that help explain why I printed out the sheet I did. As long as I can remember, we're in luck."

"We have complete faith in you, Tamara," Roddy said.

"Okay, this pile," she handed it to Roddy. "I pulled up the town records on as many houses as I could. This morning Pete told me that Whitney came by a few weeks ago to talk about putting her house on the market."

"Ernie said she was doing some painting—"

"He called her last week, and it ends up she had the house assessed, and wasn't happy with the results, so she decided to hold off for a bit."

"Why?"

"I wondered that too. So I called the assessor Pete suggested, you know Don, and asked what happened. He told me that the house was mortgaged to the hilt. She'd done a lot of improvements, which had affected her tax rate, but none of them added much value to the home. To be fair, the house was so much a part of the business that selling it separately didn't make sense, and he told her that. Anyway, if she'd sold the house, she would have lost money."

"Why was it mortgaged like that?" Lilly asked. "I thought Sam owned it outright. He used to talk about the freedom of owning the properties and putting money back into the business."

"The house was in Whitney's name. She'd been taking out mortgages to make improvements, and to keep up her lifestyle. Her clothes, those cars? They don't come cheap," Tamara said, handing Lilly some papers. "I looked at Sam's will while I was going through records. The business is mostly Sasha's."

"I'd heard that. But Whitney must have had a share, otherwise why would she have stuck around?"

"Maybe she was on salary," Tamara said.

"Or perhaps her side businesses made it worth it," Roddy said. He looked back down at the sheets Tamara had passed him and flipped through them.

"Whose house is this?" he asked Tamara, handing her a sheet of paper.

She glanced at the sheet and handed it back. "Mac Townsend. He's been there for years. After I talked to Don and he mentioned that Whitney's house had been reassessed, I did a search to look at the tax assessments that took a leap this past year. Mac was on the list."

"I wonder why was he on the list," Lilly said.

"I asked Don. Turns out Mac was one of those folks who keeps the house looking run-down on the outside, so drive-by assessments didn't notice any changes. But someone tipped off the assessor that he'd redone the kitchen and added another bathroom. His property value went up, as did his taxes."

"I wonder who called," Lilly said. Normally those changes were "caught" when a house was sold and were the problem of the new owners.

"I asked Don to ask around, and he did. Whitney called the assessor's office and told them about the other work her contractors had been doing around town. Don said they had to move on the tip, even though Mac had retired."

"Can't he get a new tax rate because of his age?" Lilly asked.

"Age was raised to seventy last year. He's only sixty-eight."

"Is that all?" Lilly said. "How's he only two years older than we are?"

"Careful of the *we*, my friend. The new receptionist thinks I'm forty-seven."

"Why does he think that?"

"Cause I told him I was forty-seven."

"And you explained your grandchildren and thirty-something children how?"

"I haven't had to, yet. No one in my family visits me at the office, Lilly. Now, where were we?"

"Whitney. Mac. House taxes," Roddy said, shuffling papers into an order that made sense to him. Lilly handed him hers and he sorted them into the pile.

"Right. Okay, this stack has the other town records I pulled—hold on, my client is here. Go ahead, read through these piles. They're kind of stream of consciousness, but if anyone can follow my stream, it's the two of you."

Chapter 29

Lilly left Roddy and the papers at Tamara's office and walked over to Bits, Bolts and Bulbs. Roddy was suited to the sorting it required, and he was asking Tamara all sorts of questions. Lilly was a more narrative learner. She could read about Mac's reassessment, but she wanted to see the house.

The pull of the garden center had called to Lilly. Digging in dirt always helped her think. She hadn't been by this week, and missed it. Not that she didn't have enough in her greenhouse and gardens to keep her busy, never mind Roddy's. But Lilly loved seeing all the new plants arrive and find a home, helping the neglected ones come back to life, and having the freedom to create arrangements that she'd never use at home. Helping Ernie out over the winter had gotten her through the fallow months, and given her something to focus on as she healed from her fall. She'd become attached to the garden center and all that was possible there.

"I thought I'd find you here," Ernie said. "Tamara

said she and Roddy would be by in a half hour to pick you up to go home. I told them I hadn't seen you, but then I figured you'd snuck in."

"Not snuck," Lilly said. "You were busy out front showing several young people around."

"The sixth grade science club. They each have fifteen dollars to spend to build a robot that has to perform a function. I was showing them all the different departments, to help inspire then to explore. They've got their baskets and are going through the store now."

"That sounds like a fun project," Lilly said.

"Should be. I had to ask Mary to put in an emergency order of paint sticks, since anything free was taken in bulk amounts, but it's going well. I'm going to be one of the judges."

"Of course you are," Lilly said. "I hope you don't mind. I moved some things around, watered, created some clusters to give folks ideas."

"You are amazing."

"I thought that I could create some how-to cards you could post if you're interested. Sometimes people are afraid to mix and match, or they want to make sure a garden looks good all summer."

"We could use the cards for social media, help bring people in."

"However you'd like to use them. Just don't use my name," Lilly said.

"I'll say they are tips from the anonymous gardeners," Ernie said. "Your being back here explains the rush on plants."

"I may have helped a few people who were dithering."

"Lilly Jayne, the anti-ditherer."

"I'm not sure that's true today. Tamara did a bunch of research and I couldn't be bothered to look at it all. When I left Roddy and her, they were going through tax records with a fervor I couldn't muster."

Ernie laughed. "You've got Delia and Roddy to process the data for you."

"I don't know, Ernie. I feel like I've lost a step these days," Lilly said. She moved around a group of pots and misted them, and then coiled the hose and put it on a shelf.

"Nonsense. If you'd lost a step, this place wouldn't turn into magic every time you came in."

Lilly smiled at her friend and impulsively gave him a hug. He'd been such a support for her when she lost her husband. He understood her pain, having lost his own husband a few years prior. Now they pushed each other back into life, and picked each other up when they felt lost.

"Ernie, you said that Tamara and Roddy were coming over to give me a ride? What's that about?"

"Apparently Warwick came to borrow Tamara's car, because he had to drop his at the shop, and Roddy told him to borrow his and Tamara would drive everyone home."

"That's complicated, isn't it? We could have walked."

"It's starting to rain. Mary was going to give me a lift home, since I walked today, but I'll jump in Tamara's car and go for a ride."

"Sounds like a plan. I'll keep fussing back here, if you don't mind."

"I don't mind at all. I'll text you when they're here."

* * *

They met Tamara and Roddy in the parking lot of the Triple B. Ernie was going to put the compost that Warwick had ordered in the back of the car, but Tamara nixed the idea. "I'm not driving around with compost seeping into these seats."

"We can load up the Jeep tomorrow," Lilly offered. "I'm used to the smell in my car." She saw Tamara shiver and smiled. Lilly's end-of-season fertilizer included cow manure, seaweed, hay, and other ingredients. Her car smelled terrible for a couple of days, but the results were worth it.

"Roddy ordered pizza," Tamara said. "We're going to take a ride before we pick it up."

"I love taking rides. Where are we going?" Ernie said, climbing into the back seat with Lilly and buckling up.

"To see some of the properties I've been researching," Tamara said. "The pizza is deep-dish, so it's going to take a while."

"From that new place across town? I've been wanting to try it out," Ernie said.

"I had a Realtor lunch there," Tamara said. "So, so good. Anyway, we're going to go by the Garrett house first. Helen Garrett owned the house outright. I'm not sure who she left it to—"

"Her cousin Jackie came in today and I talked to her," Ernie said. "She left the house to Jackie, with some cash disbursements to the next generation. Problem is, to meet the cash disbursements, Jackie's going to need to sell."

"It's much better to leave percentages to people," Lilly said.

"Jackie said the same thing. She'd really like to keep the house, but doesn't know how that's possible. I suggested she not make any rash decisions. Here's the house. Slow down for a second, Tamara. Jackie said that it's been updated with electrics and plumbing, since Helen had to move to the first floor and they needed to put a bathroom in downstairs. Apparently the taxes alone are a killer."

"And they went up last year," Tamara said. "A lot. And remember this, Helen got a senior citizen discount."

"Why was it reassessed?" Lilly asked.

"Possibly the same contractor did work at the Garrett house as did work at Whitney's," Roddy said, looking at papers.

"I can probably look at permits," Tamara said. "Roddy, send me an email and remind me to do that before we all forget."

"Done," Roddy said, looking out the window. "I haven't really been back here. Where are we? I was reading and I've lost my bearings."

"This is the street that runs right behind our houses," Lilly said. "Her lot is wider, but narrower thanks to our backyards. See that tree on the back of the lot? You can see it from your upstairs."

"Yes, of course. So, this is what's beyond the wall."

"It's an impressive wall," Ernie said. "Jackie said her family built it?"

"They did. They built it up against my stone wall so it would look uniform."

"I wish they'd used stone," Roddy said. "The brick appears to be bowing in places."

"Years of ivy have probably damaged the mortar," Ernie said.

"It's on my summer list to get it fixed," Roddy said. "What's that building on the side?"

"The gatehouse," Ernie said. "Jackie told me about it. It was built for relatives who wanted to visit in the summer, so they wouldn't have to stay in the main house. She told me I should come over to visit, to give her some ideas to get it ready to go on the market."

"She'll get a pretty penny for it," Tamara said. "Though I think it will probably be a teardown, unfortunately. This isn't waterfront, but it's close enough. And this back neighborhood has a lot of charm." She pulled away and continued down the road until it connected with Washington Street again. "Next stop, we're going over by the old church."

"To Mac Townsend's house?" Lilly said.

"Another area I don't know well," Roddy said.

"That part of town is interesting," Tamara said. "It was one of the older neighborhoods—we're talking Colonial houses—and then there was a fire in the 1910s. When the neighborhood was rebuilt it was by the same company, using three basic designs. For a lot of people the sameness made it undesirable, but now it's one of my favorite parts of town. The houses are large but not huge, tall ceilings, beautiful finishings. A bit run-down these days, but folks like it that way." Tamara kept up a running narrative of the house history of Goosebush on their way, prompted by Roddy's questions.

"This is Mac's street. And there's his house." Tamara rolled to a slow crawl and stopped the car.

"Forgive me, but from the outside it doesn't look like much," Roddy said.

"That's to fool the assessors," Lilly said. "Folks let

the outside look run-down so that their property values don't go up."

"That doesn't work as well these days," Tamara said. "Social media being what it is. People love to show off their new bathroom, or bar sink, or indoor gym. Besides, Goosebush property values keep going up, even on the houses that are in need of some TLC."

"Still, he probably thought he could get away with it," Ernie said. "It really does look like a wreck. Nice cars in the driveway, though."

"They are indeed," Roddy said. "Where's next?"

"Let's go by Whitney's house," Lilly said. "It's not far from here."

"I learn about these back roads from these rides," Roddy said. "And when Lilly helps me elude someone who's following us."

"The best way to explore Goosebush is by bike," Lilly said, ignoring everyone's laughter. She'd had to outrun the press a couple of times last fall, and was grateful that she knew Goosebush so well that it was easy to do just that. "That's how Tamara and I know all the different roads and paths. By Vespa isn't bad, either, though some of the side roads aren't as easy to explore. It's a pretty little town."

"It is," Ernie said. "Though it can be a hard place to fit in when you first move here. I remember it took Steven and me years to feel like folks didn't see us as tourists."

"How long have you lived here?" Roddy asked.

"Twenty years," Ernie said. "Hard to believe. Steven spent summers here as a kid and loved the town. He was so thrilled when we got the chance to buy the Triple B and moved here. I'm glad he was able to enjoy it for a few years, at least."

"You both made some magic with the Triple B," Tamara said. "Honestly, you made it a fun place to shop, and that helped the entire business district. Okay, here we go. This is the Bradford house." They drove up and parked.

"The house belongs to Whitney, but the business belongs to Sasha," Tamara told Ernie. "And the house is mortgaged to the hilt."

"Which is the business and which is the house?" Ernie said. "The front lawn is a parking lot for the funeral home. Who'd want to buy it?"

"See over there? That used to be another house, but Sam got permission to tear it down and turn it into the embalming section of the business," Tamara said. "Then they built that addition so that they could have more room for viewings. I agree, they'd need to sell the entire business. I doubt these additions are all zoned."

"That's a large business footprint," Roddy said. "Are they that busy?"

Lilly shrugged her shoulders. "Busy enough. When the town decided to build the crematorium, folks from other towns started to come to Goosebush, and it was just as easy to use Bradford's."

"Where's the crematorium?" Roddy asked. "We keep talking about it, but I don't think I've seen it."

Tamara put the car in *drive* and pointed out what was what: the house, the business, the funeral parlors. "The crematorium is over there," she said, pointing to a building behind them, closer to the cemetery.

"What's that?" Ernie asked, pointing toward the back of the buildings.

They drove around to look. There were two large rental trucks parked in the back. One of them had a flat tire and both were covered in pollen. There was crime scene tape on the back door, but it had been pulled off.

"Should we walk around?" Ernie said.

"I don't think so," Lilly replied. She took out her phone and snapped a picture, a visual reminder to ask Bash about the trucks.

"Good," he said. "This place gives me the creeps."

"Sam Bradshaw inherited an honest business from his father, and ran it the same way for a lot of years," Tamara said. "I'm glad he didn't live long enough to see this."

"If he'd been around, perhaps it would have stayed an honest business," Roddy said.

"Or Whitney would have gotten her way and taken him down with her," Lilly said. "It's hard to know. She left quite a wake, didn't she?"

"Sure did," Ernie said. "I wonder who else got caught up in it."

Chapter 30

The next morning Lilly buzzed the gate open, took a mug out of the cabinet, and poured a cup of coffee for Bash. He came in the kitchen door a minute later, and she handed him the cup.

"I'm not going to stay long," he said, taking a long sip.

"Would you like some breakfast? I have some deep-dish pizza left over from last night."

"Thanks, too early for me. Is the pizza from that new place? Any good?"

"Delicious," Lilly said. "I'll pack you up some for later. We have fresh rolls, if that sounds better."

Bash smelled the air. "Very fresh, from the smell of things."

"Ernie's a good housemate," Lilly said. She walked over and got Bash a plate, and put the bread basket on the table. The tray of jams and butter were still there. She'd had breakfast with Ernie and Delia, but would have another roll, happily.

"Maybe just one," he said, taking two and putting

them on his plate. "I came over here to ask you a favor, off the record."

"I'm happy to help if I can," Lilly said.

"Would you go through your notes and pictures of the cemetery again, and make notes of what's changed?"

"Again? Didn't we send you those files? And we did the walk-through with Darlene—"

"I was wondering if you remembered anything else," Bash said. "It's been a couple of weeks."

"I'm not sure I trust my memory at this point, Bash. I may have been imagining things."

Bash laughed and slathered some jam on a piece of roll. "I'd trust your memory more than anyone else's. I'm grasping at straws, but I thought it was worth a shot."

"What's going on, Bash?"

"Things aren't making sense. The fraud case is falling apart, now that Dewey's taken a runner."

"I'm sorry to hear that. Still no sign of him?"

"Someone used his Starbucks card to order coffee for pickup yesterday."

"Did he pick it up?"

"The store was wicked crowded, but the camera caught someone with a bright green jacket with *Bradford Funeral Home* on the front with a Bradford hat pulled down low," Bash said. "We couldn't see the face, but no one else had that color jacket. He had it ordered special. Didn't want to get yellow like the rest of the workers at the cemeteries. Not that he did the hard labor."

Lilly nodded. "That's interesting. About the coffee order. Maybe he'll order more soon."

"We're on the lookout," Bash said.

"I'm sorry, I interrupted you. Tell me what you can about the fraud case."

"I can't help but think the state investigations must have something to do with what happened to Whitney. But I think it's prudent to put together my own case, rather than rely on theirs."

"I'd imagine the investigations aren't only about Whitney. Perhaps her death has everything to do with what's been going on."

"Sasha and Dewey are under investigation, and they're both suspects in Whitney's murder. It's no wonder Dewey's laying low until things clear up."

"Do you think that Sasha's in trouble regarding the business investigation?"

"Probably," Bash said. "She's been in charge of the books for years. She says she had no idea what Whitney was up to, but she filed the taxes, did the town paperwork, and created the plot certificates. The paper trail leads to her."

"I have a friend who runs a funeral parlor in Marshton. She says that she's never gotten paperwork from Sasha that didn't need fixing. It's hard to reconcile both of those things."

"Maybe Whitney interfered at some point in the process."

"Maybe Sasha knew what was going on, but didn't want to know," Lilly said. "She got hit by a lot at a young age. First her mother, then her father. And Whitney being part of her life."

"And Dewey. I can't get a straight answer on whether he and Sasha were an item or not. She's sure protective of him."

"I heard from a friend of mine that Dewey was a player."

"Yeah, that's consistent with what I've been finding out. I wish I had a handle on where he's gone. These days, being off the grid is hard. To disappear completely, except for a coffee run?"

"I wonder if he'll reach out to Sasha."

"He may need her help," Bash said. "He's in more trouble than she is. I have a forensic accountant looking over the business, and it seems like Dewey was skimming from here, there, and everywhere. For all I know he may have been the mastermind, and Whitney may have been an innocent bystander."

Lilly cocked her head. "Not completely innocent. Tell me, have you spoken with Stan?"

"Not recently. Should I have?"

Lilly shook her head. "Just wondering."

"I'm going to trust you to keep me apprised of anything I need to know, Lilly."

"I will, I promise," Lilly said, buttering her roll some more.

"Anyway, you did send me all sorts of records on the cemetery. Would you go over them and write up any updates, or new thoughts?"

"If you think it would help, of course I will," Lilly said. "Is my family mausoleum in order?"

"All cleared out," Bash said. "It's still the site of an ongoing investigation, so you can't get in there for a while longer. It's actually out of my jurisdiction, but I'll check on it for you."

"That's fine. Let me know when I have it back," Lilly said. "Do you need me to look over the cemetery paperwork immediately?"

"Whenever you get a chance. I mostly want you to see if you remember anything else. Thanks for doing that, Lilly. Like I said, I'm grasping at straws, looking for something I'm missing. What else have you found out?" Bash asked.

"What do you mean? Nothing."

"Lilly—"

She sighed. "I'm not sure what it all means. Did you know that the tax assessment went up on several houses this past year? Including Whitney's? The same contractor did work on them all."

"And reported back to the town?"

"Not sure the order of occurrences, but it seems reasonable that Whitney got reassessed, and then told someone about all the other work her contractor had done."

Bash took out a notebook and wrote himself a note. "She was in wicked debt," he said. "I wonder how she afforded any work that would raise the assessment."

Lilly smiled at his favorite Massachusetts saying. "That's the question, isn't it? Why was she in such debt?"

"Whitney liked to gamble," Bash said. "High stakes."

"Wow. I had no idea."

"Not sure anyone did, except for Dewey. I just saw some footage of him down at the casino from a few weeks ago."

"That explains the need for infusions of cash, I guess. Dewey was skimming, Whitney was getting money from different sources."

"Yeah, lots of possible motives. Anyway, I will take that pizza if you're offering. Going to be another long day. You take care, Lilly. And let me know what you come up with, no matter how insignificant it seems. I want to get this sorted out."

"And make sure justice is served," Lilly said, smiling. She got up to wrap up some pizza.

"Exactly," Bash said.

"Sure, no problem. I'll be right over and take a look," Ernie said, walking into the kitchen. He shut off his phone and looked around the kitchen. "Did I hear you talking to someone?"

"Bash just left," Lilly said. "He wants me to write up what I remember about the cemetery."

"To help with the state investigators?"

"To help figure out what happened to Whitney," Lilly said. "I got the sense he was being frozen out of the state investigation. Since he's looking for suspects, other than Stan, he has to piece things together."

"I'm glad he's still looking," Ernie said.

"Me too. Who were you on the phone with? I thought you had the morning off."

"Jackie. She needs some help getting the screen windows down and the storm windows up. I told her I'd go over. I'm dying to see the house. Want to come with me?"

"I'd be happy to," Lilly said.

"Great. I'd rather walk, but I'm heading into work afterwards, so I'm going to drive. Can you go now?"

"I can," Lilly said. "Let me tell Delia where I'm going—"

"She's at the historical society."

"Again? What's she working on?"

"Somehow the cemetery research expanded into something else. She didn't want to go into it until she did some more research."

"We have that to look forward to, then. Lead on, my friend."

"Ernie, this is above and beyond," Jackie said, opening the door. "I didn't expect you to do house calls on your own. I thought you could give me someone to call."

"No worries," Ernie said. "Jackie, do you know Lilly Jayne? She's an expert at these old windows, so I brought her along."

"Jackie, I am sorry for the loss of your cousin. She was a wonderful neighbor for many, many years."

"I appreciated the note and basket," Jackie said. "And the gardening you did, to help brighten up cousin Helen's view. She always spoke highly of you and your family. I remember meeting your mother on several visits up here. What a lovely woman."

Jackie kept talking as they walked into the house. Since Helen had started to live on the first floor a few years ago, the rooms were well kept, with fresh paint and polished floors. But Jackie was leading them to the second floor, where Lilly had never been. "I've been cleaning these rooms and desperately need fresh air."

"Let me see what we've got here," Ernie said, going over to lift the window. It wouldn't budge. "Lilly, could you hand me the thingamajig?"

Lilly rifled through his toolbox until she found the five-in-one-tool and handed it to him. He ran the sharp edge along the side of the window.

"Hopefully this will break the paint seal," he said. "Lilly, can you push on the other side?"

After a few minutes the window stopped resisting

and let the weights help lift it up. The storm windows were newer, and after some lubricant the storms went up and the screens came down.

"That air is lovely," Jackie said. "That should be enough."

"Nonsense," Ernie said. "Once you figure out the steps with these windows, the rest will be easier."

"I don't know why she didn't replace them years ago," Jackie said.

"These rope and pulley windows work very well, especially when the window is oversized like this one," Lilly said. "Helen replaced the old ropes with chains several years ago. She took a class somewhere. She was proud of herself. With the new storms, they were actually very efficient."

"Unless they get painted shut," Ernie said. "You ready, Lilly?"

"Ready," Lilly said. She'd grown up fighting old windows and was happy to help. These windows were stunning, six feet tall, two-over-twos. "You know, I always used a bar of soap growing up, to keep the windows running up and down."

"I have some beeswax that will do the same thing," Ernie said, holding up a cake and handing it to Jackie. "Why don't you follow behind us and wax the side of the windows so that they open and close easier next time."

"Won't it make them close?"

"No, the weights will keep them up."

"I can't tell you how much I appreciate the help," Jackie said, doing as she was directed.

"These rooms are in good shape," Ernie said, looking around.

Jackie turned toward him and laughed. "No, they

aren't. This is such an odd old house. Not that big, which is why they built the carriage house. But it's got good bones. Bless Helen, leaving it to me. I wish she'd only left me the carriage house, but they come together."

"Why just the carriage house?" Ernie said.

"It's much smaller. All one floor, with extra space upstairs for guests. It's where I always stayed. She left me both houses because the other members of the family would have fought over them, so she thought leaving them money would be easier. Turns out, I'll need to sell them anyway."

"Why don't you talk to Tamara O'Connor. She may know of some options that are available to you. I'll write down her number," Ernie said.

"Would you mind meeting her with me?" Jackie asked. "I get overwhelmed."

"Of course," Ernie said. "I'd be happy to."

"If she hadn't been so hell-bent on clearing out before she died, I'd have something to sell," Jackie said. "But that's what happens when you live to be almost one hundred and you don't want to be a burden to people. You give all your things away."

"To relatives and friends, I hope," Lilly said.

Jackie continued to wax the windows with a fervor that belied her years.

"It makes me so darned mad," Jackie said. "I hate to feel like they took advantage of her."

"Who?" Ernie said, pulling the last screen in the room down.

"That Dewcy Marsh. She'd told me about him. That he was a charmer. Reminded me of my first husband. Who, I might add, lead me to rack and ruin, and did the world a favor by dying young. I know that sounds terrible, but trust me, you would have agreed. Helen never had children of her own, but was the family matriarch in many ways, helping kids go through school and—I'm sorry, that's not what we were talking about. We were talking about Kevin—"

"Dewey," Lilly said gently.

"Dewey. Kevin was my ex—oh, never mind. Helen had some beautiful Royal Doulton figurines. A huge collection of Pretty Lady figurines, some of them quite rare. And a Romeo and Juliet piece that I'd always loved. Anyway. When I came to visit last Christmas, I asked her about them, but she was vague. She said that Dewey was getting them appraised. When I came last month to be with her, I looked around but they still weren't there. I asked Dewey, but he said he didn't know. After Helen died, I went by their office to make arrangements and got the runaround. Over and over again. Dewey wouldn't see me, so they stuck me with Sally—"

"Sasha?"

"That's her. Sweet, but a bit dim. I mentioned the Dewey situation with the figurines, and she mentioned that he had a shop on eBay. Even wrote down the name. I checked it out and sure enough, there were a dozen Pretty Ladies up for sale as a set."

"Do you think they were Helen's?"

"There was a chip in one that was my fault. Yes, they were hers. Part of the set. I hope the rest didn't sell."

"What did you do?"

"I called my daughter. She filed a claim on them. Thankfully, he was asking a small fortune, so there weren't many bids."

"Did you tell Bash?" Lilly asked.

"Who's Bash?"

"The chief of police," Ernie said.

"Oh, I talked to him all right. But not about the figurines. He was too busy asking me for an alibi for the day Whitney was killed. I got the distinct impression that he thought I killed her. Which is ridiculous, even if I did say what they said I said."

"What did you say?" Ernie asked.

"That she should drop dead, and I'd be happy to help her with that," Jackie said.

"I can see how that might be a problem," Ernie said, smiling to offset his words. "You should reach out to Bash and tell him about the Royal Doultons. He's trying to do his job."

"We know the young man who is being blamed for her death," Lilly said. "We're trying to encourage the authorities to keep looking."

"I keep thinking I can't be the only person who had problems with her," Jackie said.

"Do you mind me asking about those problems?" Lilly asked. They'd moved to the next room and Ernie was working on the windows. Like the previous room, it was mostly empty and needed paint, but the bones were good. High ceilings, untouched woodwork, amazing plasterwork around the ceilings and the fireplace.

"First off, there was someone buried in Helen's spot. Whitney kept insisting that the spot didn't belong to the Garretts. Which, of course, it did. I'd been to all the family funerals. We knew where the plots were. Unfortunately for them, I found the paperwork bearing that out. But only yesterday. I'm not sure what to do with it now. I called Sasha this morning, but she told me she couldn't help me."

"Why don't I give you the name of another funeral home, over in Marshton. A friend of mine owns it. She may be able to help you," Lilly said. She was running the knife along the sides of the window, and helping Ernie force it up gently.

"I sure hope so," she said. "I'd like Helen to be able to rest in the place she's always wanted to. Soon."

"Had this happened to other people? Do you know?" Ernie asked.

"My daughter contacted a lawyer, and she's filed a slew of complaints. Seems like there are a few others, but it's hard to get a straight answer. She sent me some emails, but I haven't gone through them."

"Jackie, would you mind if I took a look at those emails?" Ernie said. "I'll keep you and your daughter out of this, but I'd love to get Bash some more leads."

"I'll send you everything I've got," Jackie said. "But I can't imagine you'll be able to make heads or tails of it."

"You'd be surprised," Ernie said. He stepped back and ran his hands down his jeans. "This side of the house is done."

"Thank you so much. Maybe now that I've seen how you did it, I can get the other windows open."

"Why don't you let Lilly and me help?"

"That would be wonderful, it really would. How about if I get us all some lemonade?"

"Sounds perfect," Lilly said, smiling at Ernie as Jackie fluttered out the door. She waited until she was gone, and then turned to Ernie. "Why the desire to open all the windows? She's got a nice breeze with these."

"But I want to see the rest of the house," Ernie said. "Don't you?"

Lilly smiled and took out another putty knife. She did, indeed, want to check out the rest of the house.

Chapter 31

"I just got the oddest call," Roddy said to Lilly as he walked in the back door.

"Well, hello to you too," Lilly said, laughing.

"Sorry, good afternoon. Oh, hello Delia. What are you both up to?"

"I'm showing Lilly some of my research on the cemeteries. I'm going to do some more today, with Minh."

"Bash has asked me to look at all of the notes, and see if I remember anything else that seemed off."

"I'm glad I took so many notes that first day, Lilly. Your memory is holding up to what I'm finding, so trust yourself," Delia said. "I'm hoping we can find some of the minutes from the cemetery board meetings. They've gotten very sloppy about filing them recently."

"Do they normally file committee notes?" Roddy asked.

"For a lot of years, the cemetery committee filed meeting minutes with the town, but it's been spotty. I called Portia for clarification. She said when Sam Bradford was on the cemetery committee with her, she wrote up all the notes and put them in the official files to keep him honest."

"Portia has a way with words, doesn't she?" Lilly said.

"She doesn't think that minutes are part of the by-laws for the committee, though. They should be, don't you think?"

"I'd imagine after all of this they will be," Roddy said.

"When did the changes in the cemetery really start happening?" Lilly asked Delia.

"Nineteen eighty-seven," Delia said, without hesitation.

"When did Sam's father die?" Lilly wondered aloud.

"Nineteen eighty-six," Delia said. "There's a flurry of changes from 1987 to 1994. Then the changes slow down until 2012."

"I'll bet those dates correspond to Sam's marriage to Gloria," Lilly said. "She was a few years older than Sam. Honestly, most folks thought he was going to stay single. He used to joke that his business chased people away. He met Gloria at some event. She worked for a chain of funeral homes in Maryland, so she understood the business well. They had Sasha right away and built up Bradford's, together."

"But you stopped using them," Delia said. "Can you tell me that story again, so that I can have some context around these dates?"

"Gloria got sick and stepped back from running the business day-to-day. My father, being my father, wanted to go over his plans with Sam, make sure that

the details were all worked out so that my mother
wouldn't have to worry. He called me after the meeting, beside himself. Sam kept trying to upsell him on
things, told him that it would cost him extra to use
the family mausoleum, you name it."

"Did you talk to Sam?"

"I was hoping things would blow over, honestly.
But then a friend of Dad's lost his wife unexpectedly,
and Sam talked him into a very expensive funeral.
Between that and the hospital bills, his friend almost
went bankrupt. Dad was furious. He refused to give
him the family business, so we found Evelyn."

"What happened to his friend?" Roddy asked.

Lilly sighed. "When I started making money and
helping with the house upkeep, my father had a little
more spending money. He started to invest and had
a nice little nest egg that built up. Whenever he or
my mother heard about someone who needed help,
they'd figure out a way to pitch in. This time, my father got someone at the wife's work to pretend that
she had a life insurance policy with a payout. They
went along and he got out of debt."

"That's a nice story," Delia said. "Your father
sounds like a really good man. It must have had some
weight when he decided not to use Bradford's."

"It was a blow to the Bradford business. After Dad
died, Sam spent a couple of years trying to make it
up to my mother, but she wasn't having it. Though
she wasn't as vocal about using another funeral home."

"When did Gloria die?" Roddy asked.

Delia tapped on a few keys. "In 2010. Makes sense
that things started to get hinky again if Gloria was
keeping him on the straight and narrow." She tapped

a few more keys and looked up at Lilly. "He married Whitney in 2011. Check out these past few years since she got into the picture. There were a lot of building permits put in on the house, the businesses, and the cemetery itself. I took copies of all the permits to add to the information we have."

"Tamara was going to pull the permits to look at contractors."

"I already emailed her the list. What's interesting to me is that Sam put in for some of the permits for the cemetery, but the work was never done."

"What kind of work?"

"New water pipes. Work on the walkways. Expansion into another location—"

"When did Sam die?" Roddy asked both women.

"Four years ago?" Lilly said. "It was during the fuzzy time in my life." The fuzzy time was after her mother, then Alan, got sick and died all within five years. Lilly hadn't focused on much else.

"Four years ago this December," Delia said. "Look at the changes in these past few months." She flipped through three images.

"How did you get these records?" Lilly asked.

"Every time they put in for a permit, someone goes out to take pictures. Digital photos are great for details, so I started to check on the background where I could. I'm using it to help with the cemetery modeling. I'm hoping I'll have something to show you this afternoon."

"You've done a lot of work on this," Lilly said.

"I agree with Bash," Delia said. "I think the cemetery has everything to do with Whitney's death."

"Wait, that's what I came over to talk to you

about," Roddy said. "You'll never believe the call I got from Sasha Bradford. Do you remember when she sent me plans? She was following up. Seems that a spot opened up and she wanted to give me first dibs."

"Aren't they shut down?"

"Apparently not," Roddy said. "I told her I'd come by the office this afternoon."

"What are we waiting for?" Lilly asked.

"Mr. Lyden, it's nice to see you," Sasha said. Her face froze when she saw Lilly. "Lilly, I didn't know you'd be here."

They walked into the office and sat down in the chairs facing Sasha. Lilly noticed a layer of dust in the streaming sunshine. There were folders piled up all over the office.

"Roddy is a friend," Lilly said. "He asked me about the plot, and I wondered about the location. I thought all of the space near Bertram's Folly was taken."

"Technically, yes. But Mr. Lyden indicated that he was planning on being cremated and wanted a marker. It's much easier to make room that way. Especially if he wants to be buried at sea. Markers can go anywhere."

"Surely not anywhere," Roddy said. "Don't people buy an entire plot?"

"They do, but they don't use it all, especially in the past. The plots were generous. We feel, on behalf of the Goosebush cemetery, that giving as many people their desired resting place is important. We've been rethinking available space."

"You've quoted me a price that seems in line for a full plot," Roddy said.

"There's still work, maintenance, and more that is folded into that price," Sasha said, freezing the smile on her face.

"Sasha, that doesn't sound right," Lilly said. "Isn't that tiny plot of land you're going to sell him right on top of another family plot?"

"It's all completely legal—" Sasha said.

"But surely a gray area," Lilly said. "If I went to the town hall, would this plot be registered with the cemetery committee?"

Sasha took a deep, ragged breath. "We're behind in paperwork."

"Weeks or months behind?"

"Months. I'm trying to catch up. Whitney said this spot was sold, but I don't have a certificate for the sale, and I need to have one. Please don't tell anyone—"

"Sasha, you can't make things up so that the paperwork works out. What would happen if Roddy bought that plot, and the person Whitney sold it to showed up?"

"I don't think they would," Sasha said.

"Because Whitney pretended to sell plots, but didn't."

"Oh Lilly, it's all so terrible," Sasha said, sitting down. "Sometimes she'd come in and make me run a credit card for two or three thousand dollars and she'd tell me she sold a plot, but then she wouldn't tell me where. I could never keep up, and now it's even worse. I thought that if I sold a few plots this week, it would make the books work out."

"Sasha, that's going to make it worse. You have to stop trying to cover up for Whitney."

"It isn't just Whitney—" Sasha stood up again and turned around to look out the window.

"I was telling Roddy about your mother earlier, and what a wonderful job she did running the business," Lilly said gently. "I wonder, would she be happy about the way things have been going?"

Sasha shook her head but she didn't turn around.

"Did Dewey sell plots as well? Sasha?"

"Sometimes, but Whitney signed off on all the sales." She turned back around and sat at the desk.

"Sasha, did you know that Dewey used you as an alibi for the afternoon Whitney was killed?"

"He did?" she whispered.

"He did. Do you know where he is? Dewey?"

Sasha looked up at Lilly and started to cry. She ran out of the room.

Lilly stood up and walked around the desk. She looked at the paperwork strewn across it and at some of the folders. She was careful not to touch anything.

"She's got Post-its in these folders. There's a few on these documents. Questions that need to be answered on old paperwork, clarifications. I can't tell if this is part of an audit, or part of the investigation," Lilly said. "Sasha's going to need a good lawyer."

Roddy and Lilly waited for a few more minutes, then they decided to leave. Roddy had walked around the office and took some pictures of files, using a pen to open folders.

"Sasha, we're leaving," Lilly called out as they

walked to the front door. "Call me if you want to talk." She stood and listened for a few seconds, but didn't hear anything.

"I suppose I should have been gentler with her," Lilly said.

"I think you did her a favor. It looked like she was making several calls like the one she made to me. She would have spent the afternoon digging herself a bigger hole."

"She must be desperate to fix things," Lilly said. She opened the front door and looked back at Roddy. "What's all this?"

The swirling lights were barely visible in the afternoon haze, but Bash had them on as he drove up to the office. He got out of his car and lumbered over to Roddy and Lilly as they moved down the steps.

"What are you two doing here?" Bash asked. He wasn't smiling.

"Sasha called about selling me a plot," Roddy said.

"The area she mentioned was barely a space," Lilly said.

"We decided to come down here and ask for more details."

"Which you're going to share with me, correct?" Bash said.

"Naturally," Lilly said.

"Did you buy it?"

"No."

"She's in over her head, Bash," Lilly said.

"You think?"

"She left the room and didn't come back. I think I upset her," Lilly said.

"Lilly mentioned her mother and that seemed to do her in," Roddy said.

"I'm not going to help calm her down," Bash said. "I've been sent by Darlene Daniel."

"To ask Sasha more questions?"

"To arrest her," Bash said. "Seems like she's been forging people's names on some paperwork."

"I don't suppose you could say whose?" Lilly said.

"Mentioning Mac Townsend wouldn't be appropriate," Bash said, looking at Lilly. "Mac had to sign off on all burials until he retired last winter."

"I doubt she'd do anything like that on her own."

"Whitney's dead and Dewey's gone, so she's going to get the blame," Bash said. "Darlene sounded almost giddy at all the boxes that were being ticked."

"Sounds a little too convenient," Roddy said.

"Agreed, but I have to serve this warrant," Bash said.

"I've got some information to share with you later," Lilly said. "Delia's putting it all together now. Do me a favor. Don't let Sasha talk to anyone without a lawyer."

"You're awfully protective of her."

"Listen, she's not the sharpest knife in the drawer, but I don't think she should bear all of the blame for what Whitney, and probably Dewey, did," Lilly said.

"From what Delia has been researching, it looks like her father may have been doing shady things. Which means those are the business practices Sasha was taught," Roddy said.

"Poor girl is a useful idiot," Lilly said.

Bash sighed. "Can you get her a lawyer? I'll make sure she asks for one."

"You're a good man, Bash Haywood."

"I hope you've got some other ideas I can share with Darlene. Because she's not going to be happy."

"None yet, but we'll keep working on it, I promise."

"I'll be looking forward to your call," Bash said. He straightened his hat and went over to the office door and knocked. Roddy and Lilly drove away, not waiting to see how this would end for Sasha.

Chapter 32

"I appreciate the help with this, Lilly," Roddy said a little while later. He had rolled up his shirt-sleeves and was digging holes in his garden. "Emma is coming down this Sunday, and I'd like the garden to look a little bit more put together."

"I'm sure she's coming down to see you, not the gardens," Lilly said, but she didn't push. Roddy's relationship with his daughter was getting better, especially since he moved to Goosebush and made an effort to see her and his granddaughter regularly. His daughter was still wary about trusting her father, though, waiting for him to be called away on business for months at a time. Roddy blamed himself for their relationship issues, and tried his best to be patient.

"Still, it would be nice if they were in better shape."

"Roddy, it's only May. You're starting from ground zero, and you see it every day. I don't see it as often, and I see changes every time I'm over here. The grasses will fill in some spots and also add heights. But they do spread, so let's be judicious. I've sorted them into the three types I had in the greenhouse. Why don't you put the pots around the garden, and we'll step back and make sure it looks good. Then we'll get them in the ground."

Over the course of the next half hour they moved plants, stepped back, and moved them again. Roddy was much more precise in his garden planning, but then the original plan had been designed by Florence Winslow, an apprentice of the famous garden designer Forest Hunter.

Lilly occasionally checked her phone to see if there was any news from Bash, but there weren't any texts.

"We can always get more grasses," Lilly said. "I gave some to Ernie to sell. I can check if there are any left—"

"No, I think you were right. These will be lovely spots of color, but more would be overwhelming." He muttered to himself as he picked up two more pots to put them in the garden.

"Do you have Sasha's cell phone number?" Lilly asked.

"I might," Roddy said. He took off his gardening gloves and checked his emails. "It's in the signature of her email to me. I forwarded it to you."

"Thanks," Lilly said. "Are you almost ready to plant?"

"Three more minutes."

She smiled. He'd said that five times already. She opened her email and copied Sasha's cell phone number. She put it in the text messenger, but then she stopped.

"I want to send Sasha a text, but I'm not sure what

to say," Lilly said. "I feel badly that she's all alone. At least Stan has us."

"He does," Roddy said. "I suspect for both of them, the loss of Whitney or Buzz must be complicated. I hope, and pray, that when my time is up, my daughter doesn't have complicated feelings."

"She won't," Lilly said. "But you're right. From what Stan told me, Buzz complicated his life, and not in a good way. Having Buzz's death investigated likely adds fuel to the speculative fire."

"I thought that they'd decided Buzz died of a heart attack?"

"Two deaths in as many months, with the relationship between the two? I'd be surprised if they weren't doing more investigating."

"Wouldn't the *they* be Bash?"

"It would be, but Whitney was under state investigation. I'd imagine there are a lot more people looking at the cases now. Especially if Stan told Bash everything he told me."

"I hope he took your advice and came clean," Roddy said. "I hope he appreciates your discretion."

"I sent him two texts and left a message. The message said that if he didn't tell Bash, I would. I know it complicates things for Stan. I really hope he understands that the only way through all of this is by telling the truth," Lilly said, taking her phone back out of her pocket. She started another text to Stan, but didn't hit *send*. "How are you doing back there?"

Roddy placed the last two grasses and he walked over and stood next to Lilly. "What do you think?"

"Go upstairs and look at it through one of the windows," she said.

"Upstairs?"

Your bedroom's on this side of the house. So is the hallway, and your office. Make sure that view is as wonderful as it is down here. In fact, you may want to design some parts of your gardens for your view. Maybe taller plants, or brighter colors. A pattern that makes you smile."

"You can't see your gardens from your rooms, can you?" Roddy asked.

"I used to be able to, when Alan and I had our rooms on the other side of the house. But I switched rooms, and now I have a wonderful water view that I'd be hard-pressed to give up. Delia and Ernie can both see the gardens. That's why Delia's meditation bench is where it is—she can see it from upstairs."

"I hadn't thought of the upstairs view. My plan is to redo the bedroom in the front of the house, but there's a lot of water damage in there," Roddy said, looking up behind him and smiling. He loved his renovation projects, none of which had overwhelmed him to date.

"You know, I hadn't really paid attention to that wall," Lilly said. "It does need some work."

"The bowing is concerning, but I've been told that some well-placed braces could help."

"I'd imagine so," Lilly said, walking toward the back wall. "The first thing we need to do is to continue fighting the ivy fight, though you've made great strides in the effort."

"I hired people to help with that twice last year. Our discussion about boxwoods got me thinking. A thicket of trees or shrubs would help hide the wall and may be interesting, especially if they were a well-planned garden. That said, I need to deal with the wall soon. I'd hate to do all this work and have the wall crush the gardens."

"Bracing can be added to reenforce the wall, but it would need to be done on both sides."

"Perhaps it would serve me to offer to pay for the wall to be repaired before the Garrett house is sold, so that it stays in place. I'd imagine the house may be torn down and the lot divided, don't you think."

"I think so, which makes me sad," Lilly said. "That street doesn't have as many building codes. Since the lot is long, but narrow, you're right. They could fit three houses back there. Ernie and I got a tour this morning and the house is charming. It would be a real shame to lose it."

"I'd love to see inside," Roddy said.

"I'm sure it can be arranged. Hello, what's this?"

Lilly and Roddy had been walking along the back wall toward Lilly's house. There were several over-grown cedars in the corner, so she'd never ventured behind them. Or thought she could. But she walked close to the back wall and looked to the side.

"What's that?"

Roddy pushed the branches aside. "It looks like a door in the wall."

"It does indeed," Lilly said. "I'll tell you what, let's walk over to the Garrett house and see if the door is there. I have a question I want to ask Jackie, and this will give me a good excuse. But first, let's get these grasses in so that they can settle into their new home."

"That can wait until tomorrow. I want to think about the upstairs view. Why don't we see what we can find out about the door?"

* * *

"Thank you so much for helping us satisfy our curiosity," Lilly said and she walked into Helen Garrett's backyard with Jackie and Roddy. "I was helping Roddy get some grasses in, and we noticed that the wall was bowing—"

"Oh dear, that doesn't sound good," Jackie said.

"Ms. Ross—" Roddy started.

"Jackie, please."

"Jackie, you and I share this wall. Its repair was in my plans anyway, so I'll take on the work."

"That's a relief. Thank you, Mr. Lyden—"

"Roddy," Roddy said, smiling.

"As you can see, my cousin and her family had quite the gardens back here. I've been enjoying working in them, though they are overgrown. Helen was always good about keeping up with them, even in her waning years."

"She loved gardening," Lilly said, smiling. Neighbors, friends, and the local Girl Scout troop had helped her with the work, especially the last few years. Helen had been good at asking for help when needed, a trait that Lilly admired. She hoped she did the same when her gardens got to be too much.

"Now tell me about what you're looking for," Jackie said.

"We were looking at the wall, and noticed that behind three cypresses in his backyard the wall changed a bit, and then we saw what looked like a door," Lilly said.

Roddy looked up and saw the three cypresses reaching up over the wall. "The door should be over this way, though it may be challenging to get to it," he said.

The Garretts had been fond of rosebushes. The front bushes flourished, but the climbing roses that had been on the back wall were long since dead, though the branches still hugged the wall.

"Good thing we brought our gloves," Lilly said, smiling.

"I'll go get mine," Jackie said. "I've wanted to clear some of this. You can help me figure out what's worth saving. If you have time?"

"We have an hour or so," Lilly said. "Let's see what we can get done."

As it turned out, the climbing roses were very, very dead. Jackie brought out some gardening tools and they cut the branches, and then started to pull them away from the wall. There were some scratches, but the three of them came up with a system and the work went quickly.

"That's a big mess," Lilly said, pointing to the debris in the middle of the yard. "I'll get someone to come by and haul it to the town chipper."

"The town chipper? What's that?"

"Part of the dump," Lilly said. "Not everyone can use it, but on chipping days people bring branches and the like down to the dump. The mulch that is created is added to a large pile that anyone can use."

"That would be wonderful. There are a few branches that came down this winter—"

"Ernie can get a cleanup crew here," Lilly said.

"I'm not sure I can afford that—"

"The crew is volunteer," Lilly said, smiling. She'd talk to Ernie about it, but helping Helen Garrett's family out seemed like a good plan, and one that Lilly could underwrite if necessary.

"You are wonderful," Jackie said. "What a difference clearing those branches made. Helen kept wanting those roses to come back, but they were obviously beyond hope."

"They were," Lilly said. "The trees back here created shadows as they grew. The front roses do well because they get enough sunlight. You'd be better off planting a garden of shade plants. Or you could trim the tree branches back a bit."

"Sadly, this will all need to be decided by the next owner. Thank you for your help, Lilly. Between fixing windows and clearing a thorny thicket, this has been a full day for you."

"It has," Lilly said. "In between Roddy and I went by to see Sasha Bradford."

Jackie straightened up and shook her head. "And I thought that unclogging the upstairs sink was a gruesome task this afternoon."

Lilly laughed. Roddy had waded toward another section of the wall, and Lilly and Jackie collected the branches as he hacked them away.

"Poor Sasha, that wasn't kind. She's not really that bad. Just dim, but that's nothing new, poor dear," Jackie said.

"Do you know her?" Lilly asked.

"I've known her for years. The Bradfords went to the same church as my cousin, and they'd go to the same service, so I always saw them at the coffee afterwards."

Lilly smiled. A lot of Goosebush business got done at those coffee hours.

"Sasha always seemed a bit lost, especially after her mother died," Jackie said.

"Had she been helping you with your cousin's . . . um, situation?" Lilly asked.

"She was trying to get me answers. Whitney was a roadblock on that front."

"What do you mean?" Lilly asked.

"The Garretts had a huge family plot," Jackie said. "There was room for Helen and one more Garrett. I thought about using it myself, ever since my last husband and I divorced. The last thing I want is to be laid to rest next to him, let me tell you what. But then Whitney tried to tell me it was only a double plot, or that I was mistaken, and her brother's plots were part of what her father had bought. Which I knew was a lie. Why was Helen's name on the tombstone already? I asked her."

"What did she say?" Lilly asked.

"She didn't. Sasha mentioned that Whitney was looking through all the records, trying to figure out where the mix-up had been."

"Maybe the plots got sold, and Helen forgot?"

"No, not sold," Jackie said. "Helen owned them outright, and paid to have all six plots tended to."

"What's happened to Helen?" Lilly asked gently.

"I'm trying to get this straightened out, but until then, everything's on hold. The other bodies have been there for about ten years."

"So they predate Whitney," Lilly said.

"Yup. Again, I got this from Joe—he and his son dig the graves—but it looks like the bodies aren't even Bradford jobs. He did some research for me before they locked down all the records. They were buried by another funeral home over in Kingsfield."

"Have you told this to the people who were investigating the Bradfords?" Lilly asked.

"Have I? I'm the reason they're investigating the

Bradfords," Jackie said. "When all of this happened I raised holy hell."

"I'd imagine you did—"

"Found it!" Roddy called out.

Lilly carefully made her way to where Roddy was standing in the garden. "The door?" she asked.

"The door," he said. "It looks like it needs a key. Though the wood is in terrible shape. I wonder why there's a door here?"

"I know why," Jackie said. "I'd forgotten all about this. This used to be a large wrought iron fence. During the war, World War Two, a lot of the ironworks were donated for the war effort. The entire fence was taken out and melted down."

"I wish I could have seen the fence," Roddy said.

"I'm sure there are pictures. I'll find them for you," Jackie said. "During the war there were people who needed work, so the Garretts had the brick wall built. But Helen and the son of the family who lived behind here, I don't remember their name. Dammit, sorry, I just thought 'Oh, I'll ask Helen.' I forgot I can't. Anyway, Helen and the son were in love, so they asked that a door be built in the wall so they could visit."

"What happened to the young man?"

"He didn't make it through the war," Jackie said. "Helen never talked about him much, but she did keep a picture of him by her bed. Imagine that. She lived to be almost a hundred and he didn't see thirty. All those years missing him, loving him. Of course Helen would be really ticked off that I thought her life was sad. She always said she'd been lucky to have a great love, and that was enough."

"She always struck me as very happy," Lilly said gently. "She worked, traveled, volunteered."

"Yeah, listen to me. I've been married twice and neither time took. She was happy, our Helen. But that's the story of the door. When she knew he wasn't coming back, she must have planted that rosebush. Now that it's down, I see what you mean about the wall. It shouldn't dip like that, should it?"

"I'll have someone come and look at it," Roddy said. "The wrought iron wall intrigues me. If you don't mind, I'd love any pictures of my house you can find. I'd be intrigued to see it from this angle. It may give me some gardening ideas."

"I'm going through her things now, and I'll take out anything you may be interested in."

"Jackie, are you going to have a service for Helen?" Lilly asked gently. "I understand if it's private, but I'd love to be there to pay my respects."

"Just as soon as the investigation wraps up," Jackie said. "If I'd known what can of worms I was opening up, I would have kept my mouth shut like Whitney asked."

"Whitney asked you to stay quiet?"

"Not asked. She threatened me. Did a little research on me, and found out some trouble my ex had a few years back. She said she'd tell Helen and everyone else. Like I cared. I told her to take a flying leap. She got me so mad I could have killed her."

Chapter 33

"**I** wonder if she could really kill Whitney?" Lilly asked. She and Roddy had helped Jackie clean up the gardens a bit more before they left. Roddy had taken some pictures of the wall, and promised again to get someone in to look at it. In return, Jackie said she'd put aside anything that had to do with his house.

"I'm sure it was an exaggeration, though she is feisty. She and Helen were first cousins?" Roddy asked, taking a left. They'd decided to drive the long way back to Lilly's house. Lilly had felt lazy driving to Helen's, but was glad they had. Wrestling rosebushes was exhausting.

"No, second or third. Helen didn't have any direct relatives left. She'd outlived them all."

"A hundred years old is a long time," Roddy said. "I'm not sure I want to live that long, myself. Losing everyone you knew would be difficult."

"Helen was very good at making multigenerational friends," Lilly said. "She and my mother were the same generation, but she was a friend of mine. She volunteered with the Girl Scouts up until ten years ago, and taught art for years. Up until the last year, she was going strong."

"Did you know about her wartime love?"

"No, I didn't," Lilly said. "I wonder if my father did. He lived here then. He had a heart ailment that kept him from going overseas, but he had a brother who served. I'm sure either he or my grandmother knew the story."

"The idea of the iron fence in the back of the house fascinates me," Roddy said. "It also helps explain the cypress trees. You said there used to be more?"

"Yes, all along the back. I'm sorry now that I didn't ask Helen more about her house when I had a chance. Oh, that's right, Delia—"

"Delia what?" Roddy said, pulling up to Lilly's driveway. He put the code in the keypad and waited while the gate slowly opened.

"I'd forgotten about one of Delia's projects. She went to all the neighbors and asked questions about their houses," she said. "She took it on right after Alan died. She'd been exploring our family archives and got curious. I also think she wanted to keep me distracted. I believe she went and spoke with Helen. We can ask her about that."

"That's wonderful," Roddy said. He slowly drove down the driveway, closing the gate behind him while opening the garage door. He didn't turn down the curve of the driveway until he knew the gate was completely closed. "My curiosity was piqued."

"I saw that," Lilly said, smiling. She looked down at

her phone and back up at Roddy. "What's this? Sasha sent me an email." She handed him the phone.

"Did you send her one?"

"I did, a quick one, apologizing for upsetting her. I let her know that I was here if she needed help."

"Even if she's a murderer?" Roddy said.

"Even if," Lilly said. "I don't think Sasha is a cold-blooded killer. Far from it. But I do think that she may have felt pushed by Whitney, and possibly by Dewey. She may be feeling desperate. I don't want her to feel alone."

"She seems to have taken you up on the request for help," Roddy said. "It's hard to see on the phone, but it appears that she sent you a spreadsheet of cemetery plots." He handed Lilly back her phone and pulled into the garage, driving the car up the ramp.

"Delia has the official town records," Lilly said.

"It will be interesting to see if they are the same," Roddy said, smiling at Lilly. "But it will have to wait until I go home and take a shower."

"Good idea," Lilly said. Roddy raised an eyebrow and she laughed. "For both of us. You did a lot of work in Jackie's yard."

"We all did," Roddy said. "Many hands make light work, as you've taught me many times this past year."

Roddy made no move to get out of the car, so Lilly sat.

"You know, I went through my life believing that I had to figure everything out on my own, and then live with the decisions I'd made. Coming here, buying a house that needed repair, I decided to try and live differently," Roddy said, turning and looking at

Lilly. "Ask for and accept help. You've made that easy for me. You are a generous spirit when sharing your knowledge, and your friendship. Thank you, Lilly. I count the day I crashed your garden party a year ago to be one of the best days of my life."

Lilly reached over and took Roddy's hand. She held it for a moment and smiled at him. "Roddy, that day was one of my best. Our friendship is something I didn't expect, and am grateful for."

"Lilly, should we—" Roddy was interrupted by his ringing phone. He let go of Lilly's hand and picked it up, immediately hitting the speaker button.

"Delia, hello, we're—"

"I think I found something," she said. "I'll be home in fifteen minutes."

"Where's Roddy?" Delia said as she came into the kitchen. The cats followed her and she put her backpack down, leaned down, and patted them both. "It's not time for dinner, so you may as well go back and nap."

Max and Luna looked at her, then back at Lilly, who shrugged her shoulders. "Can't help you," she said. "Delia's right, dinner's an hour away. Though I'm making tea for the humans. You wouldn't like it." She smiled and went back to setting cookies on a plate.

"Roddy's next door taking a shower," Lilly said. "We ended up helping Jackie Ross with some gardening while we were looking for the door."

"What door?"

"A door in the wall between his house and hers,"

Lilly said. She told her about the wall and the reason for the door.

"That's interesting and a new-to-me story," Delia said. "It's kind of sad too."

"It is," Lilly said. "Though I want you to remember that Helen lived a long, full life and seemed fairly happy to me. One path was closed, but she explored others with great success."

"You're right, I guess," Delia said. "It's only that— do you think people only have one great romance in their life?"

"Are you thinking about Stan?" Lilly asked, turning toward her young friend with her full attention. Delia didn't share her feelings easily, or often.

"I guess," Delia said. "I'm still pretty sad about all of this."

"Of course you are," Lilly said. "When Pete left me I was devastated. As it turns out, of course, that was a blessing and left me open to meet, and appreciate, Alan. In answer to your question? No, I don't think there's only one great love out there. I also think that there are many kinds of love. If you're asking me if Stan was your only chance at love, the answer is no."

"Thanks, Lilly," Delia said. "That's good to remember, that there can be more than one great romance in our lives. How about if I set up out on the porch?"

"Please," Lilly said. "I'll be right there."

Lilly put the rest of the food on the tea tray and carried it out to the porch. Delia had pulled out the whiteboard, a huge monitor, and piles of paper that she left on the table. Roddy came into the porch and hurried over to Lilly, taking the tray from her and giving her a smile.

"Sorry it took me so long," Roddy said. "My muscles needed extra time in the shower."

"Mine did as well. That rosebush was a lot of work," Lilly said.

"I heard you found a door," Delia said. "That's exciting."

"It is," Roddy said. "I'm not sure there's a need for it now, but the story is lovely. I look forward to seeing what the iron fence looked like between the houses. Jackie is going to try and find me pictures."

"I'll see if I have any, but I don't think so. I gave you what I had. Please share what she finds with me," Delia said. "I thought that the wall along the back of your house was from the same period as the wall at Lilly's. An iron fence, open, shows that Lilly's relatives really did buck the norms of the time."

"Of course they did," Lilly said. "I can't say as I'm not grateful for that. I like my privacy."

"Now that our gate's open, I like it too," Roddy said. "Now, Delia, don't keep me in suspense. What did you find?"

"I found the original charter for the cemetery," she said. "Plus the official records for the past hundred years. Minh's been scanning them. Here they are." She hit a couple of keys on her computer and an image popped up on the monitor.

"Hello, a new toy?" Roddy asked, leaning forward.

"I've been teaching online a lot," Delia said. "I can use this to stand up and teach, or as a way to share my screen so that I can see it, but also be looking at the camera. I thought it would be helpful for Garden Squad working dinners."

"Indeed it will," Roddy said. "Sorry to interrupt, go on."

"Ready, Roddy? I'm going to blow your mind even more. Let's split the screen." She hit another button and the layers of cemetery layouts she'd been working with came up on different windows. "I've been using that design software you taught me. See these numbers? They're the original plot numbers. Here's the listing from the original charter. Lilly, here's your family plot."

She circled some numbers on her tablet, and Roddy smiled. He and Delia loved tech gadgets. Lilly knew she'd have to work hard to keep them on task.

"Over here? These are the costs for a plot. All public record. I'll email you both copies of the charter, but there is a part that says if a plot wasn't used within seventy-five years, it would revert back to the town unless other arrangements were made."

"Arrangements?"

"A fee to the town," Delia said. "They also added plots over time. See here? Plot D 522-A? Section D, row five, plot twenty-two, and then another plot was added. In this case, it was for another family member."

"Those are pretty meticulous records," Lilly said.

"Very. Until here." Delia flipped through layers, and then records, and then came to another screen. "See? Plots were added, but the location wasn't clear. I mean, they used the same codes, but some of them went to a J subset, which would mean that one plot was divided into ten, which doesn't make sense. Then the costs went from numbers to codes. I can't find out what they mean."

"When did the records start to go awry?"

"Nineteen eighty-six or so," Delia said. "The year Sam Bradford's father died."

"Sasha Bradford sent Lilly an email earlier," Roddy said. "Have you had a chance to look at it, Lilly?"

"Not yet. I thought I sent it to you both," Lilly said. "Here you go." She took out her phone and forwarded the email to both Delia and Roddy.

Delia opened it up and put it on the monitor.

"Whoa," Delia said. "Look at all of those color codes. I wonder what they mean?"

"Scroll down," Lilly said. "Do you see how there are blocks of that blue color? Can you do a search on a name? Try Garrett?"

Delia input the search and found several names came up. There were six original entries and then one in blue, and one in purple and one in red.

"That may help you figure them out," Lilly said. "I think these are Bradford records, not public."

"And Sasha sent them to you?"

"She's in trouble," Lilly said. "She may have sent them out so that I can help her."

"Or, perhaps, so that you can make it right?" Roddy said. "It could be that her family's business practices have given her pause. You may have awoken some guilt in her."

"Perhaps," Lilly said. "Do you see over there, the Garrett blue entry? That was done in 2014. See the note on the side? It says *DCM*. I wonder what that means?"

Delia scrolled for a few minutes and then looked back at Lilly. "I don't know, but the blue entries I've seen have the same three letters in the notes section."

"More mysteries," Roddy said.

"But lots of ways to try and solve them," Delia said, tapping away at her computer. Roddy sidled his chair closer and they began to talk. Lilly smiled and poured everyone a cup of tea. It was going to be a long afternoon.

"Do you need me to walk you through it one more time?" Delia asked Bash later that evening. Lilly had called him, inviting him to dinner and telling him they wanted to talk to him, unofficially. He'd arrived at the same time as a food delivery and had helped Lilly bring the Greek food to the back porch. They'd set up a separate table for eating their very late lunch, and let Delia and Roddy use the dining table for their computers. Because of the monitor, Lilly could sit on the couch and pay attention, while using the fresh pita to capture the feta cheese.

"No, thanks," Bash said, smiling at Delia. "Three times through and I think it's finally sunk in. This must be what Darlene was crowing about earlier. Sasha spent hours with her. Though she doesn't have all of your records, Delia, so she probably doesn't have the full picture you've put together."

"To be fair, talking it through helped me understand it better," Delia said. "I would have liked to go over it more by myself, but Lilly insisted we call you."

"Once you and Roddy started to understand Sasha's spreadsheet, it seemed to me that this was evidence that Darlene would find useful, but she wouldn't share the information, so calling Bash made sense."

"I appreciate that, Lilly," Bash said. "She'd probably find it really interesting. Will find it interesting. But first I have to figure out how it helps me solve Whitney's murder."

"You think that one has something to do with another?" Roddy asked.

"If I've learned one thing over the past year or so, it's this: Assume that everything has something to do with everything until you prove something different. Too many coincidences."

"Do you think Buzz's death has anything to do with Whitney's?"

"Buzz's death is still inconclusive, but I can't see how they're related. Whitney and Buzz barely knew each other." Bash looked around the room. "Right?"

Lilly took a long sip of tea. So, Stan still hadn't told Bash about Whitney's blackmailing his father. What should she do? On the one hand, it gave Stan a motive. But on the other hand, it showed another side to Whitney. Surely Buzz wasn't the only person Whitney was blackmailing. And that could be important. She took another sip of tea.

"Buzz drank a lot," Delia said quietly. "Sometimes I'd drive him home to help Stan out. One night we walked by Whitney and Dewey in the parking lot. Buzz started screaming at her, called her a filthy cow who was bleeding him dry. Dewey helped me get him in the car. I asked Buzz what that was about, and he said that she was a blackmailing bitch. Then he passed out."

"Did you hear this story?" Bash asked Lilly.

"I didn't tell Lilly," Delia said. "It made Stan seem—"

"Guilty?" Bash said. "Because if he knew Whitney was shaking down his father—"

"Had you heard that Whitney was a blackmailer from anyone else?" Roddy asked, looking over at Lilly and furrowing his brow for a moment before recovering.

"The forensic accountant said that her expenses far outweighed her income, even if you included credit cards and mortgages. By thousands of dollars. Blackmail makes sense. Dammit, I wish I had her computer."

"Doesn't murder outweigh bad business practices?" Lilly asked. "Shouldn't you have access to that?"

"I should," Bash said. "They're telling me that I'll get to go over it in the next couple of days. I think that Darlene wants to solve the whole enchilada herself. She's dragging her heels. That's why I didn't want to meet at the station, or have you send me an email. She's moved into the office."

"What do you think?" Lilly asked.

"I think that Dewey did a runner," Bash said. "Sasha admitted to me that she and Dewey weren't together, so he didn't have an alibi."

"Neither did Sasha," Delia said.

"She met with her therapist," Bash said. "I verified the alibi a little while ago."

"Why didn't she tell you earlier?" Lilly asked.

"Because I think the poor kid believed Dewey when he said he loved her. Problem is, I can't close the investigation without questioning him."

"So you're at a standstill?" Lilly asked.

"Yeah, but maybe all of this will close a few of the loops I have open," Bash said, standing up. "Or at least it gives me something to trade with Darlene."

"Keep us posted?" Lilly said.

"I'll tell you what I can," Bash said. "Thanks for the food. No, don't get up. Thanks for recording that last run-through, Delia. Unofficially, I'm going to look it over a couple of more times, and I'll text you any questions. Night, all." They heard him say goodbye to the cats, as he left through the kitchen.

"I need to buzz him out of the gate," Delia said, looking down at her phone and reading a text from Bash. "We really should give him a code, don't you think?" She scurried into the kitchen to hit the button.

"Do you think Dewey killed Whitney?" Roddy asked.

"I think that someone sure wants him to take the fall," Lilly said. "Question is, should he?"

Chapter 34

"Honestly, would it kill them to call me, rather than send a text?" Lilly asked, hitting the gas a little heavier than needed. "And a little advance notice would have been nice. I'm glad that someone let me know that the mausoleum was basically open. The only thing that's been keeping people out is crime scene tape, according to the picture. Hardly a deterrent."

"Ernie's sending someone right over," Roddy said, looking at his phone. "Though getting a locksmith in who can change the key is specialty work. He mentioned welding—"

"I don't really care that it's pretty or not," Lilly said. "I want the family to rest in peace, and not be bothered by interlopers. Bash had me believing that it was secure."

"Maybe we should call him—" Roddy said.

"Roddy, jump out and see if you can open the gate from out here."

"Yes ma'am," he said, opening the door to the car and trying the front gate.

"Sorry, I don't mean to be bossy," Lilly said, leaning out of his side of the car.

"No worries," he said, coming back in the car. "I can't get the gate open from out here. Should we wait until morning?"

"I don't want to wait. Maybe you can open it from inside," Lilly said. "Good thing I have another way to get in. Hopefully you can open the gate for the locksmith."

"We're not going to climb over the fence again, are we?"

"We most certainly are. We've still got an hour or so of daylight," Lilly said, taking a right and pulling over to the side of the road. "Though I really need to talk to someone about this fencing. Anyone can get in this way."

Roddy laughed and waited for Lilly by the fence. He held her bag as she climbed over, holding her elbow to keep her steady. They'd had a full day of gardening and both were feeling aches and pains. Roddy swung one leg over, and then the other.

"How do you do that?" Lilly asked.

"I used to ride horses," Roddy said. "It's sort of the same principle."

Now it was Lilly's turn to laugh. "Of course it is. Okay, cowboy, I guess we should head over to the gate." She looked over to her left, toward the large gray block in the distance.

"Tell you what: Why don't you head over to the Jayne crypt, and use your key to lock the door. I'll go to the front gate and try to open it. That way if, for any reason, the locksmith finds another way in, the work can get started."

"All right," Lilly said, smiling. She walked over to her left, along the side road. When she arrived she was breathless. She realized she'd been running, or as close to running as Lilly got these days. When she got there, she went to the door and opened it. It swung easily, and she cursed.

"Sorry, everyone, didn't mean to swear," she said, looking around. There were bits and pieces of crime scene tape still stuck to the door. She put her bag on the ground and fished through it until she found a trash bag. She started carefully pulling the tape off the door, cursing softly while she did it.

She had one foot on the lip of the mausoleum and was reaching up for the last bit of tape when she felt a hard shove. She toppled a bit and grabbed onto the door. She felt an arm go around her waist and clawed at the bright green jacket that was crushing her ribs. The arm shifted and she reached down and dug her nails into the hand that squeezed her waist. Her feet were lifted up off the ground and she was pushed inside the crypt. She fell on her hands and knees and looked back. She saw another flash of green, then darkness. The door was closed and she heard the lock turn.

The term *dark as a tomb* took on new meaning for Lilly. She crawled over to the door, reaching out in front of her. When she felt the steel door, she pulled herself up. Her back seized, and she leaned over with her hands on her thighs, breathing through the pain.

She straightened up as much as she could, and felt along the door for the handle. There wasn't one. She swallowed the bile that had risen in her throat.

She patted down her pockets, but they were empty. Her phone was in her bag, which was outside. There were tiny shafts of light from the grates at the top of the building, but not enough for her to know where she was. Afraid to move, lest she trip and fall, Lilly let out a scream. The heavy granite building absorbed the sound. Surely Roddy would be there soon.

Breathe in, breathe out. She knew she was starting to panic, and hoped that old trick would help. Breathe in, breath out. Problem was, the air was still and musty. She heard a sound behind her and turned. She stepped backward, but lost her footing, falling again. Pain seared up her side, and she passed out.

"Lilly, Lilly! Wake up! Lilly!" Lilly looked up and saw Roddy's face. She realized he was kneeling on the floor, holding her hand.

"Roddy?" She tried to move, but her back seized again.

"I'm here, darling, please don't move," he said. "An ambulance is on the way."

"I don't need an ambulance," she said. She turned and used Roddy's arm to pull herself up. She felt woozy and fell back. He caught her and held her close.

"Who locked you in?" Roddy said.

"Dewey. I think it was him," Lilly said.

"Lilly, hang on, the ambulance is coming." Mary

Mancini was standing in the doorway with the light behind her.

"Did you know there's no handle on the inside of that door?" Lilly asked, squinting. She sat up a bit more, with Roddy's help.

"I think that was part of the design. To discourage tomb robbers," Mary said. "The door is hard to open or close, so the chances of getting stuck inside are minimal."

Lilly shivered. "Unless someone locks you in. It was awful. I thought I heard a sound, and was worried it was a rat."

"Not likely," Mary said. "But I'll make sure everything's sealed up. Good thing Roddy knew the key was in your bag."

"We'll need a new one made," Lilly said. She turned a bit more and moved her arms and legs. "Or maybe a padlock."

The ambulance siren got closer, and in a moment a young woman was asking Mary to step aside, and came into the tomb.

"Any way we can get some light in here?" she asked.

Mary took out a flashlight and turned it on. The EMT took over from Roddy and asked him to wait outside. The second EMT came in, carrying a backboard. In a few minutes, they came back out, with Lilly walking between them. She blinked in the fading daylight, surprised to see so many people there.

"Lilly, what the hell happened to you?" Bash said, walking toward her.

"Bash, would you tell these lovely people I'm not going with them?" She stepped forward on her own, shaking them both off. Roddy rushed forward and gently put his arm around her waist.

"Lilly, you've been hurt," he said.

"My back seized," Lilly said. "The rest are bumps and bruises. I'm not going to the hospital. Though I could use a seat. Bash, may I borrow your front seat for a moment or two?"

She sat in the cruiser and the EMTs continued to check her out. After a few back-and-forths they agreed that she could go to her own doctor, as long as she signed a waiver, which she did.

"Are you sure you're all right, Lilly?" Bash said. He was squatting beside her, holding her hands. "I wish you'd go to the hospital."

"My doctor will be able to check me out," Lilly said. "I'm fine, now. But I panicked in the dark. I never thought I would, but I did."

"You think it was Dewey?" Bash said. He'd taken out his first aid kit and was cleaning her up. "You've got pretty big scrapes on both knees. Roddy, can you take over here?"

"Of course," Roddy said.

"I can do it myself," Lilly said.

"Lilly, let people help you," Bash said, holding his cell phone up to his ear. "Yeah, Steph? I'm down at the cemetery. Dewey Marsh attacked Lilly Jayne. Can you put an APB out for him? I'm going to drive her home."

"Bash, you don't have to do that. Shouldn't you be looking for him? Roddy can drive me home. Mary, will you stay and make sure this place is closed up?"

"Hold on, hold on. Mary, I'll need to do another inventory of this place. Do you have some lights with you?"

"Sure do."

"Lilly, you sure you don't want a ride to the doctor's? Don't be stubborn about this. Promise me you'll go."

"Oh, she's going," Roddy said, standing up and looking for a place to throw the bloody gauze in his hand. "I'll go get the car."

"Be careful jumping the fence," Lilly said to Roddy's quickly retreating form. "Don't ask, Bash. You do your work. Roddy will be along in a minute."

He looked at her and shrugged his shoulders. He went to the hatchback and opened it, taking out a tablet, which he turned on. "I've got pictures from this morning."

"You were here this morning?"

"With Darlene. She was doing a final walk-through with me and wanted a witness."

"A witness?"

"To what was left."

"Did you lock the door afterwards?"

"Of course," Bash said.

"I got a text with a picture of the door, open. It said I needed to come down and lock it up."

"Who was it from?"

"I don't know. My phone is in my bag," Lilly said, pointing to the bag by the door.

Bash was back a few minutes later. "Sorry that took so long. I wanted to take a quick look inside. One of the seals was broken," he said, handing over her phone.

"What seals?" she asked. She searched her texts and handed Bash the phone. "Go ahead and forward it to yourself."

"The vaults that are used have seals on them, complete with the date it was sealed. I took a look and one of the seals was broken. It wasn't this morning." Bash took some notes and handed Lilly back her phone.

"You didn't check them all?"

"No, if the seal was intact, we left it as is. They were all at least seventy-five years old. But obviously something was in one of them. Lilly, what are you doing?"

"Sitting isn't good for my back," Lilly said. "Help me stand up. So, someone faked a seal on a vault? But why?"

"It would be an excellent hiding place. Who'd look in a used vault?" Bash said. He let Lilly lead and held onto her waist while she straightened up. "Someone must have a key."

"Mac told me that mine was the only one. Then I got one for you."

"Mac was wrong," Bash said. "Question is, how did someone get a key, when, and why?"

"Why would someone send me that picture?" Lilly asked. "Did you call the number?"

"Not yet," Bash said.

Lilly sighed, took her phone, and hit the number that the text was sent from. "It goes straight to voice mail," she said.

"Thank you, Nancy Drew," Bash said. He checked the number and flipped through his notebook. "That's Dewey Marsh's phone number."

"So it was Dewey," Lilly said.

"I'll get some forensics folks here to see if they can find fingerprints on the door. I'd like more proof."

"There's not much daylight left."

"We'll get some lights set up," Bash said. "Good,

Roddy's here. You sure you shouldn't go to the hospital?"

"I'm fine," Lilly said, wincing as she got up.

"I called the doctor's office and he's waiting for us," Roddy said.

"Roddy, I don't need—" Lilly went to take a step and then held on to the car door for support.

"Let people take care of you, Lilly," Bash said again. "I'll talk to you later."

"What do you think was in the vault?" Lilly asked as Roddy drove out of the cemetery and took a left. She shifted in her seat to get more comfortable, but realized that was impossible, so she stopped.

"I have no idea," Roddy said.

"Someone was in there this afternoon . . ." Lilly stopped and reached into her pocket for her phone. She opened the texts and held her phone out so she could read it. "I wonder if Dewey really sent that text."

"You said he pushed you in?"

"I saw a green jacket," Lilly said. "I don't know if it was Dewey. But it was someone pretty strong. He picked me up and tossed me in. But why would Dewey text me, then push me in?"

"He might not have expected me to come with you," Roddy said. "It would have gotten you out of the way for a while."

"That's terrible," Lilly said. "Why would he want to lock me in the family tomb?"

"I have no idea," Roddy said. "Maybe to confuse things?"

Lilly's phone rang and she turned it on.

"Hey Lilly—"

"Hello, Warwick," Lilly said. "Can I call you back? I'm with Roddy—"

"Sure, I wanted to tell you what I just texted Bash. I was out on the walkway, looking at the nests, and I saw a rowboat go out to the Whaler."

"This late? Was it Mac?"

"Thought it might be. I had some binoculars, but it was hard to see. I saw a green Bradford Funeral Home jacket. The kind Dewey wears."

"Was it him?"

"Hard to tell. Might have been. That's not the only odd thing, though. He drifted up to the Whaler, but he didn't get on. He did drop three boxes over the side of the boat, though."

"Are you sure?"

"Yup. I tried to take a picture with my phone, but it's pretty grainy. Like I said, I texted Bash. Tried to call him, but he wasn't picking up. I thought you should know."

"Could you text the picture to Roddy and me? Is Dewey still out there?"

"No, he rowed back in. Ty went down to the docks to see if he could see him, but he wasn't there."

"Keep an eye out," Lilly said.

"You bet. Where are you headed?"

"To the doctor's—"

"The doctor's? Are you all right?"

"Roddy's with me and I'll be fine. I'll check in with you later."

Chapter 35

There were two ways to handle her aches and pains the next morning. Lilly could either pretend they weren't there, or she could give in and use the cane the doctor had given her. She'd intended to do the former, but gave up after she had to hold on to furniture in order to get dressed.

When Alan had gotten sick, they'd installed a staircase lift to help him up and down stairs. Lilly had it removed, but now she thought about how useful it would be as she got older. Or maybe she should let Ernie look into installing an elevator. The trip downstairs took a long time, and by the time she got to the kitchen door she was exhausted again.

"Lilly, why didn't you call me to help?" Delia said, running to the door.

"I'm not sure what you could have done," Lilly said.

"Maybe make sure you didn't fall downstairs?"

"Well, I didn't, so the effort would have been

wasted," she said. "Though I will confess, I won't be going upstairs again until bedtime."

"Maybe we should set Alan's library up so you could stay in there?" Alan's library and the family archives were one and the same. Toward the end, they'd set up a hospital bed in the room so that Alan could be surrounded by his books, and also be on the first floor. Lilly had barely been in the room since.

"No, I'll be fine. Though I'm warming to the idea of an elevator."

"Why don't you go out to the porch?" Delia said. "Ernie went to his storage unit with Warwick, and they brought you over a recliner."

"I don't need—"

"Lilly, it was a lot of work," Delia said. "At least try it."

"We haven't had a recliner in this house, ever," Lilly said, walking slowly. "I hardly think this is the moment. Wait, is that a recliner?"

Delia smiled and led her friend over to the Shaker-style chair. "Did you think Ernie would own an ugly piece of furniture? He had two, so they brought them both over. Here, sit down. I'll get you a cup of coffee and some breakfast."

"How do I recline?" Lilly asked.

"It's electronic," Delia said. "Here's the remote."

She waited until Delia had left to try it out. Elevating her feet took the pressure off her sore hip. After a few minutes of trying different poses, she found the perfect one and closed her eyes. Ernie was never getting this chair back.

"Comfy?" Ernie said, coming into the porch carrying a tray, which he put down on the table. Delia followed and set up a television tray next to her.

"Very. But both of you, stop fussing," Lilly said. She leaned over to get her coffee and winced.

"Lilly, you're going to have to let us take care of you for a few days," Delia said.

"From the look of those bruises, you're really lucky it isn't worse," Ernie said. "It's amazing that nothing got broken. I'm glad you didn't hit your head."

"It's a good thing I landed on my rear end, since there's plenty of padding there." She tried to laugh, but the effort hurt. "I guess it is amazing. But I feel like I've aged a hundred years. Though that coffee smells wonderful. And what wonders are in that basket?"

"Fresh cinnamon rolls," Ernie said. "I made them last night. There's extra frosting in that bowl."

"You're spoiling me."

"Good. That's the plan for the day."

"Don't you have to go into work?"

"I'm taking the day off," Ernie said. "And before you say anything, just stop. Bash is on his way here, and if you think I'm going to miss this conversation, you're mistaken."

"He's on his way?" Lilly tried to sit up and winced.

"Where are you going?" Ernie said. "Use the remote. The chair can even help you stand up if you want. We'll meet out here. Roddy's on his way over."

"Show me how to use this, and help me sit up a bit," Lilly said, handing him the remote. Once she was satisfied, she accepted the cinnamon roll and took a bit. "Perfection."

"Oh, you," Ernie said. "I'm glad you like it. What's this?" He checked his phone. "A text from Bash. He's here. And there's Roddy, coming through the gardens. Perfect timing. Lilly, here are your pills. I don't want to hear it, missy. The doctor said you should keep taking the pain meds for a few days. Delia, would you make another pot of coffee and buzz Bash in?"

"On it," she said. "I'll also make some tea."

The two of them scurried out, just as Roddy came up the back stairs and let himself in. He carried a huge bouquet of flowers and offered them to Lilly.

"I know that bringing you flowers is redundant, but I thought they might brighten up the room." He leaned down and gave Lilly a kiss on her forehead. "How are you this morning, my dear friend?"

"Sore. The flowers do help."

"Let me go and find a vase. I assume you'd like to arrange them?"

"Actually, that's one of Ernie's special skills," Lilly said. The thought of moving her arms around made her exhausted.

Ernie came in, carrying a vase and some scissors, followed by Bash. "Roddy, I saw you coming so I got supplies. Those are gorgeous. Now, be a doll and help Bash move the table closer to Lilly. We'll move it back later."

"You hanging in there, Lilly?" Bash said, lifting one side of the table while Roddy lifted the other. The heavy oak was cumbersome, but they made it look easy.

"I'm very cranky, but my flowers and cinnamon rolls are making me feel better. I am looking forward to updates," Lilly said.

"That's one of the things I like about you, Lilly. All business. Where should I start?"

"Have you found Dewey?"

"Not sure we're going to," Bash said.

"What does that mean?" Lilly asked.

"Let me rewind a little first," Bash said. "After I got Warwick's text and voice mail and heard about the green jacket, I got a dive team out to the mooring. We found a lot more than we expected."

"Last night? You have been busy. What do you mean?"

"There were a dozen waterproof chests down there. Most of them were chained to the mooring, which kept them in place in case of tides. It's hard to tell what was dropped when, but some of them had been there for a while."

"That's probably why they had that mooring, so that it was as far from shore as possible. What was in them?" Lilly asked.

"Jewelry, some small statues. The Romeo and Juliet Royal Doulton figurine Jackie Ross told me about, thanks to you."

"Do you think all of the items were stolen?" Roddy asked.

"We're checking into that now. The three boxes Warwick saw get dumped over the side of the row-boat? We found three boxes near the mooring. Two of them contained ashes."

"I wonder whose?" Ernie asked.

"And one of them contained a cell phone and wallet. They both belonged to Dewey Marsh. We're checking them for prints, but the boxes weren't waterproof, so there's a lot of damage."

"Dewey's cell phone? The one he used to text Lilly?" Delia asked.

"The one someone used to text me," Lilly said. "We don't know it was Dewey. It could have been someone who wanted us to think it was him."

"Maybe Dewey was cleaning out the crypt and someone got hold of his phone, and wanted to get him in trouble?" Ernie said.

"Then that someone texted from Dewey's phone, put on a green jacket like Dewey's, and pushed me? That doesn't make a lot of sense."

"Maybe it was Dewey?" Delia said.

"That doesn't make sense either. Why would he text me, and then try to—whatever his plans were by locking me in the crypt. Even if he wanted to cause a distraction, why would Dewey implicate himself?"

"He wouldn't," Ernie said.

"He didn't," Bash said.

"You sound very certain. How do you know that?" Lilly asked.

"Dewey Marsh had a steel screw in his arm," Bash said. "It had serial numbers. One of the boxes of ashes had a steel screw in it. The serial numbers match."

"That was quick," Lilly said.

"Damn," Ernie said.

"They had a John Doe a couple of days ago, and the ME pulled Dewey's medical records to check. She was ready."

"Why dump the boxes so close to the mooring?"

"Whoever did it was in a rush, but also I'd imagine that he, or she, wanted to have them close by in case they needed to retrieve them."

"You've had a long night," Delia said. "Would you like more to eat?"

"I'm fine with these rolls," Bash said. "But I will take more coffee. I didn't have that long a night. There are a lot of people, and agencies, involved with this case. I'd sure like to solve it first."

"Which is why you're here," Ernie said. He took a flower back out of the vase and cut it down a bit more.

"So, it wasn't Dewey who pushed me in after all," Lilly said. "Have you questioned Mac yet?"

"Mac? Why Mac?" Ernie asked.

"There aren't that many people who can use the crematorium," Lilly said. "Dewey was one, Mac was the other. And whoever pushed me into the crematorium was a man."

"He's coming in, but we don't have any proof he's involved. There are a few other people who know how to use it. Sasha for one."

"Jackie found some Royal Doultons she swears were Helen's on an eBay auction site," Roddy said. "The site was likely run by Dewey."

"Right," Bash said.

"I wonder if he had a partner?"

"We're looking into that. And we're confirming Stan's whereabouts."

"Stan? Stan didn't push me into the crypt," Lilly said.

"We don't know who did what," Bash said. "I've got to make some calls, but I'll keep you posted, all of you. Please, do the same, okay?"

* * *

"Thank you for seeing me," Sasha Bradford said as she walked into the back room, following Delia.

"I was surprised to get your call," Lilly said.

"I heard what happened to you. Are you all right?"

"I will be, eventually," Lilly said. "Please sit. Would you like something to eat or drink?"

"I'm fine," Sasha said.

"I'm going to go back to my work then," Delia said. "Call out if you need me."

Sasha kept looking down at her hands and wringing them.

"How can I help you?" Lilly asked.

"Did my spreadsheets make sense to you?" Sasha asked.

"They did," Lilly said. "I did share them with Bash. From what I could understand, it seems like the business practices of Bradford's were not stellar."

"I swear to you, I had no idea what was going on."

"You may not have, but there's a case to be made for it all making you look guiltier," Lilly said. She sounded harsher than she'd intended, but Sasha had interrupted her nap.

"I know this isn't an excuse, but I only did what they told me to do. I filled out forms like my dad taught me. Did invoices like Whitney taught me. Sold plots like Dewey taught me. Dealt with issues like Mac taught me. I guess I thought some of it wasn't on the up and up—"

"Keeping that spreadsheet proved that."

"That wasn't my spreadsheet. It was Dewey's. He called it his insurance."

"Insurance in case anyone accused him of over-selling plots?"

"Dewey never sold plots. His initials aren't on the sheets."

"Yours are," Lilly said. "And Whitney's."

"Any my dad's. And Mac's."

"Mac sold plots?" Lilly asked.

"His initials are DCT. David Cormac Townsend."

Lilly closed her eyes and tried to see the spreadsheet in her mind. "Of course he must have. He was the caretaker."

"He found new plots and then sold them," Sasha said. "That's what the spreadsheet is about. Not legitimate plots that are registered with the town. All of the others."

"Why are you telling me this?" Lilly asked.

"They told me . . . Is it true that Dewey is dead?" she asked.

"He appears to be," Lilly said.

"I think I may know who killed him," Sasha said. "But I'm not sure what to do."

"You should tell Bash," Lilly said.

"It makes me look guilty too," Sasha said. "I thought I'd tell you and then you can tell whoever should know."

Lilly took a deep breath and looked over at the door to Delia's office, which was slightly open. Bash would be making his own decisions, since he was on the other side of the door, listening to their conversation.

"Tell me what's on your mind," Lilly said. "But, Sasha, I will tell Bash if I need to."

"The thing is, the night Buzz Freeland died?"

"I remember."

"We were sitting next to the bar. It was really noisy.

Buzz and Mac were sitting at the bar, but we could hear them. Buzz made sure of that. Buzz was going on and on about Whitney getting hers, and Mac was laughing. Whitney went up at one point and said something to Buzz. She came back to the table and I saw her put a bottle in her bag. Then Buzz left and collapsed."

"Did you see the bottle?"

"I did. It was eye drops."

"Eye drops?"

"After Buzz died, Mac came into the office one day, and he said that Whitney's eyes looked bloodshot. He asked if she'd run out of eye drops. I never saw someone go pale like that. The thing is, everyone thinks I'm stupid, but I'm not. I looked up what eye drops can do. Did you know that if you drink them and have a bad heart, it can kill you?"

"Why would anyone drink eye drops?"

"They wouldn't, on purpose," Sasha said. "But if someone put them in a drink?"

"Do you think Whitney put eye drops in Buzz's drink?"

"I think maybe she did," Sasha said. "And I think Mac saw her do it."

"Why?"

"Buzz kept telling Whitney that he was coming after her, that he had the goods. He said that the police were going to find it all very interesting."

"I still don't understand. How did Mac find out?"

"I told Dewey what I saw," Sasha whispered. "He told me it was our chance and that he'd take care of it. I think he must have told Mac."

"What do you think Mac did?"

"I know he wanted his job back. I heard Dewey and him fighting right after Whitney died, and he kept telling Dewey to lay low and stop panicking. He told Dewey to give him the bottle of eye drops and he'd make sure they'd find them in Stan Freeland's house if the cops needed more evidence."

"So Stan would get the blame," Lilly said.

"Lilly, do you think Mac killed Dewey?"

Lilly looked at the younger woman for a few moments, and then closed her eyes. Mac may have done something to Dewey's body, but maybe he was cleaning up after Sasha? Or maybe—

"Lilly?"

"Sorry, Sasha. You need to tell Bash about the eye drops. Have you done that?"

"No."

"For heaven's sake, Sasha."

"Would you tell him?"

Lilly opened her eyes and looked at Sasha. She nodded and closed her eyes again.

Chapter 36

"Show me that spreadsheet again," Lilly said to Delia. Delia had rolled out the monitor and whiteboard, and set them up so that Lilly could see them from her chair.

Sasha had left after Lilly promised she'd tell Bash about the eye drops. He'd come out of Delia's office rubbing his hand over his short haircut.

"I'll call the ME and ask them about the eye drop thing," Bash said. He walked outside and sat on the back stairs to make the call.

"We looked at this spreadsheet assuming that Sam Bradford had started the bad business practices," Lilly said. "But look at those dates. What if Mac did them?"

"Mac?"

"At one point, Mac had something to do with all aspects of the business," Lilly said.

"He also had the trust of everyone," Bash said, coming back in the house. "Here's a question: What if Whitney was blackmailing Mac?"

"Maybe this spreadsheet was started by Whitney," Delia said.

"Let's think about this," Lilly said. "Maybe Mac Townsend has been playing both sides against the middle for years. Taking a bit from here and a bit from there. Whitney caught on—"

"And she wanted in," Bash said.

"Or she wanted a cut. Eventually she'd tried to do what he'd been doing. Making more graves, moving things around—"

"But she was greedy," Bash said. "And she wasn't as good at covering her tracks. Makes sense. But Mac's house and records were searched. They didn't find anything. You'd think that Mac would have more to show for this than new plumbing."

"The mooring is too big for a Whaler, but it's far from shore," Lilly said.

"What?"

"Mac's mooring. You said that you found several boxes chained to the mooring. Maybe there's more there? Or perhaps he was storing things in the Jayne crypt? Where they would be safer? Suppose he's been collecting things over the years? He waits for a while and then sells them."

"So Mac's been running a slow, under the radar, business for years. Then Whitney comes along—"

"And presumably Dewey," Lilly said. "Remember, Dewey got the Royal Doultons from Helen Garrett. Maybe Mac was his business partner?"

"If he was, he couldn't have been happy about Dewey getting sloppy," Bash said. "I've been going on the assumption that Whitney was the leader of this gang of thieves. But what if it was Mac?"

"And Whitney tried a power play and got him fired last fall," Delia said.

"Mac's nothing but patient," Lilly said. "She made a mistake when she killed Buzz. Maybe Dewey told Mac, or maybe Mac saw her do it?"

"We need evidence," Bash said. "Until we get some evidence, it's all hearsay. I've had people going through the mausoleum, looking for evidence, but so far all they found was a chunk of granite like the one from the headstone that was near Whitney's body. But that could have been found anywhere, and from anything."

"What was the name on that headstone?" Lilly asked.

"Roy. Madison Roy. He died in 1927," Bash said.

"Delia, look at that spreadsheet. Can you find the name *Roy*?"

"Wait a minute. I found it on the spreadsheet. But let me check—yes, in the official records the location is A 1-15."

"Now, can you look at that area? Is there anything amiss?"

Delia looked at different programs and checked the spreadsheet Sasha sent, along with other records. "Nothing's amiss. In fact, this area hasn't changed at all."

"Bash, have you had a police presence in the cemetery since the murder?"

"Yes, guarding the crime scene, off and on. They're back now, going over the crypt."

"Do me a favor and pull them out tonight," Lilly said. "If it is Mac, he must be getting anxious. Let's see if we can force his hand. Oh, and you might want to bring Sasha in for questioning, and somehow let Mac know she's going to be charged."

Sunday brunch was out on the back porch. Lilly was in her recliner, and everyone else was sitting around the table. Lilly's phone buzzed and she read the text.

"Bash is here," she said.

"I'll buzz him in," Delia said. "We should really—"

"Give him a code, yes. We'll do that. Go open the door. Luna, you stay here, young lady. Max, watch her. Why she thinks she should be an outside cat is beyond me. Roddy, could you pour me a bit more coffee. I'm having a terrible time waking up today. It's probably these pills."

"But you are feeling better?" he asked, pouring her coffee and then putting the mug beside her.

"I am. I know I don't look it," Lilly said.

"You're pale is all," Ernie said. "We'll get you up and walking today. Bet you're glad we had Mary put the ramp in, aren't you?"

"I am," Lilly said. "I wonder how long it will take for me to feel better—"

"How did you know?" Bash said as he crossed the threshold into the back porch. He was carrying two bouquets of flowers and a large box of chocolates. He put the chocolates on the table, in between Roddy and Ernie. "These are for the house. The roses are for Lilly. The tulips are for you, Delia. A token to say thank you. Now, how did you know, Lilly?"

"Ah, so it worked. He went to dig—"

"Right where you said he would. Now, spill."

"Hold on, everyone. You forget that Roddy and I were working in his garden yesterday. We missed the Sasha conversation," Ernie said. "And neither of these women would talk about it last night."

"You didn't tell them?" Bash said.

"You told us not to," Delia said.

"That doesn't usually work with you," he said to Lilly.

"Of course it does, when catching a criminal is at stake," Lilly said. "Mind you, I went to bed right after you left, and slept through the night. If I'd been downstairs, I might have spilled. But Delia gave you her word, and she's a much better person than I am. Why don't you catch Roddy and Ernie up?"

Bash spent a few minutes telling them about Sasha's visit. Lilly noticed that he left out a few details, but assumed he had a good reason.

"So last night, per Lilly's suggestion—"

"Which I hope that you are taking full credit for," Lilly said.

"People think I'm a genius this morning," Bash said, smiling. "Last night, we made Mac think that Sasha had been arrested. I also closed up the Jayne crypt and pulled the detail from the cemetery. Sure enough, around three o'clock in the morning, Mac shows up, starts digging, and a half hour later we turn on the floodlights, and he's in a grave that's full of money, gold, jewelry, and the like."

"Did he confess?"

"You first. How did you know that's where he stashed his stuff?"

"I guessed, based on a few different things. Bash, you mentioned that they'd found another piece of the Roy tombstone in the crypt. I remembered how troubled Mac was about the bench being moved, and going back there and noticing that some pieces of sod had been picked up, but not rolled completely. The edges were dry." She took a sip of coffee and looked around.

"Lilly, come on. Don't keep us in suspense," Ernie said.

"I asked Delia to check that area. And unlike almost everywhere else, no graves had been moved or added around there. I thought about the rat that Whitney had Sasha put on my door. Childish and dramatic. It certainly seemed that those sorts of efforts were very much like Whitney. Then I thought about the Roy headstone. That always bothered me: Why was it there, and broken? What if Whitney had moved the headstone and put it on the bench? Perhaps as a demonstration that she'd figured something out."

"A demonstration for Mac? To show him that she'd figured out—"

"Where he'd been hiding his loot. You've all said it. His house got fixed a bit, but not much. If he'd been skimming for almost forty years, surely he'd have more than a second bathroom to show for it? When I met him, he still had a key to the cemetery, so he could let himself in and out easily."

"He could have jumped the fence," Roddy said. "Like we did."

"Yes, but the key to the gate also opened the back gate, and he could drive in and out of there."

"And had, for years," Bash said. "They're still looking at the site, but it looks like there are three or four graves' worth of treasure."

"He probably used the Jayne crypt to keep things in storage," Delia said. "I can't imagine digging back there was a frequent occurrence."

"Probably not. But somehow Whitney figured it out—" Bash said.

"And it got her killed," Roddy said.

"He claims it was self-defense," Bash said. "She'd brought the gun with her and they wrestled with it. That's also how the headstone got broken. She wanted him to show her—"

"But she had the headstone," Roddy said.

"He'd moved the grave, years ago," Bash said. "But you must have known that, Lilly."

"I recognized the name from when I was younger, but I hadn't seen it recently," Lilly said. "That made me wonder."

"Apparently Mac mentioned to Buzz that Madison Roy was taking care of his fortune. That night, at the bar, Buzz told Mac that Madison Roy should buy them a round of drinks so that they could toast Whitney when she went to jail. Whitney did some research and found the grave. She had it dug up, but there was nothing there but a body. Actually three bodies, but that's another investigation."

"What about Dewey?" Delia said. "Did Mac confess to that?"

"He isn't saying anything, but we did find Dewey's jacket. They're running it for DNA. We're hoping to find his blood on it. Lilly, for what it's worth, Mac did have a scratch on his hand."

"Why did he throw me in there?"

"He didn't confess to that. But here's what I think. We keep talking about how methodical he was and slow-moving. But here's his downfall: He doesn't think well under pressure. When he saw Whitney kill Buzz, he started to unravel."

"Why didn't he tell you what he saw?" Delia said. "That could have saved so many people a lot of grief."

Lilly looked over at her young friend, and thought of Stan. If Mac had come clean that night, would she and Stan still be together? That had to be weighing on Delia.

"I'd imagine that Mac was concerned about what Whitney would do if she was cornered," Lilly said. "She'd make his life miserable."

"What about Dewey?" Ernie asked.

"Mac's not talking about that, but we've got folks looking into the records of the crematorium. Turns out there's a record of Helen Garrett being cremated."

"But she wasn't. Jackie said that they were holding off until they could bury her where she should be."

"Exactly," Bash said. "By the time someone figured it out, it could be chalked up to another mistake by the Bradford Funeral Home."

"What about the topsoil?" Lilly asked.

"The what? Oh, the stuff from Alden Park?" Bash said. "Thanks for that tip, Roddy. Turns out that the subcontractors were skimming materials, just like you thought."

"Not I, Lilly," Roddy said.

"I always expect the worst of people these days," Lilly said. "Did that have anything to do with Whitney or the rest of the case?"

"I suspect Whitney's going to get the blame for a lot of the Bradford misdeeds. Sasha's cooperating fully. She may not have to go to jail, but that's to be determined."

"So that's that?" Lilly said.

Bash laughed and reached over to take Lilly's hand. "That's that."

"How did Sam Bradford die?" Delia asked.

"Heart attack, I think," Lilly said.

"I can check," Bash said. "Why?"

"I'm looking at the dates on this spreadsheet. If I shifted my mindset to Mac being the driver of all of this, it makes me wonder if Sam started to ask questions. See here, where things slow down right before he died? Then he died and they picked back up."

"You think Mac killed Sam?"

"Or maybe Whitney did?" Delia said.

"Okay, Delia, now you're stuck with me for a few more hours," Bash said. "I may need to hire you as a consultant on this case. You're going to have to walk me through all of this a couple of dozen more times."

"Bash, believe it or not, it would be a pleasure," Delia said, smiling.

Lilly smiled, leaned back, and closed her eyes.

Chapter 37

"**D**id you have a good nap?" Delia asked Lilly a couple of days later as she walked into the back porch. "I heard you back here talking to the cats."

"I did," Lilly said, gently rolling over on her side and pushing herself up to sitting position on the couch. "I slept longer than I intended. Where is everyone?"

"Over at Roddy's," Delia said. "They wanted to give Stan and me some privacy, so they made up an excuse about checking the garden door."

"Stan came over?" Lilly asked. She looked at Delia and patted the seat beside her. "Oh, sweetheart, what happened?"

Delia sat down and Lilly lifted her arm to put it around Delia's shoulder. Delia leaned her head on Lilly's chest and started to cry. Both cats jumped up on the couch and joined the circle.

"Thanks, everyone," Delia said after a while, sitting up and patting Max, and then Luna. "I'll be okay at some point. Stan wanted me to tell you thank you. He's been cleared of all charges."

"That's good news," Lilly said. "Isn't it?"

"It is," Delia said. "He seems lighter and more like himself. He says he's a new man. And that he wants me back."

"He does?"

"He made a pretty good case for me forgiving him."

"But you're still sad."

"I told him that I think we were better friends than lovers."

"I see. How did he react to that?"

"He tried to talk me out of it, but I've been thinking a lot these past few weeks. I'm right. Eventually I'd like us to be friends again. But it's going to take me a while."

"Are you sure?" Lilly asked.

"I'm sure. It's something that Roddy said to me one night when we were doing dishes. He said that I deserved to be loved deeply, and to be happy. I do deserve that."

"Of course you do," Lilly said.

"I keep thinking about the way Alan used to look at you. Like you were the best thing that had ever happened to him, and that he was lucky to have you in his life. Stan never looked at me like that. I want someone who looks at me like that."

Delia put her head on Lilly's shoulder, and Lilly rested her head on top.

"Delia, you'll have someone who looks at you like that in your life," Lilly said.

"You know, Lilly, I've seen two people look at you

like that," Delia said. "Roddy looks at you like you hung the moon."

Lilly took a deep breath and smiled.

"I mean it," Delia said, sitting up. "It's okay if you feel the same way. I've seen you looking at him."

"Delia, I hit the jackpot once in my life. I don't think I could hit it again. Not at my age."

"Lilly, it's okay to fall back in love with life. You're not being unfaithful to Alan. You know that, right?" Delia looked at Lilly so seriously that Lilly's breath caught, and she started to cry.

"The feeling scares me to death," Lilly said, dabbing her eyes.

Now it was Delia's turn to hug Lilly. "If you don't mind me offering an opinion? Roddy's worth getting past the fear. He's a really good man. Give life a chance, Lilly."

"You're never going to guess what," Ernie said, walking into the kitchen several days later, carrying two pizzas.

"What?" Lilly said, smiling. "Please tell me that's an eggplant pizza."

"Of course, I know that's your favorite," he said. "I wanted to celebrate. I went over to Jackie's today to clean up the yard."

"We would have helped you," Lilly said.

"You're still resting, and Roddy was there. Anyway, we got the debris in the truck and then she invited us in. She wanted to show Roddy pictures of the fence. Which, of course, he loved, since it showed him his backyard."

"Of course he did."

"Anyway, she started to talk about how overwhelming she found the work that needed to be done on the house. She's moved back to the carriage house. She said she felt more comfortable there. Roddy asked her if she'd considered separating the properties, keeping the cottage for herself, and selling the house to meet the family obligations."

"That's really smart. Do you think it would be allowed?"

"The lot is big, and there are separate driveways. We've all been saying that the houses would be torn down if they were sold. Anyway, Jackie was thrilled with the idea, but she was worried about who would move into the house and take good care of it. That's when Roddy mentioned that I'd been looking for a house."

Lilly smiled. "And?"

"And we're going to talk again tomorrow, but the numbers we discussed felt good to both of us. I may have a new house."

"You know I don't want you to move, but if you have to—"

"Why not next door?" Ernie said. "On the way home, Roddy said we could work on the garden gate door, so I could come by anytime."

"I love that idea," Lilly said.

"Plus, you'll need to give me lots of gardening help."

Lilly gave Ernie a big hug. "Oh, the adventures we'll have."

* * *

"Where did Bash and Delia go?" Roddy said, walking out to the porch with two glasses of wine, handing Lilly one of them. He sat down next to her on the couch.

"They're in her office. She's helping him make his case against Mac Townsend," Lilly said, clinking glasses with him.

"If anyone can do it, Delia can," Roddy said.

"I think she intimidates Bash, but this is a good way for him to get to know her better."

"What are you up to, Lilly?"

"Me? Nothing. Just letting two of my favorite people spend more time together."

"I see," Roddy said.

"I hope you're not too hungry," Lilly said, smiling. "Tamara and Warwick are over at Jackie's house with Ernie. He's very excited to get Tamara's opinion. Well done, Roddy. This may be a perfect solution for Ernie and Jackie."

"The house is delightful, but quirky," Roddy said. "I couldn't help but notice that it was grand, but not terribly big. And in much better shape than the Preston house."

"Plus, he'll be next door," Lilly said.

"Next door is good," Roddy said. He took Lilly's hand and held it gently. "How are you feeling?"

"Better, thanks," she said, giving his hand a squeeze. "I am feeling every one of my years, though. I don't bounce back like I used to."

"Lilly, when was the last time you got pushed into a crypt, and then locked in?"

"You have a point there. I'm lucky that you were there to save me."

"I can think of no one who needs saving less than you," Roddy said. "But I'm glad I was there to help. I'm always glad I'm here."

Lilly looked over at his handsome face, with the cleft chin, sparkling eyes, and gentle wrinkles that showed a life well lived. Her heart skipped a beat and she lost herself in his gaze for a moment.

"Roddy, I—"

"Lilly, do you know what today is?"

"What?"

"The anniversary of our meeting," he said.

"Is it really? How can you remember the exact date?"

"One seldom forgets the day that changed their life," he said gently. "I'd like to take you out to celebrate."

"We have pizza for dinner tonight," she said.

"I'd like to take you out for a proper dinner. It doesn't have to be tonight," Roddy said. He picked up her hand and kissed it. "What do you say, Lilly Jayne? Would you go out on a date with me?"

Lilly smiled at Roddy, feeling happier than she thought possible a year ago. She leaned over, and gave him a kiss as an answer.

Acknowledgments

A writer has two different journeys, the writing journey and the publishing journey. I've been blessed on both.

John Scognamiglio, Michelle Addo, Larissa Ackerman, and the entire team at Kensington Publishing have supported, championed, and celebrated both myself and the Garden Squad series. Thank you to the cover artist, Elsa Kerls, who does such a wonderful job capturing Goosebush. I am so grateful.

John Talbot, my agent, helps me navigate this publishing journey in dozens of ways.

I blog with five amazing women. Sherry Harris, Barbara Ross, Liz Mugavero, Edith Maxwell, and Jessie Crockett are sounding boards, cheerleaders, wise counselors, and wonderful friends. My dear Wicked Authors, I wouldn't be able to do this without you.

In a brainstorming session, Barbara Ross mentioned the idea of the Garden Squad clearing off graves. That spark and a few others helped me create the book you're holding.

Jason Allen-Forrest is my first reader. He responds to my "is it a book?" email with insight, enthusiasm, and encouragement. Thank you, dear friend, for being part of this journey.

And thank you to Scott Forrest-Allen, Jason's wonderful husband, for his title help and love of puns.

I joined Sisters in Crime early on my writing journey, and am so grateful I did. The organization has helped me with both my writing and my publishing journeys, connected me with friends, taught me about craft and business, and given me great joy.

Friends and family make any journey easier, don't they? Friends like Deb Brown, Scott Sinclair, Megan Keeliher, Tracy Stewart, Stephanie Troisi, Marianne Troisi, Ruth Polleys, Craig Coogan, Mal Malme, Sandra Wong, Amy Gauger, and all the other wonderful people who cheer me on.

Sisters like Kristen and Caroline, parents like Paul and Cindy—I was blessed from the start.

The next generation gives me such joy and faith in the future. Being Aunt Julie is the best role I've ever had. I love you Emma, Evan, Chase, Mallory, Harrison, Tori, and Becca. You are the lights of my life.

As I write this, it's the spring of 2021. The past year has seen so much loss. I was happy to visit Goosebush to create this story, a place free of pandemic where justice prevails.

Dear readers, I hope that you enjoy visiting Goosebush in this story. Connect with me at JHAuthors.com @JHAuthors

Gardening Tips

Thank you Edith Maxwell, Kay Garrett, Barbara Harrison, Lauren Heiy, Caroline Lentz, and Angela Deitcher for the gardening tips!

Spring cleaning is necessary for your gardens. Prune and move plants. Use compost and moisture to get your beds ready. Remember the mulch.

April is the time to direct seed cool weather crops like lettuce, spinach, kale, and chard.

Leave last fall's leaves on the garden until the end of April. Yes, it looks messy, but it provides cover for beneficial insects.

Grow more veggies in the same amount of space by using the Japanese ring system. Instead of planting one tomato inside tomato cage, plant a few plants around the outside of the cage. Line the inside of the ring with burlap. Place a mixture of cow manure and compost inside the cage. When it rains or in the heat of summer if you water (inside the ring), the rich nutrients seep out and nourish the plants. As the plants grow, use strips of pantyhose to tie them up. The pantyhose has enough give not to cut into the plant and work better than any other form of ties.

If you use the ring system, you may want to make your own cages. Use concrete wire to make them taller. A diameter of 2–3 feet will give you enough space for 5–6 tomatoes around the ring.

Remember that trees GROW, both the roots and the crowns, so do NOT plant them anywhere near septic drain lines, wells, or foundations. Choose where you plant carefully, since eventually the shadows will impact your gardening options, particularly for vegetables.

Stay ahead of your weeding. Also, be careful when/if you compost them, because if they're invasive they'll grow there as well.

There are some plants that are as invasive as weeds if they get out of control. Plan on container planting mint, bee balm, lemon balm, catnip, valerian, and others.

You may know that planting marigolds near your vegetables will attract the pollinators. Here are some other plants pollinators love: borage, a butterfly bush, coneflowers, cow parsnips, dahlias, daisies, dandelions, goldenrod, lavender, milkweed, snapdragons, and sunflowers.

Speaking of pollinators, create a source of water for them. One idea to consider is using a shallow bowl with marbles. The bees will use the marbles to rest while drinking.

Lilly uses sculptures and other items to decorate her garden. Use your imagination to make your garden special. Do you have a set of old dishes, or did you find a set at a yard sale? Use them to edge the garden!